Shikar

JACK WARNER

Shikar

A Tom Doherty Associates Book
New York

SHIKAR

Copyright © 2003 by Jack Warner

This book is printed on acid-free paper.

A Forge Book
Published by Tom Doherty Associates, LLC
175 Fifth Avenue
New York, NY 10010

www.tor.com

Forge® is a registered trademark of Tom Doherty Associates, LLC.

Library of Congress Cataloging-in-Publication Data

Warner, Jack.
Shikar / Jack Warner.—1st ed.
      p.   cm.
"A Tom Doherty Associates Book."
ISBN 0-765-30343-4 (alk. paper)
1. Sheriffs—Fiction.   2. Georgia—Fiction.   3. Tigers—Fiction.   I. Title.

PS3623.A863S54   2003
813'.6—dc21
2002045495

ISBN 0-765-30343-4

First Edition: June 2003

Printed in the United States of America

0 9 8 7 6 5 4 3 2 1

For my love, Donna, who showed me how,
and to the memory of Lieutenant Colonel Edward James Corbett,
who inspired it

Acknowledgments

Some of the characters in this book are based on living people. They know who they are. Most important, the character of Graham is based on the great, and nearly forgotten, Jim Corbett. However fantastic readers may find Graham, be assured that he does nothing in this book that Corbett did not do in real life. Corbett's first book, *Man-Eaters of Kumaon*, was a Book-of-the-Month Club selection in the United States right after World War II and was made into an abominable movie. There followed *The Man-Eating Leopard of Rudraprayag*, *The Temple Tiger and More Man-Eaters of Kumaon*, *Jungle Lore*, and *My India*. In 1987, Martin Booth's excellent biography, *Carpet Sahib*, shed long-awaited light on parts of Corbett's life never mentioned in his own books. He was a man of enormous courage, loyalty, and uncanny skill in the forests of northern India. As of this writing, *Man-Eaters*, *Temple Tiger*, and *Jungle Lore* are available in the United States in paperback. The others are out of print but can often be found used or in libraries.

I should like to thank Peter Mantius for his invaluable suggestions and criticisms, Norma Duncan for her judgment and unflagging support, and Andrea Boc for her eagle-eyed proofreading.

I have had a great many editors in my life, none so skilled or so encouraging as Patrick LoBrutto. I've had only one agent, and thank God it was Richard Curtis. It was their faith in *Shikar* that has seen it into print.

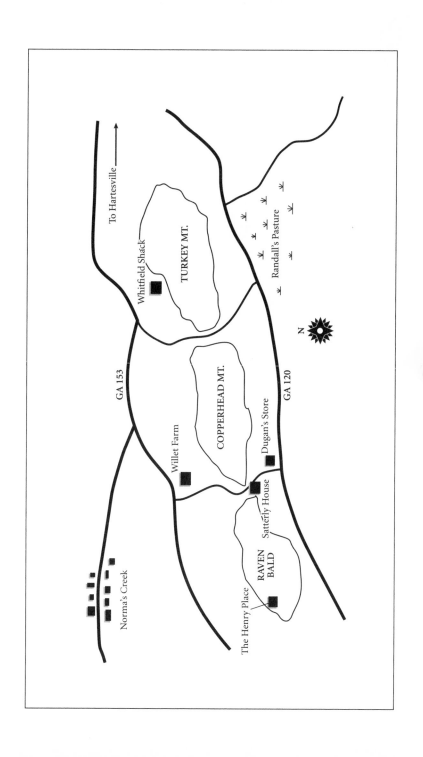

Shikar

Prologue

From the veranda of the government bungalow, he could see across the forest-draped valley of the Ladhya River all the way into Nepal. The headman of Kot Kindri told him the tiger had come from Nepal, swimming across the river in the dry season and establishing a territory of several hundred square miles along the Indian side. That was what people said, the old man told him.

Whether it had been a man-eater before it changed nationalities, no one knew. In any case, it was now officially the Kot Kindri man-eater. The government's records showed it had killed 273 people before the district officer asked him to take the field one last time. To that, he thought grimly, we can add the boy and his sister, and the old man, all killed since he arrived. And of course the government does not count people who simply vanish, never to be found.

He lifted the teacup to his mouth, watching the hand that carried it. It was dark and seamed from a lifetime out of doors, contrasting starkly with the white specks of age on the back. He sipped the strong tea and then held the cup in front of him until the surface of the liquid became as still as if it were sitting on the table.

The screen door of the bungalow, built for touring government officials, slapped softly against the frame. A tall, gray-bearded man in a turban stepped into the morning light flooding the porch.

"More tea, Sahib?"

"No, Ram Singh. Thank you. I'm going down to that nullah where we tied out the youngest bull. Perhaps we shall be lucky today; maybe the tiger has taken that bull, or one of the others. What is it the people always say when I botch a chance? 'Do not worry, Sahib, for if you did not kill the tiger today, surely you shall kill him tomorrow, or the next day.' "

"And you know that is true, Sahib. You have never failed. You will not fail now."

"Rather portentous this morning, aren't we, Ram? Time to go."

He rose slowly but effortlessly from the chair and picked up the heavy double-barreled rifle propped against the wall. From his pocket he brought out three cartridges, examined them carefully, loaded two into the rifle and returned the other to his pocket. Then he picked up the battered pith helmet sitting on the porch rail and put it on his head.

"Shall I come, Sahib?"

"No, Ram. It's only a little way. If I need help, you'll hear me. In the meantime, pack up my tent and tell the men to be ready. If nothing happens today, we'll move downriver and join young Jim at Pathangiri."

"Very well, Sahib."

It took the hunter only twenty minutes to reach the clearing beside a dry creek bed where the bull had been tied to a log. When he came in sight of the log, he stopped and watched. The bull was nowhere to be seen. Glancing up, he saw a big Himalayan magpie alight high in a *sal* tree overlooking the clearing. The bird sat there, peering around curiously.

Slowly, rifle at his shoulder, the hunter approached the log and found the bull on the other side, sleeping peacefully. After making sure the bull could still reach plenty of graze, he trudged back to the bungalow, propped the rifle against the wall and sat down.

The hunter remained relaxed, almost motionless, listening to the murmurs and exclamations of the forest. A pair of pheasants came to the edge of the trees, scratching industriously for a late breakfast. The shrill, catlike cries of peafowl wafted over the valley. After nearly an hour, a cowbell clanked somewhere down the hill. The man arose, picked up his rifle, and walked into the forest.

A well-beaten path skirted the foot of the hill. Beside it the hunter sat on a fallen log, listening to the dull clank of the bell grow louder until, to his left, a small boy appeared around a bend in the path, leading a large bullock by a rope tied to a ring in its nose.

The hunter rose, smiling, as the boy and his bull approached.

"Good morning, Ravi," he said.

"Good morning." The mass of tangled hair on the boy's head did not reach as high as the bull's shoulder. He did not smile. His eyes were black and bottomless, and his teeth gleamed white against his coppery skin. His only garment was a ragged loincloth.

"On your way to Uncle's house again?"

"Oh, yes," the boy replied as the hunter fell in step with him, rifle under his arm.

"And how many more days do you think you'll have to take your father's bull to your uncle's house?"

"I do not know," the boy said. "Until he is through with Uncle's cows. Until Uncle tells Father he no longer needs Bundar bull."

"I wonder that your father makes you walk so far in the tiger's country."

"He tells me to be careful."

"What would you do if the tiger came?"

"The tiger did come," the boy said, not looking at the hunter.

"When did this happen?" the hunter asked, keeping his tone casual despite his surprise.

"The day before yesterday. The day after I met you back there."

"And what did the tiger do?"

"He talked to me for a while."

"What did he say?"

"He told me not to be afraid. I think he must have talked to Bundar bull, too, because bull did not seem afraid. He said he would never harm us."

"Did he say why?"

"Yes."

"Why?"

"Because I am me. Because he is my teacher."

"Your teacher? What is he teaching you?"

The boy shrugged. "About being a tiger."

They walked on in silence until they reached a village of four huts, and Ravi freed the bull in a field with a dozen fat cows. The hamlet, which had no name, was about five miles south of Kot Kindri. The hunter started north, pondering the boy's tale. He was certain Ravi was telling him the truth, as he understood it. But he was not certain that Ravi was able to separate reality from dreams. He wished it had not rained yesterday. The rain would have washed the path clear of tracks.

He was still lost in thought when he heard men yelling from somewhere ahead. He sang out his long, high *"Cooooeeeee!"* and broke into a trot. In a few minutes, two villagers came tearing down the trail to stop and clutch at his shirt.

"Sahib," they gasped, nearly in unison. "Come quickly. The tiger—the tiger—"

The hunter held up his hand.

"Catch your breath while we walk," he said. "Calm yourselves and tell me what has happened."

Gradually the hunter drew out their story. An old woman was missing from Kot Kindri. She had apparently awakened before the rest of her family and, heedless of the danger, gone outside to relieve herself. Upon awakening, her family had thought she had gone to her brother's house and did not worry about her until midmorning. When a search was begun, they found a pool of blood a hundred feet from their hut. There were tracks, but none dared follow them.

Kot Kindri was a village of two dozen huts and houses on a terraced hillside. When the hunter arrived, most of its hundred residents were gathered around the spot where the woman had apparently been seized, obliterating any tracks. Several old women were wailing. The missing woman's daughter was holding two small children, rocking back and forth in silent grief. Her husband approached the hunter, his arms outstretched in supplication.

"Please, Sahib. Please."

"Yes," the hunter replied. "I shall do my best." He knew

what the man wanted—vengeance for his mother-in-law and, more immediately, the return of at least some part of her body for a proper Hindu ceremony.

He also knew the village would have sent runners to the forest bungalow nearby, and his men would arrive soon. He cast around for tracks, and soon found the marks of a drag going directly through much of the village and up the hill above it. He found a clear print and stopped to examine it.

"Slashfoot," he murmured. He never confused the track of one tiger with that of another, but this man-eater had the most distinctive set of prints he had ever seen. A cut on the pad of the left front paw had left a welt that angled like an angry knife slash across the massive pugmark.

Reaching the tree line, he stopped, broke open his rifle, withdrew the cartridges and examined them carefully before returning them to their barrels, closing the breech and moving up the hill beside the drag.

The sun had reached its zenith and the midday heat gripped the hills. Sweat drenched the hunter's shirt, but he moved silently along the track. The tiger, carrying the woman by the neck, had angled up the hill for nearly a mile before cutting around it and down the other side. In a long, deep ravine almost two miles from the village, it had stopped and eaten a small portion of her hips and legs before covering her body with grass and leaves to hide it from vultures.

The hunter did not wince at the sight of the old woman's pathetic remains. He had seen their like many times. Concerned only with scavengers, the tiger had left the kill in plain view of a dead tree that projected out of the hillside at almost right angles, overlooking the length of the nullah. The Kot Kindri man-eater had a reputation for never returning to a kill, but it appeared this time might be an exception. It would be unlikely to take the trouble to hide its kill if it had no intention of coming back. The hunter sat on a fallen log to rest and await Ram Singh and his men.

They brought him word that his son, upon learning of the kill, had set out from Pathangiri, and they also packed a cold lunch, which he ate while Ram Singh brewed tea over a small fire. When the sun was low in the sky and the heat was beginning to lift, the hunter sent two of his men up the nearest tall tree with instructions to make a racket in case the tiger was watching. When they were in place, shouting and banging with sticks on the trunk, Ram Singh helped the hunter up the almost verticle bank to the trunk of the dead tree. He eased out along the trunk until he had a secure perch about fifteen feet from its base and twelve feet off the ground. There were enough branches projecting from the trunk to break up his silhouette. When he had settled, the two decoys climbed down from their tree. Talking loudly, Ram Singh and the men left for the village.

The hunter sat crosslegged on the broad trunk, his back to the bank and facing the kill, so he could cover either end of the ravine the tiger chose to use. It was not a comfortable position but he could maintain it indefinitely, although he hoped the tiger would come before full darkness fell. Rifle in his lap, he sat motionless, like a huge burl, waiting.

About an hour before sunset, a cool breeze came blowing down the nullah from the hunter's right, bringing the damp, earthy smells of the forest. With a small smile, he adjusted his position slightly toward the left. The tiger would make its approach from upwind, or from some angle within the upwind side of the kill. It was a good omen; he could bring up the rifle and fire much more easily to his left. The breeze stuck his damp shirt to his body like a clammy blanket. He ignored it.

The nullah was in total darkness, moonrise more than an hour away, when a langur monkey sounded its alarm call from upwind, at least a mile away. The man-eater was coming.

The langur's calls died away after fifteen minutes or so, which meant the tiger had finally moved out of its sight. Within what the hunter estimated was another quarter of an hour, a kakar deer uttered its sneezing bark and stamped the ground. Three more barks and he heard the kakar family fleeing up the hill in front of him and to his right, as expected. Silence descended on the ravine. The hunter waited, for the tiger and the moonlight. If it came now, he could do nothing. It was too dark to see the kill.

When the half-moon finally rose above the hills, the hunter's legs were beginning to cramp, but he could tolerate that as long as necessary. Gradually the nullah came into view, and he could see the lumpy shape of the kill, under its sparse covering of forest debris. It appeared undisturbed, but he knew the tiger was at hand. It would wait and watch until it was certain it could go safely to the kill.

His eyes scanned back and forth over the moonlit scene, alert for the slightest movement, but it was a scene different only in detail from dozens of others in his memory. He had hunted the foothills of the Himalayas since he was barely old enough to lift a rifle. Years ago, dismayed by the wanton slaughter of tigers, he had stopped hunting for sport, refusing even to organize elephant-back hunts for visiting royalty. He responded only to government pleas to dispatch animals that had turned to killing man, and even then only reluctantly. He harbored an abiding love for the hill people of India and an equally abiding love of tigers, and he wondered that the majestic animals did not kill men more often. They were the rightful rulers of these hills, not the people who were denuding them for farms and grain fields. Gritting his teeth against the pain in his legs, he hoped fervently that this night would be the last he would spend sitting in a tree with a rifle on his lap.

It was at least two hours after the langur's first alarm call when the hunter's finely honed forest sense broke into his reveries. The man-eater was no longer watching the kill but had located him and now was stalking him.

The hackles were rising on the back of the hunter's neck even before he felt the tree trunk move slightly under the pressure of great weight. He did not need to turn to know the tiger had come down the bank above him, despite its impossible angle, and was stepping out onto his tree. Slowly he turned his head to the right until he was looking over his shoulder, while he eased the safety off the rifle in his lap. The tiger was at the base of the tree, just off the bank, one plate-sized paw poised for its next step toward him. Their eyes locked, the man-eater's blazing with an inner yellow fire. It seemed to be smiling at him.

Slowly the paw came down, and the tiger came a step nearer. Two more steps and it would be at his shoulder, or it could easily pounce and carry him off the tree from where it was. The sudden movement required to twist his torso further and snap the rifle to his shoulder would bring the man-eater upon him before he could complete it.

Smiling almost benignly, the tiger lowered itself to spring. Willing life into his cramped, nearly numb legs, the man kicked himself backward off the tree to the right. The tiger's rush knocked his helmet away as he fell, and he tried to gather his legs under him to keep from landing on his back. The man-eater's angry roar shattered the silence just as the hunter's right heel hit the ground. Pain shot up his leg and he fell backward. It knocked the breath out of his chest, but he kept his hold on the rifle.

The tiger's leap carried it almost to the spot where it had left the old woman's remains, and when it hit the ground it appeared momentarily disoriented, giving the hunter time to get his legs under him. But as the man-eater whipped around, roaring again, the man's right leg crumpled, and he fell onto his left side. Seeing him, the tiger gathered itself and rushed. On his side, his left elbow propping up his body, the hunter fired the right barrel. The rifle's recoil knocked him back, and the tiger crumpled, legs flailing, but swiftly regained its feet and with a mighty roar made its final leap. On his back, the hunter fired the left barrel and then whipped the weapon sideways in both hands, ready to thrust it into the man-eater's mouth.

The tiger fell on him with enough force to drive the rifle back into his face, smashing his nose. But it was deadweight, and he could feel warm blood pouring from its mouth onto his chest and neck. He lay quietly under the animal for a while, feeling the beating of his heart, surprised to be alive. Then he heard shouting in the distance and saw the glow of torches glimmering in the trees in the direction of the village. His men, hearing the shots and no call from him, were coming.

He was struggling to get out from under the dead man-eater when the men reached the nullah. All but Ram Singh stopped in dismay; the Sikh, with a scream of anguish, charged forward and began beating the dead tiger with a club before he realized that it was not the tiger but the hunter who was moving.

"Sahib!" he cried. "Lie still! You are hurt!" He sobbed with joy, tugging at the tiger and yelling at the others to help free their master.

"No, Ram. It's all right," the man said weakly. "All this is the tiger's blood. I've hurt my leg and bunged my nose is all."

By the time the hunter was free of the tiger's carcass much of the village had arrived. Their torches lit the nullah like a stage. The family of the Kot Kindri man-eater's last victim gathered her remains. The hunter's men had to struggle to keep the crowd from tearing the dead tiger to bits. When Ram Singh had restored order, the men lashed the carcass to a long pole and enlisted some of the villagers to help carry it. Ram Singh helped the hunter to his feet, one arm firmly around the man's shoulder.

"Ah," the man grunted. "It's just a sprained ankle. Nothing serious. When we get back you can help me get my nose back where it belongs, old friend."

A huge bonfire was burning at Kot Kindri when they returned. Runners had gone out to neighboring villages to announce the death of the man-eater. The gray-bearded head-man, wearing a red army dress coat, greeted him by the fire and solemnly prostrated himself before the hunter, touching his forehead to the man's boots. After the men laid out the tiger's carcass by the fire, the hunter, with the aid of a stick a villager had put in his hands, knelt to examine it. The teeth were in good shape; it was not an old animal. He would skin it tomorrow, and that would reveal any injuries, such as im-bedded porcupine quills, which might have led it into man-eating. Finally, he lifted the left forepaw and turned it toward the fire.

"God in heaven!" he gasped. Ram Singh dropped to one knee beside him.

"What is wrong, Sahib?"

"This is not the man-eater! You see? There's no scar on its pad. This isn't Slashfoot."

"But Sahib, it came to the kill, and it tried to kill you. Surely you are mistaken."

"No mistake, Ram. This is not the tiger we've been hunting. The man-eater is still alive."

He used the stick to pull himself painfully to his feet, watching the glimmer of the bonfire on the tiger's glazed eyes. He looked up and saw Ravi standing on the other side of the fire. The boy was staring at the dead tiger with his fathomless eyes, and there was a tear glistening on his cheek. The hunter was hobbling toward the boy when, from somewhere along the ridge far above the village, a tiger called.

"*AAAaaoooonnnnghh,*" it cried, just once, and echoes bounced back from the valley below, silencing all conversation. The boy looked up and a little smile seemed to flash across his face, although it might have been an illusion of the dancing firelight. Then he turned and disappeared into the crowd.

The hunter and his son returned to their home fifty miles away and waited for news of the man-eater of Kot Kindri, but none came. Two years later, the old hunter died peacefully in his sleep. His son soon became known in his own right as a conservationist, woodsman, and, when necessary, hunter. The hills around Kot Kindri never again experienced a man-eater's reign of terror.

September 8

Only three houses overlook Georgia Road 113 on the thirty-mile stretch between Sandville and Fairview and each of them is abandoned and nearly collapsed, gray, rain-fissured wood with no paint like the bones of a shattered skeleton.

The farmhouses still occupied sit hundreds of yards back from the two-lane road, only a break in the tree line and a mailbox to announce the dirt lanes leading to them. At night a driver could easily overlook most of them, dimly outlined by the floodlight set in every yard and a few lights in the windows if someone's still up.

No one was up at two A.M. on the ninth of September along the highway where it crosses the Sallisaw River ten miles north of Richey. No one saw the line of nondescript trucks of various sizes and colors trundling over the bridge.

No one, except the driver behind it, saw the seventh truck in the procession, a panel truck with small round ports lining both sides of the cargo box, edge slowly toward the shoulder of the pavement. Its front tire caught the gravel and it plunged down the embankment, spinning until the cab was pointed back at the river. Then it hit the other side of the ditch with the panels, making a mushy kind of "whump," and fell over about forty-five degrees, its headlights pointed upward, skimming the outermost edge of the trees. The only sound came from the right front wheel, still spinning.

The next driver pulled over quickly, picked up his CB microphone as he did, spoke briefly and then leaped out of the truck. The whole line pulled over, and men came running back, some with flashlights.

The driver of the truck in the ditch was cursing in a steady monotone as he punched off the lights, turned off the engine and clambered awkwardly out the passenger door.

"You okay?" asked another driver, softly.

"Yeah, I'm fine," grunted the driver, a small man with a stubble of beard. He was rubbing his shoulder.

A rail-thin man in a fedora instead of the prevailing baseball cap trotted up to the knot of drivers.

"What happened?" he snapped.

"Well," the driver said, "I went to sleep."

"Went to sleep? You drunk?"

"Hell, no."

"What about Andy?"

"He oughta be all right," said the little driver. "We hit soft."

"Well, for God's sake make sure," the thin man said.

The little man inched back down into the ditch and walked along the side of the truck, looking into the dark ports in the white side panel. He grunted, then turned to the men on the road. "Throw me a light," he said. One of the men tossed him a flashlight. He shined it in one of the ports, angling around, and then moved quickly to the back of the truck.

"Oh, shit," he said.

"For Chrissake, what is it?" the thin man asked. "Is he hurt?"

"No," the little man said. "He's gone."

"Gone? Whaddya mean, gone?"

"Door's open. Must've gotten knocked open when we hit the ditch. No sign of him."

There was silence. The wheel had quit spinning, and the little man turned slowly to look back up at the road.

"What'll we do?" one of the other drivers asked.

The thin man turned, walked to the other side of the road and stared up at the sky as if he was counting the stars hanging over the ridges to the north. The others waited, some looking nervously up and down the road.

After a few minutes, the thin man turned around, adjusted his hat and began issuing orders.

"Carl, get Jimmy up here with the winch, get that thing outta the ditch. It looks like it'll drive. If it will, flash your lights and we'll get going."

"You gonna call, let somebody know?" Carl asked. The boss had a phone in his truck.

"I do that, we're finished, done for," he said, looking at Carl. "That what you want?"

"No," said Carl, after a while. "I guess not."

The men drifted back to their trucks and a big Ford pickup, the last in line, moved up near the truck in the ditch. A winch motor moaned briefly and the truck was righted. The cable was reconnected, the winch started again and the truck heaved up out of the ditch like a mammoth escaping a tar pit. Its engine started, its lights blinked, and the entire procession returned to Highway 113, headed toward Alabama.

September 10

On Sunday the *Atlanta Journal-Constitution* truck gets to the Easy Way truck stop on the interstate five miles from Richey at about four A.M. There are always three people waiting for it. The driver never turns off the engine; he waves at the three people standing outside the truck stop, and the man in the back of the truck kicks out six bales of newspapers, each secured with two bands of thin, tough white plastic.

As soon as the last bale hits the ground the man in the back rolls down the cargo door, and the driver puts the truck in gear and heads back to the interstate.

Lanelle Jackson picked up her three bales, one at a time, and dumped them in the back of her Jeep. It wasn't a slick new Jeep like the one Paul Hudgins used or the red Blazer that Len Granger delivered his papers in. Her Jeep was a dirty red, and the seats were covered with canvas that had, at some point, been more or less green. The red paint did not quite obscure the stenciled U.S. ARMY legend. The Jeep was old, ancient perhaps, but it still ran—better on muddy dirt roads than the newer ones did.

When Lanelle finished her forty-mile route, which took her two hours on a dry day, she would go home, get her two boys out of bed, feed them, and send them off to school. Then, after a cup of coffee by herself, she would drive her Jeep downtown and open up Jefferson Drugs and start the big coffee urn. There hadn't been a man at Lanelle's breakfast table since her husband died on the interstate four years ago. On Sunday, she'd just go back to bed for a while.

Lanelle made sure the folds of the paper were pointed toward the front of the Jeep and then, with wire cutters, broke the bands holding the paper together. It was a fairly cool morning, but she still had the sheet-metal top off the Jeep. If the papers were stacked with the fold at the back of the Jeep they'd blow all over hell when she got to going.

All three left at the same time, waving to each other. Lanelle pulled out of the truck stop onto Georgia 58 and headed east. Every couple of miles or so there was a mailbox, and at the ones where there was a round metal tube emblazoned with "Atlanta Constitution" she stopped, rolled up the Sunday paper, and shoved it into the tube.

She turned north at Georgia 82, and the breeze from the west lifted her hair up a little. She pulled her jacket closer around her neck.

Almost two-thirds of her route was on good paved roads. Just the last of it was on dirt roads, washboarded and rutted and miserable to drive on. The ruts, baked hard by the sun, could throw a vehicle out of control. But the paved portion of her route was okay, almost a pleasure on a morning like this.

Things were beginning to stir. Occasionally a dog barked when she stopped to stuff a paper, but it was still pitch dark when she turned back west on Georgia 113. She had gone about a mile when a car with Alabama plates pulled out and passed her. She never saw many cars this time of morning.

The Sallisaw smelled like fresh mud and dead fish when

she crossed the bridge. It always did when things got dry. She began humming "Strawberry Fields Forever." She could never get the song out of her mind for long.

At Suddarth's place, three stops before she had to turn back south on the dirt road, she shoved a paper into the tube and, to her astonishment, the paper flew right out the back of it. She looked into the rear of the Jeep and saw that one of the big inserts had slipped out when she picked the paper up. That happened once in a while.

"Shit," she said, swinging out of the Jeep. She walked around the front, outlined briefly in the headlights, a slim woman in a white T-shirt and jeans, and stepped down into the drainage ditch to retrieve the fallen newspaper.

The sun was just clear of the horizon when Sally Suddarth waddled down the lane to get her Sunday paper. Ray would be back from milking their three cows in about fifteen minutes, ready for his breakfast. Things ran on rails at the Suddarth place.

She came out of the tree line and saw Lanelle's old Jeep.

"Lanelle," she said, "you sure runnin' behind this morning."

No answer, and she could see Lanelle wasn't in the Jeep. She walked up to it and heard the engine, idling kind of rough.

"Lanelle? LAAAA-NELLLE!"

She looked in the paper tube. It was empty. She walked over to the passenger side of the Jeep and saw the newspaper in the ditch. A small clump of weeds lay on the front page.

There was, however, no sign of Lanelle. Sally went back and got Ray, who climbed on his tractor and drove down to the highway, but he couldn't see anything, either. He turned off the Jeep's ignition—the key was still in it—and went back to the house to call Sheriff Barnes in Richey.

Sheriff Barnes, a tall, heavy man of fifty years, all but twenty of them in the sheriff's department, came out himself. Lanelle was a popular woman.

The sheriff walked carefully around the Jeep, watching where he stepped, although he could see nothing on the pavement. He pulled a pen out of the pocket of his brown shirt and hooked Lanelle's little purse out from between the front seats. It was open, and he could see her wallet. The wallet obviously had some bills in it, so he assumed no one had tampered with it. He pulled out the wallet and found her driver's license and a single MasterCard inside.

"What time she usually come by here?" he asked the Suddarths, who were watching from the foot of their lane.

"Around five, five thirty, I guess," said Sally. "We get up at six, and the paper's nearly always there when we get up."

"You hear anything around then?"

"No, sir. We was asleep," said Ray.

"What about the dogs? They usually bark at her?"

"Well, we just had the one," Ray said, "and I don't think he ever barked at her. Anyways, I ain't seen him for a few days now."

The sheriff radioed back to the office for a deputy with a fingerprint kit and a camera, and told his dispatcher to call the state prison at Alto and the Georgia Bureau of Investigation at Gainesville. Sheriff Barnes hung around the Suddarth place, drinking coffee and watching his deputy dust the Jeep, until an agent from the GBI, a crime scene specialist, arrived about eleven A.M. in a white panel truck.

He was mostly interested in the ditch. He picked up the newspaper with a clear plastic glove on his hand, hefted it, and then pulled another paper out of the heap in the back of the Jeep and hefted that.

"This isn't the whole paper," he said, looking around until he saw the loose insert lying in front of the pile of Sunday editions. "Here's the rest of it."

Then he got back into the ditch, which was about four feet deep at the very bottom, but not hard to climb in and out of. The last rain was two weeks ago.

"This clump of weeds here was on the paper," he said finally, "and there's a couple more little clumps over here look like they're fresh-pulled. Like maybe there was something like a scuffle down here. But the ground's hard. I don't see anything coming in or going out."

There wasn't much left to do on Sunday but issue a south-wide bulletin for Lanelle, putting a picture of her on the wire to police departments all over the region.

The next day, another GBI agent, Phil Edge, came back out to the Suddarth place followed by a corrections department truck. With him was a dog handler, Sergeant Walt Sandlin, and in the back of the truck there was a forlorn-looking bloodhound.

Sheriff Barnes met Edge, Sandlin, and his dog there at daylight. He had gone back to town on Sunday, picked up Lanelle's kids, and taken them out to his house to stay with his wife. He had a deputy start trying to find Lanelle's family, somewhere down near Columbus.

On his way out to the Suddarth house, he stopped at Lanelle's again and found the dirty-clothes hamper. He rummaged through the kids' jeans and T-shirts until he came up with a pair of Lanelle's white cotton underpants. He put them in a plastic bag and took them with him.

At Suddarth's, he gave the bag to Sandlin, who pulled out

the underwear, nodded with approval, and held it out to the bloodhound. "Find 'er, Porky," he muttered in a ritual chant. "Find 'er for me, find 'er now."

Porky sniffed the underwear with interest, and then Sandlin pulled him by his leash toward the Jeep, still chanting. The dog put his front paws on the side of the old vehicle and sniffed the driver's seat. With an eager whimper, he stood down and began twisting about, then trotted, nose to the ground, around the front of the Jeep toward the ditch. Sandlin had trouble keeping up with him.

Porky scrambled into the ditch, casting about anxiously, and then stiffened. Very slowly, he walked east a few paces, sniffing heavily, until he seemed to reach a decision. He cleared the side of the ditch in two bounds, trotted back to Edge's pickup truck, and sat down.

"What the hell," said Sandlin. He pulled on the leash. Porky was willing, in a sullen sort of way, to walk up and down the pavement. He would walk reluctantly up the Suddarths' lane, and he could even be coaxed into the ditch on the south side of the road. But the dog would not go near the ditch on the Suddarths' side of the road again.

Deputies scoured the area later that day, and the next day, Tuesday, about a hundred people from Richey and the nearby farms showed up to search, but they found no sign of Lanelle Jackson. There were no fingerprints on the Jeep but hers and her boys'. As far as anyone could tell, Lanelle Jackson had climbed down into that ditch and somehow fallen clear through to China.

September 17

The disappearance of Lanelle Jackson was on television every night for almost a week in North Georgia, and there had been stories in the Atlanta and Gainesville papers. People who never knew Lanelle became quite familiar with her face in her wedding picture and with the image of her old Jeep sitting so mysteriously beside the mailbox in front of the Suddarth farm.

It was still a major topic of conversation when Fred Jenkins, a farmer in Hawkins County forty miles north of the Suddarth place, lost a pig.

Fred and his wife, Mae, who lived about ten miles out of Foster, the only real town in the county, were sitting in their living room after dinner, talking about the Jackson disappearance. Actually Mae was talking about it and Fred was thinking about how he'd better bring in some wood for the old iron potbellied stove that crouched in front of them, its galvanized chimney disappearing into the ceiling.

"Well, I was talking to Ruth this morning, and she says maybe those satanists from up that place in Tennessee is in it, but I don't know," Mae was saying. "I kinda think she must have picked up some hitchhiker."

Fred grunted, trying to recall how many hitchhikers he'd

seen at five A.M. on two-lane country roads, when old Buster started to bark out back. Fred always paid attention when Buster spoke. He'd cornered a kid trying to steal chickens once.

Fred was sixty-seven years old, but he was an active man, and when Buster's normally deep, rhythmic bark suddenly changed to a frantic, high-pitched yammer he bounded out of his big reclining chair. A cow bellowed in agony, once, and he grabbed the 12-gauge off the wall. Snatching the flashlight, he threw open the kitchen door to be greeted by a God-awful scream that stopped abruptly, a scream that could have been human but Fred knew was a pig.

"Somethin's after the stock," he yelled at Mae, who rushed into the kitchen. "Stay inside. Shut the door."

Whatever was there was gone by the time Fred got to the barn. Buster was standing by the door, no longer barking but growling now and then and, to Fred's amazement, trembling a little. At the pig lot, Fred tried to count his stock—he had twenty animals in the big pen—but it was so dark and the pigs so agitated he couldn't get the same number twice. He had the feeling one was gone, but there was no damage to the fence. The gate was still locked. There was nothing to do but wait for morning.

Shortly after sunup, he counted nineteen pigs in the pen. The barrow he had intended to slaughter for winter eating was gone. There were signs of blood in the trampled mess inside the pen, but Fred couldn't see how the hog had been removed. When he went to his small herd of cattle, which gathered near the barn for the night, he found a cow with a strip of hide hanging off her flank.

Fred called the sheriff, but nobody ever came out. He patched up the cow and spent most of the day splitting firewood for the stove and bringing it to the porch, and thinking about what had happened. He couldn't believe thieves had taken his hog. How could a man rip a foot-square piece of hide off a cow's butt like that? He couldn't think of an animal likely to do it either or to get a two-hundred-pound pig over a four-foot fence.

Black bears occasionally wandered down from the mountains, but they never attacked stock. Every so often there was talk of bobcats and wildcats and even panthers. Nobody in his lifetime or his father's had ever seen a panther, and while a few people did say they had seen a bobcat, none ever reported one that would have been up to this work.

As he stacked the firewood Fred realized in a slightly shameful way that he had no particular interest in trying to find out what had happened to his animals. He knew he could cast around the pen, and if he looked hard enough he ought to find some blood sign, maybe some kind of tracks or prints, but he wasn't going to. Maybe it was age, maybe winter coming, maybe the way old Buster had trembled, but he'd as soon not see what had taken the barrow.

Live in the country all your life, some strange things happen, and there aren't always answers. He only hoped it wouldn't come again.

September 26

Thirty miles northeast of the Jenkins farm, the Appalachian Mountains rise out of the stony ground. By the time they march into Harte County they have reached their full stature, rarely more than four thousand feet high.

In the spring and summer, densely forested with rocky outcrops and occasional boulder fields, the mountains have the dark, brooding air of old men who have seen bad things and expect to see worse, and they yield little to the people who live among them.

The southern terminus of the Appalachian Trail is here; early in the spring, it is crowded with hikers determined to follow the trail all the way to Maine. In the fall, those who chose to brave late winter in the Northeast, and who stuck to the trail all summer, straggle in to finish their pilgrimage. Thousands of others hike the trail for only a day or two. Between spring and late fall the cabins and camping grounds at Echota State Park are usually full.

In the fall the hardwoods turn bright orange and yellow and red before their leaves drop, baring them like bristles on a worn brush against the gray winter sky along the ridgelines. Those two weeks of brilliant color in October draw thousands of flatlanders from Atlanta and other places where people have money to drive a couple of hundred miles to look at leaves. For a couple of weekends the two-lane highways of Harte County are jammed.

Leaf time looked to be only a few weeks away when old Coddy Turner called the sheriff's department in Hartesville to report the disappearance of Washburn Whitfield.

Whitfield lived alone at the foot of Turkey Mountain in a half-crumbled shack that had been his daddy's, and not many people knew him. He and Coddy had grown up together. Coddy and his wife lived around the other side of the mountain, and Mrs. Turner scarcely approved of old Wash. Wash, she always liked to say, was a strange name for a man who seldom did.

Wash rarely came around, but Coddy felt sorry for him, even as strange as he had gotten since they had gone off to join the Marines together fifty years ago and fought the Japanese on the other side of the world. So he stopped in to visit once a week or so. After all, old Wash probably wasn't any odder than he would have been himself if he hadn't married.

On the 26th of September Coddy stopped at Wash's place on the way to Hartesville, and Wash asked him to bring back a box of salt and some baking soda. But when Coddy came by on his way home to deliver the stuff, he couldn't find Wash, which was odd since his '72 Chevy pickup was sitting next to the house. Coddy left the two items by the sink in the kitchen and went on home.

Worried, he went back the next day and nothing seemed to have changed. He yelled and got no answer. He even looked in the privy, fearing the old man's heart had quit on him there, but it was empty except for a couple of spiders. The salt and the baking soda still sat on the old porcelain sink.

Wash had never gotten a telephone, so Coddy went home and called the sheriff.

Ellen Mashburn, the day-shift dispatcher, took the call, a brief one because Coddy wasn't a big one for talking. Checking her board, she saw that Deputy Grimes ought to be around Turkey Mountain somewhere.

"Seventeen, ah, what's your twenty?" she said into her mike in the sweet sing-song voice she'd been using for the Harte County sheriff for thirty years.

"Seventeen. I'm at mile 12 on Highway 30," came the answer.

"Seventeen, you hidin' behind Lucy's Market again?" asked Ellen. "Listen, you know the Turner place out offa 153?"

"Ah, yeah. Coddy Turner you mean?"

"That's ten-four. He just called in a missing person report on old Wash Whitfield. Says he hasn't been able to find him. Like you to go pick up Mr. Turner and drive over to the Whitfield place, see what you can find."

"Ten-four," replied the deputy.

Half an hour later he pulled up to the Turner double-wide, where Coddy was waiting for him on the porch, and twenty minutes of silent driving got them around the mountain and up the set of ruts that served the Whitfield place as a driveway.

"I looked in the house yesterday and today," Coddy said, "and he ain't there. He ain't in the privy. That there's his only vehicle, and it ain't moved in two days. I been comin' round to see Wash 'bout all my life, and only times he wasn't around the place, then his vehicle wasn't neither."

"You got a key to the house?" Grimes asked.

Coddy looked at him. "Ain't no key," he said. "Go on in."

The two men entered, Grimes, in his khaki uniform, leading. What appeared to have been a two-bedroom house had decayed to a kitchen and one room, sealed off from the rubble with sheets of unpainted plywood. There was a stove, a chair and a bed, and a small table with two chairs in the kitchen. The place smelled of stale food, mold, and old man.

What dishes, pots and utensils were available were washed and stacked in a drainer. The sagging old bed was made, a blanket over the gray sheets.

"Looks like he ain't been here in a while," the deputy said.

Coddy grunted and then stopped, looking at the wall by the stove. "Now that's somethin' I didn't notice before," he said.

"What?"

"He kept a old .22 bolt-action on that rack, right under the 12-gauge."

The shotgun, Grimes saw, was about the cleanest thing in the house. "Doubt if somebody would've stolen the rifle and left the gun," the deputy said.

"Somethin' else I didn't think to check," Coddy said, stepping to the bed. He reached under the mattress up to his elbow, and pulled out an envelope. It was full of cash.

"Old Wash's bank," he said, a faint note of grief entering his voice. "Wouldn't have left this behind. Guess you better take it," he said, handing the envelope to Grimes.

The two men walked back to Grimes's patrol car, where he put the envelope in a plastic bag after counting the money—a total of $735—and having Coddy initial it. Then, being the official on the scene, he peered into the cab of the pickup, which was empty, its seat covers ripped and the roof fabric hanging down, then opened the door to the privy. The stench almost brought him to his knees before he could slam the door shut.

"No dog?" asked Grimes.

"No, never saw one," Coddy answered. "Just some chickens."

They walked down the ruts past the house toward the caved-in barn. The remainder of a SEE ROCK CITY sign could just be deciphered on its roof. Half a dozen chickens ambled in and out of the wreckage, clucking disconsolately. What used to be a small cornfield was overgrown, waist-high with grass. The remains of an old mechanical shucker rusted behind the barn.

A faint path was visible through the grass to the tree line at the foot of Turkey Mountain. "Where's that go?" Grimes asked.

"Wash'll go up in the woods, see can he get a squirrel," said Coddy. "Can't afford much groceries."

"Would've taken the rifle, he was after squirrel," Grimes said, and began walking slowly through the grass.

Coddy just grunted and followed the deputy.

At the edge of the woods, hickories and maples and poplars, Grimes stopped, looking around. "You smell something, Mr. Turner?" he asked.

Coddy sniffed. "Yeah, a little. Don't smell very good."

"You got that right," Grimes said, tension in his voice. "You up to helping me look?"

"Hell, yes," said Coddy. He might be eighty-five years old, but he wasn't going to turn his back on a friend, alive or dead and starting to stink. "I seen plenty of corpuses. I was a Marine in '43."

"Good. You go up that way," Grimes said, pointing up the mountain to the right. "I'll take the left. Don't get out of sight. You lose the smell, holler."

Turkey Mountain at this point was a very mild grade, and

neither man had hard going. Deputy Grimes was beginning to think he had lost the scent when he heard Coddy's strangled shout.

He could see the old man staggering out of a hollow at the base of a big hickory, and he appeared sick, gasping for air. Grimes ran to him.

"Him?"

"Think so," Coddy said, his eyes bulging and his face a sickly gray. "What I could tell."

"What's wrong, Mr. Turner?"

Coddy reached out and held on to a sapling as though he might be about to fall.

"Somethin's ate him."

Within an hour, every element of law enforcement that Harte County could muster—four of the sheriff's twelve blue-and-white Crown Victoria patrol cars, the county coroner's car, and an EMS truck from Harte County Hospital—was arrayed behind Wash Whitfield's shack, all under the command of Sheriff Grady Brickhouse.

Coddy Turner's wife, considered by her neighbors something of a wit, often said that Brickhouse was an odd name for a man who wasn't built like one. Grady Brickhouse was built more along the lines of a ripe pear, which was only one of the things that kept getting him elected. Brickhouse was probably the most popular sheriff in Georgia.

He was a local boy who went away to school at Athens and came back to teach English at Harte County High, and within ten years was principal of the school. When the DEA peeked into the pocket of a Miami drug runner and found the sheriff of Harte County, Grady Brickhouse ran for the office and was elected in a landslide. No one had bothered to run against him since.

Sheriff Brickhouse wore the same khaki shirt and pants and hat as his fourteen sworn deputies. In fact, any of the six deputies on the scene, including Chief Deputy Mark Weinman, would have been taken for sheriff more quickly than Brickhouse; they were trim, fit, and mostly young, while the sheriff was lumpy, easily winded, and on the far side of middle age.

He was also somewhat sickly that afternoon, having gone up a carefully prescribed trail, the one already tramped out by Coddy Turner, to view the remains of Wash Whitfield. There was not much to see—just his head and the upper part of his shoulders, his feet in their boots, and four fingers scattered around, all lying in a pool of congealed blood and covered with late-season flies. The remains had only recently begun to smell.

His .22 rifle lay six feet and four inches away from his head, by tape measure. It had not been fired. The coroner, Emory Hadfield, was no medical man and had no idea what had happened to Wash Whitfield, but Hadfield, Weinman, and Brickhouse had all dealt with bodies found outdoors after being dead much longer than old Wash, and nothing had done this to them. An army of raccoons and foxes would have been required for this.

Brickhouse summoned one of the EMS paramedics.

"Jimmy," he said, "I hate to lay this on you, but I want you to put Mr. Whitfield in a bag and take him down to the crime lab in Atlanta. Be real careful; use those gloves and don't lose any of the fingers. Get it down there right away. We got to know what happened to him. And Jimmy, not a word of this to anyone. Far as you know, Mr. Whitfield went up there after squirrel, died, and the animals got to him, which is probably what did happen. But we don't want rumors."

"Okay, Sheriff," said Jimmy without enthusiasm.

"Don't forget, when you radio back to the hospital, have them call your mom and tell her you'll be gone overnight. County'll pay for your hotel bill, but it won't pay for anything you spend in that Cheetah Club place."

"Okay, Sheriff," said Jimmy again, considerably brighter. He pulled a silvery bag from the back of his orange-and-white truck, put a surgical mask on his face and surgical gloves on his hands, and walked up the trail toward the hickory.

Brickhouse turned to the chief deputy, a thin man in a mustache and perpetual Ray-Bans who looked like anybody's idea of a lawman. "Unless Bill turns up some strange fingerprints inside that dump, this doesn't look easy, Mark."

" 'Fraid you're right," said Weinman. "Got four men up there fannin' out around that mess and they haven't found diddly. Ground's too rocky for tracks. Whitfield didn't leave any going up there; no reason to think the perp did either."

"You think somebody killed him?"

"Come on, Grady. What else?"

"Well, I was hoping maybe heart attack."

"Now that'll be damn hard to show, without a heart, won't it? I could buy it, maybe, if what's left of him wasn't six feet from his rifle. Man had a heart attack, he'd drop the piece where he stood. Wouldn't fling it six feet. More likely he was hit a hell of a blow from behind, sent the rifle sailing."

"Why?"

"God knows, Grady. People do it for fun now."

"Not in Harte County."

"Nobody says the perp has to be a constituent, Grady. Gangbangers down in Atlanta, they got good cars, you know."

"Well, shit, Mark, you gonna try to convince me some fifteen-year-old kid from one of them projects loaded himself up on crack, drove up here, crept out in the woods, and killed that old man? Hell, that road out there don't lead from anywhere to anywhere. You got to know where you're going to get here. Besides, what about the money under the bed? Place wasn't turned over at all."

Weinman had no reply, and they both stood watching the deputies scouring the ground and the EMS technician, under the eye of the coroner, collecting the remains.

"Anyway, we're both pissin' in the wind with all that," Brickhouse said. "The how and the why aren't the biggest problems right now."

"Yeah."

"You think somebody butchered him?"

"If they did, they used a damn strange tool to do it with. It didn't look like cutting to me."

"Maybe Coddy was right. Maybe something did eat him."

"You know anything out here that hungry, Grady?"

Harte County had, on the average, three homicides a year, and one and a half of those took place within Hartesville and thus were the responsibility of the Hartesville Police Department. There was also an average of four bodies each year in the county that had to be shipped to Atlanta for an autopsy to determine the cause of death. Most were unskilled hikers who got lost, died of hypothermia, and were found weeks or months later.

So Grady Brickhouse was not a major customer of the scientists at the Georgia Bureau of Investigation headquarters on

Panthersville Road outside Atlanta, but the chief pathologist, Dr. Herman Steinberg, counted the mountain sheriff among his better friends, a professional who could talk about things besides perps and power, and who never got pushy.

Steinberg ran a lab that was always about a dozen corpses behind and backed up a weeks on tests, so he valued sheriffs who weren't pushy. He didn't hesitate to pull down his mask and pick up the phone on the wall in the autopsy room when the intercom told him Sheriff Brickhouse was calling.

"Grady, how are you?"

"I'm fine, Doc. How 'bout you?"

"Well, I got an ugly sonofabitch staring up at me on table no. 1 here, but otherwise not too bad. What's up?"

"I got a real strange one headed down to you."

"Hell, Grady, the ones we get, they're all strange. I tell you about that stiff came in from Waycross with a hamster up his ass? New intern opened him up. You shoulda heard her scream when she saw that damn thing."

"Hamster killed him?"

"Naw, heart attack. Matter of fact, I'm pretty sure somebody put the hamster in there post mortem."

"That surely is a strange one, Doc, but the one I'm sending you isn't so funny. Fact is, it's got me scared shitless."

"What is it?"

"It's what's left of an old man who went squirrel hunting behind his house yesterday. At least he was last seen yesterday morning and wasn't around yesterday afternoon. We found him today. All we found was his head, his shoulders, which were still attached, his feet, and some fingers."

"Goddamn, Grady, isn't anybody feeding those crows up there?"

"Doc, how many outdoor stiffs you get that only got the head and feet left?"

"Well, to be honest, I can't think of one. But what about wild hogs? They can play hell with a corpse, you know."

"Yeah, but it'd be strewn all over the mountain. What's left of this old guy was all in one place. I don't know what we got here, but it doesn't look good. I was hoping, since there isn't all that much to look at, you might be able to slip it in ahead. You know how I hate to ask a favor like that, but there it is."

"Grady, you're a mensch. I'll do what I can for you. You say it's on the way?"

"Yeah, Harte EMS is on the road now. Ought to be there before closing time, he doesn't get hung up at one of them nudie joints down there."

"Good. I'll try to get back to you tomorrow."

"Thanks, Doc. I surely appreciate it. You take care."

"Don't mention it, Grady. Stay well."

Weinman walked into the office, Ray-Bans still in place, as the sheriff hung up his phone.

"Anything?" Brickhouse asked.

"Only prints Bill came up with in the house were Whitfield's, Turner's, and a couple of Grimes's. Nothing but Whitfield's on the .22."

Weinman pulled an evidence envelope out of his shirt pocket and tossed it on the sheriff's desk. "Only thing we got is this. Jameson found 'em ten feet from the remains."

"Hairs?" Brickhouse asked, looking at the packet.

"Yeah. Stuck to a bush about three feet off the ground. Seem too stiff for human hairs. Maybe a bear."

"Uh-huh," agreed the sheriff. "No telling how long they

been there, either. Well, pack 'em up and send 'em down to the GBI. I'm not gonna ask for a rush on them. Wouldn't do any good, and besides I got Doc Steinberg to more or less agree to take a look at the remains tonight or tomorrow." He paused, thought of something, and looked up.

"Whitfield have family anywhere?"

"Haven't found any yet. Turner says he never knew any but the father, and he died in '57. Bill went back out to the shack, gonna look through things, see if he can find papers or anything might show some relatives. Took some tools with him, too, put a padlock on the door. Not much in there, but I expect it belongs to someone."

"You're a good man, Mark."

"Damn right," said the chief deputy, "and I'm going home for some dinner."

"Me too, pretty soon," Brickhouse said. The sheriff and his wife had never been able to have children, and although Weinman was a little old for the role, the sheriff often caught himself thinking of the chief deputy as a son.

Mark Weinman had been an all-state end on the Harte County High football team while Brickhouse was principal. He had gone on to the university—too light to play college ball—and upon graduating joined the FBI.

When Brickhouse was elected sheriff, he was dismayed, if not surprised, at what he found in the department, and quickly set about convincing Agent Weinman that leaving the feds and coming back to Harte County as chief deputy would be more interesting than chasing white-collar criminals in Tulsa, Oklahoma. Weinman brought professional law enforcement training to the department, and Grady could forgive him those damn Ray-Bans glued to his head.

It was only a little after five, so Brickhouse worked on the duty roster for leaf season a while, then closed up his office and drove home. He couldn't get his mind off Wash Whitfield, especially the way the old man's eyes had seemed to bug out of his bodyless head as though the last thing he'd seen was a hell of a surprise.

September 27

A little after ten the next morning, Ellen turned on the intercom to tell Brickhouse that Doc Steinberg was on the line from Atlanta.

"Morning, Doc," the sheriff said. "Stuff get there okay?"

"Oh, yeah. I came in a little early to look at your old fellow this morning. Tell you what, Grady, you're right. You've got a strange one up there."

"What killed him, Doc?"

"Grady, dammit, you saw that mess. No way anybody can tell what killed him. Find the rest of him, maybe we can get an idea. But not from what you sent me."

"You think somebody cut him up?"

"No. He wasn't cut up. He was chewed up."

"You mean something ate him?"

"There's no way I can testify to that. For all I know whatever chewed him up may have spit him out and carried him off in a crocus sack. But I would testify that in my best judgment, what separated these various body parts was a chewing, tearing action. They were not severed by a knife, ax, saw, or any kind of blade known to me," Steinberg said, falling by habit into the formal language of the witness stand.

"Anything else?"

"There were some odd hairs, looked like animal hairs. I sent them to the lab, but they're covered up. Be a few weeks before we get a report."

"Yeah, one of my deputies found some hairs stuck to a bush. Mark mailed 'em to you this morning. A bear, maybe?"

"May be. I'm not a hair man, except to say they weren't human. But don't get your hopes up about bears, Grady."

"Oh, I know. Bears won't usually bother a human corpse. Probably just sniffed him over."

"Yes, and I can usually identify bite marks—human, dog, raccoon, rat, fox, things that tend to gnaw on our stiffs. Never saw one chewed by a black bear, but I'll tell you this, Grady. If a bear did that, then to coin a phrase, it was a nightmare bear."

"Come on, Doc."

"Grady, if I judged the breadth of the bites right, whatever separated that old man's carcass could have bit a bear's head off in one snap."

"Doc, you sure as hell aren't cheering me up. Any ideas?"

"Yeah. Keep your doors locked."

Brickhouse sagged back in his chair, rubbed his face for a minute, then got up and walked down the short hall to the chief deputy's office.

"Morning, Mark," he said.

"Morning, Sheriff. Ellen says Doc Steinberg called."

"He did. It was not good news," Brickhouse said and repeated the pathologist's report.

"What the hell are we gonna do, Mark? I can't even think where to start."

"Far as I can see, Sheriff, there isn't much we can do. We don't really know if what tore him up was what killed him, and we can't even think of what it might have been that tore him up. We've examined the scene as best we can, and came up with half a dozen hairs that may mean nothing at all. By the book, we've done everything, and if we start going around the county asking people if they've seen something big enough to bite a bear's head off, we're going to be up to our ass in alligators. I don't think there *is* anything to do now."

"So we just wait and see what happens?"

"That's about it," said the chief deputy from behind his Ray-Bans.

The intercom squawked. "Sheriff, you in there?"

Weinman punched the button. "Yeah, the man's here, Ellen."

"Jason Tanner wants to see you, Sheriff."

Weinman punched the button off and looked at Brickhouse. "Started already," he said.

"Maybe," said Brickhouse, turning to leave. "Tell her to send him in."

Jason Tanner was the only reporter at the weekly *Harte County Herald*, a young man of small ambition and mild curiosity. Jason Tanner was not a digger, but he could probably detect a story if it was thrown into his lap, and Grady Brickhouse had a strong aversion to lying. He could live with not telling the truth, but he would not lie.

"Jason, how are you this morning?" he asked, leaning over the desk to shake the pudgy young man's hand.

"Just fine, Sheriff. And you?"

"Well enough, son. What's up?"

"Understand you found a dead body out by Turkey Mountain yesterday. Man named Whitfield. What can you tell me?"

Brickhouse paused, mind racing.

"Not much to tell, Jason. Old fellow, Wash Whitfield, eighty-seven years old. Lived alone out there on the family place, what was left of it. Appears he went up the mountain a ways hunting squirrel and died."

"What of?"

"Well, we haven't been able to tell yet. He was pretty far gone."

"Pretty far, eh? Smell real bad?"

"Yeah, pretty bad. Found him by the smell. Too far gone to tell for sure, but no evidence it wasn't natural causes."

"Know anything about him?"

"Well, he was born in Harte County, only child as far as I know. Went off to the Marines in the war, fought in the Pacific. Came back here, lived with his daddy. Daddy died in '57. Been alone since then. Most folks knew him said he was a little strange, but really not many knew him. Kinda kept to himself, you know."

"Okay, Sheriff, thanks," said the reporter, rising. "Anything else going on?"

"Nah, it's quiet. Just trying to get ready for leaf season."

When Tanner was out the front door, waving good-bye to Ellen, Weinman walked into Brickhouse's office, a grin under the Ray-Bans.

"I listened, Sheriff. You're a weasel, you know that? 'Pretty far gone.' "

"Did I lie, Mark? Did I?"

"No," the chief deputy said, laughing, "but you oughtta be ashamed. And if this shit gets down to Atlanta and you try it on them, you will be."

"Well, we'll hope it won't ever come to that. We'll just sit tight and hope the whole damn thing goes away, right?"

"I can't think of what else to do. You got any ideas?"

"Me? Last idea I had was hiring you, and you turn out thankless as a serpent's tooth. How's the leaves look?"

"You didn't hire me to be a leaf reader, Sheriff. Call old lady Carter. Ask her to look at her woolly buggers, you want a leaf reading. I'm gonna go arrest somebody."

"Who?"

"Now how the hell you expect me to know that? I can't tell you who I'm gonna arrest 'til I find 'em breaking the law, can I?"

October 1

Where the Appalachian Trail crosses the summit of Bloody Top Mountain there is a hiker's shelter, a simple, windowless log hut with a door at one end and a fireplace at the other. Most hikers stay out of the shelter unless weather forces them in.

The shelter is clean enough, but the lack of ventilation gives it a musty odor, and it's home sometimes to bats and always to mice. It didn't look very inviting to the young couple from Atlanta when, gasping for breath, they reached the boulder-strewn crest of the mountain two hours before sunset.

"I'd rather stay out here in a sleeping bag," Emily Sturdivant said, mopping her forehead with a stylish bandanna. "Kinda creepy in there."

"Yeah," Jon Derico replied, turning away from the door. "We didn't come up here to sleep under a roof anyway."

"Somebody's had a fire over here," Emily said, pointing to ashes between a couple of big rocks.

"Looks like a good place to make one," Jon said. They spent half an hour roaming around gathering up twigs and sticks and an occasional large dead branch. Jon, concentrating hard to remember the articles he'd read, built a fire big enough for cooking but not big enough to get out of hand.

Once it was burning Emily opened her small pack and pulled out a package of buns and a dozen Oscar Meyer wieners. Jon had the mustard and relish in his pack. Emily laid it all out while Jon whittled a couple of sticks to a point.

They sat together on a rock, watching their franks swell and sizzle over the fire.

"Look there," whispered Jon. "To your right."

A fat groundhog was hustling across the rocks, oblivious of their presence, or unconcerned by it. He never gave them a glance. But as he crossed the highest point of the mountain he stopped and, his head moving slowly left to right, surveyed the panorama before him. Then, seeming to shake himself, he waddled swiftly down the other side of the mountain, his glossy fur rippling in the slanted light, and disappeared into the trees.

They ate their hot dogs and sipped warm beer in silence

for a while, then unfurled their sleeping bags in the failing light, arranged their small packs beside them, and slid into the bags. Jon pulled the rubber band off his ponytail and let his long hair hang down. Emily reached out for Jon's hand and held it.

"Look at the stars," she whispered.

"Yeah. Never look like that back in Atlanta, do they?"

They lay quietly, gazing at the sky. Both were juniors at Georgia State, Atlanta's big urban campus. They had grown up in the city, gone to different schools, and met as freshmen at State. They lived with their parents but had vague plans to get married after graduation.

Emily jumped as something flew low and fast over her, creating a slight "*woosh*" and making the stars blink.

"What was that?" she asked, frightened.

"Damned if I know, Em. Musta been a bird or maybe a bat. Wasn't very big, whatever it was."

There were more small whooshes, one after another.

"Chasing bugs is what they're doing," Jon said. "Kinda scary at first, but they won't hurt us."

"Feels like we're being dive-bombed," Emily said.

A screech owl called from the woods, its hollow, trilling, downward-falling cry piercing the darkness.

"Oh, God, now that's scary," said Emily, a shiver in her voice.

"Hell, Em, it's just an owl. You can hear them in your backyard sometimes."

"I've never heard one before."

"Trust me."

"Why's it called Bloody Top Mountain?"

"Indians called it that. Supposed to have been a big battle up here hundreds of years ago."

"Okay. G'night, Jon. I love you."

"Goodnight, Em. I love you too."

The night was pleasantly cool. The moon had not risen above the mountains, and the darkness was nearly complete. Occasionally something whooshed low overhead, and there were stirrings within the trees. Emily, who had never spent a night outdoors in all her twenty-one years, reviewed memorable outdoor moments from horror films she thought she'd forgotten and all the lessons learned from *Deliverance* about the inhabitants of the Georgia mountains.

"You awake?" she whispered, and jumped a little when Jon replied in a normal voice.

"Wide awake. Feel like I'm trying to sleep standing up."

"I don't think I can sleep out here, Jon. Maybe we better try the shelter."

"That's fine with me, honey," he said. He slipped out of his bag and turned on the flashlight he had kept with him.

They picked up bags and packs and, stumbling occasionally on the rocks, went to the shelter. Jon probed every corner with his light; nothing was stirring.

Leaving the door open, they unfurled their bags, dropped their packs beside them, and tried to get comfortable.

Emily leaned over and kissed Jon on the cheek. "G'night again, sweetheart. Thanks for humoring me."

"No problem, Em. We're both new at this."

The dirt floor was level, and the solid walls of the shelter damped the sounds of the night. Sleep came readily to both this time.

Some time later Emily awoke with a start. She had been sound asleep, and suddenly she was wide awake. She lay looking at the rafters, puzzled by the lack of transition. She recalled that before she went to sleep, the rafters were lost in darkness. While she slept, the moon had risen, its light streaming through the open door.

She raised her head enough to look around and saw there was something at the door, something low and bulky. She caught a strangely rank, penetrating odor, something she'd never smelled before.

I'm dreaming, she thought. That's why it seemed so strange to wake up. I didn't really. I'm still asleep. Her right arm was out of the sleeping bag. Slowly, inch by inch, she moved it until she felt Jon's bag. She pressed her fingertips against it. He was still there.

She held her breath and listened. She heard Jon breathing, making the little whistling noise he often did. She thought she heard something else breathing, too. She wasn't sure.

Her neck was getting stiff from holding her head up. The bulky thing in the door was still there. She put her head back down and listened hard. She heard it then, heard it under Jon's whistling. It wasn't something else breathing, really. It was sniffing. It was smelling them, or smelling for them.

Oh God, let this be a dream, please. Let it be a dream.

She stiffened the fingers of her right hand and poked at Jon. He didn't respond. She poked a little harder. He snaffled and squirmed away from her touch, but he didn't wake up.

She lifted her head just enough to look at the door again. The thing was still there. It wasn't outside looking in now. At least part of it was in the cabin. It was so big it blocked out all light at the lower part of the door. The moonlight kept it in silhouette. She let her head back down.

It had to be an animal. Probably a bear.

Let it be a dream, please, please, let it be a dream.

Okay, Emily, if it's a dream, all you have to do is wake up. Wake up.

Nothing changed.

She heard a small sound from the door and raised her head. The thing seemed to be moving toward them. Fear and anger galvanized her and she jerked herself into a sitting position and reached wildly for her pack.

"Get out!" she screamed hoarsely. "Get out get out get out!"

The thing lowered itself and growled. It sounded like an explosion in the little cabin.

Emily hurled her pack at it. Jon leaped up, fighting to get out of his bag, yelling incoherently. The thing whipped sideways, banged itself against the door frame, made a snarly, woofing noise, and disappeared into the night.

"Shut the door, Jon," Emily cried. "Shut it quick."

Jon lurched out of his sleeping bag, fell to one knee, picked himself up, grabbed the door, and slammed it shut. "What's wrong, Em?" he gasped. "What is it?"

"Something was coming inside," Emily sobbed. "Oh, God, it was huge, and it was sniffing, smelling for us."

"Oh, Em, I'm sorry," he said in a consoling voice. He left the door and started toward her. "It must have been a nightmare." The door began to swing open.

"Don't leave the door!" Emily screamed. "Close it! Close it!"

Jon leaped back to the door, felt around the frame, and found a bar. He dropped it into place, locking the door, then returned to Emily.

"It wasn't a nightmare," she sobbed. "I hoped it was, but it wasn't. It was coming after us."

"Okay, babe. Okay. It's all right now," he said, holding the trembling girl, rocking her. "It's gone."

As he comforted her, Jon remembered the noise that awakened him. It hadn't been Emily's shrieks. It had sounded like thunder, under the roof and not above it.

"Musta been a bear, Em," he said. "Just looking for our hot dogs."

"It's still out there," she sobbed.

"No, it's long gone."

"You don't know. It could still be out there."

"The door's locked, Em. It's okay. Go to sleep, now. It's okay."

Eventually, exhausted by terror, she fell asleep, and he lowered her back onto the sleeping bag. He went to the door and listened. He could hear nothing. He got the flashlight and looked at his watch. Three hours, maybe, until daylight.

He got out the Boker Tree pocket knife he bought for the trip, opened the biggest blade, and sat down in front of the door.

He sat there until the sun was fully up, then awakened Emily. They rolled their bags roughly, tied them to their packs, left the cabin, and went down the trail on the south side of Bloody Top Mountain at a near-run. Two weeks passed before they told anybody what had happened.

October 8

Harry Buchholz shifted uncomfortably on the weathered pine boards and wondered what was happening to his luck. Every year for the last six he had taken one whitetail buck from this stand on Copperhead Mountain, and he had taken it within three weeks of season's opening.

But this was the fourth Saturday of the season he had rolled out of bed at four A.M., dragged on his camo suit and boots, driven twenty miles to the mountain, and walked two more in the darkness to his handmade stand, and he had yet to see so much as a doe.

The bushes had quivered now and then at the edge of the clearing, but Harry Buchholz felt he was a cut above the average deer hunter and intended to remain that way. Killing does had long been legal, but Harry would never do it. Nor would he even raise his old .30-06 to his shoulder until he had absolutely, definitely identified his target as a buck worth shooting. And when he had taken that one buck, he would put the carcass in his truck, take it over to Harlan's for butchering, and kill no more deer that year.

This usually meant firing only once each season, because Harry was still a good, if not outstanding, marksman, and he never ventured half-assed snapshots. He hated the idea of chasing a wounded buck all over Harte County and then losing it.

Harry considered himself a hunter, not a killer. He felt a sense of loss, almost of grief, every year when he walked up to his kill, more often than not staring at him with dead eyes. No one, not even his wife, knew that. A man didn't talk about those things, for various reasons, but he wasn't ashamed of it.

Buchholz Appliances would probably never sell enough washers and dryers and refrigerators to finance his dream— an African safari, where he could go up against something that could fight back. It damn sure wouldn't if all the beerbellied bozos who spent the season shooting at anything that moved, often each other, discovered that old Harry was one of them bleeding hearts.

A movement in the undergrowth to his left brought him back from daydreaming, but the small tremor of the brush died quickly and there was nothing more. What in hell had happened to all the deer on Copperhead Mountain? Was the forage bad? Was this side of the mountain shot out? Hunters over in the eastern part of the county were doing all right, from what he had heard, but Walt Hanks, the banker, who had a stand over on Turkey Mountain a few miles away, had said he wasn't having any luck either.

Hanks, however, was not a man Harry thought very highly of. The banker—and the bank—had laid out some pretty serious money a few years ago to keep it quiet about how Hanks had mistaken the Bates boy for a deer and taken a good-size chunk out of his butt with a 12-gauge ball. Old man Bates had told the kid that for that much money he could damn well tell all his buddies he couldn't sit down because he had a boil on his ass.

The sun had driven all the mist off Copperhead Mountain when Harry finally decided to pack it in for another week. He removed the magazine and then popped back the bolt on his rifle, softly ejecting the chambered round into his lap. He lit a cigarette, smoked for a while, and then tied a piece of clothesline rope under the forward sling ring so the rifle would hang butt down, and lowered it carefully to the ground twelve feet below. Then, moving slowly because he was still stiff, he began inching down the ladder nailed to the maple where he'd built his stand.

Grady Brickhouse was reared back in his old Naugahyde La-Z-Boy, an immense ham sandwich on a plate balanced on his gut, a bag of chips shoved between his thigh and the arm of the chair, and a Bud Light in hand, watching Vanderbilt kick Georgia's ass all over the field.

Brickhouse was thinking he might need another sandwich to get him through this torture when the phone rang.

"For you, Grady," Mary yelled.

Brickhouse put his beer down and picked up the portable phone.

"Brickhouse," he said.

"Weinman here," said the chief deputy unnecessarily. "I'm just leaving the house. Pick you up in ten."

"What's going on?"

"Big trouble, probably. I'll explain when I get there. Anyway, you've seen enough of that shit down at Athens by now, haven't you?"

The sheriff heaved his recliner upright and stood, shedding bits of bread, lettuce, and chips, and took his food to the kitchen. "Some kind of trouble, honey. Gotta go."

"I thought so," said Mary. "I'll put dinner on hold until I hear from you. Be careful, now, Grady."

"I don't think it's that kind of trouble," the sheriff said, "but I'll let you know soon as I can tell when I'll be home."

Brickhouse didn't have to change clothes. Mary often groused that there was nothing but khaki shirts and pants in his closet. He checked the mirror, decided the day-old beard wasn't all that bad, clipped on his sidearm, stuck his badgeholder on his belt, picked up his hat, and went out on the porch to wait for Weinman.

The blue-and-white Crown Vic was backing onto the highway when the chief deputy told Brickhouse he'd had a call from the weekend dispatcher.

"Said Dora Buchholz, Harry Buchholz's wife, called in and she was frantic. Said Harry went out to his deer stand this morning and hadn't come home by noon, so Dora drove over where he leaves the pickup and found it still there. She didn't go any further because she wasn't exactly sure where his stand is, but she was sure something was wrong because he's never stayed there anywhere near that long.

"Ray said he sent Jameson over to meet her where she found Harry's car. 'Bout two hours later Jameson radioed in and said he had a full-blown crime scene and asked for all the help he could get. Ray asked him if he'd found Harry, and he said no, but he was acting kind of cagey, I guess because Dora was with him.

"I told Ray to get Bill and Monroe going, and to call Dora's sister and get her over there. Bill's supposed to bring Dora out to the road and wait for the sister—Jean, I think it is—to get there and take Dora home."

"So something's happened to Harry?"

"Sounds like it."

"It's been twelve days, Mark."

"Right."

"If something had to happen to Harry, I'd damn sure rather it'd happened in his bathroom."

The little pullover on an overlook at Copperhead Mountain was nearly full of cars by the time Brickhouse and Weinman arrived, parking beside three blue-and-whites that flanked Harry's big Ford pickup. Dora Buchholz's sister had already picked her up.

Deputy Banks led the sheriff and the chief deputy up the faint trail toward the clearing where Harry Buchholz's stand was fixed to the big maple. When they entered the clearing, Brickhouse could see Jameson sitting on a fallen tree with another deputy, Monroe Tolbert. Thirty paces away was the maple that held the deer stand. Buchholz's rifle, still tied to the rope, rested upright against the tree.

"Where'd you walk, Phil?" he asked Jameson as the deputies came over to meet them. "Along that line there, Sheriff," he said, moving off to the right and sighting down his hand to the tree. "I kept Mrs. Buchholz fairly close to it, too."

"Okay, string some tape, mark it off."

Brickhouse and Weinman went on to the tree. A pair of steel-rimmed glasses lay beside it. Blood was congealed on one lens. A spray of blood arced over the bark about eight feet up the tree, some of it streaked on the butt of the rifle. The ground had been trampled and torn.

"Oh, shit," said Brickhouse.

"Yeah," said Weinman, sighing. "I don't reckon he had a lot left in him after he lost all that."

"Unless it's somebody else's," said Brickhouse.

"My, you do think of everything, Sheriff."

"You see anything in that mess resembles a footprint?"

"No, but the ground's pretty damp after that rain Thursday. What with that and the blood maybe we can pick up something."

Fifteen minutes later, the searchers, fanned out on the compass points from the tree, heard Weinman shout, and found him standing on a grassy shelf overlooking a clear, fast-running stream about twenty yards from the deer stand.

"What, Mark?" asked Brickhouse, panting.

"There," said the chief deputy, pointing at a small depression ten feet away and somewhat back from the edge of the shelf. Dry grass, sticks, and leaves appeared to have been raked into a pile at the back of the depression. After Brickhouse stared at the debris a few seconds, he realized there was a human hand sticking out of it.

"Go real slow, now," said Weinman. "Search on the way in. Don't take a step until you've covered the ground you'll walk on."

The men took twenty minutes to reach the pile, and they found nothing but earth that appeared to have been scraped with a leaf rake. Carefully, they removed the sticks and leaves.

Under them was half of Harry Buchholz. From the navel down, he was missing. So was his throat. The spine was visible through the gaping wound. Jameson whirled away, staggered a few feet and vomited. Brickhouse held himself together by sheer will.

Weinman, apparently immune to the sight, rose and began casting about.

"Sheriff," he called as Brickhouse brought his gorge under control. "Over here."

The chief deputy had found a way down the four-foot drop to the stream and was crouched on a yard-wide, pebbly bank next to the creek. Brickhouse struggled down and joined him.

"Ever see anything like that?" Weinman asked, pointing at a clearly defined print in the bank. A little water had seeped into it.

"Sweet weeping Jesus," wheezed Brickhouse softly. "What the hell made that?"

"Something with a foot big as a bread plate," said Weinman. "Tell you what, I reckon if it's got teeth it could bite off a bear's head."

The Harte County Sheriff's Department could remain quiet about the death of old Wash Whitfield, oddball and semihermit, but the abrupt decease of Harry Buchholz, well-respected businessman, member of the Hartesville Chamber of Commerce, and secretary of the Lions club, was a different matter.

Grady Brickhouse talked to the widow, her sister, and Harry's brother for two hours Saturday night. It was, he told Weinman Sunday morning, the most miserable two hours he ever spent.

"You mean you couldn't just tell 'em Harry was too far gone?" the chief deputy said with a grin.

"Shit, Mark. Dora was damn near hysterical, and Jean started acting like I was hiding a murderer in the trunk of my car. I just kept saying that we had no idea of what killed him or how, and that his body wasn't fit for them to view. I sounded like a broken record.

"Finally, I asked the brother, Don, to step out on the porch. He seems like a fairly level-headed guy, although I don't really know him, he lives over at Fort Hodge. I said to him, 'Look, I am *not* lying. We do not have the foggiest idea what in hell killed your brother, but we don't think it was murder.' So he says, 'Why not?' Finally, I said, 'Look, you seem to be about the right age, were you in Nam?' He says, 'Yeah, I was there.' I asked if he saw combat; he says lots. So I tell him, 'Okay, you can look at the body, and then you can tell me what you think killed your brother.'

"So we went down to the hospital and went to the basement, and Gary down there pulled that mess out for him to see. He stood up to it good, I'll say that, and when he was done we walked outside, and all he says, 'Was there an explosion of some kind, like a mine,' and I said, 'No.' He looks at me a while and then he says, 'You won't just let this go, will you.' I told him, 'Hell no, not in a million years.' But I didn't tell him Harry wasn't the first. So he just thanks me and says he'll take care of the women."

"Good for you, Grady," said Weinman, sitting in Brickhouse's office. He had brought in the plaster cast made of the footprint at Bucktail Creek. The print measured a little over six inches wide by eight and a half inches long.

"Now what? This is Sunday. I figure our people will keep quiet enough, but you got half a dozen people at the hospital saw the remains. So I give it until maybe midday tomorrow before it's all over the county that we don't have but about half of Harry Buchholz."

"I'm taking this cast down to Atlanta tomorrow morning. Ought to be able to find somebody down there who can identify it," said Brickhouse.

October 10

Brickhouse swung his Crown Vic into an empty parking space at Zoo Atlanta a few minutes after ten A.M. Monday. A desultory rain was falling and the lot was nearly empty.

The sheriff identified himself and said he was looking for an expert to examine an animal's footprint, but refused to show it to the five people who passed him ever onward until a tanned, muscular man in a dark beard and pony tail walked into the waiting room.

"Hi, I'm Sam Woodward, curator of mammals," he said with a smile, extending his hand. "Can I help you?"

"I expect you can," Brickhouse said after identifying himself, "but it's a confidential thing, you see."

"Okay," said Woodward, whose khaki outfit wasn't creased and starched as briskly as Brickhouse's. "Come on over to my office."

Once there, Brickhouse took the cast out of a brown paper grocery sack, unwrapped the bubble packing and handed it to Woodward. "Can you tell me what made that print, Doctor?"

Woodward stared at the cast, absently murmured "Not doctor, just Sam," and pulled a heavy volume off of his bookshelf.

He thumbed quickly through the book, stopped, compared the cast to a drawing Brickhouse could not quite make out and nodded.

Grinning, he handed the cast back to Brickhouse.

"Where'd you get this, Sheriff? Is it a joke of some kind?"

"It damn sure isn't any joke, Mr. Woodward. You tell me what it is, maybe I'll tell you where I got it, but I'll tell you right off it's an emergency."

Woodward shrugged.

"Sheriff, that print was made by the right forepaw of a full-grown Bengal tiger."

Brickhouse collapsed onto the chair beside Woodward's desk, nearly dropping the plaster cast.

"My God in heaven," he whispered. "I musta walked into one of those time warps. This just can't be happening."

"Assuming you did make that cast, Sheriff, will you tell me where you made it?" Woodward asked.

"We made it Saturday afternoon, on the bank of Bucktail Creek in Harte County, Georgia, twenty yards from the body of a man whose bottom half was missing."

Winslow paled under the tan. "You really aren't joking, are you?"

"No, Mr. Woodward, I deeply regret to say that I am not. In fact, two weeks ago and about ten miles away, we found the remains of an old man. All that was left of him was his head and shoulders, his feet, and some fingers. The GBI pathologist told me he appeared to have been chewed up."

"You're saying you have a man-eating tiger loose in northeast Georgia?" Woodward said.

"No, sir. I don't know what the hell I've got, other than

bits and pieces of two bodies. You're the expert. You tell me this footprint was made by an abominable snowman, I'd probably believe you."

"This is incredible."

"No shit," Brickhouse snapped. "Pardon me that, Mr. Woodward."

"No problem, Sheriff. You forgive me. I'm just trying to get my mind around this."

"Once you do, I'd be glad of any suggestions."

"Where did you find the body?"

"In a little depression, about twenty feet across and a foot deep. Something had scratched up sticks and leaves and grass from all around onto the body."

"Tigers will do that sometimes, trying to hide their kill from vultures and so forth. Probably intended to come back and finish it up."

After a long silence, Brickhouse looked up with a wry smile. "Don't suppose you're missing one, are you?"

"No, Sheriff, afraid not," Woodward said with a chuckle. "We don't have any Bengals. We have Sumatran tigers. Not much difference except they're noticeably smaller. Want to see one?"

Brickhouse stood up, and they walked out and up a path to a covered area with a huge glass window looking onto a forest scene, soggy with rain. Thirty feet away, under an overhang of fake rock, lay a tiger. Its head was held high, eyes half closed as if about to fall asleep. The tip of its tail twitched occasionally; otherwise it might have been a statue.

"That's Raguno," Woodward said. "He's our male."

"Where's your female?"

"Next enclosure," Woodward said. "Tigers are solitary animals. Males and females only get together in mating season, and even then it can get pretty bloody."

"Rough sex, eh?"

"Indeed."

"Now, you say old Raguno there is smaller than my problem appears to be. What are we looking at in terms of a Bengal tiger?"

"I'm afraid you are looking at the largest and the most powerful cat in the world, with the exception of the Siberian tiger, which is nearly extinct. A male might be 450 to 600 pounds, perhaps 12 feet long, nose to tip of tail, 4 feet high at the shoulder. Generally, a forest animal, and diurnal, by which I mean it will hunt day or night alike."

"They don't normally eat people, do they?"

"No. I'm not a tiger expert by any means, but from what I understand, they generally turn man-eater only when they're forced to. Old age, injury, something that keeps them from killing their normal prey."

"And what's that?"

"In India, several kinds of deer or elk, large and small, buffalo, or, as a next-to-last resort, cattle."

"Why isn't that happening in Harte County?"

"You sure it isn't?"

"Well, we haven't had any reports of cattle missing. Fellow out in the western part of the county did mention he had a couple of sheep disappear about three weeks ago, but he didn't make out a complaint about it."

"Maybe sheep and people are all your tiger's up to."

"Not my tiger, Mr. Woodward, please. My problem, but not my tiger. I'm still having trouble believing this."

"Of course."

They watched Raguno in silence for a while. Finally, Brickhouse said softly, "I'm waiting for suggestions."

"Yes," said Woodward. "Tigers are endangered animals, but obviously someone is going to have to kill this one. The problems of trying to take it alive are insurmountable. Anyway, I suppose public opinion, when it gets out there's a man-eating tiger loose, would rule it out."

"You know any tiger hunters?"

"Tigers are no longer hunted, Sheriff. I can't think of anything but the Department of Natural Resources."

"Yeah. I thought of them too," Brickhouse said without enthusiasm. "One other thing, Mr. Woodward. Any idea how there came to be a tiger in North Georgia?"

"It had to have escaped from some sort of attraction. It's against the law in Georgia to keep that sort of animal privately, although I've heard of places that do. My guess would be a circus or carnival or something like that."

"You heard of any missing a tiger?"

"Hardly. But on the other hand, I can envision some small operation skipping out without reporting it. What would you do to some carny owner who knocked on your door up there and said, 'Pardon me, but I've lost my tiger?' "

"At this point, file two counts of murder against him."

"Given the premise as a whole," Woodward said, "the strangest thing to me is the animal's behavior. Most animals born in captivity don't know what to do with freedom. They have no idea how to provide for themselves, and they generally just hang around the vicinity where they escaped until someone finds them. Makes me wonder if your animal—pardon me, your problem—was a live capture smuggled out of India and into this country."

"Well, I guess it really doesn't matter much where it came from or how it got here, although I'll ask the FBI to see if they can find out. Problem is what to do about it. Like you said, DNR is the only thing that comes to mind. Guess I'll go over there now," Brickhouse said, then stopped as a thought came to him.

"You know, they may not believe me. Can I have them call you for confirmation?"

"Certainly, Sheriff," said Woodward. "Let me ask you one thing. When are you going to announce this?"

"Announce it? Jesus Christ, do I have to make a proclamation of some sort?"

"I think you've got to tell people what's going on, tell them how to protect themselves. Sort of like being party to murder if you don't. That is the technical charge, isn't it?"

"Yeah, it is. You're right, of course. So what do I tell them to do?"

"Stay home. Lock their doors."

"Yeah. Somebody already mentioned that. Thank you, Mr. Woodward."

As Brickhouse drove toward the twin towers that house, among other things, the Department of Natural Resources, he thought briefly about walking into the governor's office and asking for the National Guard. No, he told himself, maybe it'll come to that but not now. Just follow the dotted lines. That's what the dotted lines are there for, for people who've run out of ideas or never had any to start with.

The reception he expected at the animal control section was quick in coming. One man laughed so hard he got hiccups. Finally he found Bud Gorman, promoted a couple of years ago from a game ranger's post that included Harte County. Gorman looked at him closely, as though inspecting his head for holes and then at the cast.

"Well, Grady, whatever made this sure as hell don't come natural to Georgia. Now, you mind if I call this fellow over to the zoo?"

"Go right ahead, please," Brickhouse urged.

He listened to the brief conversation, after which Gorman sat at his desk, scratching his head.

"Well?"

"Well, much as I hate to admit it, Grady, I guess you have an animal control problem."

"Bud, I prefer to think that *you* have the animal control problem and that you will do something about it."

"I just wish you had a picture of this damn thing or something."

"Goddammit, Bud," Brickhouse flared. "I just *wish* I had its fucking skin on my wall. I just *wish* I didn't have two bodies look like they went through your grandma's sausage grinder. I just *wish* I was sheriff of Abernathy County, where man-eating tigers are unheard of. I just *wish* I was out in Hollywood in bed with a movie star instead of sitting here talking to a bunch of goddam peckerheaded civil service time servers." The sheriff sagged back in his chair, out of breath.

"Awright, Grady, awright. I'm gonna do the best I can here, but you got to realize that the people we hire are usually paid to thin out nuisance deer or trap problem 'gators. Baddest things they come up against are wild hogs once in a while. Lot of them are going to find out their farms need a shitload of farmin' or their trucks need an overhaul if I mention man-eating tiger to 'em. But I got a guy in mind. I'll try to have somebody up there in a few days."

"Thank you, Bud," said the sheriff. "Sorry I blew up. It's good to find somebody in this joint isn't a laughing jackass. Now I gotta go back to Hartesville and say the same things to my constituents that I said to those turkeys out there. I don't know whether they'll laugh at me or kill me."

"Politics is a bitch, Grady," Gorman observed.

Brickhouse spent the two-hour drive back to Hartesville trying to decide what he would say at a news conference and wondering how he could get people to believe him. As it turned out, that had already been taken care of.

There were four television trucks, two of them with their remote satellite antennas already extended, two Blazers from the *Atlanta Constitution* and a car from the *Gainesville Times* in the parking lot at the sheriff's office. Reporters and cameramen were milling outside the front door. It looked as though the circus had come to town.

Brickhouse drove right on by, went around the block, and parked in the back. He slipped through the hedge and into the back door without being seen.

"What the hell?" he bellowed as he closed and locked the door.

"Sheriff, where have you . . ." began Ellen, but Weinman cut her off.

"What the hell, indeed, Sheriff. What can you tell us about man-eating tigers?"

"What? Where'd you hear about that?"

"From the ladies and gentlemen of the press, Sheriff. I assume you saw the party out on the lawn."

"I don't understand," said Brickhouse.

"No, you don't, Grady," said Weinman, his face red. "You've lived up here all your life among friends. Jason Tanner is your idea of a reporter. Grady, you've got to realize that Jason Tanner is a goddamn armadillo, and those people out there are wolves. Somebody you talked to down in Atlanta picked up the phone and called his buddy the reporter, and the wolves beat you back home.

"It ever occur to you maybe you ought to call up here and let me know what's going on? First time that phone rang and a reporter asked me what we're gonna do about our man-eating tiger, I like to shit."

"Okay, Mark. I get your point. I'm sorry. I left all of you high and dry."

"Lecture's over, Sheriff. Now tell us what's going on."

When he had finished, nobody had anything to say for a few minutes.

"You think a DNR bounty hunter can deal with this?" Weinman asked.

"I don't know. Got to let him try. I'm damn sure no tiger hunter. You know of any?"

"No, but I can think of at least a dozen damn fools who'll start to think they are. Any idea what to do about them?"

"I thought about that, and I don't see there's anything we can do. It's a free country, and there's no closed season on tiger in Georgia. If this animal would be good enough to confine his activities to a square mile or so, maybe we could cordon it off. All we can do is warn people that this tiger is a better hunter than they are."

"You going out there?" Weinman asked, nodding his head toward the front.

"Yep. At least saves me the trouble of calling a news conference."

"Grady, once more," said the chief deputy. "Don't bandy words with those people. Don't tell them about how far gone old Wash was. Tell them the absolute truth about what you want them to know. What you don't want them to know, keep your mouth shut. Say, 'I can't comment on that,' or if you don't have an answer, say 'I don't know.' The longer they think you're honest, the longer they'll play along with you. The minute they get the idea you're blowing smoke up their asses, they'll start doing their own investigating, and then God knows what'll happen. You don't want to see a story about how your momma used to go talk to the tigers in the zoo, do you? And remember, those folks out there are Georgia people. This time tomorrow, every motel in the county is going to be full of reporters from all over the country. Be careful, for God's sake."

"This is going to piss little Jason off," Brickhouse said.

"Probably," Weinman agreed. "That doesn't matter. I hate to be callous, but Jason Tanner and the *Harte County Herald* don't mean much now. Joe Wells won't let Tanner get out of hand even if he knew how. The rest of them, though, they're here to get out of hand."

"Okay, Mark, I'll be careful."

When Brickhouse stepped out of the front door, there was a shout, and the crowd converged on him. For a fleeting moment, the chief deputy's wolf analogy became real, and he saw himself crippled and abandoned to the pack.

He raised his hand against the clamor and shouted, "Okay, okay, folks. I'm Grady Brickhouse, sheriff."

"Sheriff," bellowed a cameraman. "Before we start, you mind moving out by the flagpole? Light's bad here."

As he was trudging to the pole, he heard the door open behind him and turned to see Tolbert bring out the speaker's stand they used for safety lectures. Silently the deputy set it near the pole. "Thanks, Monroe," Brickhouse whispered.

The cameramen fussed with the stand, arranging it and then festooning it with microphones. There was no jockeying or elbowing; they were all from Atlanta. They all knew each other and did this together every day.

When they moved back and hoisted their cameras onto tripods, Brickhouse stepped to the stand. As though on signal, the hubbub started again, every reporter trying to get his attention.

"Wait, folks, now wait," Brickhouse shouted. When the shouting subsided, he said "Why don't I just tell you what we know, and then you can ask questions."

"Good," said a young woman with a notebook.

"All right," he began. "We don't know much, and the facts we do have are not very well connected. But as far as we know, this started two weeks ago when we found the remains of a man named Washburn Whitfield in the woods behind his house out at Turkey Mountain.

"It appeared Mr. Whitfield had gone squirrel hunting. He had a .22 rifle with him, which had not been fired. The thing was, and I'm not sure how to put this tastefully, but there wasn't very much of Mr. Whitfield left. Doctor Steinberg down at the GBI couldn't make a guess as to cause of death, but he said the remains appeared, in his words, to have been chewed."

A little ripple of satisfaction ran through his audience.

"Mr. Whitfield was about eighty years old, I forget exactly, but he lived alone out there. No witnesses, no tracks, no prints, no evidence of any kind but some hairs we sent down to the lab. Frankly, we didn't know which way to turn.

"Then on Saturday, Harry Buchholz was killed at the foot of his deer stand over on Copperhead Mountain. We found his remains down the mountain, near Bucktail Creek. There was a little more of him than there was of Mr. Whitfield, but the body looked in the same condition. Something had scraped debris—twigs and grass and so forth—over it.

"Down on the bank of the creek, our chief deputy, Mark Weinman, found a footprint. We made a cast of it, and today I took it down to the zoo in Atlanta. Mr. Sam Woodward, the curator of mammals there, told me there is no doubt that it was made by a Bengal tiger."

The uproar started again. Grady looked out over the dozen reporters and camera people—cameramen was incorrect; one of them was a woman—and saw Weinman and Jameson standing well back.

Then a stentorian voice boomed over the rest. "Sheriff, you got that cast with you? Can you hold it up for us?"

Weinman whispered in Jameson's ear, and the deputy loped off behind the building. Moments later he returned with the grocery bag. Brickhouse pulled out the dull white cast and held it up.

Cameras whirred and clicked.

"Sheriff," said a blond reporter. "What're you gonna do now?"

"Well, Miss—"

"Kathleen Bentley, *Journal-Constitution*," she said in a husky voice.

"Well, Miss Bentley, we're going to have to assume, crazy as it seems, that we have a tiger loose around here who's killing people and eating them. We have no idea how it got here or where it came from. Nobody's seen it that I know. Frankly, I still kind of think this is going to turn out to be something entirely different. But we have the fact of two mangled bodies.

"As to what we're going to do, well, obviously we have to look for this animal and kill it. The Department of Natural Resources has agreed to send us a professional hunter as soon as possible."

"They don't have much experience with tigers, do they, Sheriff?" asked a man whose hair appeared to have been glued in place.

"No," Brickhouse replied. "Do you?"

That drew a laugh.

"Mr. Buchholz had a lot of family around here, I understand," said another reporter. "How have they reacted to this news?"

"Well, sir, I just got back with the news myself, and I guess I was a little naive not to realize it would get here ahead of me. But I expect Chief Deputy Weinman"—he looked over the crowd, and Weinman nodded slightly—"has informed them. I cannot tell you their reaction, and I hope you'll try not to bother them."

As soon as he said it, Brickhouse realized that was a forlorn hope.

"What are you telling the people of Harte County to do, Sheriff?" shouted a well-dressed woman.

"Well, ma'am, about all we can tell them is to take every precaution they can. It's my understanding that tigers hunt whenever they're hungry, day or night. I'd suggest that people, especially those in the western part of the county, go outdoors as little as possible, and I realize how ridiculous that will sound to farmers who have stock to care for. But I would a lot rather see cattle and sheep killed than farmers. I expect it would be wise for those who must go out to tend their farms to go armed and in groups.

"But I do want to emphasize that the last thing we need is

a bunch of hunters running around in the woods looking for this animal. The potential for an accidental shooting would be enormous, and they would be exposing themselves to terrible danger from the tiger. We have a professional hunter coming, and we need to give him room to do his job."

"Sheriff," asked another man, "what are you doing about finding where this tiger came from?"

"I'm going to ask the federal agencies, the FBI and the fish and game people, and the DNR to handle that end of it. I expect you know it is illegal in this state, and I think in most states, to keep animals like this privately. Any reputable attraction would have informed authorities immediately if they had lost one, and we know of no traveling show that has exhibited a tiger around here this fall. So we think it probably got away from people who were just passing through, which means they'll be hard to find, and finding them has to be secondary to eliminating the animal."

"What will you do if the owners of this tiger are found?" the man asked.

"Charge them with the murders of Mr. Whitfield and Mr. Buchholz."

"Do you think more people will be killed?"

"I pray not."

"Where's the hunter going to look for the tiger?"

"He's the hunter, not me. But all the evidence we have suggests western Harte County."

"Sheriff, I understand that in India, hunters used to sit in trees over human kills to shoot man-eating tigers. Is there a chance you'll take Buchholz's body back out there?"

Brickhouse stared in disbelief at the reporter.

"No sir, no chance of that. We were hoping you'd volunteer."

"You ever hear of man-eating animals in this part of the country before?"

"No sir, nor any other part of the country. In Harte County we get more reports of flying saucers than we do tigers."

"Any chance it might just go away?"

"If it goes away, it's got to show up somewhere else, unless it dies of old age, and wherever it goes it'll get hungry again. I won't wish Harte County's problem off on any of our neighbors."

"Have you asked the governor for help, for troops, maybe?"

"No. I'd like some expert to tell me it might do some good before I ask for the National Guard."

"Sheriff, you seem awfully calm."

"Well, I still have the feeling this is a bad dream and I'll wake up before long." Brickhouse said. "But the people I've talked to up to now say we're doing the right things."

"Tha-ank you, Sheriff," said the blonde with a wicked grin, and the reporters dispersed. Television crews began setting up their live shots—Brickhouse politely declined to be part of any of them—and print reporters left to file their stories.

Inside, Weinman patted Brickhouse on the shoulder. "That was pretty good, Sheriff, pretty good. That last line may come back to haunt you, but overall you did good."

"What'd I say wrong?" Brickhouse asked.

On the phone in her room at the Best Western, Bentley was talking to her editor after unloading her story.

"Kathy, this is a hell of quote here where he says, 'I'll wake up before long.' I mean, all they're doing is bringing in some DNR deer hunter and telling people to hide in their homes. Sounds like maybe he needs to wake up. What do you think about working that into the lead?"

"I thought about that, Alan. It is a damn good quote, but that isn't what he meant by it, and actually he seems to be a pretty sharp guy. I talked to some people who know him before I drove up here and they're all real high on him. I wouldn't feel right making him out to be an idiot right now. Let's give him some rope."

"Okay, I'll go along with that. Now what we need is a mood-of-the-county piece. Talk to people in town, go out to some of the country stores, stop at some farms, get lotsa quotes. Get back to me before six thirty.

"You need some help, Kathy? I want you to be careful up there."

"Come on, Alan. You think I'm scared of this tiger? Tell you this, I feel a damn sight safer in Harte County than I do in John Hope Homes. I don't need help, honey. Just don't even think about pulling me off this."

"Well, all right, but don't go to sleep under any trees."

"Shit," she snorted.

Mary Newton was an Atlanta girl when she met Grady Brickhouse at the University of Georgia. They were in the same class, both going for a degree in education, and the day after they graduated they were married in the Methodist church where her father was pastor. They both got jobs at Harte County High.

Mary still had blond curly hair, although it took a touch of coloring to keep the gray out, and she'd put on a little weight over the years. She still taught English at the high school.

The only regret she had was the lack of children. She and Grady never tried to find out what the problem was. They decided it was better not to know whose reproductive system was flawed. That way there couldn't be any blame.

Lacking children, she had just gone on babying Grady, who accepted it gratefully. She had been so proud of him when he was made principal of their school and even prouder—and astonished—when he decided to run for sheriff. He was such a gentle man, she thought, and it was still sometimes a shock to see him in that lawman getup with a gun on his belt. But the job hadn't changed him much, not personally, at least.

It had just about ruined his use of the language, however. He had gradually started talking like a hillbilly gumshoe. Now he didn't talk the way her old Grady used to talk unless he got mad, and he hadn't been mad at her in a great many years. They knew each other so well, adjusted to each other's peculiarities so thoroughly, that there was nothing left to get mad about.

She heard about the tiger in the teacher's break room between fourth and fifth periods. Old Mrs. Jameson—her son was one of Grady's deputies—was almost hysterical. She was afraid of house cats, and they couldn't convince her the tiger wasn't going to show up on Maple Street and scratch on her door. They had to send her home. The principal came in and handled her class. He said he was glad to get away from the phone.

When school was out, the drive was lined with cars from out in the county, parents picking up students who normally rode the bus. Some people seemed downright scared, and a lot more on the verge of it.

Mary stopped at the A&P on the way home. It looked like this might be the worst time ever for Grady, worse than the time they found those boys selling amphetamines in the restroom. She wanted to fix him a sirloin and mashed potatoes for dinner, and if there was time, a German chocolate cake.

Brickhouse wasn't surprised when the phone began ringing at five minutes after six. In fact, he had the cordless at the dinner table.

"Grady? Cal Heflin. You lost your goddamn mind?" started the county commission chairman.

"Not quite."

"What is this man-eating lion shit? I come home, perfectly nice day, leaf season maybe a week off, county got a chance to make a little money for a change, and next thing I know my goddamn phone's ringing off the hook, people wanna know what about this man-eating lion, Grady says we got a man-eating lion loose. You gone completely crazy?"

"Cal," Brickhouse said when Heflin slowed down, "in the first place, I never said anything about lions. It's a tiger."

"Now that sure 'n' hell makes me a lot happier, Grady."

"Cal, I've made some mistakes today, but I've caught a lotta crap for them and I don't need this ragging. Now you just calm down."

"The biggest mistake you ever made in your life was going on that damn teevee cryin' about man-eatin' whatevers. You done ruined leaf week and prob'ly made us out to be the laughing stocks of the whole damn country. I didn't see the Atlanta stations, but I figure that sonabitch Brokaw's gonna come on and say, like, "Folks, you wanna think twice about going up Harte County see them leaves, 'cause all them hillbillies is runnin' round scared o' tigers.' Jes-us, Grady."

"Now I'm gonna tell you a few things, Cal," Brickhouse interrupted, his voice flat. "First, I was elected to protect the people of this county, not to enhance the goddamn economy, and if you don't think they need protecting, you go get in your car and drive over to Howard's Mortuary before they get Harry Buchholz fixed up and take a look at what's left of him. Second, don't worry about your damn leaf week. I learned a few things about human nature today, and there's gonna be so many people swarming into this county they'll trample those half-assed apple stands of yours. And third, get off my back and stay off or I'll throw your fat ass in jail for highway mopery." He punched the phone off and dug into his mashed potatoes.

"Grady, this is really going to be awful, isn't it?" Mary said.

"Ah, Mary, I'm not upset. I just don't let pompous fools like Cal Heflin get away with anything. Not good practice. But, to be more direct, unless we get lucky it's going to be a long, hard pull, and it'll probably have an effect one way or another on everybody in the county. You know, it's so incredible, so unreal, that I still haven't accepted it.

"Think about it, Mary. You remember, it wasn't more'n twenty-five years ago or so we first started climbin' up to the top of Turkey Mountain with a lunch basket, havin' a picnic up there where it seemed like the whole world stretched out around us. Doesn't seem very long ago the last time we did. But tonight, there's something up there that'll kill you. Kill you and eat you too.

"How many counties of ten, fifteen thousand ordinary, English-speaking people with telephones, teevees, cars, and all that you ever hear of having a man-eating tiger loose? Isn't that a hell of a thing?

"Remember back when we were kids, that leopard got loose from the zoo in Oklahoma City? There were things in the papers about it, and, God, it caught my imagination. A leopard loose! I kept thinking, what if that was here? What if it was Atlanta? Would it come up here? Would I look out the window and see it? As I recall, everybody with a gun in Oklahoma was out leopard hunting."

"I don't remember that," Mary said. "What happened? Was anyone hurt?"

"Nothing. Found the poor damn animal starved or nearly so right outside the zoo. But the point I'm making is that this is the information age now, and by tomorrow this town, and this county, is gonna be under a microscope.

"But, no, I'm not upset. You remember two years ago, that crazy bastard from over at Johnstown took that little Upton child and raped her and killed her? Now *that* upset me. I never yet fired a weapon anywhere but a practice range, Mary, and I never told you this before 'cause I was ashamed of it, but when Mark and I went out to get that creep I was hoping for a chance to kill him. This, though, this is an animal, an honest-to-God animal, and it's only doing what it has to do to survive. It's gotta be put down, but it's kind of hard to get mad at it.

"What I am, Mary, is scared. I don't recall seeing anything in any of my how-to-be-sheriff manuals that talked about man-eating tigers. I got a pretty good idea what to do about terrorists or civil unrest or snipers. I know what to do about a rabid raccoon, but I'll be damned if I can think of anything to do about a man-eating tiger holed up in the mountains. That's a lot of country. So if anything comes to you, the high sheriff would appreciate you sharing it with him."

The phone rang again.

"Sheriff? Is that Sheriff, ah, Brookhouse?" asked a voice that seemed to be crying faintly from the bottom of a barrel.

"Yes, this is Brickhouse."

"I say, Sheriff, my name is Westerby, at the *Times* of London. We have just dispatched a reporter to, ah, Hartesville, but he cannot get there until tomorrow, and we're wondering if in the meantime you could tell us. . . ."

Brickhouse covered the receiver, looked across the table and said, "Here we go, Mary," then took his hand away and began, "Well, sir, I really haven't anything to add to what I said. . . ."

Every Atlanta television station led its evening news with the Harte County man-eater, as it became known, and each had an elaborate graphic of the county, showing the sites where Whitfield and Buchholz had been found and emphasizing that the sheriff felt the primary danger lay in the western half of the county.

Country families with relatives in town made arrangements for their children to stay in Hartesville. Those without relatives nearby made plans to move wife and children out of the county altogether in the morning. Older people, and younger ones without children, tended at first to accept the threat of a man-eating tiger as just one more burden to be borne by country people in a liberal regime. After all, for people inured to televised fantasy, a newscaster talking about something they'd never seen wasn't much different from a *Mission Impossible* rerun.

That attitude tended to change abruptly with experience. Late that night Garner Hadley and his wife Sue were watching television in their double-wide off Georgia 153. Garner, getting up to go to the bathroom, glanced out the window.

Thirty yards away, under the pole that held a floodlight illuminating the front yard, was the tiger. It was simply standing there, looking around, like a shopper just arrived at the mall. It was huge. Garner, his bladder under pressure, nearly lost control. He tried to call Sue, but like in his nightmares, he couldn't talk. He could only squeak.

Sue heard him squeaking, saw the color drained from his normally florid face, and ran to the window. As she did, the man-eater took a couple of steps toward the trailer. The Hadleys fled to their bedroom, locked the door, and huddled in a corner until dawn. Then they packed what they could carry, ran to their pickup, leaped into it, and drove to Sue's sister's house in Hartesville.

The news did not penetrate every corner of Harte County that night, for in Harte as in most mountain counties there are recesses so deep that little ever penetrates them. Raven Cove was such a place. A high cut between Copperhead Mountain and Raven Bald, only a ten-mile-long, dirt forest access road passed through it, and there was only one dwelling—the shabby, three-room tarpaper house where Rose Satterly and her nine-year-old son, Roy, lived.

The news of the man-eater didn't reach the Satterly house because it had no television and no radio. If Rose had been able to scrape together the money for either one, it wouldn't have mattered because there was no electricity. The closest electricity was three miles away, at Dugan's store, where the forest road emptied out onto Georgia 153.

The social services of the county and the state had not reached the Satterly house because the people who ran them were unaware of Rose and Roy. Rose had only the vaguest knowledge of such services. She was only vaguely aware of most things.

Four or five times a week Rose walked down to Dugan's store and washed the windows and the glass cases and cleaned the bathroom. Then she went across the highway and cleaned Fred and Annie Dugan's double-wide trailer. She went home with a couple of bags of groceries, a few dollars in cash, and whatever magazines the Dugans were through with.

The Dugans were the only people Rose really knew. Fred and Annie didn't think Rose was all there, for it took a while for her to understand things, but she was quiet and gentle and Annie knew a good thing when she had it going. She had to keep an eye on Fred, though. Life had ground the girl down pretty bad, but she was there, and Fred was always alert to his chances.

Once in a while Rose would meet a man at the store, and he would go home with her. Getting a ride was good, because the walk home was all upgrade. Some would only stay an hour or so, some longer. One stayed nearly a month, and he was nice, helping out around the house and taking Roy out hunting. But one day at the store he saw a state trooper drive by, and he went out the back door and she never saw him again.

Rose was a small, plain woman, thin, wan, and rather ethereal, with faded brown hair. She spoke, generally, when spoken to. No one knew where she came from or what had happened to her.

The only thing Rose really had in all her life was Roy. She wasn't sure who his daddy was. She'd borne him back there in her bedroom. She realized when she had had Roy that she needed a way to keep track of things. Rose didn't have a very good memory. She could remember yesterday just fine and last week pretty good, but after that, things kind of faded away. Rose herself had no idea where she came from or how old she was or who her parents were. She was always amazed when people started talking about things like that.

But they did talk about them, and she understood from

their talk that it was important to know some of these things. So the week after Roy was born, when she took him down to the store with her to do her chores, she asked if she could have one of the free calendars.

She took the calendar home and hung it on the wall in the kitchen and marked off every week, and every year she got a new calendar. Thus she was quite sure that Roy was nine years old, because there were nine marked-up calendars in the bottom drawer of her old dresser plus the one on the wall. When she needed to remind herself of his birthday, she'd go back to the first calendar, where it was marked.

Roy hadn't started school yet. Rose didn't know if she had been to school or not, but she guessed she must have been since she could read, slowly, and write, even more slowly, and do simple sums. She knew Roy needed to go, but she wasn't sure when he should start going, and she kept forgetting to ask Annie.

Rose was determined that Roy would grow up to be a gentleman. If he grew up to be a gentleman, he could go out into the world, and well . . . she wasn't sure what gentlemen did, really. She knew they spoke quietly and were nice to everybody. They were clean, and their clothes were nice and looked new, and they drove nice, clean cars. They paid for their gas and their snacks with little cards, not cash money. Annie had pointed out these gentlemen to her until she could pretty well pick them out herself. None of them ever came home with her. She did her best to teach Roy to be a gentleman.

Rose had found a tattered old dictionary somewhere, she didn't remember where, but she knew how to use it. When Roy started talking, she began bringing home the magazines, mostly *National Geographics*, and reading to him as best she could. Before very long Roy was reading to himself, and she showed him how to use the dictionary. The book was in two pieces now, but most of it was still there. Roy kept it in his room, with their best oil lamp. She also taught him to add and subtract.

Roy loved his mother fiercely. One day a year or so ago— back when the calendar showed some horses running around on what looked like a western prairie—she came home with a fellow from down at the store, and Roy went out to play. But he heard a thump, and his mother cried out, and he ran into the house with a thick branch in his hand and saw her trying to get off the floor. Her lip was bleeding. The guy she had brought home drew back his foot like he was going to kick her, and Roy yelled and whacked him on the back of the head with his stick, hard as he could, but it was a long way up there and it didn't do the damage he had hoped for.

The man howled out, staggered forward a few steps and then turned around and came for him. Roy was about to swing again when Rose landed on the guy's back and sank her teeth into his neck. The man really screamed then, like a woman, whirled around once and went running for the door, Rose on his back like an Indian on a bucking horse in one of Roy's favorite pictures. He ran outside and she dropped off, slammed the door shut behind him and locked it. Roy ran to her and saw her lean toward the sink and spit out something bloody. She grabbed him up and hugged him and told him what a hero he was, and Roy had never felt so good. When she put him down he looked in the sink, and what he saw there, he guessed, was a pretty good chunk of that bastard's neck.

Rose loved Roy just as fiercely, but she wasn't like most mothers. She never worried about him. In fact, she never worried about anything. It never occurred to her that anything might happen to Roy. Roy could come and go as he pleased. Roy, however, knew how to worry. He realized the day he saved Rose that he had to worry about her. She needed him once, she might need him again. So Roy was always around the house when she came home from Dugan's. If she brought somebody with her, he'd hang around outside, but that didn't happen hardly at all any more. Usually he'd just make sure she was okay and then go on about his business.

Although Rose didn't know, Roy had friends. There were farms here and there along the highway on the other end of the access road, and several had kids around his age. Every so often he would walk up there and play with them. They never came to see him, because he never quite told them where he lived, and he never went into their houses. A mother came out the back door once and tried to talk to him, but he smiled at her politely and backed away.

His friends asked him why he wasn't in school. He told them he was in school, it was just a different one from theirs. They didn't pry.

Most of his friends, however, were animals. He'd been hunting that one time, with Bob, his mother's friend, but he knew he wasn't going to like it and he didn't. He shot at a couple of squirrels but missed—by a lot. He only went to make Bob happy, because Bob was nice and treated Rose good.

A couple of cottontails would come to the house most days in the evening and sit waiting for something to eat. Rose and Roy didn't waste much, but in the summer, when Rose's garden was producing, he could find something for them. Most of the deer on Raven Bald would show themselves to him without concern, although they didn't like him getting too close. He even knew where a roly-poly old black bear usually hung out on the other side of the mountain, but it took a long time to get there and back.

Up toward the rocky crest of Raven Bald there were, in fact, ravens, great big black birds, a whole lot bigger than crows, and they kind of croaked. Roy loved to watch them fly. He'd read a creepy kind of poem that had a raven in it.

In his room, Roy separated all the *Geographic*s into two piles—the regular ones, which he generally discarded when he had read everything in them, and the ones that had articles and pictures of birds and animals that interested him. He kept all those and read them over and over again.

The night the rest of the county learned about the man-eater in its midst, Roy was in his room reading an old *Geographic* article about wild pigs. That morning, while Rose was at Dugan's, he had gone wandering partway up Copperhead Mountain and had found the remains of a pretty big boar. Only the head was left, and the bones were scattered around. Ugly one, it was, and smelled terrible, but Roy rarely got to see one so he poked around at it a little, examining the big tusks and the hard, coarse hair. Must be mighty uncomfortable to have teeth growing right out your mouth like that, he thought.

He still had the boar on his mind when he got home, so after dinner when Rose went to bed Roy started hunting for the *Geographic* about wild pigs. Took him half an hour to find it. When he finished, he was sleepy, and night had fallen.

Roy picked up the flashlight Rose had given him for Christmas last year and walked outside. He didn't need the light, although there wasn't much moon, because he knew exactly where he was going—to the privy. A little way toward Raven Bald, an owl called. Looking for his dinner, Roy thought.

———

The privy was pitch dark, and Roy turned his flashlight on briefly to make sure there weren't any bugs on the seat. He'd read once about somebody who got bit by a black widow spider in a privy and nearly died. Those were ugly customers.

It wasn't too bad in the privy. Awful cold in the winter, but he and Rose spent some effort and a little money trying to keep it clean. Every so often Fred Dugan would bring up a bag of lime for them. Annie always came with him. Roy didn't care much for Fred, but Annie was kind and he was always polite to both of them. Rose had nearly burst with pride one day when Annie called him a little gentleman.

The owl called again and then again, spacing his hoo-hoo-hoos very neatly. Far off, Roy could hear dogs barking. Chasing 'coons, probably. Some of Roy's best friends were 'coons. They were a lot of fun.

Something brushed the wild azaleas behind the privy. Idly, Roy wondered what it was. Must be something fairly large. Boar? Not likely. Way too wild to come this close to a house. Deer? Possible, but mostly they'd be bedding down by now. Couldn't be a dog; dogs didn't know how to be quiet. Well, maybe he could find out. He rose, cleaning himself with pages from a big old phone book that said "Atlanta" on it, buttoned up, and walked out.

Whatever had brushed the azaleas was nowhere to be seen, and Roy didn't want to scare it by turning on the flashlight. He smelled something sort of sharp, a strange smell that faded almost immediately.

Roy was no more scared of the darkness than he was the daylight, and the idea of an animal wanting to hurt him had never occurred to him. Spiders, sure, and snakes maybe if you stepped on one, but there wasn't an animal in the mountains would hurt you if you didn't try to hurt it first, and the mountains were Roy's world. No animal had ever so much as threatened him.

So, after looking for the azalea brusher, Roy walked on back to the house. In the kitchen, he worked the pump to get enough icy water to wash his hands and face, took a drink from the old mug they kept on a hook there, and went back to his room.

Peeling off his T-shirt and jeans, Roy pulled back the covers of his bed and rolled in. He kept the bed up against his window, which was a little lower than the top of the bed. He liked it that way because he could smell and hear and sometimes even see things in the outdoors before he went to sleep; sort of like camping out without the red bugs. He kept his window open until the first snow. It got cold sleeping by that window, and sometimes when he woke up his nose was numb, but he never moved his bed.

A gentle breeze was blowing through the screen as Roy stretched out and relaxed and let his mind wander. He began thinking about the boar again, wondering how it had died. Did it get sick? Did it just get too old and drop down dead there? The magazine said boars fought in the rutting season. Maybe a bigger, younger boar had killed it. Be quite a fight, really something to see. Maybe something else, he thought, rolling over with his back to the window. But that's silly. What else? Copperhead bite, maybe.

Roy was nearly asleep when he caught that smell again, sharp, almost stinging his nose, bringing him fully alert. He didn't move. He lay there quietly, breathing softly, trying to figure out the smell, which had to be coming in the window. Gradually, he became aware of a sound. Was he breathing that loud?

He held his breath, and the sound went on. Something else, something big, was breathing, outside the window.

This realization sent a tingle up Roy's spine. No animal— at least no animal this big—had ever come to his window. He lay there, forcing his breathing down, forcing himself to contain his excitement. It was the grandest feeling he had ever known, and he reveled in it. In a minute, now, he was going to roll over and meet a new friend.

He gathered himself inwardly, closed his eyes, and wiggled just a little like he figured he did when he was asleep and looking for a more comfortable position. Then, eyes still closed, he rolled over.

The pungent smell was even stronger, about enough to make his eyes water. As he completed his roll, he heard a strange sound, a sound like thunder a long, long way off, but different, like maybe if you heard it coming out of a barrel, like it was being held in, way down inside something. He opened his eyes just enough to see through his lashes.

At first there was nothing, nothing but the breathing and the smell. Then, he saw eyes, a foot from his own. They were kind of yellow, and they were huge. With a start, he realized he had seen nothing at first because he had been looking for something normal size, something that would have fit in between those eyes. Roy knew he was looking at the biggest wild animal he had ever seen. He was so startled his eyes popped open.

The yellow eyes narrowed and gleamed, and there was a noise that reminded him of a little model steam engine one of his friends had, only a whole lot louder, kind of a steamy "*Haaaaaaaaaaaaaaaahhhhhh*" starting out loud and dying away, accompanied by a strong odor of rotten meat. The whole thing was so far beyond what Roy had expected that a minute passed before he understood that he had heard a cat's hiss. An enormous cat.

As all this ran through the boy's head he kept perfectly still, and the eyes outside dropped their squint. They just stared at him, blinking occasionally. Roy wasn't scared, but neither was he sure he was awake. He thought he was probably dreaming.

He had heard, a year or two ago up nearly to the top of Turkey Mountain, a yowl that he took to be that of a wildcat. He had also heard an old roaming tomcat set up a clamor outside the house once in a while, and there wasn't a lot of difference. His mind raced through his memory of *Geographics*, and he decided he had to be dreaming. There was no such cat as this around here.

But it was a very fine dream, the best he had ever had, and he hoped, as he slid away, that he could keep on having it. Right there at the end, he thought he heard the dream-cat purring.

October 11

Roy awoke shortly after dawn. There was nothing outside his window but morning mist and the chatter of birds. Rose, as usual on days she didn't go to Dugan's, was still asleep. She needed a lot of sleep.

As he pulled on his clothes Roy thought he could still smell his dream-cat. In the kitchen he pumped up a glass of water and got a couple of pieces of bread, wolfed them down and went outside.

He walked around the house to his window. Kneeling down, he felt the patchy grass, but he couldn't detect any unusual warmth. He kept looking, crawling around carefully, until he came to a spot of ground kept soft by the roof drainpipe. There was a footprint, like a cat's, but his own hand fit inside it, with plenty of room to spare.

A real tingle ran up the boy's spine. Not a dream. Not a dream after all. It's real. Roy was flopped back on his butt by the drainpipe, lost in wonder, when there came a sound that made the hair rise on his neck.

The sound seemed far off but came from everywhere. Starting as a deep, impossibly deep moan, it rolled around and sharpened into a mighty roar—"*aaaoouuuunnNNGGGHHH!*" It was repeated three times.

For the first time, Roy Satterly wondered if he ought to be afraid of an animal.

Sixteen miles away, Coddy Turner and his wife, at breakfast in their double-wide, heard it and froze. It seemed to rattle the trailer. "Holy God," gasped Coddy, coffee sloshing onto the table. "What was that?"

Deputy Monroe Tolbert, easing his cruiser down a state road halfway to Hartesville, heard it, pulled over, cut the engine and leaped out. He heard it three more times. The rising mist seemed to quiver each time.

When Brickhouse walked into the office Tuesday morning, Ellen said she'd been swamped with calls from the western end.

"People scared outta their wits, Grady. Saying they heard some God-awful noise a little while after sunup. Monroe heard it, too. Said it was the scariest thing he ever heard. Figures it musta been the tiger."

"Advertising now, is it?" Brickhouse said.

"Didn't do much good. Nobody seemed to be able to give us a location on it. Most folks said it was coming from all around them, no matter where they were. Monroe was headed into town when he heard it, and all he could say was somewhere to the west."

"Sound bounces off those mountains," Brickhouse said.

"I guess so."

Brickhouse went down the hall to the chief deputy's office, where Weinman was just hanging up the phone.

"That was your buddy Gorman down at DNR," he said. "Hunter's supposed to be here tomorrow. Fellow named Elmer Ponder from down around Colquitt County somewhere. Gorman said he told him to look us up first thing."

"Well, that's pretty quick work. Everything seems fairly calm this morning to me. How's it look to you?"

"I stopped at some schools on the way in. Some of the elementarys are so empty they're talking to the superintendent about closing for the duration. Harte High didn't seem too sparse, though. Oh, yeah, and the Best Western is booked solid. Mrs. Patel out at the Rest-Easy said she's filling up pretty fast."

"Patels from India, aren't they?"

"Yeah, I talked to her a little. They're from Bombay. They don't know shit about tigers, except they saw some in a zoo once."

"You hear the tiger this morning?"

"No, too far away and too sound asleep."

"Yeah, me too. Listen, Mark, all the cars have shotguns in the trunk, right?"

"Yeah."

"Double-ought buck?"

"Uh-huh."

"What about getting some 12-gauge slugs, loading the guns with alternate rounds? I don't want our people to come across this thing without any firepower. I expect it'll take a lot of killing."

"Fair enough. I'll tell 'em to keep the guns in the backseat too, instead of the trunk."

"Yeah. I hope they take it out before they put a prisoner back there."

The intercom crackled. "Sheriff with you, Mark?" Ellen asked.

"Yeah."

"Ray Estes and Howard Gieske are here to see you, Sheriff."

"Gimme a couple of minutes, then send them to my office, Ellen. Thanks."

"Come on, Mark," Brickhouse said. "You might as well be in on this." Ray Estes was mayor of Hartesville and Howard Gieske the chief of the town's small police department.

The two visitors walked into Brickhouse's office, shook hands all around, and sat down.

"Grady," Gieske said, "my phone's been ringin' all mornin' about this tiger."

"Mine too," said Estes.

"Question is," the chief continued, "what do we need to do here in town? What's the likelihood this tiger might come into Hartesville?"

"Gentlemen, I'd say there's no chance at all," Brickhouse replied. "I can't imagine why a jungle animal would come into a place full of cars and trucks, can you? Right now the closest we know it's gotten to town is a good twenty miles. I expect if it can't get anything to eat in the area where it is now, it'll just move on to another part of the mountains. It's not gonna leave the woods and come in here."

"Well, that's what I figured, but we got old ladies swearing they saw the damn thing in their flower gardens this morning," Gieske said.

"What's the situation out around Turkey and Copperhead?" Estes asked. "I was wondering if we needed to set up a shelter for folks in one of the schools."

"I figure there's no more'n about twenty families in the area of greatest danger right now," Brickhouse said. "I've got deputies checking all the houses this morning. I understand a lot of those folks have sent their children away, and some have picked up and left altogether. Only the stubborn ones and the ones with livestock are sticking it out. I don't think there's any need for a shelter right now, but it may come to that and I sure appreciate you thinking about it, Mayor."

"What else you doing?" Gieske asked.

"We've shifted most of our patrols out that way. But mainly we're just waiting for the DNR hunter. He's supposed to be here tomorrow. You got any suggestions?"

"Me, I'd think about putting out some poison," Gieske suggested. "Go over to Harlan's, get some sides of venison or whatever he's got, salt it up good, and put it out there."

"Kill a hell of a lot of small animals, Chief, but it's still a damn good suggestion. Mark, will you take care of it?"

"Right," said the chief deputy, adjusting his Ray-Bans.

That afternoon Bob Willet, who ran a small farm near Copperhead Mountain, heard his dog begin barking hysterically.

His son Bob Junior, who happened to be one of Roy Satterly's sometime playmates, dashed out of his room for the door.

"Bobby, no!" his mother yelped.

"You sit right down there, Bobby," his father ordered. "Why you think we kept you home from school?"

Bobby sat down, a sullen look on his face, and they heard the dog's barking stop suddenly. Then they heard the bleating of the two dozen sheep Willet had driven into the barn the night before. Something was after them, damn sure, but Bob Willet valued his life and the lives of his family a good deal more than those of his sheep. Tiger wanted 'em, he could have 'em. Anyway, he didn't own a gun big enough to hurt a tiger. Tiger, for God's sake. What was the world coming to?

He waited for an hour and a half after the noise died away, then walked out to the barn.

"Sheriff," said Ellen over the intercom. "Bob Willet from out to Copperhead Mountain's on the phone. Says the tiger's been there. You wanna talk to him?"

Brickhouse picked up the phone.

"Hey, Bob, Grady. Trouble?"

"Yeah, somethin' killed my dog and took one of my sheep. Musta been the tiger. We heard it all, couldn't see anything from the house, though. I waited awhile 'fore I went out there.

"Had the sheep penned up in the barn, but there's no doors on the back, just a big gate, you know. Evidently ole Ace tried to go for the tiger. He's behind the barn there, skull just about mashed flat. Damn tiger apparently went over the gate, took a big fat sheep, and jumped back over the gate with it. I expect it went into the woods behind the barn."

"You got good sense, Bob, not going out there when trouble started. Now, you sit tight and don't try to look for that sheep.

The DNR hunter's supposed to be here tomorrow, and I expect he'll come to your place first. Okay?"

"Grady, I'm more likely to grow wings 'n' fly than I am to chase this tiger. I'll wait for the hunter."

Roy Satterly stayed home, thumbing through the *Geographics* in his animal stack. As he went from the magazines to his ripped dictionary and back, it appeared to him that the biggest cats in North America were the cougar and the jaguar. The jaguar seemed to be pretty big, but it lived way down at the bottom end of Mexico and mostly in South America. The cougar, on the other hand, lived in the west and wasn't so big, either. Whatever his dream-cat was, it didn't belong here.

When darkness fell, Roy got into bed and stayed awake as long as he could, hoping the dream-cat would visit again. It didn't.

October 12

Elmer Ponder drove into Hartesville Wednesday morning in a big, new, king-cab Ford pickup with a rifle on a rack in the rear window.

He angle-parked the truck in front of Ruby's, got out and locked it. Ponder, a small, wiry man in a forage cap, brown cord jacket and blue jeans, went into Ruby's and slipped into a booth. Half a dozen businessmen were sitting around a table drinking coffee. At the front, by the window, four out-of-town reporters and a photographer were finishing breakfast. At both tables, the talk centered on the Harte County man-eater.

Helga started to put a menu in front of him along with his glass of water, but he looked up at her and said, "Ham 'n' eggs. Two, over easy. Black coffee." He didn't smile, but he didn't frown, either. He just looked at her until she pulled back the menu and hurried away.

"Who's that guy?" asked Ruby, looking out of the kitchen service window. "Don't believe I've ever seen him."

"Damn if I know," said Helga. "I know I've never seen him, and I don't mind if I never do again. Mean-lookin' bastard. Ain't polite, like them reporters. Ain't funny, like Cal and his gang. He's just there."

Helga served him his ham and eggs over easy and his coffee, and Ponder ate them slowly and deliberately. He looked down at his plate to cut his ham and stab a bite, then stared straight ahead as if he was counting the times he chewed. After a while, Ruby agreed the guy was kinda creepy.

Helga refilled his mug and left him the ticket, and when he rose to leave he dropped two quarters on the table.

"Everything okay?" Helga asked brightly at the register.

Ponder rolled a toothpick out of the machine, accepted his change, and looked at her evenly.

"Okay," he said in a flat voice and kept on looking at her for a few seconds before walking out to his truck. His eyes were a strange watery blue.

Five minutes later Ponder pulled his truck into the lot at the sheriff's department, and met the sheriff and chief deputy in Brickhouse's office.

"Elmer Ponder," he said. "DNR."

"Got some ID? Just to be safe?" Weinman asked.

"Gorman said he'd call you," Ponder said, offering a driver's license. "I contract by the job. They don't give me no ID."

"That's fine," Brickhouse said. "Just wanted to make sure you're really Ponder."

Ponder stared at him as he put the license away. "Gorman said you'd fill me in," he said finally.

"You know you're after a tiger, a man-eater? Killed two people?"

"Yeah."

"You ever see a tiger before?"

"Yeah."

"Where?"

"Stopped by the zoo, way up here."

"This one's a lot bigger, we think."

"Okay."

Brickhouse got up and walked over to the big survey map of the county on the wall.

There were two red pins on it, where Whitfield and Buchholz had died, and a blue one at the Willet farm. Brickhouse explained the map, described the ground.

"Okay," said Ponder, turning to go.

"Where you figure to start?" Brickhouse asked.

"Go out to that farm first, see can I find the sheep."

"You want any help?"

Ponder stared at him for a while.

"No," he said.

"Very good, then," Brickhouse said. "Good luck."

"One thing. Gorman says I keep the skin."

"And welcome to it," said Weinman. "Just kill the damn thing."

Ponder stared at him.

"Sure," he said finally, and left.

Brickhouse looked at Weinman. "Reckon DNR's getting down to the bottom of the barrel?"

"Well, didn't Gorman tell you he might have trouble finding someone?"

"Yeah," said Brickhouse. "Stupid sonofabitch, isn't he? But he looks like he could kill things, for sure."

Brickhouse was only half right about Elmer Ponder: He wasn't stupid. What he was, was careful.

Elmer Ponder killed things for a living. He did it efficiently and just as ordered, and no one ever complained about his work.

Which is not to say no one had any complaints at all; it was just that those who did have grievances were no longer in a position to lodge them. Ponder killed what he was paid to kill; it didn't matter to him. But those high-paying jobs didn't come along very often, because Ponder was very careful about them.

DNR could always pick up the phone and find him, and they'd work out a deal to thin some deer or some wild pigs. But people who wanted him for other jobs never knew his name, and they had to go through a lot of other people, who knew him by other names, to find him. Ponder didn't work for just any crackpot with a wad of dough. Get your ass in trouble for sure that way.

Ponder had thought Gorman was using some kind of code when he called and asked if he was willing to hunt a tiger. Maybe Gorman had suddenly become one of those other customers, which made Ponder very uneasy.

"What'dya mean, tiger?" he asked.

"Tiger, believe it or not," Gorman replied. "They got a Bengal tiger killin' and eatin' people up in Harte County."

"Tigers in India, ain't they?" Ponder asked.

"Yeah, Elmer, that's where they belong, but one's got loose from somewhere. I ain't pullin' your leg. You want him? Top bounty, best we've ever paid, since there's some danger attached."

"Always some danger 'tached," said Ponder. "Fucker near put an arrow in my gut down at Jekyll couple years ago in that deer thinnin'."

"Yeah, Elmer, I remember that, but he wouldn't have ate you," said Gorman, getting a little exasperated. Elmer really was kinda thick sometimes.

"Okay," said Ponder.

"You'll do it?"

"Yeah."

When Ponder arrived at the Willet farm, Bob Senior came out on the porch. "You must be the DNR hunter," he said.

"Yeah," Ponder said. He didn't offer a name.

"What can I do to help?"

"Tiger get your sheep?"

"Something sure did."

"Show me," Ponder said, pulling the rifle out of the rack in the cab. It was a big Remington 700 in .300 magnum. He loaded four rounds into the weapon's internal magazine and racked the bolt to chamber one.

They walked out behind the barn, and Bob could see his wife and Bobby looking out the window at them.

He took Ponder to the gate holding the sheep in the barn. "Took a ewe out of there. Took her over the fence. Killed my dog first."

"You follow up?"

"No."

"Okay," said Ponder, turning toward the tree line, chambering a round as he walked.

Willet watched him for a minute, wandering in a wide zigzag, looking for sign. Then the farmer shook his head and walked back to the house.

By midmorning there were more than thirty reporters and cameramen gathered in front of the sheriff's department, and after discussing it with Weinman, Brickhouse decided to bring a little order to things.

He walked out to the flagpole, and the crowd descended on him, yelling and shoving.

"Hang on," he said. "Just hang on."

"First off," he said when things were quiet, "I want to welcome all of you to Harte County. It's not a real rich area, as some of you may have noticed, and visitors are much appreciated. Don't be stingy with those expense accounts."

There was general laughter.

"Okay. Now here's what I'd like to do. Every day at ten in the morning and four in the afternoon, we'll have a briefing right here. If it rains we'll figure out something else. If I'm not available for the briefing, Chief Deputy Weinman will handle it, and if neither of us can do it, Ellen will explain to you why not and when we can do it."

"It's my intention to be completely honest with you. In return for this, I ask you not to follow me or my deputies when we leave here, and not to bother us at home. If you really need something, ask the dispatcher to call one of us. If there is a major development at some odd hour, one of us will call the Best Western and the Rest-Easy and ask the clerk to wake the reporters. If you want to be wakened, tell the hotel desk that, and I'm sure it'll work out. Any questions?"

"How about live shots?" an Atlanta television reporter asked.

"No live shots. Neither I nor any of my people will do live shots under any circumstances unless you want to go live at one of these briefings. We're not trying to be ugly. There are just too many of you. If we do a live shot for you, then we've got to do them for everybody else and it won't ever end. Understood?

"All right. Now there's not much to tell you this morning except that the DNR hunter arrived about two hours ago, and he's already on the job."

"Who is it?" asked Bentley, the reporter from the *Constitution.*

"Elmer Ponder."

He had to spell "Ponder" for them.

"Where's he from?"

"He didn't say, but I understand it's from down around Colquitt County somewhere," Brickhouse said.

"What do you know about him?"

"Not one thing. I never heard of him or saw him before, which of course doesn't mean anything. Maybe Bud Gorman down at DNR can tell you something."

"Can we talk to Ponder?"

"When he comes back to town, you can ask him."

"Where is he?"

"That's the other thing I was going to tell you. A farmer reported one of his sheep taken out of his barn yesterday afternoon. Ponder said he'd start there."

"Where's this farmer?"

"Off-limits, folks. I'll ask the man if he wants to talk to you. Otherwise I'm not going to give you information like that. People up here value their privacy."

As Brickhouse walked back into the radio room, Ellen said, "Willet called."

"Yeah?"

"Wanted to know where you found Ponder."

"What'd he do?"

"Didn't do anything. Willet just thought he was sort of weird."

"He is sort of weird," Brickhouse agreed. "I hope you told him he was DNR's and not ours."

"Sure. He said Ponder's gone into the woods with an elephant gun."

"Good," Brickhouse said.

He was about to go to lunch when a technician at the GBI lab called. "Sheriff, considering the trouble you've got up there, we decided to put these hairs your office sent at the top of the queue.

"There's nothing in our collection to match them, which means whatever left them is not native to Georgia. So one of our guys went over to the zoo and collected some hairs—lion, tiger, gorilla, and orangutan. Your hairs are not lion, orangutan, or gorilla, but they are a pretty close match for the tiger. So it looks as though you're on the right track."

"Well, thanks a lot," Brickhouse said. "I really appreciate you going to all that trouble. Tell Doc Steinberg hello for me."

Right track, he snorted after he hung up. Can't see we're on any track at all. All we got going for us is that DNR creep. "Ellen, I'm going to lunch."

Ponder was no great shakes as a tracker, and he knew it, but the blood trail wasn't hard to follow once he picked it up. Sheep was leaking like a sieve.

The hunter was only a hundred yards into the forest when he saw something white sticking up behind a fallen tree. He froze and scanned the area quietly. A couple of cardinals were bouncing around in a bush near the tree. Nothing seemed to be bothering them, so he walked slowly toward the white patch.

About thirty feet away he realized that what he was seeing was the lower part of a sheep's leg. He stopped again, wary, but detected nothing and went on. On the other side of the log were the remains of Willet's sheep, almost entirely eaten. Ponder sat down and smoked a Camel.

Another fifty yards to the west, on a steep grade up Copperhead Mountain, he found a pile of congealed vomit. There was wool in it. He kept going up.

Ponder moved as quietly as he could, avoiding overhead branches and bushes. After a while, the way seemed to level out and then dip a little, and he heard water running. The noise tended to block smaller sounds, so he walked more slowly.

The source of the sound was a little rill no more than four feet across, rushing over rocks that created foot-high waterfalls. Most hikers would have thought it lovely and sat beside it to eat their lunch. Lovely was not a concept that often occurred to Elmer Ponder.

He scrambled down the little bank, stepped across the rill using a big rock in the middle, and clambered up the other bank. As he did so, he heard a noise from a dense rhododendron patch to his right. He stopped, listened, and then moved on. Three more paces and something in the rhododendrons growled at him. He'd heard the sound before, on the Discovery Channel. But this was deeper and louder, and he froze.

The edge of the rhododendron thicket was fifteen feet to his right. Very slowly, he turned to face it, and was greeted with another, louder, growl. Bastard's in there for sure, but where? He took a step back. No response. A step forward, another growl.

Elmer Ponder snapped the Remington to his shoulder, throwing off the safety as he did, and fired at the sound.

The boom of his heavy rifle was drowned by a roar that shocked him as though a mortar round had landed at his feet. A massive red blur burst out of the rhododendrons. It covered fifteen feet in one bound and was upon him with the next, just as he yanked back the Remington's bolt.

Brickhouse stopped off at the public library and found a big picture book on tigers and took it to Ruby's, where he chose a back booth. The place was full of reporters, squeezing out a lot of disgruntled downtown businessmen. They all greeted him jovially but left him alone. They were a raucous bunch, like ill-raised teenagers. Maybe wolves are like that until they're on the hunt.

Helga brought him the country-fried steak, which he munched slowly while looking at the book. It was about a place called Ranthambore in India, which used to have a fortress in it that had fallen to ruins and was now a tiger preserve. It talked about how close tigers were to extinction, and all the efforts being made to save them.

The pictures were stunning, and eerie. Tigers peering around decayed columns, lying in broken stone doorways. Incredible animals. Beautiful, powerful. The setting made him imagine one walking down the street where he lived, smelling the tires on his Crown Vic. He shivered, just as someone settled into the seat across the table.

Paul Grimes. He grinned and said rather loudly, "Studying the enemy, eh, Chief?"

What the hell, Brickhouse thought, but smiled back.

Then Grimes started talking very quietly; the sheriff could barely hear him under the reporters' din.

"Weinman sent me, Chief. Willet just called. Thinks maybe the hunter's bought it, or hurt. Said he'd been gone in the woods about an hour when they heard one heavy-caliber gunshot up the mountain aways. Waited two hours; he ain't come out."

"Jesus," Brickhouse grunted. Then he laughed hugely for the benefit of the reporters. "Go over to the counter and get a candy bar, Paul, and then go on back to the office. I'll finish up here."

Grimes grinned and sauntered away. Brickhouse cleaned his plate like a righteous sheriff, picked up his book, and went out, waving to the reporters. "See you at four," he said.

He and Weinman piled into a blue-and-white, and Jameson and Bill Banks into another. They spaced their departure by five minutes, using no lights or sirens.

At Willet's place, the farmer showed them where he'd last seen Ponder, and the spot where the hunter had entered the woods. Weinman picked up the blood trail right away.

"He was following this," the chief deputy said. Brickhouse sent Jameson and Banks back to the cruisers for the shotguns. Every man pumped a round into the chamber of his Remington 870.

"Safeties on?" Brickhouse asked before they entered the woods.

They immediately found the remains of the sheep and saw that Ponder had stopped there for a smoke.

"Willet said the shot came from up the mountain," Weinman said, adjusting his Ray-Bans, "so I guess up is the way to go. We'll spread out, ten feet apart. Keep your ears open as well as your eyes."

They began trudging up the mountainside. Banks found the vomit with the wool in it.

"Well, we're on the track," Brickhouse said, "even if he wasn't."

"Water ahead," Weinman said after another twenty minutes.

"Very good, Mark," said Brickhouse, panting. "I thought it was maybe cows with bladder trouble."

"There he is," Jameson said as they approached the little creek. "On the other bank." They could see the soles of two boots.

"Go careful, careful," cautioned Weinman. "Tiger may still be here."

But there was no challenge as they crossed the creek and gathered around Ponder's body. His scalp was peeled forward over his face, the skull exposed. Teeth had nearly met in his neck, front to back, just missing the jugular. His head lay at an impossible angle to his shoulders. The Remington was behind him, the bolt open.

"Didn't eat him," Banks said. "Reckon it didn't like the taste?"

"It just ate that sheep yesterday," Brickhouse said. "Maybe wasn't hungry."

"Sure was pissed, though," Jameson said.

Weinman was examining the rhododendron patch. "Tiger came out of this," he said. "Hairs stuck here and here."

"You reckon Ponder wounded him?" Brickhouse asked.

"I circled around," Weinman said. "No blood sign, if he did." The chief deputy picked up the rifle. There was some grass in the open chamber. A few feet away near the edge of the bank was a spent brass cartridge. Weinman emptied the magazine. "He got off one shot, couldn't get the bolt closed before the tiger got to him.

"He's got to be a decent shot. If he fired when the tiger came out of that thicket the range would've been maybe twelve, fifteen feet at the most. Can't see how he'd miss entirely that close, and a slug from this would have to do some damage.

"I'd think maybe he heard something and fired for effect," Weinman continued. "Didn't get the effect he was looking for."

"Yeah," Brickhouse said. "That sleepy old Raguno down in Atlanta, I guess he can be kinda misleading. Banks, you and Jameson go on back to the cars, call the hospital and have 'em send Jimmy out here, no emergency, but get here quick. Don't tell 'em what it's about. Mark and I'll wait until he gets here."

"We will, huh?" said Weinman with a grin after the deputies were over the creek and out of earshot. "What if that sonofabitch decides all this exercise made him kinda hungry after all? How long's it been since you climbed a tree, Sheriff?"

"You climb, I'll give him my lily-white body to save yours. Hell, I couldn't tell Phil and Bill to stay here while we left, and little as I cared for this creep we can't leave his corpse unattended. He's probably got a momma somewhere."

"Yeah, he visited her, too, while he was at the zoo," Weinman said. "You know what this is gonna lead to, don't you?"

"I expect we'll hear . . ." the sheriff began, breaking off at a sound on the other side of the rushing creek. "What's that?"

But Weinman was already on one knee, the stubby black shotgun at his shoulder, thumb on the safety. Brickhouse quickly joined him.

Their tension increased as more sounds of movement drifted to them over the noise of the creek. "Can't be Bill and Phil," Brickhouse whispered.

"Not unless they turned around," Weinman agreed.

"Tiger make that much noise?"

"How the hell would I know?"

Suddenly a blond head appeared over the opposite bank.

"Put those things down, you crazy bastards," came a husky voice. "We ain't no damn tiger."

It was Kathleen Bentley. With her was a black man festooned with cameras, peering out from under dreadlocks clamped down with a black-and-yellow knit cap.

"Jesus wept," groaned Brickhouse. "Miss Bentley, what in the hell are you doing here? This is a crime scene. And who is this?"

Bentley, in white shirt and jeans, hair pinned up, skipped across the creek and up the bank. "It looks more like the woods to me, although I see a body on the ground there. This here is R. L. Street, best news photographer in Georgia. Did you actually think not telling us where that hunter had gone was gonna keep us from finding out?"

Brickhouse was stunned, and Weinman remained silent, a small grin on his thin face.

"That the great white hunter there?" Bentley asked, coming closer. "Deputies down the hill didn't want to say anything, but I gathered the tiger got him. Jes-us. Somethin' sure did."

"You must be Weinman," she said, turning to the chief

deputy and thrusting out her hand. "Little dark in these trees. Can you see me through those shades?"

"Oh yes," Weinman said, shaking her hand.

"He can see you, but I bet he can't see me," said Street, snapping various views of Ponder's body.

"Now wait a minute," the sheriff began, shocked.

"Chill, Sheriff, chill," said Street. "*Journal-Constitution* wouldn't publish pictures like this. It's just for the record, y'know, just for the record."

"Didn't the deputies tell you not to come up here?" Brickhouse asked.

"Oh, yeah," said Bentley. "Said you'd throw us and them both in jail. Gonna be kinda hard to string yellow tape all around the mountain, Sheriff."

"Well, where's the rest of the herd?"

"Oh," Bentley said, batting her eyelashes, "I think most of 'em are around the other side of the mountain. I shared what I had with 'em, you know, but I'm just really bad at givin' directions."

"Now," she said, pulling a notepad out of her hip pocket. "What you reckon happened here, Sheriff?"

"Mark, give her your estimate of the situation."

"Well, Miss Bentley, did you see the sheep down there?"

"Uh-huh."

"Well, we believe Ponder decided to move uphill from there. And did you see the vomit with the wool in it? No? I'll show you on the way down."

"I can pass on the tiger puke," Bentley said. "What next?"

The grilling continued until Jimmy arrived with his partner and a body bag on a stretcher.

As they walked back down the mountain, the sheriff said,

"I hope you didn't harass the Willets, Miss Bentley."

"Harass 'em? Shit, Sheriff, they invited us to dinner. You go on back and brief those talkin' dogs by the flagpole. I really do appreciate you being so kind," she said sweetly, "just as long as you don't tell them a damn thing you didn't tell me."

"I wouldn't dare."

"You better not, darlin.' "

The crowd had swelled to about forty-five reporters and cameramen. They made so much noise they could scarcely hear Brickhouse. He brought out Weinman to discuss what he made of the signs on the mountain and the coroner and the emergency room chief from Harte County Hospital to discuss Ponder's wounds. While the doctor was talking, Ellen came out and whispered in his ear for a minute.

When the doctor was through, Brickhouse stepped back up to the stand.

"Meeting here like this obviously isn't going to work any more," he said. "I've just learned that Maude Mayfield Elementary over on McClatchie Street is going to close until the emergency is over. The school system has agreed to let us use the auditorium there. So I'll see you there in the morning."

He went back to his office and called Bud Gorman.

"Bud, this is Brickhouse."

"Hey, Grady. Ponder get there okay?"

"Yeah, he got here okay. Now where would you like me to send him?"

"Send him? Don't he know where to go?"

"Yeah, Bud, he knew where to go, all right. But now he's dead. I need to know where to send his body."

Gorman's voice went up a few notches.

"Dead? Jesus Christ, what happened?"

"Tiger killed him. Official cause of death was a severed spinal cord and a broken neck."

"Oh, God. I . . . I don't know if he's got family or not. Only one I ever talked to when I called was him. I'll see what I can find out. Nothing like this has ever happened before."

"Yeah, those whitetails don't fight back much, do they? Bud, you worried about a lawsuit?"

"Damn right I am."

"Well, I don't think you oughta worry too much. One of my men with nothing better to do went over Ponder's truck. Up under the front seat in a special-made rig he found an H&K 9-millimeter, silenced; five thousand dollars in twenties and fifties; and four brand new driver's licenses. They had different names and addresses, but they all had Ponder's picture. What'd your boy do in his spare time?"

"No idea, but it don't sound like it was anything to make us proud. Thank you for that, Grady. I'll get back to you on the body. You gonna give that stuff to the GBI?"

"Thought I would."

"Fine. Sorry this didn't work. I ain't got anybody else to send you."

"Okay, Bud. I know you did your best. You sure you don't want to send up a few of them laughing jackasses you got down there in the office? We could use 'em as bait."

When he hung up, Brickhouse called Weinman in.

"Tiger three, Harte County zero, Mark. We gotta come up with something better to do than retrieve bodies. How the hell can we stop this?"

"I was looking at the map, Sheriff. There's no way to know the extent of the tiger's range, but it's at least two hundred square miles. Probably more than that, maybe a lot more. Now, there's a few theoretical possibilities. First, poison. I was gonna go out to Harlan's this afternoon and see about getting some meat; that'll have to wait until tomorrow now. Second, tracking. I don't know of anybody in the county or anywhere else good enough to do that, even if they were willing. Third, sitting up for him, the way deer hunters do. We could scatter deer stands around, put deputies in them. We'd have to get lucky, but it may be our best shot right now. At least we'd be doing something. I imagine one of those companies that makes prefab stands would be glad to let us have some for the publicity."

"Check into it tomorrow, Mark. Be ready to do it by the end of the week."

Bentley, with several hours in hand over her competitors, filed her story early. Street, the only photographer with pictures of anything but the news conference, transmitted half a dozen prints back to Atlanta.

They ate a late lunch at the motel. The solid beat she had scored by tracking Brickhouse down at the scene of Ponder's death put her on an emotional high that was still running, and she wasn't ready to call it a day. She talked nonstop through the unremarkable meal and when it was gone looked at her watch.

"It's only three," she said. "Why don't we go out there and just drive around on some of those forest service roads? Hell, we're on a roll. We might get lucky again."

"Get lucky and what?" Street asked.

"Oh, hell, I don't know, R.L. But we damn sure aren't gonna turn anything sittin' around here in town. Come on."

"Why not?" said Street. "I'll drive."

They headed west out of Hartesville. "You got a map?" he asked.

"Naw," Bentley said. "Highway map isn't gonna show those forest service roads anyway. Let's just drive around on 'em until it starts to get dark, see what we can see."

"See a lotta dirt roads is what we'll see."

They drove past the Satterly house without even noticing it; it sat well below the road. They came to the rutted lane leading to the Whitfield place but ignored it; it was obviously a private trail.

They drove halfway up Turkey Mountain before the road got too rough for the poorly maintained Blazer, which had no four-wheel drive and very little two-wheel pull left. Back on 121, they drove past the Willet place—the invitation to dinner was contingent upon the death of the tiger—and found a road winding up Copperhead Mountain.

It was good for about ten miles at thirty miles per hour and another five at ten miles per hour before it began to peter out. Dusk was half an hour away.

"R.L., this little cruise has just about beat my kidneys to death," Bentley said. "It was my idea, but I think I've had enough. Let's turn around and go home. Be dark pretty soon anyway."

"Good enough," Street said. He found a place wide enough to turn the Blazer around, and they started back down the mountain.

They were on the western side, a little more than halfway back to GA 121, when the Blazer lurched around a bend and Street stood on the brakes.

"Holy shit," he whispered.

Bentley, who had been examining her makeup in a small mirror, looked up sharply and gasped.

The tiger was stretched out in the middle of the road, fifty feet away, looking at them with the annoyance of a man awakened from a sound sleep.

Bentley had trouble getting her breath. Street turned off the ignition.

"What the hell'd you do that for?" Bentley whispered. "Start this damn thing up and run over it."

"Be gone long before we'd get there," said Street. Slowly he unbuckled his seat belt and groped with one hand for his bag in the backseat.

"Then start the goddamn truck and back up out of here," Bentley said. "That thing is enormous and it looks hungry."

"You got yours," Street said, lifting his bag over the seat. "Now I'm gettin' mine."

"R.L., you crazy bastard—"

"Shut up."

"You're gonna get us both killed!"

The tiger watched them with interest but didn't find it necessary to rise. As Street fished a longer lens out of his bag and clapped it onto a Nikon, the tiger yawned hugely. Street made several exposures through the windshield, then slowly unlocked the door and began pushing it open. He stopped every time it creaked.

"Oh, God. R.L., don't!"

"Hush, dammit. Shootin' through glass ain't worth shit."

In painfully slow motion, he got the door open far enough to slide out of the car. He rested the lens on the top of the door and began shooting.

At the first "click-whirrrr" the tiger leaped to its feet and faced the car. Bentley was rolled into a ball in the front seat, trembling.

Street continued to shoot and the tiger took several steps toward the car. About thirty feet away, it dropped into a crouch, and its tail lashed from side to side, twice. Its mouth opened in a menacing snarl.

"R.L., get in here!" Bentley screamed.

Street slid back into the driver's seat and slammed the door, and the tiger leaped to one side, bounded off the road and disappeared into the trees.

Bentley was quivering. Street looked at her, grinned and said, "Damn fine idea you had, Miz Bentley, goin' out for a little ride."

A full-color photograph of the tiger, standing on the forest service road as if he owned it, covered four columns at the top of the front page of the *Constitution* the next morning, and the back page of the A-section was quickly switched to color and devoted to more of Street's pictures. The Harte County man-eater was no longer faceless.

The dream-cat came back to Roy's window about an hour after nightfall. Roy was lying on his right side, waiting, and suddenly it was just there. Again, he smelled it before he really saw it. There still wasn't enough moon to make out anything but the eyes. He didn't move. He didn't think the cat liked for him to move. He just watched it, and the dream-cat watched back, the huge yellow eyes blinking only once in a while.

This time he knew he heard it purr. It sounded almost like one of those big trucks down on the highway. Roy wanted badly to know more about his dream-cat, to really see it, but he knew it would probably go away if he moved, so he was still until he fell asleep, listening to that deep rumble.

October 13

Brickhouse got to the office at eight fifty-five. At nine, as he expected, Ellen transferred a call to him.

"Sheriff Brickhouse, this is the governor's office. Will you hold for the governor, please?"

"Certainly." Five beats of silence.

"Sheriff? This is George Munson."

"Good morning, Governor."

"A better one down here, I expect, than in Harte County. At least our problems aren't eating us."

"No, sir."

"Sheriff, I want to send you some help. The death of that hunter has shocked the whole world. I think a lot of people thought of this as some kind of circus until they saw this morning's paper."

"Yes, sir," Brickhouse said. He hadn't seen the Atlanta paper yet.

"I called General Bland half an hour ago and asked him to mobilize the best troops he's got for the job. He told me he'd have men in Harte County this afternoon. He'll be in touch with you before noon on the details. I expect you'll have to arrange a suitable place for them to bivouac."

"Of course, sir."

"Sheriff Brickhouse, you don't sound very enthusiastic about these troops, if I may say so."

"Governor, I guess I'm not. I don't really know why. Maybe this doesn't seem like a National Guard problem. But to be honest, I don't have any better ideas, and I sure hope they get results."

"You may very well be right, Sheriff, but we've got to do something. Neither you nor I can sit by while this damned animal scarfs somebody up like a hamburger every few days. Please call me if there's anything more I can do, anything at all."

Brickhouse hung up the phone and leaned back. The implied criticism stung, but he couldn't deny it. He'd tried to act like Whitfield's death hadn't happened, and what had he done since Harry Buchholz died? Not one damn thing but wait around for Ponder to come along and get killed.

Truth was, he had no idea what to do. Ellen had been getting calls from all over the country from people who said they were big-game hunters. He told her to ask them if they had ever shot a tiger. One had, she reported. From the back of an elephant. Great, he had said. Do we have to supply the elephant? He couldn't let a bunch of outsiders come in and play tiger hunter.

Okay, he thought, we're doing something. Mark is setting up the deer stand thing; he's going to put out some poison meat today.

Weinman came in while he was staring at the map. "Mornin', Mark."

"Sheriff. You been on 121 this morning?"

"No, I swung around the other way. Why?"

"Steady stream of traffic from down south. As bad as peak leaf season weekend. Some guy's set up a stand down by the city limits sign selling hot dogs, Cokes, and T-shirts. Ones I saw had a happy-looking tiger on them and said 'I Had Lunch in Harte County, Ga.' "

"Oh shit," Brickhouse groaned. "Can we run him off?"

"He's on private property, and he's got the licenses."

"Well, maybe at least the troops can direct traffic."

"Governor called already?"

"Yeah, first thing. Adjutant general's gonna call back in a while, tell us exactly what's coming. Be here this afternoon."

"What do they know about tigers?"

"What do you know about tigers? What do I know about tigers? That's the goddamn problem, Mark. None of us knows anything about tigers. Maybe they'll get lucky, who knows?"

"Yeah. I hope they don't get unlucky."

"Whatever. We've got to find a place for them to set up camp. Can you do that?"

"Yeah. Ken Randall and his whole family decided to go visit relatives in Florida. He left a number to call. I'll see if we can use his pasture out by Copperhead. I don't think he grazes anything on it anyway."

"Good. I gotta go down to the school and tell the press the cavalry is coming."

While Brickhouse was holding his morning briefing, the adjutant general called. He told Weinman he was sending elements of the First Battalion of the 122nd Infantry; perhaps 250 troops, depending on how many were able to answer the hurry-up activation. Weinman told the general how to find Randall's pasture.

On Thursday, Rose Satterly went down to do her chores at Dugan's. Roy thought about walking over to the highway on the other side to see if maybe the kids over there had seen the dream-cat. He tried to figure out how he could ask without them thinking he was weird. Previous conversations had taught him that the other boys didn't think about wild things the way he did. When he talked about watching 'coons or possums, they wanted to know why he didn't shoot them.

He was still pondering that when the clouds began to gather in early afternoon. Seeing that, he gave up the idea of the trip, because if it started raining he needed to go down to Dugan's to help his mother home with the groceries.

A family of raccoons lived in the stump of a lightning-killed tree just up the mountain a little way, and Roy hadn't checked on them in a while. The youngsters would be ready to get out on their own some by now. He decided to walk up there and see what he could see.

Roy was strolling along a path that ran by the 'coon stump, practicing bird whistles and watching the ground for sign, when he looked up to check his bearings.

Sitting right in the middle of the path, in a break in the canopy about one hundred feet away, looking right at him, was the dream-cat. It had to be the dream-cat. Except for cows and horses, it was the biggest animal he'd ever seen and by far the most beautiful. He was excited, more excited than he'd ever been.

He examined the dream-cat as well as he could at the distance, in the poor light. It was reddish, with black streaks. There was white on its face and its belly. Sitting there on its haunches, it appeared to be a lot taller than Roy. He had to get closer; he had to.

Slowly, he stuck out his bare right foot, put it down, swung his weight onto it. The dream-cat's eyes narrowed, and its ears dropped back along its head. Its mouth opened, like a smiling cave, and there came that vast, steamy, hissing noise. Its tusks, he noticed, seemed to be as long as his fingers, and very white. Roy noticed the tail for the first time, because the end of it twitched.

Obediently, he put his weight back on his left foot and brought the right back under him. The dream-cat's ears popped back up, the hissing stopped, and its mouth closed. The eyes resumed their huge roundness.

They stood there in the path, looking at each other. Roy thought somehow the dream-cat wanted to say something to him, maybe was saying something, but he couldn't hear anything. In fact, he realized, he couldn't even hear birds or insects. The forest was silent, as though everything in it was holding its breath.

Roy thought he felt a drop of rain on his head and looked up. When he looked back, the dream-cat was gone, like it had never been there. Roy stood for a while, looking. He thought about going up to where the dream-cat had been. He decided that might not be a good idea, although he wasn't sure why. He went back to the house, to his animal *Geographics*.

Rose got home before the rain. She was always tired on chore days and didn't feel like cooking. Roy took a peanut butter sandwich back to his room, and he was almost finished when he found out what his dream-cat was.

In Randall's pasture, Lieutenant Colonel Winshiser, commanding officer of the First of the 122nd and the man placed in command of the operation, gathered his company commanders around the tailgate of a truck while the troops set up their tents. It looked like rain was coming, so he wanted to lay out his plans for tomorrow. The forecast was clear for Friday and Saturday.

Winshiser, an Atlanta advertising executive, knew very well that this operation was more of a publicity stunt than a serious mission. Trying to find a single tiger, which presumably didn't wish to be found, with the men of the First Battalion in the two hundred square miles of mountain and forest that the sheriff had shown him was absurd.

However, there was nothing he'd love more than to make this work. So, before reporting to guard headquarters, the colonel had called a few old friends in the regular army at Fort Stewart. He had some surprises up his sleeve.

When his officers were gathered around the map on the tailgate, Winshiser started.

"Gentlemen, none of us has any illusions about the probability of success in this mission. Nonetheless, we're going to do our best to nail this animal, and here's how.

"First, I want each of you to pick his five best machine gunners tonight. Tell them to gather right here half an hour before first light tomorrow with their assistant gunners. That should be about 0530. They will be issued M60s, and they will be placed in intervals along the ditch, facing Turkey Mountain, there. They need to provide themselves with materials for thorough camouflage.

"At first light, Blackhawks will arrive in this pasture to pick up the remainder of the troops. You will go with them to the summit of Turkey Mountain. Debark them, fan them out so they cover the better part of the mountainside, and send them downhill, screaming and yelling and making as much noise as they can. They must hold their fire unless they plainly see the tiger and have a straight downhill shot at him. Make that very clear. We don't want accidents. Sprinkle radios along the line. The Blackhawks will remain at low level behind you, with gunners in the door. I don't expect they'll do much good, considering the canopy, but at least they'll add to the racket.

"There will be a fifth chopper, an Apache gunship, at a higher altitude ahead of the line. It will be carrying FLIR and may well be able to spot the tiger if it is running toward us. The Apache will be in radio contact and ready to strike if the target is spotted and if they can reach him. Our best hope, of course, is to run the tiger ahead of the line and into the M60s at the road. Questions?"

"Jesus, Colonel," said one of captains. "You're playin' hardball here. Where'd you get the Apache?"

"Friends in high places, Mr. Bonelli. Lots of people would like a crack at a tiger."

"Ah, sir, Sergeant Richards told me some of the men would like to go over to that hot dog stand we passed on the way in. Would that be permitted?

"They crave hot dogs? I believe the cooks can roast them some."

"I, ah, understand they want some of those T-shirts, sir."

"Tell the sergeant and the rest of your noncoms that if we kill this tiger, my agency will see to it that every man has a T-shirt proclaiming him the killer of the Harte County man-eater. On the other hand, if I see anyone wearing that "I Ate Lunch in Harte County" shirt, I personally will have *him* for lunch. Anything else?"

October 14

Dawn was still a quarter hour away and the sharpshooters of the Harte County Army, as it quickly became known, were snuggling down in the ditch by the road, festooning themselves with tufts of dried grass, when an old yellow bus marked Harte County Schools loomed out of the darkness, escorted by two blue-and-whites.

Colonel Winshiser gaped as the bus doors folded open and groggy-looking men and women, clutching notebooks, still cameras, and video equipment, filed out, shepherded into a ragged line by deputies. Some held paper cups of coffee.

Winshiser's face began to redden as he saw Brickhouse and Weinman approaching.

"What," he said, trying to keep his voice under control. "What is the meaning of this, Sheriff?"

"This, Colonel, is the press corps, which by sometime this afternoon will probably outnumber your corps. They are also very aggressive, and they have a tendency to get into all kinds of mischief if they think they're missing something. I figured you'd rather have them nice and comfy in one place, like that ditch across the road behind your machine gunners, than maybe wandering around up on Turkey Mountain."

"I did not give permission for this, Sheriff."

"No, sir. You don't need to. This is Harte County, and that is a Harte County road there. No military emergency has been declared. Now, with all due respect, Colonel, certain realities have to be faced. Your operation here carries enough risk of accident to your own troops without adding the possibility of one of them mistaking a *New York Times* reporter for the tiger and blowing his ass off."

"Perhaps you're right, Sheriff. Can your men keep them under control?"

"Yes."

"Do all of them understand the danger? There may be gunfire, and there is the tiger to be considered."

"Yes, sir. Most of them are bored and anxious to see some action. We don't have many worldly attractions in Hartesville."

Two miles away, a line of helicopters clattered out of the mist.

"Get 'em in the ditch, Sheriff," Winshiser said. "Move the bus. Do you have the road secured?"

"Right."

"Very good," the colonel said, turning to his men and barking orders as he walked.

"Just like the Nam," said the *Miami Herald* to the *Washington Post* as they watched the choppers settle into the field. The blast of their rotors sent the *Post*'s leonine mane streaming back like a windsock. Battle-dressed troops ran to the dark green helicopters, crouching low. Down the line, a CNN cameraman hugging his minicam to his shoulder bitched about the lack of light.

With a ragged, deafening roar the laden helicopters rose and swung in the direction of Turkey Mountain.

A cheer went up along the press line. "Waste the man-eater," someone shouted.

"Here they come," the *Herald* observed when the yelling and shouting drifted down the mountainside. The helicopters rose above the tree line and hovered. High overhead, another, smaller, chopper circled. The reporters could hear the faint chatter of radios in the ditch across the road, where the machine gunners squirmed into firing positions. The tree line was about one hundred and fifty yards from the ditch. If the tiger was coming, that would be the killing ground. The gunners had a clear field of fire along a three-hundred-yard front.

"It'll take them a few hours to get all the way down the mountain," Brickhouse said to reporters on either side. "Long time to keep your concentration."

"Indeed," said the *Times* of London.

"I may go to sleep," said Bentley.

The press corps soon lost interest in gaping at the mountainside and listening to faint, hoarse yells. Some of them gathered in a knot around Brickhouse, notebooks out. A few cameramen, using an equipment case for a table, opened a deck of cards and began dealing five-card stud.

"Jesus, look at that," a television reporter shouted, pointing upward.

The smaller helicopter was in a near-dive toward a point midway down Turkey Mountain.

"He's gonna crash!"

"No, he's seen something!"

Radio noise in the camp increased sharply. Brickhouse thought he heard Winshiser yelling.

The gunship was within two hundred yards of the treetops

when smoke erupted from under its pylons. Two white plumes hurtled into the trees.

"Holy shit!"

"Rockets!"

Two sharp *whump*s. Smoke, chunks of earth, and pieces of trees rose above the canopy and then settled gently back down. The helicopter veered gracefully up and away, climbing back to its station.

Weinman climbed out of the ditch and scurried to the command post. Five minutes later he trotted back to the ditch.

"Colonel says the gunship's infrared imager mistook a couple of deer for the tiger. He's not happy. Rockets came within about a hundred yards of his troops up there."

"Venison for dinner?" someone asked.

Roy heard the helicopters Friday morning, but he never saw them. He'd heard them before. He'd seen them on the Dugans' television when he went with Rose to do her chores over there.

He paid little attention to the sound now. His mind was filled with his tiger. No longer his dream-cat. His tiger. Somehow, he knew, it was his friend. He thought about his tiger all morning. He wondered if someday he'd be able to pet him, if he liked being scratched behind the ears, like tabby cats did. He'd noticed yesterday that the tiger was male.

In the warmth of afternoon Roy decided to go back up that path to the 'coon stump, more because he hoped to see his tiger than to see the 'coons.

He stopped where the tiger had sat yesterday. He dropped to his knees and examined the ground. Couple of hairs, nothing else. He got up and walked on to the stump. He watched for an hour, and finally saw the mother 'coon peek out, then duck back. Roy had never seen her act like that. She sure was nervous. He didn't think she was afraid of him. She hadn't used to be, anyway.

He noticed how quiet the forest still was, remembering its silence yesterday. Lotta birds gone south, he guessed. He saw a flash of red in a mountain laurel patch. Cardinals. Tough little guys, stay the winter with us.

Oh well. Might as well go back. Too late to do much of anything else. Be pretty cool again before sundown, and bare feet get awful cold. He had a pair of shoes, but he saved them for when it snowed. Shoes, Rose told him once, cost an awful lot.

Roy was about halfway home when he stopped suddenly. He smelled tiger. His friend was near. He looked around, but he couldn't see anything. Slowly, he turned all the way around. You're there, buddy. I know you're there. Where? Come on, where?

He started turning again. Off to the side a blue jay glided down to a laurel thicket, feet braced to land, then veered off, flapping its wings hard, rising back to the trees. Roy stopped turning and watched the thicket. He stared until his eyes burned. He saw a tiny movement, then another. Finally, part of the laurel resolved like magic into the tiger's face. The movement he had seen was his friend's ear twitching.

The tiger was a lot closer than he had been yesterday. Roy figured he could have thrown a rock over his friend in the thicket. He could see the tiger was lying down. As usual, it was watching him, staring at him.

After a while, Roy realized that he was standing on a twig or something that was poking his foot. As soon as the thought occurred to him, he got to be real uncomfortable. Watching his friend carefully, he squatted down. That really hurt, but all the tiger did was lay back his ears a little. So Roy reached his hands out behind him and let his butt drop to the ground. Better. He plucked the twig away from his foot. Gradually, the tiger let his ears rise back up.

Roy and his friend resumed their silent communion. The boy had dropped down by a small dogwood, and he leaned back against it. If he looked away from the tiger, he had trouble picking him up again. He thought that maybe this really was a kind of dream-tiger, a magic tiger, an animal that very few things could see, and that even he, the tiger's friend, could only see once in a while. Didn't seem to go along very well with the hairs, or with that smell, which was even worse than Rose's treasured little bottle of perfume. But it was fun to think about, and thinking about it, Roy fell asleep.

Asleep, he dreamed the tiger smell got stronger and stronger and then he felt breath, like a hot breeze, puffing at his cheek and arms, and a sound like his friend was sniffing at him. And he thought he heard the tiger say something, right in his ear, a little garbled voice from far, far away.

When he awoke, the sun was nearly down, and he knew the tiger was gone. His toes were so cold they were numb. He got up and hobbled home.

The line of soldiers came hurrahing out of the forest line well past lunch, having been sobered and slowed in their progress by the gunship's rockets. None of them had seen a thing, not even the deer the helicopter fired at. It was a dead loss, but Ruby, grateful for the best week she'd ever seen, sent sandwiches and beer out to the reporters for lunch, and while they had no real news, the print people could write plenty of color and the TV contingent had great war video. Most had come to life in time to tape the rocket launch.

"Only to be expected," Colonel Winshiser told the assembled reporters. "Tomorrow morning, we'll hit Copperhead Mountain. Maybe we'll have better luck. See you all at sunrise."

October 15

Saturday morning the parade to the camp at Randall's pasture was augmented by a second school bus, which Colonel Winshiser estimated was at least half full.

Camaraderie among the media was high; Winshiser walked over and told the reporters that things were going to work pretty much the same as usual today. The assault this time would be on Copperhead Mountain, to the west of Turkey Mountain, which meant to their left as they faced the mountains. They'd shift about a mile down the road.

Morale was not so grand among the troops, last trained for desert warfare. Most were unaccustomed to stumping down mountainsides and none cared to have rockets fired around them.

"I ain't havin' any more fun than you girls are," Sergeant Orval Howe told his squad. "Now get them vests on and get your asses in that lead chopper the minute the man gives the signal."

The six P.M. and eleven P.M. news and the morning papers had feasted on the military operation and the rocket fire. Now the flakes, the nutcases, and the idle from hundreds of miles around were flocking to Harte County. All but four of Brickhouse's deputies were on duty at each end of the war zone, as he and Weinman had begun to call it, trying to keep civilians out. The state patrol was trying to sort out the traffic jams. The Forest Service and the DNR were sending up every available ranger to help with crowd control. Cal Heflin had called Brickhouse Friday night.

"Sold every apple I got, Grady. Tryin' to get a truckload in from up Tennessee. Ever'body I talked to says even if Christmas don't come, it'll be their best year ever."

"That's nice, Cal," Grady said, signaling Mary for more coffee.

"Reckon we could do this ever' year, Grady? Shit, we could have an arts 'n' crafts festival, some pickin' an' singin, an'—"

"Cal, I hope that tiger's sittin' on your goddamn bed when you wake up in the morning," Grady snapped, slamming down the receiver.

The Harte County Air Force was running late this morning. The troops slid into sitting position to wait, reporters sipped their coffee, and comparative quiet fell over Randall's pasture. Brickhouse saw the buses lumber away and walked over to his place in the ditch, behind the gunners. Most of the reporters, he noticed, had bought Thermoses and filled them with coffee. "Where's yours?" he asked Bentley.

"I'm sharin' R.L.'s," she said. "Time I got to WalMart they were sold out."

"Try Lacey's?"

"Tried there first."

"How about—"

"*aaaaoouuuunnNNGGGHHH!*"

Coffee sloshed into the ditch. The soldiers leaped to their feet, whirling around, some with their rifles at ready. The reporters huddled deeper, looking up at the mountains.

"Sweet Mary and Joseph," whispered the *LA Times*. "What is it?"

"*aaaaoouuuunnNNGGGHHH!*"

It was like thunder made of pain and rage and came from everywhere, surrounding them. Bentley trembled, pulling her jacket around her neck. The woman from *El Diario* had pulled out a rosary and was telling her beads.

Winshiser was talking to his troops, gesturing.

"*aaaaoouuuunnNNGGGHHH!*"

Excited gabbling rose up and down the line; the reporters scarcely noticed the approach of the helicopters.

"Well, chaps," said *The Guardian*, "rather puts things in a different light, doesn't it?"

"Gets us back to old-time basics," observed the *Sun-Times*. "The saber-tooth is hungry, and we're sitting in our cave clutching our clubs and shitting ourselves."

The pilots found a good clear landing zone on the upper ridge of Copperhead, a rocky bald where they could safely hover three feet above the ground while the troops jumped out and formed a perimeter. Then they brought their lightened ships up over the trees again and backed them a little way toward the other side of the mountain.

Sergeants rushed about, forming their men into a broad line, trying to balance width of coverage with the concept of a tight net. Hard enough on bare ground, a pure bitch coming down a mountain that was virtually a jungle; in fact, it was worse than a jungle in the damp places where the rhododendron and the mountain laurel grew.

They took more than half an hour to get the line ready. Last night, after more than a dozen soldiers had yelled themselves into laryngitis, a couple of officers had gone to WalMart and bought every noisemaker they could find: party favors, duck calls, whatever.

Sergeant Howe looked at his. It had a mouthpiece, so he blew lustily into it. Accordioned paper unfurled for two feet in front of his mouth and made a noise like a camel fart before snapping back. Down the line Private Samuels snickered.

"Jesus," grumbled Howe, who was back at Georgia State studying English lit. "I'd rather yell." He stuffed the noisemaker in his pocket.

Samuels blew on his duck call. Didn't sound much like a duck, but it was damn sure loud, Howe thought. On his right, Private Anson gaily twirled a ratchet. "It's come to this," Howe muttered sadly. "God help us."

Then Lieutenant Carr gave the order to move out, and the line plunged into the woods, honking, rattling, and quacking. Down the line somewhere a guy had one of those toy fire engines with a battery-operated siren under his arm, howling and whining.

"Oh, well," Howe said to himself, filled his lungs, and began bellowing.

"Tyger, tyger, burning bright—"

He stopped when he saw Samuels and Anson drop to one knee and raise their rifles. Carr was running toward him, yelling "Where? Where?"

"Sorry, sir, that was dumb of me," Howe said. "Just making noise, didn't think."

Carr looked at him curiously and then told them to get moving, catch up. Anson and Samuels were snickering again.

"Ho! Ho!" Howe began to shout in a rhythm timed to his feet. Samuels resumed his quacking, and Anson twirled his ratchet overhead.

The fun didn't last long. It was rugged going. Men stumbled over rocks and branches, falling. One sprained an ankle. Dense stands of brush and laurel thickets forced them apart. Within forty-five minutes the line was ragged and disorganized. Some units were out of touch with their neighbors.

Howe's mighty "Ho" had subsided into a kind of grunt. Anson was having so much trouble staying on his feet he forgot to twirl his ratchet most of the time. Samuels just left his duck call in his mouth and breathed through it. "Mallard with emphysema," Howe said to himself.

Thinking about noise reminded him of the tiger's call, and that reminded him of why they were going through this. He looked up and down the line. The men were watching their feet. They weren't looking for the tiger. Howe suddenly realized they could be in grave danger.

"Hey!" he shouted. "Samuels! Anson! All you turkeys! You forget that tiger's shoppin' for lunch? Stay alert, goddamit! This is Indian country."

Samuels and Anson sharpened right up, he noticed. He couldn't see the rest.

Roy heard his friend calling in the morning. Scared the birds away. His mother was just getting up.

"What in the world was that, Roy?" she asked.

"I don't know for sure, Ma," he said cagily. "You think it might be some new kind of animal?"

"Well, Roy, I don't know why there would be any new kind

of animal, but you know more about them than I do. It was awful loud, anyway." She began sweeping the kitchen.

He went up the path toward the 'coon stump for a ways, found a good log and sat down to see if the tiger would come. He brought two peanut butter sandwiches, one of them for his friend.

In the press lounge, which is how the reporters were referring to their ditch, boredom had settled in again. The Red Cross provided brunch, and they munched while interviewing each other and lying about all the important stories they had covered. The men tried to make dates with the handful of women. One of the Atlanta television stations decided to relieve its reporter on the scene, but he didn't want to go and got into a fistfight with his replacement.

Brickhouse was asking Weinman about plans for the deer stands when they heard two sharp cracks from the mountain. Everyone whipped around, but there was nothing to be seen.

"M16," muttered Don Buchholz, who had asked to come out with Weinman. One of the helicopters was slipping sideways toward the eastern edge of the mountain. Radio traffic at the command post acquired the same urgency as it had yesterday when the rockets were fired. It didn't abate so quickly, however.

A large puff of smoke emerged from the trees, and the helicopter veered toward it.

"Smoke grenade," Buchholz said. "Marking an LZ."

The helicopter settled down through the smoke. Brickhouse heard footsteps and looked over to see an officer running to the ditch.

"Sheriff, does your hospital here have a helicopter pad?"

"No. What's wrong?"

"Not sure, but somebody's apparently hurt. Can you get an ambulance here?"

"I've got one at the eastern roadblock," Brickhouse said, "but I doubt I could get it out. How much fuel does the chopper have?"

"At least another forty-five minutes," the lieutenant said.

"Why don't you have them come back here to the field. I'll bring the ambulance up, the EMS guys can look at your casualty and start treating him. If it's bad, they'll ride the chopper to Gainesville. Hospital there's got a pad."

"Sounds good, Sheriff," said the officer, running back to the camp.

Weinman was already on his handheld to the deputies at the roadblock.

"Get the EMS truck started up here right now, code 3. Tell the crew they probably have a gunshot victim coming, may have to chopper him to Gainesville."

"Ten-four."

"Heard it, Chief. On the way," came another voice. It was Jimmy. Brickhouse heard the siren start just as the helicopter rose out of the remains of the smoke.

"I knew this was coming," Weinman said.

Reporters began climbing out of the ditch and helping their friends. Brickhouse leaped out and yelled, "Back in the lounge. Get back!"

"We gotta go over—"

"Go over and what, get your head lopped by a helicopter? You cannot go into the camp. I gave the colonel assurances that you would remain here under any circumstances.

"Now listen. Someone has apparently been shot. The helicopter there is bringing him to the pasture. That siren is an EMS wagon. The paramedics will evaluate the victim and, if necessary, accompany him to the hospital in Gainesville, where there is a helicopter pad.

"Chief Deputy Weinman will go over there for us. He'll observe the situation, he'll make every attempt to ascertain what has happened, and he'll come back here and fill you in. Now, please, go back in the ditch."

There was deep grumbling, especially from photographers, but everyone scrambled back into the ditch. Brickhouse made no objection when reporters reluctantly agreed to hoist their cameramen to their shoulders.

When the EMS truck rolled up Weinman got out of the ditch and accompanied Jimmy and his partner to the pasture. The Blackhawk flashed overhead, spewing dirt and pebbles from the roadside, and dropped sharply to a bumpy landing in the field.

Brickhouse, pacing on the road, saw the EMS techs run to the helicopter, each dragging a case of equipment, and climb in. Winshiser, one of his officers, and Weinman joined them at the open cargo door. After a few moments, Jimmy scrambled out, spoke briefly with Weinman, and ran toward his truck. He was dragging another case out, along with an IV setup. "Bad, Sheriff. Chief deputy wants to see Bill Banks right away."

Puzzled, Brickhouse called Deputy Banks out of the ditch and sent him to the chopper. When he turned back he saw a soldier had emerged from the chopper and was talking to Winshiser. Jimmy leaped back into the chopper, and Banks, after a few words from Weinman, crawled in behind him. The pilot put power to the rotors, and the group of men ducked and trotted away as the chopper rose swiftly. Weinman was trotting past the impatient reporters. "Just a second," he said to them. "Be right with you."

"Worse than we thought," he told Brickhouse. "You want a report now or you want to pick it up as I tell them?"

"Anything we can't tell them?"

"Not that I can see."

"Go ahead then. No point in going through it twice."

They walked back to the edge of the ditch and the reporters packed in. A woman jammed against the front of the ditch squawked in pain.

"All right, folks, loosen up. You aren't going to miss anything," barked Brickhouse, exasperated. "Soon as you give each other breathing room, Chief Deputy Weinman will tell you what he knows."

"Here's what I'm told," Weinman began. "Approximately twenty-five minutes ago, a soldier on the eastern end of the line observed movement to his left. He turned to face that direction and readied his weapon. He saw it again, in a large stand of dry grass, about waist high. As he watched, he saw an orange-colored object move through the grass. Believing it to be the tiger, he fired twice at it. At this point someone screamed, and a man leaped up in the patch of grass.

"Several of the soldiers ran into the stand of grass, where this man, a civilian, was screaming and acting incoherently. In the grass they found the body of a woman in an orange jumpsuit. She appeared to have been struck by both bullets, once in the left side and once in the left thigh. She was unconscious.

"The helicopter was called and both subjects put aboard it, along with two soldiers who did their best to stop the flow of blood from the wounds. Our paramedics are now accompanying them to Gainesville. I am told that the woman's chances are not good."

"The man with her appears to be drunk. He had to be

subdued before he was put into the helicopter, and by the time they reached the field he was in a stupor and unresponsive. I have no idea right now who these people are or where they came from, but I assume they are part of this horde of curiosity seekers. Deputy Banks is aboard the helicopter and has placed the man under arrest. By the time they reach Gainesville I expect he will have some kind of identification, and as soon as we can notify the woman's relatives we will pass those IDs on to you.

"Before you ask, the soldier who shot the woman will not be identified. He's in a state of shock, and I do not see any way he can be held responsible for this.

"The operation is continuing, and the soldiers expect to be at the tree line in about an hour. That's all I have."

The clamor of questions erupted immediately.

The troops had been back an hour when Lieutenant Carr trotted up to the colonel.

"Sir, we're missing a man."

"I think one went to Gainesville with the helicopter," Winshiser said.

"I know that, sir. We're missing Private Samuels. He was over on the western side of the line."

Winshiser took a deep breath, staring at Copperhead Mountain. "Get a search party going. Two squads, including his own, of course. Find him before dark. He may be out there hurt."

"Yes, sir," Carr said.

Sergeant Howe took the point for the search team. He was furious with himself. Samuels had been his responsibility, right next to him, and he'd lost him, just flat lost him and didn't know he was gone until they got back to camp and he tried to assemble the squad.

Howe knew exactly where the squad had come out of the woods. He had the lieutenant spread the men out on both sides, no more than five feet apart. He told them to watch the ground, watch it for sign. Half a dozen other soldiers had volunteered to cover them, watching their flanks for the tiger.

They hadn't been looking half an hour when Howe saw Samuels's helmet. No sign of Samuels. His weapon was under a bush five feet away. The significance of that hit him like a weight, and he fell to his knees beside the helmet. Samuels wasn't lying out here injured. The tiger had him.

The lieutenant was about to say something when Anson called out from a little way uphill. "Some blood here, Sarge."

Howe stood up, the helmet in his hands, and looked at the lieutenant. There wasn't anything to say. He walked on up to Anson.

"Looks like a trail, Sarge. Not a lot, but right on our track. You figure the tiger got him?"

"What else?" Howe said, his voice harsh.

Anson looked at him.

"Not your fault, Sarge."

"No? Whose?"

"Nobody's. Shit, Sarge, this ain't our bag. We ain't trained for it."

The lieutenant was watching them, quietly. The other men were casting around.

"We oughtta be able to handle ourselves. I oughtta be able to protect my men."

Howe looked like he was about to cave in.

"Anson's right, Sarge," the lieutenant said behind him. "We weren't ready for this."

"Damn right, Sarge," said Anson. "We ain't hunters."

"We were the hunted today," the lieutenant said. "Let's move on."

An hour before dark Private Martínez screamed.

The rest ran to the sound and found Martínez back in the woods, vomiting. "Over there," he gurgled, pointing to a big maple.

Private Samuels was mostly gone. What was left was lying on its back. His face was intact, although there was a terrible scalp wound. His duck call was still in his mouth. Howe couldn't get it out.

The lieutenant took the radio and talked to base for a while. When he came back, he said, "They can't get any more medics in here through the traffic. They don't even have a body bag down at base. They're getting a civilian Medevac chopper from Gainesville. Should be here before dark. We'll stand by until they get all this cleaned up."

Roy Satterly sat along the path to the 'coon stump all day, but his friend never showed up. He took his extra sandwich back to the house and ate it for supper.

When the reporters found it would be well after nine P.M. before the buses could get them out through the snarled traffic, there was a brief uproar before they turned to technology. At least two dozen had cellular phones with them. The TV people called their stations, which dispatched helicopters. Some of the print reporters decided to share choppers too. The rest called their papers and dictated their stories, keeping them painfully brief. Everybody was able to file before the batteries died, and most could file fuller stories for later deadlines once they got out of the war zone.

Brickhouse got back to his office at nine thirty, exhausted and depressed. He called the state patrol chief at home in Atlanta.

"Sid, I expect you know what a disaster we had up here today," he said.

"What a bitch, Grady. I never heard anything like it."

"We've got to close down the circus, Sid. Can you have your boys block every road leading into Harte County tomorrow morning, real early? There's no interstate here, just state roads. I'd like to turn back everybody who doesn't live in the county unless they've got deliveries to make."

"I'll have to check with the governor, Grady. If he okays it, we'll have the roads closed by four A.M. What about reporters?"

"We've got our quota of those, too."

"All right, Grady. Good luck."

When Brickhouse hung up, the night dispatcher laid a note in front him. "Forgot to tell you when you came in, Sheriff. Lady at that number called twice tonight."

"What's she want?"

"Didn't say."

Brickhouse looked at the number. Long distance, 202 area code. Washington. Washington could wait until tomorrow.

"I'll return it in the morning, Randy. I'm going home."

Ray's Tavern, on Highway 153 on the east side of Hartesville, was always busy on a Saturday night. The booths were full, the bar was about two-thirds full, and all four pool tables were in use, although the men shooting on three of them were wasting a lot of time watching a short, chubby woman who was running the fourth table to the despair of her burly, bearded date.

It was about ten P.M. when the now-familiar tiger graphic appeared over the anchor's shoulder on the big-screen TV over the bar and Skip, the barkeep, turned up the sound. The tavern fell unnaturally quiet. The pool players stopped their games to listen.

It took the CNN anchor a long time to recount the events of the day, with a lot of video of helicopters and people being pulled out of them in baskets. There was a long segment showing Weinman standing on the road, recounting what had happened to the couple. A soldier who appeared to have been weeping refused to talk about the discovery of Samuels's body.

"Christ a-mighty," said Bill Hall, a tall, thin man in jeans and a flannel shirt. "How lame can you get?"

"Well, it's just the National Guard," said Tommy Hancock, a wiry young man who worked with Hall at the Harte County Plumbing Company. "Ain't like it was the regular army, let alone marines."

"Don't matter," said Hall, watching his wife finish her burger and fries. There was nothing left of his but an empty plastic basket. "Believe I coulda done better'n that."

"Well, come to that, reckon we both coulda done better," Tommy agreed.

"Be a helluva thing, wouldn't it, kill that damn tiger?" said Bill.

Tommy gazed at the television set, its volume now turned too low to hear over the clack of the billiard balls and the whine of George Strait. There was a map of Bosnia on the screen.

"Yessir, it would," he nodded. "Man'd be a hero, for sure. Be all over the teevee. Be in the newspapers."

"Well, looks like rain tomorrow," said Bill. "You wanna give it a try, next good day? We can get the time off."

"Damn betcha. Let's do it."

"Awright, then," crowed Bill, slapping the table.

October 16

Rain began to fall steadily before dawn Sunday, and it looked to Brickhouse as though it might last all day. What a blessing, he thought, driving to the office.

Weinman was already at work.

"What's the word, Mark?"

"Banks called from Gainesville a little while ago. Woman died early this morning. No ID on her. He got the drunk sobered up, though, and the man said she was his wife, Irene. His name is Ferris Iberville, a short-order cook from Cobb County. Said he and Irene had a day off, thought it'd be slick to drive up here and watch the show. Brought a fifth of Old Pistolwhip, got here about three A.M., and crept out in the woods."

"What's the charge?"

"Public drunk, disorderly conduct, and reckless endangerment. Solicitor doesn't think manslaughter or murder would hold up."

"Where was the dead soldier from?"

"Newnan."

"Makes me feel like crying. Is this ever going to end, Mark?"

"We're due a break of some kind. We got five dead now, four killed by a tiger and one from being where she had no business being. I had to hold off on the poison because of the troops. Oh, Sid called from DPS, said the governor okayed the roadblocks. We're sealed off now."

"Good," said Brickhouse. He picked up the note from last night. "Guess I better return this call. Stay put; shouldn't take long."

"Good morning," a woman's voice said. "State Department."

"State Department? Maybe I got the wrong number. This is Sheriff Brickhouse in Harte County, Georgia. One of my deputies said someone from this number wanted me to call."

"Yes, Sheriff, you have the right number. We've got special instructions on this," the woman said. "Will you hold while I patch you through to the embassy in London?"

"Yes ma'am," he said, shrugging at Weinman's questioning look. "Patching me through to London," he whispered.

"Hello, Sheriff Brickhouse?" said a man's voice.

"Yes, sir, this is Brickhouse."

"Sheriff, this is James Outerbridge, here at the embassy in London. Ambassador Wright has asked us to get in touch with you most urgently to see if we can be of any assistance in your emergency. The papers and the telly here are full of it, you know."

"Well, Mr. Outerbridge, that's very kind of you and the ambassador, but I can't right offhand think of anything for you to do."

"Actually, Sheriff, we've something in mind. The British

foreign minister, Mr. Ibbotson, called yesterday morning. His father was an old India hand, out there until the Raj closed down. He had a great friend, a man who probably knows more about tigers and how to hunt them than anyone else in the world."

"Well—"

"To our considerable surprise, Mr. Ibbotson told us that this man's son, who followed in his footsteps, is now living in retirement in Yorkshire. His name is Graham, Colonel James Graham. Mr. Ibbotson said he had been in contact with Colonel Graham, and found him vitally interested in what's happening there. In fact, Mr. Ibbotson said he was finally able to convince the colonel that he ought to lend you a hand."

"Is Colonel Graham aware that this tiger has killed four people?"

"Yes, yes, he is, Sheriff. Mr. Ibbotson told us that while it has been some years since Colonel Graham has hunted tiger, the last one he shot had in fact killed and eaten 228 people."

"What?" Brickhouse yelped.

"Oh yes, Sheriff. Man-eaters are quite a problem in India."

"I'm not sure—"

"The ambassador said to tell you that if you can have the colonel met at the airport in Atlanta, brought to Hartesville, and given simple housing, there will be no other expense for you."

"Mr. Outerbridge, that is extraordinarily generous. When can Colonel Graham come?"

"Actually, Sheriff, he's booked on a Delta flight due in Atlanta at two A.M., your time. I realize what a dreary hour that is, but it's the quickest we could move."

"You seem to have thought of everything, Mr. Outerbridge. We're very much in your debt."

"Oh no, Sheriff, I'm merely the messenger boy. From what I understand, I think you'll enjoy Colonel Graham, and I've no doubt he can help you with this tiger. That's Delta Flight 312 from Gatwick. I've another call now, must run. Good luck."

Weinman had his elbows perched on Brickhouse's desk.

"That's the damnedest phone call I ever had," Brickhouse said. He repeated the gist of it.

"Weird," Weinman snorted.

"Well, look at it like this. We got a professional hunter from DNR. Tiger killed him after an hour in the field, and he turns out to be some kind of racket guy anyway. Next we get the National Guard; tiger gets one of them in two days. None of these guys knew diddly about tigers. How can I turn down a free offer of somebody who's supposed to know everything about them? Hell, Mark, we got people right here can shoot. We just don't know how to use them."

"Can't deny any of that, Sheriff. What the hell. Want me to pick him up?"

"We'll both go," Brickhouse said. "Now I got to go down to the school and talk to the wolves. With no operation out at the guard camp, they'll be restless. What should I tell them about this Colonel Graham?"

"If I were you, I wouldn't tell them anything until we talk to him. If this is a joke of some kind, we could look even worse than we do now, if that's possible. If it's not, he ought to have a say in it before we turn the pack loose on him."

"I'll just tell them an expert is coming. I won't go further than that. Then I'm going to see if Winshiser will use his troops to try to cordon off the whole area. Go home, try to get some sleep. I'll pick you up about six and we'll go down to the city and have dinner before we go to the airport."

Roy helped Rose with household chores on Sunday. It was wash day, but with the rain there wasn't any point in that, so they dusted and swept, and Roy spent several hours trying to get his room organized a little.

Roy didn't figure the dream-tiger would come around in the daytime when his ma was there, so he didn't watch for him. Sunday night he kept the lamp going late, reading some new magazines the Dugans had given him, and when he doused the flame and crawled into bed, the tiger was there by the window, waiting for him. At least he thought it must have been, because the first thing he saw when his eyes got used to the darkness was his friend's huge yellow eyes.

The tiger no longer got nervous when he moved a little bit, although he was still careful not to do anything quick or jerky. He made himself comfortable by the window and looked through the screen at the dim figure. The piercing, feral odor no longer made his eyes sting; it was a welcome smell, like Rose's sweat when she gathered him in her arms.

Finally Roy closed his eyes and listened to his friend purr. One day, he hoped, he would be able to touch his friend, to stroke him and scratch his ears, and maybe learn whatever it was the tiger was trying to tell him. He drifted away to sleep and jumbled dreams that gave him fleeting glimpses of what that day might be like.

The light, steady rain seemed to restore a degree of calm in Harte County. The wolves at Mayfield School were satisfied with Brickhouse's briefing on the details of Saturday's tragedy. Then they went to church, where reporters always go on Sunday in a traumatized town.

So many of them flocked to the Evangelical Pentecostal Church that some had to be turned away. The word had gone around, spread perhaps by a few Presbyterian practical jokers, that the Pentecostals were snake chunkers, followers of that peculiar mountain faith which dictates that the righteous may take up serpents without injury. However, the Pentecostals were not about to take up serpents. There was a church in the north end of the county that practiced snake handling, but nobody could remember its name or its exact location.

But the reputation of Brother Abel Sugrue, pastor of the Evangelical Pentecostal Church, was also well known, and the reporters were not disappointed.

Brother Sugrue approached his sermon with relish. Indeed, he had spent hours constructing it with many a whispered thanks for such an opportunity. After all, how many pastors got a chance to denounce such evil afoot in their own parish? For the beast that had so mysteriously sprouted in their midst must be possessed by Satan or one of his emissaries.

"This is no ordinary tiger!" he bellowed, his eyes bulging. "This is the Devil from Hell, Satan his own self, come to challenge the reign of Jesus Christ Almighty right here in Harte County! What are we gonna do about it?"

What they were going to do about it, Brother Sugrue told them, was to gather at the church every evening for an hour of prayer, to strengthen the hand of the hunters against the onslaught from Hell.

Reporters who attended other churches heard less revelatory sermons; some almost entirely ignored the tiger as just one more passing cross for the faithful to bear, while other pastors urged caution and some arranged work parties to offer something beyond standard rations to the soldiers.

———

At Randall's pasture, Brickhouse found Colonel Winshiser and his officers in the command and control tent, trying to come up with a new strategy. Most of their ideas, he discovered, involved operations out of the question, such as napalm or carpet bombing.

"Tell you what, Colonel. I think the most important thing you and your men could do here is to throw a ring around this area and try to keep any more fruitcakes out of it," Brickhouse said.

"Good God," Winshiser said. "Are you expecting more, after what happened yesterday?"

"Not that sort, no. But I keep picking up talk about some of our local hunters taking a notion to go after the tiger. We've got to stop offering this damn thing its dinner on a plate.

"No way we're gonna keep out anybody who knows the area and really wants to get in, but you've got enough men to make it tough on them," Brickhouse said, pulling out his detail maps of the area. They settled on blockading 153 and 120, on both sides of Copperhead, Turkey, and Raven Bald, letting motorists pass but not leave their cars.

"I think I've got enough men to put them out in pairs in vehicles—I'll get some more humvees from Stewart," Winshiser said. "I'll have to space them out so far they won't be able to see each other, but each team can see a common point halfway between them."

"Good. But make sure they stay alert, Colonel. That tiger's sure to check them out."

"I don't think caution will be a problem for them," Winshiser said.

———

Brickhouse and Weinman drove to Atlanta Sunday evening in the sheriff's personal Crown Vic. They wore slacks and sport coats.

They got in about nine and had dinner at a little place on LaVista called Nicola's, which Doc Steinberg always raved about. Nicola, a rotund Lebanese elf, came out wiping his hands on his apron to greet them as though they were long-lost cousins. When Weinman remarked on the rice, Nicola told him how it was prepared—with a touch of cinnamon—and then scurried back to the kitchen. He returned with a deep bowl of rice and scooped more on their plates than they had to begin with.

"I love Ruby dearly," Brickhouse said, "but she's not even in the hunt here."

"Not hardly," Weinman said.

They hung around until ten thirty, regretfully leaving plates still a third full. Normally they would have gone to the Cheetah III, had a few drinks, and watched the naked dancers and made bets with each other about which of the drunks was going to be the next to try to grab a crotch when a girl offered her garter belt for folding-money tips.

When they got back in the car, Brickhouse and Weinman discussed the nudie joints, but neither was really in the mood for it.

"Wouldn't it be just grand to look between one of those girls' knees and see the *New York Post* on the other side of the bar?" remarked Weinman.

"No shit," Brickhouse said. "Sheriff Drools at Naked Dancers While Tiger Eats Constituents."

They wound up killing an hour in a Peachtree Street bookstore, then driving out to Hartsfield International Airport, drinking coffee in a lounge, then flashing their badges to get to the international concourse.

The rain stopped shortly after midnight in Harte County, not long after Fergus Moody relieved his brother Ferroll in the hayloft of their barn.

"Anythin'?" asked Fergus.

"Naw. Esther seems a little restless is all."

"Hokay, I got it, then. Don't forget to wipe your damn boots before you go inside."

Ferroll snorted and shook his head in disgust, picked up his old pump-action 12-gauge, and climbed down the ladder nailed to the wall of the little barn. Closing the barn door behind him, he went slogging off to the house, thirty yards away. Fergus watched him, lit by the glow of the post-mounted floodlight, until the back door screen snapped shut.

Fergus set his Thermos and his double-barrel on the floor and sat down on a boat cushion in front of the loft's small door, which was centered over the barn door proper. There was only the one door to the barn itself, but there were little doors at both ends of the loft. By day or moonlight, the one in back looked out on waist-high weeds, discarded equipment, a few empty barrels, and, not far away, the tree line. On a night like this, nothing could be seen from the loft's back door, and it had been closed against the rain.

Fergus Moody raised goats, show goats. Some of the seventeen goats sleeping in the barn below were worth hundreds of dollars. Just that past summer, Fergus had turned down an offer of seven hundred and fifty dollars for Esther at a show down in Athens. Esther was family, about as much family as Ferroll or Cassie, his wife, who was fixing Ferroll a snack now before he went to bed.

When the tiger thing started, Cassie had convinced Fergus to ask his baby brother to come over and stay with them. Ferroll lived by himself, a little south of Hartesville, about a fifteen-mile drive away. He had a few goats, too, but that area seemed pretty safe. Fergus's place, outside Hartesville's western edge, was under the sway of the tiger, and Fergus would take no chances. He had been prepared to stand guard over his goats twenty-four hours a day. Cassie wasn't particularly fond of Ferroll, but she'd rather put up with him than have Fergus fall out of the barn or get sick. He was a hearty man, but he was sixty-five years old.

Still, Fergus insisted on taking the midnight to noon shift. You had to figure that was the more dangerous time, and the way Fergus was raised, you didn't put your baby brother into the most danger, even if he was sixty-one years old and not good for much of anything.

Fergus could still taste Cassie's fried potatoes and scrambled eggs. He opened the Thermos, poured out a cup of black coffee, and leaned back against a couple of feed sacks, watching the yard. He could see his truck and Ferroll's and the four-foot tank by the well where the goats drank. The goats had the run of the yard, and the grass was cropped down close to the ground. The fence, and the taller grass beyond it, was visible only in a few places before the shadows swallowed it.

Every morning after Ferroll relieved him, Fergus checked around the barn for signs of the tiger. He hadn't seen anything yet. Nonetheless, Fergus had a gut feeling that his goats, the finest in Harte County and perhaps in all of North Georgia, would be a prime target for the tiger. Sooner or later, it would come around. It took one of Willet's sheep, it'd damn sure show up at Moody Goat Ranch.

————

Fergus Moody's nearest neighbor, Carl McElroy, lived in a small brick house a mile up the road, and, like Fergus, he was taking care of business. Carl's principal business was women. His line of work was house building, and if he had put the same single-minded determination into building houses that he put into the pursuit of women, Carl would have been the richest thirty-four-year-old man in Harte County.

Carl was slim and handsome, with a well-tended mustache and a boyish glint in his blue eyes. He was a notorious figure in Hartsville and much of the outlying county, had been since his high school days. Carl had run through all the women willing to be seen with him. He had married two of them, one because it seemed like a good idea at the time and the other because it was the only way he could get her into bed. Neither marriage had lasted a year.

It was getting damn difficult, and at the time the only action Carl had going was Hale Causey's wife, Laura. They could only get together when Hale was on the road, pulling his rig up to Arkansas or even Chicago for some shipper or another. She would call him when Hale was on the road. She called him Sunday night, said she'd have the baby in bed and asleep by ten. Best part of the thing with Laura was convenience. She lived in a double-wide about five miles down the road.

On a rainy night like this, however, Laura didn't want him pulling up their dirt driveway because Hale might spot the tracks, especially since she made her lover park behind the double-wide so nobody could see his truck. Just after midnight, Carl doused the lights and pulled well up the driveway of the old Gander place, which had burned to the ground three Decembers ago, leaving only the chimney to mark the place where the small house had been. He turned off the dome light before he opened the door and began walking to Laura's driveway, only a hundred yards on down the highway. Carl, carefully staying on the grass so as not to leave prints in the mud, was drenched by the time he walked up to the little porch of the double-wide. Always paid to be cautious. Hale Causey was a big sucker, and ungentle.

Weinman went to a Delta gate clerk and discovered the flight from London was on time. Its gate, however, was even farther down the concourse, so he tapped the sheriff awake and they strolled off.

"How many miles you figure we are from baggage claim right now?" Brickhouse asked. "This place wears my ass out every time I come here."

"Damn if I know," Weinman said. "It wouldn't surprise me if you said it was really a big maze and baggage claim is on the other side of that wall."

"Hate this airport," Brickhouse grumbled. "Fact is, I wouldn't give two cents for the whole damn town. It's got out of hand."

"Good places to eat, though," Weinman said as they sat down in front of the proper gate.

"There is that," Brickhouse agreed.

At a quarter after two, bleary-eyed, bewildered travelers began filing out of the corridor from the plane. A Delta representative stood where they could see him, ready to give directions to connecting flights and customs. Weinman had told the man who they were, and who they were waiting for. They had no idea what Colonel Graham looked like.

The flow of arriving passengers slowed and finally stopped, and Brickhouse and Weinman stood up. "Reckon it really was a joke?" Brickhouse asked.

"Looks kinda like it. We can check Delta, see if they got

him on the passenger list." They were walking toward the woman at the desk when a tall, elderly man stepped out of the corridor.

"Gotta be him," said Brickhouse. Despite his years, the sheriff saw, the man was slim, with an erect, military bearing, and there was a feeling of strength about him. His short-cut, light-gray hair had receded, giving him an unusually high forehead. A neatly trimmed gray mustache covered his long upper lip. His eyes, Brickhouse thought, seemed clear and sharp, and his face, with what appeared to be a small, permanent smile, was remarkably benign.

The Delta rep stepped forward and asked a question. The man nodded, and the Delta guy beckoned to Brickhouse and Weinman.

"Colonel Graham?" Brickhouse said, holding out his hand. The Englishman took it in a firm grip.

"Just Jim, please," the man said in a soft voice. "You are Sheriff Brickhouse?"

"Yes. This is Chief Deputy Mark Weinman."

"Glad to meet you, sir," Graham said, shaking Weinman's hand. Their visitor was wearing a tweed jacket with leather elbow patches, cut close to the body in a style long out of fashion, and loose-fitting flannel trousers. The clothes were well-worn but good and looked exactly right on him.

They started for the escalator, but Graham noticed a restroom and asked them to wait for him. "Long trip, you know, and I seem to have an aversion to walking about in airplanes," he said.

The lawmen watched Graham disappear into the men's room. "Jesus Christ," Weinman said, blowing out a sharp puff of air. "It's an even worse joke than we thought, isn't it?"

"What do you mean?" Brickhouse asked, startled.

"What good's that old fart going to do us? He must be ninety if he's a day."

"You think so? Doesn't look nearly that old to me," Brickhouse said. "Any case, all we want's his experience, his advice."

"Well, I hope his memory doesn't run down his pants leg in there," Weinman said.

At the international baggage pickup, they waited about twenty minutes for luggage to begin showing up. "Most interesting," Graham said, watching the carousel carry the bags around as they popped up from the trucks below. Brickhouse looked at him and Graham flushed lightly. "I travel very little any more, Sheriff," he said.

An old leather suitcase with shipping-line stickers on it came around, and Graham stepped forward, lifting it easily off the carousel.

"That it?" Weinman asked.

"One more piece," Graham replied.

A long gun case, again old but obviously solid, came by, and Graham took it.

"What's that?" Brickhouse asked.

"A rifle," Graham said, with a smile that forgave the obvious question.

"Wasn't necessary, Jim," Brickhouse said. "What we need is your experience."

"I see," Graham said. "Ibby's playing tricks again, I suppose. Ah, well. Can you get me through customs with this, Sheriff?"

"I imagine so," said Brickhouse, bewildered.

At customs, Brickhouse and Weinman showed their badges

and explained Graham's business. Nonetheless, the customs officer, more from curiosity than suspicion, asked Graham to open the rifle case.

"What kind of cannon is that, Colonel?" Weinman asked as the customs officer nodded and waved them on. Graham carefully closed and locked the case.

"Jim, please. Just Jim. It's a double rifle, made by Westley Richards. It's chambered for the .470 Nitro Express. Been with me for a great many years now. It was presented to my father by the government."

"Never saw a double-barreled rifle."

"Uncommon now, even for big game," Graham agreed. "All these new magnum loads and so forth, you know. However, it's a bit late for me to consider changing weapons."

"I see," Weinman said, glancing at Brickhouse.

Graham refused to let them carry his luggage. They installed him in the backseat of Brickhouse's Crown Vic and pulled out of the parking lot.

"Aren't you tired, Jim?" Brickhouse asked.

"No, not really," Graham said. "This whole thing is really rather exciting. Thought my shikar days were long gone."

"Shikar?" Weinman asked.

"Ah, yes. Hindu expression, means "hunt." A shikari is a hunter."

As they cleared the city and drove north, Brickhouse and Weinman described the area where the tiger was operating, and Graham asked questions. Finally, after a long silence, Brickhouse asked: "I know that's pretty sketchy stuff, but just on the basis of it, what can you advise?"

"I long ago foreswore killing tigers," Graham said. "If we do not protect them, they will disappear, and we will be very much the poorer for it. But when one turns bad this way, it must be destroyed."

"We worked that out for ourselves, Jim," Weinman said rather sharply. "You're the guy with the experience, though. We need your advice on how to do it."

"Advice, eh?" Graham said with a chuckle. "Gentlemen, I'm afraid you misunderstand. I have not come to give you advice. I have come to try to kill this tiger."

Laura opened the door to let Carl in, pressing against him for a kiss. "Oooh, honey," she whispered, drawing back. "You're soaked to the bone. Come get those wet clothes off." She took his clothes to the bathroom, wrung them out and hung them over the shower curtain, turned on the bathroom heater, and closed the door. The Causeys didn't have a dryer.

After a couple of drinks to get the chill off, Carl and Laura got down to business, keeping quiet to avoid disturbing the baby in the next room. Carl hated that, because Laura was a squealer, and squealers always made him feel especially powerful. But, he thought dolefully as Laura whickered into his shoulder, you had to settle for what you could get these days.

Laura, a plump redhead with a big, sweet smile, was enthusiastic, and the way her enthusiasm and her caution were always at odds was especially engaging to Carl. It pleased Laura to think that she had her fancy man on the side, but she damn sure didn't want Hale to know about it, so she wouldn't let Carl stay the night. He had to be gone before sunup, even if Hale wasn't due back for a couple of days. Somebody might see him leaving. So at five A.M., Carl pulled on his shirt and pants in the sweltering bathroom. They were still clammy and chilled him immediately. Laura hustled him to the door, leaned up to kiss him good-bye without touching anything below the chin, and closed and locked the door behind him.

The rest of the trip back to Hartesville was spent largely in silence. Brickhouse dropped Weinman off after asking him to handle the Monday press briefing and brought Graham home. Mary was asleep, and he showed the Englishman into the spare bedroom quietly.

"A bathroom attached?" Graham said wonderingly. "The very lap of luxury, Sheriff."

Brickhouse smiled.

"Sheriff," Graham said softly, "perhaps I owe you an apology. My remark about not being here to give advice has clearly upset both you and Mr. Weinman. I did not intend to be so abrupt. It is simply that I am not only unused to offering advice, I am very poor at it.

"Were I to offer you my advice, it would not get you one step further forward. There are only a few ways to go about finding and killing a tiger, and you have thought of all of them. Your unfortunate soldiers tried beating for him, which is the term we use to describe an attempt to drive an animal out of heavy cover and into the line of fire of a gun or guns.

"From what you tell me of the ground, the beat in this case was haphazard, since there was no indication the tiger was in the area to be beaten, and virtually certain to fail, since he could easily slide out of the net before being forced into the open. The fact that he did not do so, but instead lay in wait to seize one of the beaters, is unique in my experience. It certainly shows him to be an exceptionally bold animal and probably one quite familiar with human beings.

"You have also thought of poison, which I abhor but which,

in this case, would certainly be justified. However, you have so far been offered no means of administering it to one of the tiger's kills.

"You have put in motion plans for waiting up for the tiger. To this I could only offer the suggestion that you wait up over some kind of bait, possibly a sheep tied out, since I suppose cows are rather dear and anyway the tiger has shown no disposition to kill one. This, incidentally, would indicate one of two things: that he has a physical defect that prevents him from killing so large an animal, or, more likely, that he simply does not know how to manage it.

"There is a fourth way, which is to stalk the animal. It can be done, and I have done it, but for someone without a great deal of experience, stalking a man-eating tiger is an elaborate means of suicide.

"Now, there is all the advice I can give you. Tell me frankly, Sheriff, is it even worth the drive to Atlanta and back?"

Brickhouse smiled ruefully. "No, Jim, I don't suppose it is."

"Of course it isn't. The kind of knowledge you need for this is not something that can be passed on as advice. Certainly it can be learned, for I learned it. But it requires years and years of patient study in the forest, and much experience with tigers in general and man-eaters in particular. I have that, although two things mitigate against me here," Graham said, loosening his tie.

"It has been a very long time since I entered a forest containing anything larger than a hare, but I believe the instincts formed over the better part of my life are still available. More significantly, my experience and my knowledge were developed in a forest on the other side of the world. Geologically, I think, it is similar to yours. But its inhabitants are altogether different, except for the curious presence of this tiger. Other forest animals, when he understands them, are the hunter's most valuable informants.

"So you see, all I can really do for you is go into your forest and do my best to kill the tiger," Graham said, sitting on the bed and unlacing his soft leather boots. "I quite understand how laughable this may seem to you and to Mr. Weinman. I assure you, however, that I am rather more spry than I appear to be.

"I can still walk twenty-five miles or more in a day over whatever ground I must. I satisfied myself before I agreed to come here that my eyesight has not deteriorated to a degree that significantly affects my aim. In any case, from my understanding of the conditions here a shot at long range is unlikely. My hearing, while not what it once was, is adequate to the task.

"Perhaps, too, you should understand that I have no living relatives. Should this shikar come to a bad end, no one will sue you. No relative of mine would ever have considered such a dastardly thing anyway. Finally, Sheriff, I am here because I want to be. I have spent most of my life being useful. It would be nice to be useful again.

"So. Will you let me try to help in the only way I can?"

Brickhouse grunted. "I hate the idea of sending a man your age into a situation like this. But I'll be damned if I can think of a practical reason not to do it, given what you say, and maybe it'll work. I don't know what else to do.

"So, yes," Brickhouse said. "We'll do whatever we can to help you. Just tell us what you need, what we can do."

"Thank you, Sheriff," Graham said with a smile.

"It's getting close to dawn," Brickhouse said. "I'm whipped. We'll talk more after we've slept. Good night, Jim."

"Good night to you, Sheriff."

In his bedroom, listening to Mary's slow breathing while he pulled off his shoes, Brickhouse realized he hadn't asked Graham exactly how old he was.

Carl McElroy had always heard it was darkest just before the dawn, and he could easily believe it now. Once out of range of the Causeys' floodlight, it was difficult to see where he was walking. He wished he had a flashlight and shivered under the damp shirt. At least the rain had quit.

By the time he found his truck he had slipped in the mud and fallen to one knee, and walked straight into a tree trying to find the abandoned driveway. He sighed with relief as he settled behind the wheel. He wasn't looking forward to starting his new construction on the east side of town in a few hours. It was always a bad sign to start with a muddy site.

He rolled the key over and the ignition groaned. "Oh, shit, no," Carl whispered. Again, and there was even less response. He flicked on the headlights; there weren't any. He looked at his watch. It would be light in an hour or so. Any other situation, Carl would have opted to stay with the truck until then, but if anybody saw him Laura would flip, and Laura was all he had going. Not much for it but to walk home in the dark. A mile wasn't so far, and at least there ought to be a little light to see by pretty soon.

Up to the moment he stepped out of the truck, Carl hadn't even thought about the tiger. But as he looked at the faint images of tall weeds against the blackness of the trees beside the driveway he thought he saw movement. He jerked back and his elbow whacked the mirror on the door.

However, he saw nothing else. "Coulda been anything," he

muttered. "Coulda been a possum or a 'coon or a rabbit. Been that tiger, I'd prob'ly be dead now. Wish to hell I'da brought the gun."

Carl found it comforting to talk to himself when he was nervous. He walked haltingly back up the driveway and along the edge of the road toward home, whispering a near-constant stream of reassurance. Carl owned a shotgun—to be without at least that much armament was to be considered weird— but he was no outdoorsman. It never occurred to him that his monologue might cover other sounds.

He was trudging uphill, staying on the pavement to assure his footing, when he saw oncoming headlights hit the treetops at the crest of the hill. Panicked, he leaped into the ditch and hunkered down. The car crested the hill and drove past. The headlights didn't reach him, and he didn't think anyone saw him. He was clambering up the side of the ditch when a car approached from the other direction. He ducked back down until it had passed.

Looking up, Carl could see the outline of the trees against the sky much more clearly now. People were beginning to stir, especially the ones with a long drive to work.

"Shit," he muttered to himself. "I better stay off the road. Take that path runs along the woods." Hoisting himself gingerly over a three-strand barbed wire fence, he struck out in the darkness, pushing through a stand of waist-high grass toward a trail that wound behind the houses on his side of the road.

Birds were beginning to sing in the trees, and that cheered him. Another car passed back on the road. He stopped and looked at its fading taillights and thought he saw the grass swaying about fifty feet behind him. "Must be a breeze," he whispered, although he couldn't feel one.

He walked on, trying to be quiet, until he found the path that ran along the edge of the tree line. "Pity it don't run all the way to the Causeys," he told himself. He didn't know how it came to be there. Kids exploring and playing kept it packed hard, but it was a little slippery after the long rain. Carl was beginning to wheeze a little, and his knee was sore where he had fallen on it. It was still very dark, and when something loomed in the darkness ahead he stopped suddenly, then realized it was just one of Fergus Moody's goat feeders. He knew Fergus's barn was nearby, screened by a stand of old walnuts.

"Almost home," he muttered. "Almost—"

Carl whipped around to see what had made a kind of grunting noise behind him, but there was nothing but blackness after a few feet. He could have sworn he heard something, something live. But there was nothing but silence now, except for a bird singing in the trees somewhere. "Gonna put that damn shotgun in the truck before I leave the house again," he told himself and then remembered he had to get a battery into the damn truck before he could drive it home. He'd have to call Shorty to come get him soon as he got back.

"Gonna be a long damn morning for sure," he muttered.

Fergus Moody was draining the last of the coffee out of his Thermos when he heard something approaching the barn. A strange sound, movement, certainly, and a kind of growly mumble that reminded him of a badger he'd seen once. He set the Thermos down carefully and reached for the shotgun, peering into the blackness just beyond the walnuts. Whatever it was, it was getting closer. In the barn below, a couple of goats stirred nervously.

Fergus began to wish he'd brought his rifle, too. The shotgun was loaded with double-ought buckshot and wouldn't have much range. But there was a handful of extra shells in his jacket pocket.

It sounded like the thing was in the trees now, getting closer. There were more sounds from below, and Esther bleated softly. He could tell most of the goats were awake and standing. Something definitely had them nervous. Had to be the tiger. Fergus brought the shotgun to his shoulder.

His eyes, straining in the darkness, were beginning to burn. Cassie had been after him for years to see an eye doctor. Well, man gets in his sixties, he can't expect to see as well as a boy. But there, there it goes. Movement. In the trees, coming for the barn. Knew you'd come, you bastard. Fergus yanked the trigger and the recoil rocked him back a little against the feed sacks and made him pull on the second barrel a little before he wanted.

The muzzle flashes blinded him, and the shotgun's blasts nearly deafened him. He thought he heard something crashing through the underbrush and up the hill, but then he heard it groaning out there. It didn't sound much like he thought a tiger would. Lights were coming on in the house as Fergus got up, reloaded the shotgun and climbed stiffly down the ladder. It wasn't until he was on the ladder that he realized the goats were panicked, bleating and milling around the barn. Esther was lying in a corner, her sides heaving. He started hollering for Ferrol.

It seemed to Brickhouse that he'd just fallen asleep when Ellen called.

"May have a break here, Grady. Cassie Moody called, said Fergus done shot the tiger, but she was pretty hysterical. Somethin' about Fergus and his little brother goin' after it. I got Handley headed out there. You want me to call Mark?"

Daylight was seeping under the curtains. Brickhouse rubbed his eyes and glanced at Mary. She was still asleep.

"Yeah. Tell him I'll meet him out there." He padded to the door of the spare bedroom and woke Graham before dressing.

Brickhouse had to show Graham how to get into the patrol car's seat belt. The Englishman was fascinated by the two-way radio. When Handley reported his arrival at the goat farm, they could hear a woman squawking and goats bleating in the background.

Day-shift deputies were beginning to report their locations when a breathless voice broke in.

"Twelve," it said.

"Go ahead, twelve," Ellen replied.

"I need a four."

"Oh, shit," Brickhouse groaned.

"Same twenty?" Ellen asked.

"Affirmative."

"What does it mean, Sheriff?" Graham asked, clutching the armrest. Brickhouse had accelerated and turned on the blue light, but they were out of town now and he didn't punch on the siren.

"Twelve is my deputy, Handley. Four is an ambulance, emergency. Twenty is location, so when he said the same twenty, he means he's still at the goat farm. Somebody's hurt pretty bad."

Handley's blue-and-white was pulled up by Moody's house, the roof lights still whirling and the driver's door open. Ferrol Moody was down by the barn, waving frantically at them. Brickhouse pulled round the deputy's car and drove to the grove of walnuts, leaving room for the ambulance at the barn. They could hear its siren in the distance.

"Where's Fergus?" Brickhouse barked as he got out of the

car. Graham was taking his heavy double rifle from the back-seat.

"In there," Ferrol answered, waving at the open barn door. "Poor Esther, she's havin' a difficult delivery."

"Esther who? Who's hurt? What happened?"

"Esther, she's the brood goat. Carl McElroy's the one hurt. Fergus, he shot at the tiger, but young Carl, he done took the load in the legs. Don't rightly understand it."

"Where is he?"

"Like I tol' you, in the barn."

"No, goddammit, where's Carl?"

Ferrol pointed toward the walnuts, and from somewhere behind them, Barnes yelled, "Over here, Sheriff!"

Brickhouse and Graham worked their way through the stand of walnuts and high underbrush to find Handley and Cassie kneeling beside a body lying just off a hard-beaten path at the edge of the woods. She had Carl's head in her lap. The legs of his jeans were tattered and bloody. McElroy was deathly pale but awake. His eyes shifted from Brickhouse to the trees as the ambulance's siren gave a last warble and sighed into silence by the barn.

The sheriff squatted down. "Bad?"

" 'Fraid to look," Carl said. "Hurts."

"Don't think it amounts to much, Sheriff," said Barnes. Getting up. He nodded curiously to Graham.

"What happened?"

"Fergus said he was sittin' in the hayloft, guardin' his goats. He and Ferrol been standin' guard twenty-four hours a day since all this started. Says a little before dawn, he heard the tiger comin' through the walnuts, let him have both barrels. Then he hears Carl here hollerin'." Cassie wailed and patted Carl's ashen cheek.

"What about it, Carl?"

"Walkin' home, down the path, mindin' my own business, somebody shot me. Like he says, musta been ole Fergus thought I was the tiger come for his damn goats."

"What were you doing out here in the dark?"

Carl's blue eyes shifted from the sheriff to Cassie and then to Graham, standing in the background. Two EMTs burst through the weeds. "We'll take care of him now, Miz Moody," said one of them, slipping a blood pressure cuff on Carl's arm. The other slit open Carl's jeans. His legs looked as though he had contracted a fearful rash. Blood was smeared around and coagulated in BB-sized spots from midthigh to ankle.

The paramedic ran his hand down Carl's right leg, then pinched one of the blood spots between thumb and forefinger. The drying blood popped open and a buckshot appeared.

"Carl, you were out of range for all intents and purposes," the paramedic said. "Believe you're gonna be just fine soon's they get the lead out of you." Cassie, standing to one side, wailed.

"No, ah, damage up higher?" Carl asked weakly.

The paramedic smirked. "Missed that altogether," he said. "Let's get the stretcher. Might's well take him back in style."

"Cassie, you go on back to the house now," Brickhouse said. "Looks like everything's gonna be all right."

"Now," Brickhouse said as the plump woman hurried away, wiping her eyes. "What the hell you doing out here, Carl?"

"Can't rightly say, Grady, know what I mean?"

"No, dammit, I don't know what you mean. How come you're walking around in the dark out here when we've got a man-eating damn tiger loose?"

"Grady, you know how it is. . . ."

Understanding dawned. "Woman involved? Somebody's wife?"

Carl nodded a fraction of an inch.

"Not out here, surely to God?"

"No, no, no. Like I said, I was walkin' home. God's sake, Grady, don't tell anyone. Please."

The paramedics returned with the stretcher, Weinman following them with a shotgun in one hand. "Gotta take him in now, Sheriff, get the lead out of him. You gonna put him in for a Purple Pecker?"

Brickhouse grunted, yawned, and got up. "Morning, Mark. Where'd he go?"

"You mean the old fella came with you," Handley said. "He went up the trail there and 'round the corner, where it bends back in toward the woods. Who is he, if you don't mind me askin'?"

"English big-game hunter, name of Graham," Weinman said, pushing his Ray-Bans up his nose. "Come to help out with the tiger. From what the medics say, Grady, I expect Deputy Barnes can go on home, unless you need him to do something."

"Nah. Thanks for hanging on out here, Fred."

Graham appeared at the bend in the trail. He was walking alongside the trail, not on it. The heavy rifle was under his right arm.

"Good morning, Mark," he said. "I found something back here you chaps might like to see."

They walked back down the trail, Graham pointing out the marks of McElroy's boots in the thin layer of mud on the trail. "You see him coming along, rather unsteadily. It was dark, and he was tired. He must have been rather distracted too."

"How do you figure he was unsteady?" Weinman asked.

"See here and just there, the prints are blurred where he

slipped just a little. The stride, too, is somewhat uneven," Graham replied.

"Why distracted?"

Graham smiled and motioned them along the trail.

Fifty feet from the spot where Carl had fallen, his boot prints were obliterated in places by heavy tracks. "The pugmarks of the man-eater," Graham said. "The tiger was following him. Here is where it ran into the forest when the shots were fired. But see, back here, how careless it was. A broken twig." He picked up one half of the twig and snapped it. The sound was small but sharp in the morning air. "And here, it stepped on this rock." The stone, smooth and ovoid, was set against another rock, a slight smear of mud on it. Pressure on either caused a distinct *clack*.

"Our quarry is a very large male tiger in its prime, although perhaps a bit underweight. In this instance it was remarkably careless, presumably a result of inexperience or contempt. Mr. McElroy is either hard of hearing, or was making enough noise himself to cover the sounds the tiger made."

"Making enough that Fergus mistook him for the tiger," Brickhouse said.

"Only a tiger in search of a mate makes enough noise to be heard as far as that barn," Graham said, "and a stalking tiger could very easily enter the barn without being heard. In any case, this tiger was almost certainly preparing to seize the young man. It was gaining on him steadily. Another minute or two, I should think, and it would have been upon him."

"Shall we follow it?" Weinman asked.

"Oh, yes. He'll be far away by now, but any fresh trail is worth following. I presume most of the farms hereabouts have telephones, and I can keep in touch with you that way."

"We'll go with you," Brickhouse said.

Graham looked startled. "I doubt that would be productive, Sheriff. Three people, even when they are quite skilled, cannot move together with any degree of silence. I have always found it best to hunt alone."

"Well, you said the tiger would be long gone, and we'd surely like to see how it's done."

"Vetting me, Sheriff?" Graham said with a little smile.

"No, I'm genuinely curious. I realize we'll probably just be in your way. We don't expect to hang around with you all the time. Just this once."

"Very well, but you must understand that we will be on my ground, so to speak, and you must do as I say. To begin with, Mark, leave that gun here. I shall go first, and the two of you follow in single file. Try to walk where I do."

Weinman locked his shotgun in his car, and the three set off up the slope behind the goat ranch.

Graham walked steadily up the slope, moving almost soundlessly although he didn't appear to be watching where he stepped; rather, it seemed to the two men following him, he paid attention only to the ground on his left. This part of the forest was hardwood, with little undergrowth. The older trees grew about twenty to thirty feet apart, with some understory like dogwood between them. Brickhouse and Weinman couldn't help but crunch the thin cover of fallen leaves under their boots.

Suddenly Graham held up his right hand and halted. Brickhouse managed to stop before running onto the Englishman's heels and heard the chief deputy grunt behind him. Graham looked back at him, held a finger to his lips, and walked off to the left, moving very quietly, one foot stepping where the other had been. About ten feet away he stopped, plucked something off a low branch of a little buckeye tree. He scanned the ground around it for several minutes before returning.

"Tiger's hair," he whispered and resumed the march, angling somewhat to the left.

After a quarter of an hour, they began to hear the sound of running water. Graham slowed the pace noticeably and became even more wary. Often he would stop, turning his head as if ranging for sound.

The source of the sound was a rill about three feet across, plunging down the mountainside. Graham began walking along it, keeping to the grassy area just off the soft, pebbly banks. He was watching the ground on both sides closely, but he also lifted his head constantly to look ahead and to both sides.

Brickhouse realized he was so tense he was holding his breath. He tried to relax while maintaining vigilance and just avoided stumbling over Graham when the Englishman suddenly dropped to one knee. He was watching the bank of the rill, motioning Brickhouse to get down. The sheriff squatted, looking around nervously. Weinman turned to watch their back trail.

Graham rose and moved, stooping, down to the bank, where he dropped to one knee again. He summoned Brickhouse and Weinman with a gesture.

"Tiger's pugmarks," he said softly, pointing to tracks on both sides of the stream. "It was here more than an hour ago, perhaps two hours. It paused to drink here," Graham said, pointing to two prints side by side, "then stepped over the stream and proceeded that way, toward the shoulder of the mountain. It's no longer running, but it's moving at a strong pace."

Graham stopped suddenly, stepped quickly across the rivulet and knelt to examine another pugmark. He reached out and touched it gently, as if brushing it, and his eyes seemed to widen momentarily in surprise, then lose their focus as he looked downstream.

"What is it?" Brickhouse whispered.

"An odd thing," Graham replied slowly. "Very curious. . . ." Then, seeming to reach a decision, he rose to his feet and motioned the officers across the stream. "Let's push on now."

Now and then, as they continued, Graham would point at something. Brickhouse saw a partial print in one place and a tiny tuft of hair on a bush, but generally he saw nothing at all where Graham pointed. After an hour's tracking, they saw a rock outcropping a hundred yards away.

Again Graham dropped down, motioning the officers down with him. He watched the area for a quarter of an hour without seeming to move. Then he rose slowly, brought the rifle to his shoulder with the muzzle pointed at the ground, and moved off at an angle to the rock. He motioned for Brickhouse and Weinman to follow.

The way to the rock led through a sharp cut in the mountainside. The slope to the rock was mild, but behind them an abrupt bank rose as high as twelve feet and formed a ledge about twenty feet wide.

Graham moved like a shadow, wincing when one of the officers stepped on twigs or rustled the damp leaves. Every thirty or forty paces he changed direction, always approaching the rock at an angle. However, Brickhouse could see his attention was concentrated as much, if not more, on the forest side as on the rock side of their path.

When they reached the outcrop and emerged into the sun, Graham pointed to a spot of bare earth bearing the tiger's track. "If not frightened, he probably would have spent some time here basking in the sun," the Englishman said. "But it appears he pushed on."

"What was all that back-and-forth about?" Brickhouse asked, gasping for breath. The climb and the tension had exhausted him.

"An excess of caution, Sheriff. I really do not believe the tiger is anywhere near us now, but it would be foolish to go barging straight through such an obvious ambush spot. You see that high embankment back there?"

"Sure."

"A perfect spot for the tiger to wait for us. To walk straight to the rocks here would have meant turning our backs on the ledge. The tiger has enough of an advantage without giving him more. By quartering to the rock, I was able to keep the ledge to one side or another, where I would see any movement instantly.

"It could easily take me half an hour or more to find where the tiger left these rocks, and he appears to have somewhere to go. Now, it is nearly noon, we've had little sleep, and I'd like to have those sheep tomorrow. Let's turn back and see if Esther had her kids safely."

At the farm, they found Fergus Moody washing his bloody hands and arms at a hydrant by the barn. "All that ruckus nearly gave Esther a miscarriage," Moody said sourly. "But she gave me a couple of healthy kids, and I think she'll be fine.

"Cassie tells me McElroy's gonna be okay too," he said, standing and shaking his hands to dry them. "Glad of that, although I don't know why he's blunderin' around in the dark behind my barn."

"Fergus, you're just damn lucky you didn't hurt him bad,"

Brickhouse said. "You got a right to protect your property, but you got no right to go shooting at something you can't see. I could do you for aggravated assault right now, and if some ambulance-chaser gets ahold of Carl you could lose your house and your goats and every damn thing you got. I'm gonna let this slide for now, but if you're gonna go on sitting up for tiger every night you might do better to take a brass band up there with you instead of that shotgun. You hear me?"

"Well, hell, Grady, you know I never meant—"

"Never meant don't count for a hell of a lot if you kill somebody, Fergus. Not many juries gonna set a goat's life above a man's. Try to use some sense after this."

Brickhouse turned away and walked to his car, Graham and Weinman behind him. Moody was still flapping his hands at his side. A goat bleated inside the barn.

"I notice you didn't tell him he saved McElroy's life," Weinman said with a grin as the officers reached their cars.

"What, and make him act like a hero? This is the second person we've had shot for a tiger. McElroy ain't about to start suin' over this, either, but the next one probably won't have just come from somebody else's wife. Now I'm goin' home and back to bed. Come on. Jim."

October 17

Monday morning Roy Satterly walked down to Dugan's with Rose, holding an old cast-off umbrella over them. When it rained Roy generally went with her, helped her with her chores, and walked her home. Wasn't anything else to do, and he didn't want his mother getting sick from walking in the rain. She wouldn't use the umbrella by herself.

While they were cleaning the windows a television crew came in; Roy heard the reporter identifying himself to Annie. He looked at them out of the corner of his eye. The guy with the big camera was stocky, wearing jeans and those fancy high-top white shoes and a kind of dirty-looking jacket. The rain had plastered his short brown hair to his scalp. The reporter was small and slender with a tan coat that had a belt around the waist, although it was hanging open. He had long hair that rose up and back from the front and sides. Drops of rain glistened on it just like they did on the outside of the window.

The cameraman turned on a light that brightened the inside of the gloomy store like the sun had come right through the roof. Fred looked out from the storeroom, then ducked back. The reporter started talking to Annie while the camera guy squinted into the camera, pointing it at her and fiddling with things on it.

The reporter had a big microphone. He would say something into it, and then thrust it at Annie, and she would say something. They were talking about a tiger. That startled Roy. They must be talking about his friend, his dream-tiger. Maybe he was a very famous tiger.

After a while Annie and the reporter stopped talking, and the light went off. The reporter looked around and saw Rose and said something to Annie. She said something back, Roy couldn't hear what, and shook her head, no. Then the reporter looked right at Roy, and Roy could tell the man was looking at his bare feet too. Annie grinned and nodded and then the two men came walking around the potato chip rack toward him. Suddenly Roy was frightened. He squirted Windex all over the glass, for the second time, and started scrubbing hard.

"Can you take a few minutes out to talk to me, fella?" the reporter asked.

Roy dropped his hands to his sides and turned as though he hadn't even known the men were there.

"I guess," he said. The man looked like trouble to Roy, and he was instantly wary.

The big light on the camera flashed on again, so bright it hurt his eyes and he had to squint and look at the floor.

"What's your name?" the man said into his microphone, then held it in front of Roy's mouth like he was offering him something to eat.

"Roy."

"Roy what?"

"Satterly."

"How old are you, Roy?"

"Nine."

"Where do you live?"

"Up the road a ways," he said.

"School out because of the tiger?"

Roy didn't know what he meant by that. He decided it would be best to agree.

"Yeah."

"Where do you think this tiger came from, Roy?" the reporter asked.

"India," he said proudly.

The reporter chuckled. "Very good. But how do you think he got here?"

"Dunno," Roy said.

"You walked here in the rain, Roy?" asked the reporter, looking at Roy's feet. There was some mud on top of the right one.

"Yeah."

"Aren't you afraid of the tiger?"

Roy answered this time without thinking about it.

"No,"

"You're not afraid? Why not, Roy?" The man's voice changed a little and he pushed the microphone a little closer to Roy.

Roy wished he had said yes, which apparently was what the man thought he would say. He noticed the photographer turning something, and the glass thing on the end of the camera poked out a little more toward him. He knew he had to be careful now. He remembered how the other boys had acted when he told them about his animal friends.

"I dunno," he said, looking at his feet. "Just not."

"What if he's waiting for you when you walk back home?"

Roy heard Annie start coughing loudly. He started to say

he hoped it would be, then realized that would probably be a mistake. He had the idea from what he'd heard them saying before that they thought the tiger was bad, although Annie had said how good business was because of it.

"I dunno." It was all he could think of.

"Dunno much, eh?" said the reporter. "Okay, thanks, Roy."

The light went off, and Roy saw Annie was glaring at the man. The reporter smiled and went out the door. The cameraman followed him, waving to everybody. Rose was still working on her window. Roy didn't think she'd noticed anything.

"That was no gentleman," Annie announced.

Roy was surprised. He didn't know a man could look just like a gentleman and not actually be one.

Rose and Roy walked home late that afternoon, Roy carrying a grocery sack under one arm and the umbrella in the other. Annie had given him a Goo-Goo Bar before they left, and he was saving it for dessert. There was a jar of grape jelly in the bag, along with some bread and things, and some chicken. Rose said that what with him to help her carry, she didn't think she'd be too tired to fry the chicken for dinner. Roy kept an eye out, but he didn't see his friend.

Brickhouse awoke late Monday to find Graham already up and Mary completely under his spell. They were at tea in the den.

Graham stood to greet him, holding his cup and saucer in one hand rather than setting it down first.

"Good morning, or good afternoon, Sheriff," he said. "Your lovely lady has been entertaining me most royally."

"Don't you believe that, Grady," said Mary, her eyes sparkling. "You've brought home a very fascinating man. Jim has been telling me about all the wonderful places he's lived. Have some tea with us?"

"Good day, Jim, and Mary," the sheriff said, happy that Mary was pleased. "I'll stick to coffee—don't get up, I'll get it."

Brickhouse brought his coffee into the den and dropped into his La-Z-Boy.

"So, tell me about all these places you've been, Jim," he said.

"Not so many places at all, Grady," the Englishman said. "Just India, East Africa, a bit of Europe, and England."

"Born in Yorkshire?"

"Oh, no. Born in India. Domiciled, they call it, to differentiate us from real English people, who merely came to India and soon left."

"Being born in India kept you from being a real Englishman?"

"Oh, real enough by law, certainly. But not socially. It never bothered my father, and it didn't bother me. We were content in India, more than anywhere else. I loved the country and the people."

"Where did you live in India?" Brickhouse asked.

"In the north, in the foothills of the Himalayas. I always felt it the most beautiful place in the world, and I have seen nothing to change my mind."

"I gather that man-eating tigers were a big problem there."

"Well, I wouldn't say a big problem," Graham said, "but there did seem to be quite a run of them in our area over a period of fifteen or twenty years, tigers and a few leopards, too."

"I understand your father was a hunter, too."

Graham chuckled. "My father was a hunter, yes. But to

compare him with the ordinary hunter, say a Royal Army officer on leave, would be comparing a housecat to a tiger. Father was as much a part of the forest as the tiger. I have never seen a man so brave, nor a man with so much love in his heart.

"He loved the people, and he loved the tiger. The British were not, for the most part, welcome after the Raj fell, but it was different for us. Father left anyway, moved to Kenya. But the Indian government made our bungalow a museum, and they named the country's largest tiger preserve after him. He, as much as any man, is the reason there are still wild tigers in the world."

"How wonderful," said Mary. "And he taught you to hunt?"

"I was allowed to prowl in the forest as a small child, just as he was. By the time I was old enough to carry a gun, father was sick of hunting. He would hunt only when called to destroy a man-eater. But he never lost his love of the forest. I would not say he taught me anything. He showed me everything."

"Why were there so many man-eaters in your part of the country?" Brickhouse asked.

"Coincidence, surely. But I have never known a tiger to turn man-eater without a compelling reason."

"Such as?"

"Debilitating injury, or old age, or both. If a tiger can no longer pull down its normal prey, it must take what it can, and human beings are quite easy to kill."

"Any guess as to why our tiger is eating people?"

"Difficult to say, this being such a unique situation. But your forest is not full of large game, only fairly small deer and a few wild pigs. This tiger, in captivity most or all its life, would probably have a great deal of difficulty bringing down a deer. He's killing and eating whatever he can find."

"I was told the last tiger you shot had killed, I think he said, 228 people? That seems incredible."

"Not at all, Grady. Not in India. Certainly it would be unthinkable here, but I have known man-eaters who have been credited with much higher numbers than that. The Pragnar leopard for instance, is known to have killed nearly 400 people over a period of about seven years. The Champawat tiger was blamed for 438."

"How in hell can that happen?"

"For several reasons. The only well-armed people in India at the time were the British, and not a great many of them were keen on hunting man-eaters, especially if no white people were harmed. Of those who did hunt, not very many proved to be very good at it.

"Worse still, the hill people have a kind of fatalism, a tendency to accept whatever happens. Most of them believe that man-eaters are not animals at all but devils, *shaitans* is their word, who cannot be killed by normal means. Ipso facto, the only likely result of trying to kill a man-eater is to draw its attention. Despite how this sounds, I always found them a remarkably brave and stoic people, quite ready to risk their lives to help me when I was trying to kill a tiger. They simply had not the slightest idea that on their own they could kill a man-eater.

"In fact, I recall arriving at a village where a man-eater was operating and being told that the tiger had killed an old woman near the village the previous night. The people said they had followed the blood trail to a deep thicket, and when they approached it, the tiger growled at them. One of the men in the group had a musket, and when he heard the tiger, he fired the gun into the air. The tiger burst out of the other side of the thicket and disappeared.

"I asked him why, instead of shooting at the sky, he didn't fire into the thicket. Well, the man looked at me as though I had lost my mind. 'But Sahib,' he said, 'if I had fired at the thicket I might have hit the tiger, and then he surely would have come out and killed me.'"

"Grady," said Mary, "it's getting toward dinnertime. Why don't we take Jim to Fletcher's?"

"Good idea. Fletcher's," he said to Jim, "is what passes for the best restaurant in Harte County, and actually it's not bad. Doesn't serve booze, so I think most of the reporters haven't found it yet."

As he backed the car out of the driveway, Brickhouse asked Graham what he wanted to do about the media.

"No, no, I really can't talk to any reporters," Graham said. He seemed appalled.

"It's going to be hard not to," Brickhouse said. "They know an expert's coming. They'll raise hell if I don't tell them about you, and they'll start looking for you."

"It's simply not possible," Graham said, more agitated than Brickhouse had seen him. "Look here, I'll think of something. Just don't tell them anything until tomorrow. Can you do that?"

"Of course."

Fletcher's Steak House was a couple of blocks from the Rest-Easy Hotel, and as Brickhouse parked the car, he noticed Rajneesh Patel coming down the street. Patel, a man in his sixties, smiled at Brickhouse and his wife, then peered at Jim and paled. He stopped and reached out as though to touch him.

"Grame Sahib?" he asked in a whisper. "Is it really you?"

Graham smiled at him and nodded.

Patel dropped to his knees, then prostrated himself and touched Graham's boots with his forehead. Brickhouse gawked, astonished. The Patels had been reserved, even haughty, since they came to town five years ago.

Graham flushed deeply, grabbed Patel by the shoulders, and gently hauled him to his feet. They spoke briefly in a language Brickhouse had never heard.

Patel turned to Brickhouse with tears in his eyes.

"Perhaps you do not know," he said, "that in my country this man is known so very famous and loved all. He is still call Grame Sahib. Long ago my uncle made pilgrimage to a great shrine in the high mountains. On his way home, a terrible leopard catch and eat him. Grame Sahib kill that leopard. My father have picture him. I thought never to see him."

The old man spoke a few more words to Graham, salaamed, and hurried on toward the motel.

"Most embarrassing," said Graham.

They decided over dinner that Graham would begin his shikar at sunrise on Tuesday and would make his base at Whitfield's tumbledown shack at the foot of Turkey Mountain. Brickhouse objected to that, but Graham insisted that from the sheriff's description, it would be more comfortable—and more secure—than the tent in which he used to living while in the field. And it would keep him away from the reporters.

They ate mostly in silence, however, until, over coffee, Mary remarked that the encounter with Rajneesh Patel seemed to have upset Graham.

"No, Mary, it didn't upset me, not at all."

"You must be a great hero in India yourself, as well as your father."

"Perhaps to a few, in the sense of a dentist who relieves a man of a bad and long-standing toothache. It always seemed to me, though, that for every one who blessed me and my rifle, there was another for whom I came too late.

"And that is, frankly, what is weighing upon me. I fear I will not be able to kill the tiger as quickly as you may hope."

Brickhouse looked up sharply from his cheesecake.

"You must not expect too much too soon, Sheriff," Graham continued. "So far I have never failed to kill a man-eater whose hunting I have undertaken. But of all of them, only one was killed within a week. Most took a great deal longer. The Rudrapore leopard, the one that ate Mr. Patel's unfortunate great-uncle, required two years."

"Two years?"

"Oh, not a solid two years of hunting. Good Lord, no. My nerves are as good as the next man's, but no one could stand that kind of tension for so long, and I had a living to make, too. I was in the field for probably six months out of those two years before I finally killed that leopard.

"The point is, however, that in only one instance have I been able to come to terms with a man-eater so quickly that it did not kill again while I was in the field.

"In our favor, there is the point that this tiger seems to have established a smaller territory than he would have in India. Against us is my unfamiliarity with the conditions here. But the tiger will grow hungry again very soon. If you will purchase a few sheep for me, perhaps we can induce him to dine upon them until I can get in touch with him."

"What a curious expression," Mary said. "Get in touch with him."

"That's what I must do, don't you see. I have to get in touch with him—meet him, in other words—in person."

October 18

The sun was already well up and the mist driven off Raven Bald when Roy awoke on Tuesday. He had stayed up late wrestling with the knowledge that outside people knew there was a tiger in the mountains and thought he should be afraid of it.

If they thought he ought to be afraid, that probably meant they were afraid. But he couldn't see why. His friend, to be sure, was very big, had very long teeth, and a terribly loud hiss, but he hadn't done anything to make Roy fear him.

Roy finally decided there was no way to make sense of this without more information. He pulled on his clothes and checked his mother. She was still asleep. He pumped up a drink of water in the kitchen, grabbed a couple of pieces of bread, and set off down the dirt track toward the Willet farm.

The trees were still dripping from the rain, and Roy kept to the open, watching for tracks in the soft ground. There were no deer prints, and the only legible sign Roy noticed was a family of turkeys that crossed from the direction of Copperhead Mountain heading for Raven Bald.

When he crossed the last little ridge before the Willet farm, he was surprised at the silence. He couldn't hear the dog, which had always seemed to be barking. He could hear the sheep, but he couldn't see them, and from the sound, they must be in the barn. Bobby was nowhere in sight, either.

All this was beyond Roy's experience, and it made him nervous. But he kept on walking. He was halfway between the house and the barn when he saw Bobby waving to him from a back window. He saw Bobby turn and say something to someone else inside the house, and in a minute the back door opened and a woman came running out, Bobby's mother, he supposed. Bobby was right behind her.

"Hi, Roy," he yelled.

"Bobby," his mother said sharply, "get back in the house!"

"Oh, Mom, it's okay. It's not around now. See, Roy's okay."

"You're Roy?" the woman asked but didn't wait for an answer. "You come on in the house with us. You mustn't be out walking around now. It's terribly dangerous, don't you know that?"

Roy was taken aback by all the commotion. Bobby was on one side and his mother on the other, and she took hold of an arm and marched him toward the door. "Come on in, Roy," Bobby said. "I ain't had nobody to play with in nearly a week."

"Don't say ain't, Bobby," his mother snapped automatically.

With that, Roy was in their kitchen. He'd never seen anything like it. He knew his own kitchen wasn't very nice, but the only other one he'd really seen was the kitchen in the Dugans' double-wide, and it wouldn't have filled half of this one.

"Would you like some breakfast, Roy?" Bobby's mother asked.

"Had breakfast, ma'am," Roy said.

"Well, you can talk after all, and like a gentleman, too," she said lightly. Saying he could talk like a gentleman made Roy feel good. He knew Rose would be proud of that.

"Even so," she said, taking a tea towel off a baking pan on the long, white counter, "I bet both you fellows could do with a piece of apple pie."

Bobby hopped up on a chair at the big kitchen table. Roy could see he was going to have a piece, so he supposed it would be all right. "Yes, ma'am," he said.

"Well, go and wash your hands, and it'll be sitting there for you when you get back," Mrs. Willet said. "Bathroom's right down that hall, first door on the left."

Roy went down the hall, amazed by the gleaming floor, and into the bathroom. It was amazing, too. Clearly the Willets had running water, like the Dugans, but Roy couldn't figure out how to get the water warm. There was just one faucet with one valve on it. Its handle swiveled around and up and down. Roy didn't want to waste water so he washed his hands in the cold and went back to the kitchen.

Bobby was waiting for him, sort of impatient. Roy eased up on the chair and looked at the slice of pie in front of him. There was something on top of it. He looked closer and saw that it appeared to be melting on the pie.

"Ice cream, stupid," Bobby said in a whisper.

"I figured you like your pie à la mode," said Bobby's mother.

"Yes, ma'am," Roy said. Bobby was digging in, so Roy started eating, too. It was so good he began taking very small bites to make it last longer.

Mrs. Willet sat down at the end of the table, wiping her hands on her apron. She was a stout woman with light-colored hair and rosy cheeks. She had a nice smile.

"Where do you live, Roy?" she asked.

Roy was under the spell of apple pie à la mode, and his guard was down.

"Up the road that way," he said, pointing between the mountains, and barely remembered to add, "ma'am."

"Is your mother there?"

"Yes, ma'am."

"Does she know you walked all the way here?"

"No, ma'am. She was asleep when I left."

Mrs. Willet started to ask about his father but didn't. She'd pried enough to find out something was badly wrong at Roy's house. In Mrs. Willet's world, no mother stayed in bed when her children were awake.

"Roy, do you realize what a dangerous thing you did, walking here? Don't you know the tiger could have been waiting for you?"

Roy took the last bite of pie. It was the most marvelous thing he'd ever eaten. His mother hadn't taught him about not talking with his mouth full, so he blurted out: "Really wasn't no danger, ma'am. He'd been waitin', I'd'a just said 'hey' and sat down to talk to him." Roy had no sooner shut his mouth around the pie than he was aghast at what he'd said.

Bobby guffawed. His mother, however, was alarmed. "Roy, that sounds very brave, but it's also very, very foolish. You boys go play for a while, and Bobby can tell you what happened when the tiger came around here."

Bobby related with gusto the events earlier in the week, when the tiger had killed their dog, seized a sheep from the barn, and then killed the DNR hunter who had come to shoot him. Roy considered this but decided there was nothing surprising about it.

"That guy was tryin' to kill him. What else could he do? What would you do if somebody was tryin' to kill you?" Roy asked.

"But that ain't the half of it, Roy," Bobby said. "I can't believe you don't know about this. Don't you watch TV? Shee-it, Roy, that tiger killed an old man over to Turkey Mountain and ate him, and then when the soldiers was lookin' for him Thursday he grabbed one 'a them and ate him, too. It ain't like he's just hangin' out mindin' his own business. He's havin' people for dinner."

Roy was stunned. Eating people? Why would his friend do that? The tiger hadn't acted like it wanted to eat him. Something was wrong here.

"My dad's got all the sheep in the barn and a big door on the back so the tiger can't get in. He lets them out once a day. When he gets home from his job Uncle Wes comes over, and they let them sheep out for an hour, feed 'em and watch over 'em with shotguns. Won't even let me help," Bobby said resentfully.

Bobby had a box full of toys, and the boys played checkers for an hour or so, but Roy was distracted. If the dream-tiger was eating people, that was sure enough to make them afraid, but he just couldn't believe it. The more he thought about it, the more agitated it made him.

Finally, he said, "Bobby, I got to go now."

"Ma said for you to wait until Dad gets home, and he'd take you."

"That's real kind, but I can't wait that long. Really, ain't no reason to worry about me."

"Why? You think that tiger won't like the taste of you?"

"Yeah," Roy said, walking to the door of Bobby's room.

"Roy, Ma'll have my ass—"

"It'll be okay, Bobby. I'll see ya later," Roy said and walked quietly down the hall to the kitchen. Mrs. Willet was working over the sink, her back to him. He opened the door.

Mrs. Willet turned sharply, dropping a potato on the floor. "Roy! Don't—"

"Bye, Miz Willet," he said. "Thank you for the pie all mowed." He was out the door and running.

The woman's rosy cheeks paled and she rushed to the telephone. She started to dial and then put the receiver down. "Bobby!" she yelled.

Bobby came out of his room, sheepishly. "I couldn't stop him, Ma. I told him you wanted him to wait."

"I know that, honey," she said. "But I don't know Roy's last name. What is it?"

Bobby, startled, thought for a few seconds. "He never said, Ma. I don't guess I ever asked."

Mrs. Willet picked up the phone again and dialed the sheriff's department.

Brickhouse and Graham were on the road out of Hartesville before dawn, a large basket of food prepared by Mary in the backseat of the Crown Vic. Graham was wearing old brown pants, a brown shirt, and a tan corduroy sports coat, cut like the one he wore off the plane. Brickhouse thought he was dressed more for a lawn party than a tiger hunt.

"How many sheep do you want?" Brickhouse asked.

"Three should suffice to start with," Graham replied.

"I noticed a pen that seemed serviceable at Whitfield's," the sheriff said. "I'll have Willet put three of them in there for you, today if he can."

"Excellent. Tell him the noisier the better—ones that tend to set up a row if they're separated from the herd."

"I'm also going to leave a cellular telephone for you. Have you used one?"

"No, I haven't," Graham said. "Seen a few, but they're not that common in rural Yorkshire."

"I'll show you how to use it. I expect to hear from you once a day, Jim. If I don't hear from you by midnight every day, I'll come looking for you."

"Very well. That seems a good plan."

Dawn was breaking over the side of Turkey Mountain when they reached the first National Guard roadblock, a humvee blocking both lanes. A soldier with a sidearm got out, saw it was a sheriff's cruiser, and waved to his partner in the driver's seat. The driver spoke briefly on a radio and pulled the squat vehicle out of their way. The soldier patted the fender. "Be careful, sirs," he said.

They drove on slowly, and two more humvees pulled out of their path before they drove up the rutted lane to Wash Whitfield's shack. Nothing appeared to have changed, except the left front tire of the aged pickup was flat.

Brickhouse opened the padlock his deputy had fixed to the door and gave Graham the key. The stale smell was strong inside. Graham left the door open and hoisted a window.

Brickhouse lugged the basket of provisions into the kitchen, and the Englishman brought in his rifle case and a small leather kit containing toiletries and, incongruously, eight huge cartridges. To Brickhouse they looked like miniature artillery shells. In the case with the rifle was a cleaning kit.

The sheriff went out to the car and came back with a large hunting knife in a belt scabbard. "You don't have a knife, do you, Jim?"

"Just a pocket knife," he replied.

"I'd like you to have this," he said, holding out the heavy knife. "I've never had use for it. It was my father's. He was quite a hunter. Skinned many a deer with that knife."

Graham took the knife and withdrew it from the scabbard.

"This is a fine piece of steel," he said. "Thank you, Grady. I shall treasure it and, I hope, have good use for it." Graham loosened his belt and slid the scabbard on.

Before he could buckle it again, Brickhouse held out a small cellular phone in a belt case. The sheriff showed him how to turn the phone on, the buttons to punch to call the sheriff's department number out of memory, and the button to punch to have it dialed. The phone worked well from the cabin.

Graham opened the gun case and withdrew the heavy rifle. Breaking it open, he held it up and peered through the barrels. Satisfied, he selected two cartridges, examined them carefully and slid them into the barrels, snapping the breech shut. The remaining four cartridges he slipped into a pocket.

"Only six rounds?" Brickhouse asked.

"There was a time I carried only three," Graham said. "I lost an excellent opportunity through foolish waste of that third cartridge, though, and decided to err on safety's side in the future.

"Well, I believe I shall go out now and just get the lay of the land," the hunter said, moving to the door. "I shall check in tonight as you asked. Thank you again for this fine knife."

Roy sprinted until the Willet house was out of sight, then slowed to a quick walk. He didn't want a ride home. He'd as soon nobody knew where he lived.

Roy knew there was something wrong with his mother. His encounter with Mrs. Willet had only confirmed that. He had a vague idea that people who weren't sufficiently like other people got taken away and put somewhere. It didn't matter to him that Rose wasn't like other people. She was his mother. She never fussed at him. She did everything she could for him. She loved him, and he loved her, and that was all there was to it. He wouldn't have anyone taking her away somewhere.

As Roy walked, he began to get thirsty. There was a creek a little ways off to the Raven Bald side, so he veered off the road, down the bank, and into the woods, cutting diagonally so he could still pick up some ground.

He could hear the creek long before he saw it. There were some good-sized trout in it, and Roy often fished for them at a pool further downstream, toward home. He thought, as he walked toward the watery, rushing sound, about the fancy fishermen he'd seen.

They must've been gentlemen, in their funny hats that looked like they'd sat on 'em all the way from home and the long, thin poles they had to put together, and the way they swished and twirled their lines before they dropped their funny-looking bait into the water. Some of them seemed real good at it. Others were always getting their hook caught on something behind them—one guy had hooked his own shoulder—and that started 'em really cussin' and carryin' on. All Roy used was a long cane pole one of his mother's friends had left and some fishing line and weights and hooks from Dugan's. Worms were always good bait.

Roy reached the creek at a spot where it swirled around a lot of small rocks. You could see the bottom most places. The creek was about fifteen feet wide there and running pretty fast. Roy knelt on a rock by the stream, so as not to muddy his pants, and scooped up water in his cupped hands to drink. It took three scoops of the icy water to drown his thirst.

He shook his hands dry, started to get up, and saw the tiger, standing directly across the stream from him, watching him with that calm, wide-eyed stare.

Roy, kneeling on the rock, stared back. His hands were numb from the water. "You ain't been eatin' people, have you?" he asked aloud.

The tiger cocked its ears forward as if to hear better.

"I said, you ain't been eatin' people, have you?" Roy said, a little louder.

The tiger stared at him for a while and then took a step forward. Roy remained silent, kneeling on the rock. The sound of the stream was like a roaring wind in his ears.

The tiger took another step, which brought it to the edge of the water. Without taking its eyes off Roy, the tiger lowered its massive body to the ground, craned its neck forward and down, and began lapping at the water. Its eyes never left the boy.

Roy strained to hear the sound of the dream-tiger drinking, but all he could hear was the rush of the stream. Then he picked up another sound, rising above the stream, the sound of a car coming down the dirt road.

The tiger raised its maw just above the stream, water trickling off its chin, its eyes still on Roy. Roy turned instinctively to look back through the trees and saw the top of a white car going by, crunching and spewing pebbles. When he looked back, the tiger was gone.

Roy went back to the road and resumed the walk home, his spirits higher. The way his friend had acted, he didn't think he was eating people. He'd looked him right in the eyes when Roy asked him about it. Nobody with a guilt like that on 'em could look anyone right in the eyes.

He was walking along looking to see what had crossed the road since morning when he heard a car again and looked up to see one coming right toward him. It was way too late to run into the woods. He just got off the road and kept walking. But the car stopped, and a man in a brown uniform wearing a gun got out. The car was white and had blue writing on it that said "Sheriff."

Roy stopped and the man walked up to him and crouched down so they were at eye level.

"You Roy?"

"Yes, sir"

"Roy who?"

"Satterly."

"You live around here, Roy?"

"Yes sir."

"Where?"

Roy pointed up the road.

"Place with the tarpaper sides?"

"Yes, sir."

"You know how dangerous it is for you to be walkin' out here, Roy?"

"Somebody said."

"Okay, Roy," the man said, rising. "Get in the car."

Roy was terrified.

"You arrestin' me?"

"I oughtta be. Anybody walkin' around out here with this tiger loose is prob'ly guilty of misdemeanor stupidity, nothin' else," the deputy said. "But I reckon I'll just take you home."

Roy got into the car quietly. He watched the deputy pick up the microphone hooked to the dashboard and speak into it.

"Fifteen," he said.

"Go ahead, fifteen," a woman's voice said on the radio.

"Found the boy," the officer said. "He's okay. Takin' him home now. You might call Mrs. Willet, let her know."

"Ten-four," the radio said.

The deputy turned the car around on the narrow road and rumbled the short distance to Roy's house. "You want me to come down talk to your ma?" the man asked.

"No, sir," Roy answered, even more terrified.

"All right, I'll let it go this time. Next time, you talk to your ma before you leave the house, especially with this tiger loose. Understand?"

"Yessir," Roy said, getting out of the car. He was afraid the man had already been here and talked to Rose. "Thank you," he said.

"You're welcome, son," said the deputy, dropping his mean act. "It's what they pay me for. Now you take care of yourself."

Roy nodded and ran to the house. Rose was cooking chicken again, always a good sign. Pie all mowed and fried chicken all in one day. "Hi, Ma," he said.

"Hi there, Roy," Rose said cheerfully. "Have a good day?"

"Oh yeah, Ma. Real good." The deputy hadn't talked to her after all.

"See any of them tigers that reporter was talking about?"

"No, guess not, Ma." He hated to lie to his mother, but she might say something down at Dugan's that would cause a barrel full of trouble.

October 19

"Graham checked in last night," Weinman said when Brick-house reached the office Wednesday morning. "Seems to know what he's doing, doesn't he?"

"I was damn impressed," Brickhouse agreed.

At Whitfield's place, Graham arose before dawn Wednesday, ate some of the provisions Mrs. Brickhouse had provided, heated some tea, and went out to look over his livestock. Three fat sheep, an old ewe and two geldings stood with morose airs in a makeshift pen near the collapsed barn. Several containers of feed stood nearby.

Rummaging in the debris of the barn, Graham found a length of rope and hung it on the fence, then returned to the shack. He had poured himself a second cup of tea when the tiger called.

"*aaaaoouuuunnNNGGGHHH!*"

Graham set his cup down carefully and walked out of the shack, waiting.

"*aaaaoouuuunnNNGGGHHH!*"

He turned, looking over the shack at Turkey Mountain.

"*aaaaoouuuunnNNGGGHHH!*"

Graham, his head back, seemed to let the eerie sound wash

over him. When he walked back into the shack, he was smiling, and his cheeks appeared moist. He sat down at the rickety white table, his eyes far away, and slowly finished his tea. Then he picked up his rifle, broke it open, withdrew the cartridges and examined them before returning them to the breech and closing it.

Walking back to the sheep pen, he peeled back the fence, tied the rope around the neck of one of the sheep and led it out. Closing the fence, he started up the mountain, the sheep trotting along behind him. He was still smiling.

Rose Satterly had just left for Dugan's when the tiger called. Roy wondered if she heard it.

He started up a deer track on Copperhead Mountain. The day was bright and brisk, and Roy felt sure it would be a good one.

Tommy Hancock was waiting on his front porch with a lunch box in one hand and a shotgun in the other when Bill Hall drove up in a plumbing truck.

"How come the truck?" he asked, as Hall backed onto the highway.

"Had an idea it might get us through them roadblocks easier."

"Oh. Where 'bouts we going?"

"You remember that fancy cabin we put in the plumbin' year or so ago, up on Raven Bald?"

"One that guy built for a summer place?"

"Right. Figured we'd start around there, find a good place to wait 'n' watch. Reach 'round back there and put on a different jacket. Don't no plumbers wear their camo suits to fix well pumps."

At the first humvee, a soldier got out to check them.

"Where you boys goin'?"

"The Henry place, up Raven Bald," Hall told him. "Say they ain't gettin' no water." It was a plumber's truck and they were plumbers. Hall's shirt even had a Harte County Plumbing patch on it.

"Okay," the soldier said. "Be damn careful now. You want an escort?"

"Nah," said Hall. "Folks'll watch out for us."

They passed four more roadblocks before they reached the long dirt road that ran up Raven Bald to the Henry place. As soon as Hall found a spot out of sight of the highway and wide enough to leave the truck, he pulled over and stopped.

"Let's go get this sumbitch," he said, pulled off his work shirt, and put on his camo top. Hancock took off the old jacket and pulled his shotgun from behind the seat. Hall got his Sako .30-06 from the back and loaded it. Hancock pumped a shell carrying a single lead slug into the chamber of his Remington 870 12-gauge. With their weapons and their lunch boxes, they crossed the first road, ducked under the top wire of a barbed-wire fence, and entered the woods.

They walked single file, quartering up and across the side of Raven Bald, for about two miles, saying little, looking for a likely place to wait for the tiger.

"Look there," Hancock said.

"What?"

"See over there," he pointed, "through them trees? Big poplar come down on the edge of that bank. How 'bout that?"

"Looks good."

When they reached the spot they saw they could approach the tree from the bank, walk about eight feet along its massive trunk, and have a perch ten feet above the ground. They made themselves comfortable, side by side but facing different directions. They had fairly clear sight for at least fifty yards in three directions, but the tree angled downward off the bank and they couldn't see beyond its lip. A gentle breeze was rustling the fallen leaves, blowing up the bank.

"Keep a close watch on your left," Hall said to Hancock, who was seated closest to the bank. "Don't want that sumbitch comin' down the tree after us."

It was about eight A.M. The woods seemed as always. Birds flitted through the trees. Somewhere, far away, a sheep bleated.

Graham was halfway to the summit of Turkey Mountain when he found a spot to tie out the sheep. A hickory with fairly low branches afforded a clear view for nearly fifty yards over the shoulder of the hill, and after taking a bearing from that tree, he walked the sheep almost to the limit of the view, about forty yards from the maple. There he tied the animal to a large fallen log, kicked away leaves to reveal sparse brown grass around it, and returned to the tree.

Brickhouse would have been even more impressed to see Graham climb the tree, swarming up it with the agility of a veteran climber and a much younger man, rifle slung over his shoulder. He hoisted himself onto a large branch about twenty feet from the ground, facing the sheep, and wriggled into a comfortable position. The sheep cropped the dried grass without enthusiasm, occasionally lifting its head to bleat.

Within a few minutes Graham seemed part of the tree. The only movement was his eyes, ranging slowly over the ground in front of him. He waited.

———

The press was enraged over Brickhouse's refusal to identify the new hunter.

"Folks, I can't help it," the sheriff said at his morning briefing at the elementary school. "The man asked me not to reveal his identity, and I have to respect that. Perhaps when he's through, he'll be willing to talk to you."

"Why doesn't he want to be identified?" demanded the *Times* of London, who had already put together enough references to believe the hunter was British.

"He didn't say, and I didn't ask," Brickhouse replied.

"Where is he now?"

"In the woods."

"Where's he staying?"

"In the woods."

"You mean he's camping out there?"

This shit's gonna turn me into a liar yet, Brickhouse told himself. But living at Whitfield's, in his estimation, was camping out.

"Yes."

"I understand the tiger was heard calling this morning."

"That's right."

"May be some action then," the *National Enquirer* said.

"I hope not," Brickhouse said.

Roy reached the summit of Copperhead Mountain well before noon. He saw the soldiers' camp spread below him, and it surprised him. He knew there were soldiers around, but not so many. It looked like a town.

He sat down on the rocks, watching a vulture soar overhead. Looking for lunch.

———

Graham had been waiting for about two hours when the tiger came. He couldn't see it, but he was certain it was near. He made no movement but smiled inwardly, relieved the forest sense that had kept him alive for so many years was still intact.

His eyes scanned the forest in front of him, bit by bit. Nothing moved but the sheep, apparently unaware of the tiger's presence.

The sheep bleated. Somewhere down the mountain, a pileated woodpecker hammered at a tree. It sounded almost like a machine gun. Gradually the awareness of the tiger's presence faded until Graham knew it was gone. Quite probably the woodpecker had scared it off. Formidable bird, that.

Graham knew the tiger would not return for many hours. He climbed down from the tree, kicked the leaves off more grass for the sheep and then began examining the ground behind the tree. He suspected the tiger had approached from that direction.

In about ten minutes he found the spot where the tiger had lain behind a fallen poplar to watch the sheep. The leaves were still warm. Picking up its trail, he began to follow. It was headed over the mountain. The ground was fairly hard, and it was a difficult trail to follow.

The woodpecker hammered again, farther away this time.

Hancock and Hall knew nothing of tigers, but they knew better than to talk or smoke on their perch atop the fallen poplar. They remained silent, each immersed in his own thoughts. They moved about a yard apart after finding that bringing up their weapons simultaneously caused them to bump elbows.

Shit, Hancock thought after Hall moved away. What's he think we got out here? They ain't but the one tiger. We ain't both gonna see him at once. Maybe he thinks we'll get a tiger and a deer same time. Shee-it. Ain't no deer out here any more anyhow. Say the tiger got 'em all, or they all run off.

The poplar was fat and fairly comfortable but it was hard, and after a while Hancock's left leg started going to sleep. He tried swinging it, but Hall poked him on the arm, pointed at the leg, and shook his head, no.

Dammit, Tommy, you ain't got no sense at all, Hall thought. You gotta sit still. Real still.

He had no sooner finished the silent chastisement than the right side of his crotch began itching. The longer he ignored it the worse it itched. Goddamn soap. Why can't they make some soap don't give me jock itch if I lather up my 'quipment? He couldn't stand it. Slowly as he could he took his right hand from the rifle and inched it to his right thigh. He scratched, slowly but hard. He knew Hancock was looking at him. Dammit all, I can't help it. Swingin' your leg is one thing. Jock itch is another.

Graham followed the tiger about a mile down the mountain before losing the trail. There was plenty of time before he needed to start back to the shack. He went back to the clearing, saw the sheep was napping, and climbed back into his tree.

Tommy Hancock was keeping a sharp lookout on the bank where the poplar's roots had torn out of the ground. Hall's warning when they settled onto their perch had given him a mental picture of the tiger coming down the fallen tree toward him. Don't see it come over the bank, probably be too late, he thought. Thing gets on the tree before I see it, I wouldn't have time to twist around and get the gun to my shoulder. Have to fire just about like this, gun in my lap. Be lucky to hit it, might lose the gun, and if I didn't, I'd have a hell of a time rackin' in another round from this position. He wished he could practice that a little.

But he couldn't, so he watched to his left as much as he watched in front. He tried not to move his head, just scanning his eyes left to right, right to left. It was awful quiet. He could hear Hall breathing.

A jay scolded briefly somewhere close behind the bank. It startled Hancock, who was scanning the area ahead of him, and he jerked his head around. He saw the bird fly off into the tree line. Somethin's back there. Could be most anythin'. He gave most of his attention to the area on the left. Tree hadn't been down long, he saw. Lumps of red dirt hanging to the roots here and there. Dirt was dry, but not dry enough to drop off in the wind yet.

The adrenaline surge receded. He could hear Hall's breathing again. Sounded like he was breathing through his mouth.

He was. His nose was runny, and the late afternoon breeze was getting cold. Hall wished he had put a T-shirt under his flannel shirt. Long johns under the jeans would have been good, too.

Tommy's flinch when the jay shrieked had broken him out of a reverie in which half the town was gathered around his truck, looking at the carcass of the tiger in the back. The reporters were pushing and shoving each other to reach him, yelling at him, and that little blonde he kept seeing on TV, reporting from in front of the sheriff's office, was holding a microphone under his nose. She was right in front of him, almost pressed up against him, and with her other hand she pressed a card into his pants pocket. He knew what was on it. The number of her motel room.

He went back to his fantasy, watching the clear area in front of him, trying not to think about feeling cold and ignoring his jock itch. He figured that blond TV reporter probably wouldn't do his jock itch any good. He'd have to lather up his crotch to make sure it smelled good, and there he'd be. Well, they got powder and stuff for it. I'll just have to get some of that. Maybe it'd work. Anyway, he doubted that lady would pay much attention to a little rash in the crotch of the hunter who killed the Harte County man-eater.

The reporters were all around him, pushing that little blonde right up against him. They were hollering questions at him so loud that it took just an instant to realize that high-pitched yell wasn't just in his head. At the same time something struck him on the left ear and Tommy's shotgun fell across his lap and slipped away to the ground.

Hall jerked around. Tommy wasn't there, but he could hear him screaming.

"BillBillohGod! Itskillinme!"

The screams were so harsh and full of terror that Hall couldn't recognize Tommy in them. In his panic he couldn't locate the sound. He threw himself sideways, stomach across the tree trunk, and then he saw Tommy.

He saw him just for a second, and at first Hall thought his friend was riding the tiger, like a horse. Tommy and the tiger were gone into the trees before he understood what he had seen. The tiger—somehow it looked more reddish than orange—had Tommy by the left calf. Tommy lay face up, crossways across the tiger's back, more or less astraddle it. His right leg was bent back along the ground. His hands were trying to grab anything they could find. His mouth formed a hopeless O, and his eyes were bulging as though they would pop from their sockets.

Hall screamed, too. "Tommy! Tommy!"

But he was lying across the poplar on his gut, the .30-06 in his right hand. Even if the tiger had remained in sight he couldn't have gotten off a shot. And now he was sliding backward. He dropped the rifle and tried to get a grip on the bark, but he was sliding faster. He came off the tree feet first and he tried to throw himself sideways, to land on his hands and knees, but it didn't work and when he hit the ground he heard a loud pop, like a dry branch breaking, and he knew it was his leg.

Bill Hall lay on his face in the leaves. His left leg was broken somewhere between the knee and the ankle. He didn't have to look. The initial rush of pain made him a little sick, but in a few minutes it became surprisingly tolerable. He knew he had other things to worry about.

He lifted his head and looked around. He had landed facing the bank. He looked to his left. The rifle had to be that way somewhere, but he couldn't see it. He rolled over on his back, careful to roll to the right so his left leg could stay on the ground. The pain wasn't bad, but he could feel his foot flopping. It was like having a dead trout where his foot was supposed to be.

He looked to the left again, over his shoulder, and saw his rifle. It was about ten feet away. He looked around for a stout stick, something to use for a crutch, but there wasn't anything closer than the rifle itself. Shit. No point in trying to get up.

Hall started oontzing himself backward on his rump, lifting up with both hands, sliding back, dropping down, bringing his arms back, doing it again. He made about a foot at a time and it didn't bother his leg much. His camo pants were tucked into his boots so he couldn't see whether the bone had come through the skin anywhere, but there was no sign of blood.

Finally he reached the rifle. He picked it up, and for no

good reason swung himself around in the direction the tiger had taken Tommy. He slumped onto his back, slipped off the safety, and fired three rounds into the sky, quick as he could work the bolt. He counted to five, fished a fresh magazine out of his pants, reloaded and fired three more rounds.

Hall looked at his watch. It was a quarter after four. If none of the soldiers came up from the road in an hour or so, he figured he could get back to the truck using the rifle for a cane.

He wasn't afraid. He wasn't worried about his leg. It would heal. He wasn't worried about the tiger, not now. It had Tommy to keep it busy for a while. The only thing that frightened Bill Hall was closing his eyes, because every time he did he saw Tommy's face again, hanging upside down over the tiger's back.

Graham, on Turkey Mountain, was too far away to hear Hall's shots. He waited until the sun was low and clambered out of his tree. The sheep was grazing again. He untied the rope and led it back down the mountain toward the shack. The sheep was ready to go; Graham occasionally had to hold it back. He stayed alert, but he was reasonably certain the tiger had gone far afield.

On Copperhead Mountain, Roy heard Hall's shots but paid no attention to them. Soldiers all carried guns; had to figure they shoot them off sometimes.

A couple of hours later, with dusk coming on, Roy decided to head back home. Rose wouldn't worry if he wasn't there when she got home—she never worried—but he didn't want to be very late.

Roy was nearly home, moving down a deer track, when he

looked up and saw the tiger about ninety feet ahead. He wondered why he rarely saw the animal move. One minute it was there, the next it was not.

The tiger was just sitting there, looking at him. Roy sat down. "What is it?" he whispered. "What do you want to tell me?"

He knew the tiger was there to tell him something, and he knew it would make his life different. But still he couldn't hear anything. Almost, he thought, but not quite.

He reached down to brush a beetle off his toe, and when he looked up his friend was gone.

Brickhouse was about to leave the office when Winshiser called.

"Tiger's got another one," the colonel said.

"Oh, Jesus. One of yours?"

"No, thank God. One of yours. One of your citizens, I mean. Couple guys got through our roadblocks this morning saying they were plumbers, going to some cabin on that last mountain—what is it, Raven Bald?—to work on a pump or something. They went hunting tiger instead. It took one of them. Other one broke his leg somehow, fired off a bunch of rounds. Men at the roadblocks heard and we sent a party up there. Found the injured man, fellow named Bill Hall. Said the guy he was with was Tommy, ah, Hancock. He wasn't real clear on what happened. I think he was going into shock. You need to get paramedics out here to pick him up. Getting dark now, and I'm not very interested in sending another search party up there."

"Absolutely not," Brickhouse said. "We'll take care of that in the morning. Thanks for getting the survivor out. That must've been hairy."

"We're soldiers," Winshiser said with some bitterness. "We may be weekend soldiers, but we're expected to be able to deal with hairy stuff. Pardon the pun."

Brickhouse detailed a deputy to find Hancock's family and notify them. He wasn't sure the man had anybody in Harte County. "Graham's supposed to check in on his cell phone sometime tonight," he told the dispatcher. "Tell him the tiger's killed another man, long ways from him. Tell him I'll be out to get him first thing in the morning."

October 20

Brickhouse arrived at the old Whitfield house shortly after dawn on Thursday. Graham was waiting for him. He put his rifle in the backseat, climbed in front, and waited for Brickhouse to bring him up-to-date.

"Got a call from the National Guard commander last night. Couple of hunters slipped through their roadblocks. Tiger got one. Other broke his leg. He's in the hospital. Deputy talked to him last night. He isn't sure how it happened. They were sitting above the ground on the trunk of a fallen tree. One minute his buddy's there, the next he's not. Saw the tiger going into the trees with him. Couldn't get a shot and fell off the tree.

"We'll head over to the guard camp, pick up the colonel,

and maybe you can figure out what happened. We've got to find the body, whatever there is to find."

"Of course," Graham said. "I tied out one of the sheep yesterday and sat over it. Tiger stopped in to visit but was too wary to show itself. This was in the morning. I tracked it to the west before I lost the trail."

"Yeah. The kill was two mountains over to the west from you, on Raven Bald. Happened around four P.M."

The humvees made way for them one by one as they approached Randall's Field, where Winshiser emerged from the command tent to join them.

Graham moved to the backseat of the cruiser, and the three men pulled out of the camp, Winshiser directing Brickhouse to the dirt road leading to the Henry cabin. "Heard about this place," the sheriff said as they pulled up, "First time I've seen it. Pretty fancy."

"Certainly is," Winshiser said. Brickhouse opened a back door for Graham, who was trying to find the nonexistent inside door handles.

"This way," Winshiser said, heading across the road to the east. "Sergeant who led the search party had the remarkable presence of mind to blaze a trail to the spot where they found the survivor."

When they came to the fallen poplar, Brickhouse and Winshiser remained at the tree line while Graham went forward, rifle under his arm, to examine the scene.

"Old fellow doesn't have much to say, does he?" Winshiser remarked.

"Nope," Brickhouse agreed as they watched the natty Englishman disappear behind the roots of the poplar, walk out of sight in the underbrush, and then appear again under the tree near the point where its crown lay on the ground. He beckoned to them.

"The tiger approached from the east," he began, "and probably saw the men sitting on this tree when he neared the top of that bank. He watched them for quite a while, then backed out of the underbrush and made his way rather quickly around to the west. That puzzles me, puzzles me a great deal."

"Why's that?" Winshiser asked.

"The tiger made its initial approach from upwind, as one would expect. But for some reason it decided not to press its attack from that direction, which is most unusual. Perhaps the men were watching very closely for an upwind approach. In that case I would have expected the tiger to wait for a better opportunity, but instead it made a semicircle to this point and emerged from the underbrush almost directly under the tree.

"I doubt very much if the men could have seen it from the tree. It went very slowly, on its belly, directly under the tree," Graham said, walking along its track with the two men.

"Here it reared up and took its victim by the leg and yanked him off the tree."

"Good God," the colonel said. "That's a long way up there. Ten feet at least."

"An easy stretch for this tiger, Colonel. As you can see, there is no blood here. The tiger kept its original grip and raced off to the west, slightly downhill. I expect the survivor had his back to that direction. The tiger was carrying its victim in a strange position, over its back, which must have been the way the man fell.

They walked back toward the tree line. "The man was still alive, you see. He pulled those clumps of weeds out, trying to find something to hold onto."

About ten yards inside the trees a small bush had been uprooted and blood was spattered about. "As I read it, the victim got hold of this bush, which must have caused the tiger some difficulty, so it decided to put a stop to the resistance. It dropped him and grabbed him by the neck before he could get up. There isn't a great deal of blood, so we can assume the neck was broken or the victim suffocated or both."

"How do you know he took him by the neck?" Brickhouse asked.

"See the drag marks, here, and all along here, as we go deeper into the forest. These marks were made by the heels of the man's boots. If we had dry, dusty ground I would expect to find more marks made by his knuckles. A tiger by preference carries its prey by the neck or by the back. If he carried the victim by the back, we would see toe marks, not heel marks, and they would have been made from a different angle."

"Be damned if I can see much of anything," muttered Winshiser.

"It's just a matter of knowing what to look for, Colonel," Graham said. "Now, if you gentlemen will follow several steps behind me, we shall see if this spoor will lead us to the remains."

When they saw the rhododendron thicket, Graham halted. "The tiger was headed for that," he said, pointing toward the rhododendrons. "I expect that is where it took its meal. There's always the possibility it could still be there. If you would be so kind, see if you can find a few throwing-sized stones."

Graham watched the thicket while the sheriff and the colonel quickly gathered up half a dozen rocks. With remarkable accuracy, the Englishman sailed the stones into various parts of the thicket. There was no reaction, and he continued along the blood spoor.

"The tiger took its victim into that awful thicket there, and I expect the remains are not too far from the edge." Graham made a wide circle around the rhododendron and found the point where the tiger left it.

"From the looks of this, something may have disturbed its meal," the hunter said. "I'm going to try to follow it now. There's always the possibility of making contact."

"Be careful, Jim," Brickhouse said.

"Most certainly. It will probably be hungry again quite soon."

"Where'd you find him?" Winshiser asked when Graham had disappeared into the woods.

"He sort of fell in my lap."

"Well, he seems to know what he's doing, which is a hell of a lot more than I can say for the rest of us."

"Yes."

Brickhouse radioed for paramedics and a deputy with a chainsaw. They found the remains of Tommy Hancock about six feet into the rhododendron patch. The tiger had eaten relatively little—parts of the buttocks, back, and thighs.

The tiger's trail was not easy to follow, but Graham managed to pick it up again each time he lost it. After its skimpy meal the tiger had gone down Raven Bald at a steady pace, stopping only to drink from a creek. It had crossed the narrow valley below not far from Randall's pasture and quartered up Copperhead Mountain.

Part of the way around Copperhead, at about mid-morning, Graham found a spot where the tiger had paused on a deer track. It had sat there for an appreciable time; the marks of its haunches were blurred and wavy from its frequent slight shifts of its weight. Why had the tiger stopped here? There was no water. Had there been game, it would have dropped to a crouch.

Then, to his astonishment, Graham saw a human footprint near the spot where the tiger had paused. It was made by a shoeless child, apparently at virtually the same time the tiger had been there. Baffled, Graham began backtracking the child, and found that he—Graham was fairly certain it was a boy—had come from higher on the mountain and had sat down himself on the track about a hundred feet uphill from the tiger.

Had the boy seen the tiger and contained his fear? He couldn't imagine the tiger failing to see the boy. Just disturbed over a hard-won kill, the man-eater would likely have been in an ugly mood. Graham walked back to the tiger's resting spot, comparing the age of the prints again. He felt sure they had been made at the same time

He was crouched over the deer track, still trying to piece together what had transpired there, when he heard someone coming up the trail. Standing, he saw the shaggy top of a boy's head coming up the mountain. Silently, he sidestepped into the forest.

Roy Satterly figured Rose would stay in bed all morning. She had been unusually tired Wednesday night. He had some peanut butter and grape jelly for breakfast, straightened up his room, and swept the kitchen. After taking the dinner dishes out of the drying rack and putting them away, he went out and headed up Copperhead. He'd like to find out where his friend lived.

Where his friend had sat and watched him yesterday, Roy saw a man's bootprints. They were on top of his prints and the tiger's. He wasn't sure what to do about it. He moved up the path, and saw that the man's prints came onto the deer path from the side. They seemed to end there on the path where the tiger had been.

Who was it? Nobody ever came out here except deer hunters, and he hadn't seen any at all this year. Where did he go? Roy couldn't make sense of it, and his feet were getting cold. He decided to go on up the mountain for a while.

From behind a log fifty feet away, Graham watched the boy study the prints and then cast about for a trail. He was thin, in need of a haircut and shoes, and none too clean. But he seemed to have remarkable woodcraft. As the boy moved away up the mountain, Graham moved downhill, well to the side of the path, taking care to leave little sign.

Ten minutes' walk brought him to the edge of the forest. To his left was a rundown house with what appeared to be some sort of black paper on the walls. The wooden trim hadn't seen paint in years. He walked along the forest line toward the house and, looking down, saw that he was following the tiger's tracks.

The tracks, faint and old, left the edge of the forest, moved behind an outhouse, and from there to the house. Following, he found the tracks went to a window. Graham crouched down, astonished by what he saw. The tiger had been here several times, and on every occasion, had spent considerable time. It appeared to have spent most of that time sitting, facing a window screen. Behind the screen the window was open a few inches. Peering into the room, he saw a bed against the window, a lantern, and piles of magazines. Judging from clothing on the floor, he thought it was probably the boy's room.

Graham went around to the front of the little house and

knocked on the door. There was no response. He was walking back toward the woods when he heard the door open. A woman was standing there, looking at him impassively. As he walked back toward her, she rubbed at an eye with the edge of one hand.

"Very sorry, madam, if I've awakened you."

"That's all right," she said. "Time to get up anyway."

"Madam, do you have a youngster, a boy about nine or ten years old?"

"Yes," she said.

"I suppose you aren't aware of it, and I don't know how to put it tactfully, but there is a man-eating tiger in this neighborhood. He killed another man yesterday. Your son is in great danger wandering in these hills right now."

The woman looked at him silently. She rubbed her eye again.

"You really must keep him home until the tiger is killed."

Silence.

"Are you quite all right, madam?"

"Oh, yes. I'm fine, thank you," she said brightly, although her face remained blank.

"I see. Very well, madam. Sorry to have disturbed you."

He was three steps from the tree line when he heard her say "Bye, bye, now. Nice of you to drop in."

Graham was baffled. The woman was clearly afflicted mentally. Her odd responses were ample testimony to that, but it was difficult to imagine any mother allowing her child to run such a risk. And what to make of the tiger's visits to the boy's window? His father's tale about Ravi and the bull during the time of the Kot Kindri man-eater flashed out of his memory.

He set off for home, staying on the low ground, too pre-occupied to dare the higher reaches of the forest.

When Graham reached his shack, he found Brickhouse sitting in his blue-and-white next to the ancient Chevy.

"Good afternoon, Sheriff."

"Jim. Find anything?"

"Not really. Tracked the man-eater as far as Copperhead Mountain. I intend to go back out this afternoon and tie a sheep out. If the tiger is still hungry, he may kill it; if we're lucky and he's not too hungry, he may leave enough for a second meal, in which case I shall be waiting for him."

"Waiting where?"

"In a tree, of course."

"Ah," Brickhouse said, getting out of the car, reaching back in and lifting out a box. "I hope you've worked up an appetite. Mary figured you must be getting tired of all that dry stuff she fixed you. Sent me out with a hot meal for you."

Graham looked at the box and back to Brickhouse.

"As long as there's enough for two, and you've time to join me."

"Probably enough for four," Brickhouse said. "You want to eat out here?"

"An excellent idea. We can use that stump there for a table. I'll get the chairs."

As they dug into the fried chicken, Graham asked Brickhouse about the mood of the town.

"Not good and getting worse," Brickhouse said. "They can't see that we're doing anything."

"We're doing all there is to do."

"Hard to convince people of that. I keep shutting the barn

door after the horse is gone. From now on, Winshiser's troops are going to escort any civilians through the area. If we'd done that yesterday, that plumber wouldn't have been killed."

"Hindsight, Sheriff. It's a marvelously accurate thing. But if these men had wanted to hunt the tiger badly enough, they could surely have gotten into the area. They could have walked, couldn't they?"

"I suppose so."

"If you examine the situation, at least as you have laid it out for me, that deer hunter was the last unsuspecting victim. The soldier, the plumber—all of them were actually hunting the tiger, weren't they?"

"That's right."

"It's difficult to see how you can be blamed for that. If people wish to offer themselves up out of an excess of courage and a deficit of understanding, it is scarcely your fault."

"That's good logic, all right. I like it. But people around here think they can hear that tiger sniffing at their back door every night, and they want somebody to blame for it. The logical one to blame is the one they're paying to protect them."

They finished eating in silence. Brickhouse opened a Thermos of coffee, and Graham brewed tea.

"Sheriff, have you made any progress toward finding out how this tiger got here?"

"No. I haven't even tried, to be honest. I asked the federal people, the FBI and the customs people, to look into that."

"I shall be very interested to know what they learn."

"I'll pass it on as soon as I hear," Brickhouse said, his voice nearly drowned out by the clatter of a small helicopter moving swiftly overhead.

Patrick Rolls and Bernie Oppenheimer were experts in surmounting roadblocks—Rolls the physical kind and Oppenheimer the legal kind. When their hired helicopter from Atlanta deposited them at the little grass runway that served Hartesville as an airport, a rented Pathfinder was waiting for them.

They pulled their minimal luggage from the chopper, waved good-bye to the pilot, and dumped it all in the back of the Pathfinder. In the glove compartment of the vehicle were marked maps.

Rolls took the wheel and Oppenheimer navigated. They drove through Hartesville and into what the real estate agent had been mortified to hear Rolls call "tiger country."

At the first National Guard roadblock, they stopped and told the sergeant they had rented the Henry cabin.

"Last time two men went up there, only one of 'em come back," the soldier observed.

"We heard," Rolls said. "But we aren't hunters. You're welcome to search the truck for guns. Bernie, show him the receipt for the cabin."

"That's okay," the sergeant said. "That humvee over there"—he pointed to a second vehicle, parked off the road—"will escort you to the cabin and see you safely inside. Otherwise, sirs, you're on your own. I suggest you stay indoors."

"Okay," said Oppenheimer as they resumed their trip, this time behind the olive-drab humvee, "we got Turkey Mountain, and Copperhead Mountain, and then Raven Bald. Is that a mountain, too?"

"That's right, Bernie, except it looks like your shiny dome on top."

"Don't be like that," Oppenheimer said. "All right, there's Dugan's place. Now, another mile . . . yes, see, he's turning up that dirt road."

Rolls pounded up the little-used, rock-strewn road behind the humvee.

The front deck of the Henry cabin served as a carport, and Rolls pulled the Pathfinder under it while the humvee stopped in the driveway. A soldier with a rifle got out of the passenger side and stood silently, scanning the tree line.

"Damn good," said Rolls, getting out and looking back out over the spectacular flow of mountains and forest. "Good place to start this from."

Rolls was a man familiar at least by name to every reporter back in Hartesville; a few had worked with him. His roots were in the now-moribund wire service United Press International; for that and for several of the most important newspapers of the country he had covered virtually every major upheaval in the world since the civil rights movement of the 1960s. A series of unfortunate encounters with managing editors who Rolls collectively called "whey-faced bean counters who can't take their thumbs out of their asses because they're afraid what might fall out" and who as a group called him a "wild hair" had left him on the beach. After a certain amount of milling around, he had hired on with Nova Corporation, producer of television docudramas.

Oppenheimer had worked for Nova long before Rolls came along. Oppenheimer was a lawyer, a fixer, the man who sewed up everybody who knew anything worthwhile to an exclusive contract to sell their knowledge only to Nova. Rolls figured out who needed to be wrapped up, plotted the production, and often wound up writing the script. It was his idea, when they discovered there was absolutely no lodging to be had at any price in Hartesville, to find a vacation cabin in the very area where the production would be based.

The cabin proved luxurious, with modern furniture, a fully equipped kitchen, two bedrooms, each with a bath, and a wide deck at the front. The agent had told them apologetically that although the owner had brought in electricity while the cabin was under construction, he had taken his time with a telephone line, and one had not yet arrived. "No problem," Oppenheimer had said. "I've always got my pocket phone."

Roy went all the way to the top of Copperhead again without seeing anything but the tiger's tracks in a couple of places on the path. He was pretty sure they weren't fresh. When he got back home, Rose told him about the visitor.

"Man was here, asked if I had a boy 'bout your age," she said. "Told him I did."

"Did he want me?" Roy asked.

"He didn't say so. He sort of scolded me for lettin' you run loose outdoors while this tiger thing is around. Guess I don't understand about a tiger."

"Don't worry, Ma. There's no problem."

"Take your word for it, Roy. Let's eat dinner now."

October 21

On Friday Graham was up before the sun again. He had tea and a muffin before putting the rope on one of his sheep—he chose the veteran from Wednesday—and starting up Turkey Mountain. He took the sheep further up the mountain this time, tethered it to a fallen pine, and climbed into a tree about a hundred feet from the animal, which was already bleating its unhappiness. He found a branch suitable for a long wait about fifteen feet off the ground. Once in place, he opened his rifle, replaced the cartridges, closed it, and made sure the safety was on.

Again Graham seemed to blend into the bark of the old hickory. He was nearly invisible. A blue jay settled on the branch five feet from him.

Oppenheimer dropped Rolls off at the school for the morning press briefing and went on in search of witnesses whose stories needed to be purchased. Some of the reporters who knew Rolls from previous assignments expressed dismay that he had to share a vehicle.

"Kinda money you're working for now, you both oughta be driving chauffeuered limos," said the *Sun-Times*.

"Bull-shiiit," Rolls retorted. "These jokers pinch money

tighter'n UPI did. Hell, I had to walk over here from Gainesville, you know that? And you peckerwoods got all the motel rooms, so they're makin' me sleep out in the goddamn woods with that tiger."

Fortified with coffee and donuts, provided each morning courtesy of the city of Hartesville, Rolls held court at the school until midafternoon, telling war stories and small lies from remote places of the world. When everyone decided to visit the front lines at Randall's pasture, he hitched a ride with the *Inquirer.* Brickhouse would only allow six vehicles in the caravan, so each was packed.

Rose got up late, not feeling very well, so Roy volunteered to go to Dugan's with her and help. It had been a long time since he'd seen his new friend, but he had to think of his family first.

Graham had been in the tree watching the forest around the sheep for several hours when, again, he became aware of the tiger's presence. He had estimated that its most likely approach would be along a shallow ravine, from his right to his left, that would bring it within twenty feet of the sheep unseen. He remained still. He would raise the rifle when he was sure the tiger would not detect the movement. Two small birds flitting through the trees took a sharp upward jink at the ravine, and Graham knew the tiger was there.

Graham waited. The sheep began straining at its rope, bleating frantically in the direction of the ravine. But after twenty minutes, it gradually relaxed and began grazing fitfully, looking up sharply toward the ravine every few seconds.

The hunter was growing uneasy when, somewhere behind him, he heard the whirr of wings. Some kind of bird had been disturbed, probably by the tiger. It had circled around behind him.

Graham looked down at the ground. The tiger could probably make an easy running jump to reach his boots. Slowly he drew himself into a standing position on the limb. It was a precarious perch. The limb was only about ten inches in diameter. He held the rifle under his right arm and clung to a small branch overhead for balance with his left. The tables had turned.

Slowly he twisted so that his back was against the trunk of the hickory. He could fire safely only in a narrow arc to the front; his balance was too precarious to let go of the overhead branch. Firing straight down would be an option if he was willing to risk a dislocated shoulder; the heavy rifle's recoil would almost certainly knock him out of the tree if he tried a one-handed shot directly to either side.

He waited quietly for whatever might happen. He couldn't see his watch, but he estimated half an hour had passed since he stood up on the branch when there was movement on the other side of the tree, behind him. He heard a low, rumbling growl.

"Slashfoot," he said softly, almost whispering. "Is it you?"

The growl deepened until it seemed as if the tree vibrated with it, then ended in a hissing, spitting noise. In a second there was a loud grunt and a tearing, raking noise almost at the level of Graham's feet. The tiger was reared on its back legs, sharpening its claws on the other side of the tree.

Graham's small smile broadened slightly, and he tightened his grip as the hickory quivered a little. After a couple of minutes of this territory-marking ritual the tiger grunted again, dropping back on all fours. There was a low, muttered snarl from farther away, and it was gone.

The reporters' caravan arrived at Randall's pasture with great commotion, and Winshiser hurried to lay down some ground rules.

"Stay out of the tents unless you're invited in," he said. "Most of the night-shift troops are still asleep; it's hard enough to get any rest out here without you folks barging in on them. Try to keep the noise down as best you can. Okay?"

"Are you going to make any further attempts to kill the tiger?" the *Daily News* asked.

"Sheriff Brickhouse has his own man in the mountains now, and he has asked us to cordon off this particular area to try to keep any more amateurs from getting injured. We'll let the colonel have the ground for now."

"The colonel?" shouted Newsday.

"What colonel? Are you saying this hunter is an army officer?" The reporters, who had begun to scatter, crowded around Winshiser. The colonel looked over their heads to see Brickhouse frantically waving with his left hand, shaking his head, no, no, and holding a finger of his right hand to his lips. Winshiser got the idea that the sheriff didn't want Graham identified.

"Ah, I, ah, I'm afraid that was a slip of the tongue," Winshiser said. "The sheriff has asked me not to talk about this hunter."

"Have you seen him?" Rolls asked. Some of the reporters had begun to doubt the hunter's existence.

"Yes," said Winshiser.

"What's he like?" Bentley asked. "Can't you tell us something about him without identifying him?"

Winshiser looked at Brickhouse, who shrugged.

"Well, he's an older fellow, quiet, very, oh, I guess you'd

say well-mannered, well-spoken. Very much a gentleman."

"You think he knows what he's doing?" the *Times* asked.

"From what I have seen he could probably draw an accurate likeness of you just from looking at your footprint," Winshiser said. "I believe he knows exactly what he's doing. The fact that he's been alone out there since—when, Tuesday?—and he's still alive is pretty good proof of that."

"Where'd he come from?" CNN asked.

"I've really told you all I can," Winshiser said.

The crowd shouted a few more questions at him, but when he refused to open his mouth again the reporters and cameramen scattered over the pasture, looking for other interviews.

Brickhouse had hoped to get them out of the pasture and back to town before dark, but that looked to be impossible. He hadn't kept an accurate count of how many there were, and now they were all over the place. He decided to let them get their fill. Some would want to get back sooner than others, and if he refused to take any of them back until all agreed to leave, they would ferret each other out. Reporters, he had noticed, have a deep-rooted need to know everything, and chief among the things they worried about knowing was what their competitors were doing.

Rolls, no longer a daily reporter, was the single exception. He invited Bentley and the young woman from the *St. Paul Pioneer Press* along with four of his old friends to a barbecue at his cabin Monday night. Then, the battery on his own cell phone dead, he borrowed the *Inquirer*'s, reached Oppenheimer, and asked the lawyer to pick him up.

Graham relaxed in his tree and waited until dusk was gathering before climbing down. There would have been little profit and much danger in following the tiger when it left the clearing. It would very likely have been waiting for him somewhere along its back trail.

The sheep was bedding down for the night when Graham started back to his shack. He went slowly and carefully, but his forest sense told him the tiger had gone elsewhere.

Roy was cleaning the ice cream freezer, his last chore of the day, when a big man in a soft leather jacket walked into the store. He bought a few groceries and a couple of six-packs of beer.

"Business been hurt much by this tiger thing?" he asked Annie.

"Can't say it has," she said. "Better than usual, if anything. You a reporter?"

"After a fashion," he said, looking around. "I'm staying at the cabin up on Raven Bald."

"Oh, the Henry place. Is it nice inside as it looks?"

The man's eyes wandered around the store, studying Rose briefly as she mopped the wooden floor, then falling on Roy.

"It's nice," he said. "Really quite nice."

The man walked over to Roy.

"How you doin'?" he asked.

"Fine, sir," said Roy, looking down at the glass.

The man squatted down, the way the television reporter had, but he didn't stick anything in Roy's face.

"Work here every day?" the man asked.

"No sir. Not every day."

"No cars out there. You walk?"

"Yes sir."

"You're not afraid of the tiger, are you?"

"No, sir."

"Good," the man said, making a small smile and reaching out to squeeze Roy's shoulder. "Don't you ever be afraid of anything. It's not worth the trouble."

He stood up and ambled over toward Rose two aisles away, acting as though he was looking for more groceries.

When he was next to Rose, he said, very quietly, "That your boy?"

"Yes," she said.

"Damn fine young man," he said. "You've raised him right."

Rose flushed with pleasure but then started when the man took hold of her hand.

"I think he needs some shoes, this time of year, don't you?" the man said with a grin. He squeezed her hand, went to the counter for his groceries and beer, and left.

He was out the door before Rose realized he had left something in her hand. It was a fifty-dollar bill.

She went to Annie and told her what happened.

"I'll be dogged," Annie said. "He certainly is a gentleman. Tell you what, Rose. I've got to go to town tomorrow. You have Roy ready in the morning, and I'll pick him up. Take him to Lacey's and get him shoes and a coat."

"Man said shoes," Rose observed. "Didn't say about a coat."

"Rose, be sensible. That's enough money to buy two pair of shoes, but Roy's gonna grow out of 'em before he even wears out one pair. And he needs a coat, too. Don't he?"

"I guess."

"You want to come with us?"

"No, I don't guess."

"I didn't think so. Now you get along home, and I'll see you in the morning, Mr. Roy. Be sure and take a bath."

Roy skipped around all the way home. His day had been so good that he thought his friend might be waiting for him on the path up Copperhead Mountain, so after Rose was in the house he went around back and started up the path.

The tiger was sitting in the usual spot, like it was waiting for him.

Once again he got the feeling it was trying hard to tell him something, to talk to him. He still couldn't hear. Then he did hear something, but it wasn't a voice. It sounded like the tiger's stomach rumbling. After a while, the tiger rose and walked into the trees. It was the first time the tiger hadn't just vanished.

October 22

Brickhouse was in early Saturday, but Weinman was there before him.

"I'm gonna drive out and talk to Graham, see if he found anything," the sheriff said.

"Before you go, had an interesting call yesterday from Perry down in Atlanta."

"FBI Perry?"

"Yeah. They're falling all over themselves trying to get a piece of this. They been trying to trace the tiger. He says there was a little shopping mall carnival, what they call a tent show or a mud show, over in Spartanburg first part of September, had a big tiger in a little cage. Closed there on the eighth. Opened the twelfth at one of those outlet malls outside of Huntsville. Didn't have the tiger. Guy runs the mall says he was kind of counting on the tiger, but the fellow in charge told him it took sick and died.

"Closed there on the sixteenth. Next date was a strip mall up near Memphis. Never showed up. Evidently didn't have any other dates.

"Perry said it was a fleabag outfit called Big Top Productions, home address in Sarasota. Turned out to be an empty lot. Nobody down there ever heard of it."

Brickhouse sighed. "Like somebody just put it together so it could dump this damn hungry tiger on us, eh?"

"You'd think," Weinman said. "But that's not all. Perry said they traced all the likely routes between Spartanburg and Huntsville, then ran a computer check for unsolved crimes for a couple or three weeks around the likely date. You remember what happened down around Richey about then?"

"Shit, Mark, I can't hardly remember what happened last week right under my nose, way things been going. What happened down around Richey?"

"That newspaper delivery woman disappeared down there. You talked to Barnes about it, as I recall. She dropped a newspaper in a ditch, as they figured it, went to retrieve it, and just vanished."

"Sonofabitch. So it got away down there and worked its way all the way up here?"

"That's what it looks like."

"That's nearly a hundred miles."

"Maybe it wanted to see the leaves this fall. Maybe it heard your constituents taste better than Barnes's."

"Maybe you better get over to the school and feed the wolves. I've got to get a little paperwork done, then I'm going out to see Graham."

Roy got up at dawn Saturday, dragged the big galvanized tub into the kitchen, and began heating water to fill it, which took more than half an hour. By then Rose was up, too. She got some scissors and a comb and trimmed his hair while they were getting the tub filled, then brought Roy some soap, and he scrubbed himself hard all over. While he was doing that, she heated up more water to wash his hair.

When Annie drove up, Roy had on his best pants and button-up shirt, his only pair of socks, and the shoes he was planning on wearing this winter. They were kind of small and pinching his feet. He was excited; he hadn't been to Hartesville in more than a year.

The place called Norma's Creek consists of nine houses huddled on either side of County Road 12 in a narrow valley between low mountains, a crow's nine-mile flight north of the Satterly house. The fast-moving stream for which it is named runs behind the houses on the south side of the road.

It has no post office and only one store, which was Ray Craven's living room and front bedroom before he decided to go into business. A Coca-Cola sign over the wide front porch distinguishes it from the other houses, all small frame buildings united in their need for paint.

Behind most of the houses are large vegetable gardens, some even stretching back far enough to allow half an acre planted in corn. Others have enough land for outbuildings and a few milk cows. Bo Fugard's backyard is given over to rusting automobiles and tractors.

All the children of Norma's Creek have grown and gone; its sixteen residents are retired or nearly so.

On fine weekends, half a dozen or so of the women of Norma's Creek get together in Sally Ann O'Neal's front yard and offer their quilts for sale. There is never much traffic on the county road, which peels off 153, so the ladies don't sell many quilts. But it has turned into a social tradition, and folks frequently drop by for a chat.

There is such a feeling of isolation in the valley around Norma's Creek that its residents rarely connect themselves to events elsewhere, and they didn't even discuss the possibility of canceling their quilt sale because some odd animal was causing trouble in another part of the county. At Norma's Creek, anything they can't see from the front porch is another part of the county.

So the quilt sale at Norma's Creek went on as usual. The ladies brought out their folding lawn chairs and their quilt racks Saturday morning and set them up in Sally Ann's front yard on the south side of the highway. Sally Ann's husband, Roscoe, got the QUILTS FOR SALE sign out of the garage and propped it against the poplar tree.

It was a bright morning, and by ten thirty it was warm enough that most of them took off their jackets. Two cars had gone by in an hour and a half, both driven by people who waved cheerfully but didn't stop. The ladies of Norma's Creek didn't know the county's roads to the outside had been cut off.

They were discussing the continuing ill health of the widow Hadley when the conversation stopped abruptly and everybody looked at Sally Ann as if she were the Antichrist.

"What in the world are you—" Sally Ann got out before the tiger seized her by the arm. None of them had noticed the animal until it appeared right behind Sally Ann, and they were struck dumb for a moment by the sight. The tiger yanked her backward, knocking over her chair, and Sally Ann's scream galvanized the ladies.

They leaped up, shrieking, and Olla Mae Martin threw her chair at the man-eater, which was dragging the terrified woman toward the backyard. The chair hit Sally Ann more than it hit the man-eater, but the beast dropped the woman, uttered a thunderous growl, and charged Olla Mae.

Olla Mae turned to run, and Vita Murdock threw her coffee mug, hitting the tiger in the flank. As it whipped around, Midge Partridge flung a quilt toward it. The sight of the billowing quilt and the din of the women's screams apparently unnerved the man-eater; with a snarl it dashed behind Sally Ann's house and began roaring its fury.

Roscoe O'Neal appeared at the door with a shotgun and saw his wife on the ground where the tiger dropped her, shrieking and sobbing hysterically. The arm of her blue flower-print dress was sodden with blood.

Roscoe burst out of the door and down the steps. "What happened?" he shouted.

"The tiger!" several of the women yelled. "It went behind there, toward the creek." It roared again, and the rest of Norma's Creek came running toward the commotion.

Roscoe dropped down beside Sally Ann, set the shotgun aside, and began stripping off his shirt. Sally Ann was terribly pale.

"Everybody out!" Roscoe yelled. "Get out of here! Get in your cars and get out before that damned thing comes back."

He tied his shirt roughly around Sally Ann's wounds, picked her up, and ran toward their car. "Vita," he shouted. "Can you come with me?"

The woman broke away from her husband. "Help them get Vera out," she told him, and rushed toward Roscoe's car. She jumped into the backseat, and Roscoe put Sally Ann in, her head on Vita's lap.

Lanny Murdock and Fred Martin got Vera Hadley out of her bed and helped her into the backseat of the Murdocks' Oldsmobile.

The tiger was still roaring. It sounded as though it was moving from house to house.

Within twenty minutes, every resident of Norma's Creek, including most cats and dogs, was gone. Some even neglected to close their front doors. Norma's Creek was a ghost town.

Brickhouse was about to leave Graham's shack and head home for lunch when Ellen called him on the radio. "Unit ten?" Ellen's voice called.

Brickhouse reached through the window of his car and picked up the mike. "Ten."

"Ten, can you phone?"

"Yeah."

He got his cell phone out of the glove compartment, flicked the speakerphone button, and dialed the dispatcher's number. Ellen answered on the first ring.

"Brickhouse."

"Sheriff, the emergency room nurse from the hospital called. A man just brought his wife in from over to Norma's Creek. Tiger attacked her, he said. She was one of them women having that quilt sale every weekend, you know? Tiger came right up to them and grabbed her, he said. Said the whole place lit out."

"You talk to the man?"

"No, nurse said they'd sedated him. Identified him as Roscoe O'Neal. Said his wife was in bad shape from loss of blood, shock, and infection, but they're pretty sure she'll live. Another woman came with them, but soon as they got his wife out of the car this other woman went into hysterics. Had to sedate her, too."

"Okay," Brickhouse said. "I'll go over to the hospital now. Send a couple units through Norma's Creek. Tell them to phone if they see anything, keep it off the air. And tell them to stay in the car."

"Where is this place, Sheriff?" Graham asked when Brickhouse put the mike back on its bracket.

"Little clutch of houses about a twenty-minute drive from here," Brickhouse replied. "You want to go look at it?"

"No, I don't think it would be productive," Graham said. "The tiger probably hasn't eaten since Wednesday, and then only lightly. I doubt it will remain in an abandoned locality. I believe I'll pay a visit to my sheep."

Annie brought Roy home at midafternoon. She let the boy out, waved at Rose, and continued toward the store.

Roy was wearing a pair of new boots that laced up over the ankle, one of three new pairs of socks, and a new corduroy jacket, and gave Rose the $4.33 that was left over. He was so excited from the trip he couldn't sit still.

He bounced around the house, telling Rose of what he had seen in Hartesville and what it was like in Lacey's Department Store. Rose tried to understand and even asked a few questions. She was proud of her boy. He looked so nice in his coat and boots. They were soft boots, not hard and shiny, but they smelled like leather. Roy said they were swayed. He didn't know what that meant, but both Annie and the salesman had called them swayed.

———————

Graham carefully stalked the clearing where he had left the sheep. The rope was still tied to the fallen tree where he had tethered it, but that meant nothing, He waited, watching the scene silently, then backed away and worked around to the ravine he had expected the tiger to use.

After another careful stalk, Graham could see the rope was broken and the sheep gone. He stood up and walked to the tree, which was spattered with the sheep's blood. He followed the blood spoor for about a hundred yards. The tiger had taken its kill into a small ravine and eaten it out. The legs and head remained, attached to the skin.

A dollop of blood on a maple leaf was not quite dry. The tiger had returned to Turkey Mountain after its fiasco at Norma's Creek and had left its kill not much more than an hour ago. The sheep would not allay its hunger.

Graham found the tracks of the tiger leaving the ravine. It had gone up the mountain a short distance and stopped to rest a bit in the sun, within sight of the ravine where its kill lay. It had departed to the west, no more than half an hour ago.

At the hospital, Brickhouse found Fred Martin, who had come to check on Sally Ann after depositing the widow Hadley with her son in Hartesville.

"I don't believe any of us will be going home until this is over," Martin said. "Most of us have family we can stay with, and those who don't are welcome in lots of homes around here. We're all old, and going back for a shirt or a toothbrush ain't worth whatever life we've got left."

"Hell of a time to be having a quilt sale," the sheriff observed.

"Reckon so, Grady. I guess we just didn't think. . . ."

At the pasture, Winshiser told Brickhouse he was catching some heat.

"Had HQ on the line this morning, wondering why we're not doing anything but manning roadblocks."

"What'd you tell them?"

"That, one, it was what the local authorities asked me to do, and, two, in my estimation it's about all we're capable of doing. My officers are getting some pressure from a few non-coms who fancy themselves as hunters, want permission to go out on their own. Far as I'm concerned, going into those woods after that tiger would be offering it more food. I've been thinking of having a razor-wire perimeter set up around the camp."

"Well, Harte County certainly appreciates what you and your men are doing out here, Colonel. We'd be having a hell of a time without you."

Sergeant Ted Luck, at the wheel of a humvee on one of the interior roadblocks near Copperhead Mountain, waved at the sheriff after moving his vehicle out of the road. Brickhouse waved back as his blue-and-white moved on to the next roadblock.

"Seems like a nice fellow," said Private Gene Dorsey, who had been riding shotgun with the sergeant since the roadblock operation began.

"Yeah, seems like."

Luck backed the humvee across the road again and shut off the engine. They were at the apex of a mild curve on the highway, with a view of about a quarter of a mile in either direction. The road was bound by a ditch on each side, then barbed-wire fence, which seemed to be trying to hold the forest back. On the side nearest Copperhead, there were NO HUNTING signs tacked to the fenceposts.

It was cloudy, and a cool breeze was coming from the west. Dorsey kept the canvas door closed on his side of the humvee. It kept the breeze out, but he would have kept it closed anyway. Dorsey was a city boy, and he wanted no part of tigers.

Luck, on the other hand, was a hunter, a gun collector and a marksman. He was one of those pressuring his superiors for a crack at the tiger—although preferably not with his M16. "Got a couple of rifles at home would be better," he had said. "Or I could borrow a 12-gauge from the sheriff."

But, even undergunned, he figured he could hold his own with the tiger. Put enough of those little .223 slugs in the right place, you'd stop him. Luck wished the damn thing would come along. He kept his door flap open in case it did.

Base was doing its quarter-hourly check. Dorsey picked up the radio microphone and waited their turn.

"Base to Unit Eight," the radio said.

"Unit Eight. All clear," Dorsey answered, then put the mike back in its rack.

"When you reckon we'll go home, Sarge?"

"Who knows? Doubt the state can afford to keep us out here a whole lot longer. Operation like this costs the taxpayers a lotta money." Luck was reading the latest issue of *Guns & Ammo*.

A mile to the east, in Unit Six, Sergeant Howland Jackson had a new partner, Private D'Antonio Laney. Jackson, who stood six feet four and weighed 250 pounds, was trying to stretch out in the passenger seat. It wouldn't work. It never worked, but he never gave up; the laws of geometry, he figured, had to have a loophole somewhere.

"Sarge," said the private. "How come the other noncoms, they all call you Howlin', like Howlin' Jack?"

" 'Cause I play guitar a little and sing some," the sergeant said.

"Whassat got to do with it?"

"You never hearda Howlin' Wolf?"

"Who he?"

"Shit. Where you from, Laney?"

"Lizella."

"What kinda music you listen to in Lizella?"

"Oh, you know, Ice-T and Snoop and TLC, like that."

"That rap shit?"

"Yeah. Mostly."

"You ever heard of Lightnin' Hopkins?"

"Don't think so, no."

"I think we got us a generation gap here, my man. Howlin' Wolf an' Lightnin' Hopkins an' Muddy Waters an' them, they sang the blues. You never hearda the blues?"

"Oh, yeah, I heard of 'em. Never listen to 'em much. Old-timey stuff. Ain't got that beat, ya know?"

"Shit," Jackson snorted.

"So, okay. I can see the Jack, 'cause you name Jackson. But where they get the Howlin'? That's a big stretch, ain't it?"

"Not if your name is Howland."

"Howlind? With a D?"

"Howland. H-o-w-l-a-n-d. Howland."

"How you get a name like that?"

" 'Cause my daddy read the comics. He name me after a owl in the comic strips."

"Owl? Name Howland?"

"Tha's right."

Laney began to giggle. "That funnier'n shit, Sarge."

Jackson swung his head around and looked at Laney squarely.

"An' where you get a name like D'Antonio? You got an Italian in the woodpile somewhere?"

Laney stopped laughing. "No. My momma, she just like the sound of it."

Jackson looked at him. "That funnier'n shit, too," he said, without smiling.

Graham looked up. Clouds muffled the sun, but he guessed it was nearing midafternoon. The ground over which the tiger had gone was rocky, and it had been difficult to follow. But it was headed in the general direction of the highway and Randall's pasture.

The hunter stopped to rest on a boulder briefly, looking out over the side of the mountain. The leaves were turning: There was yellow and orange, and some red was beginning to appear. It was a beautiful sight, but he had the feeling it would not be a good day.

At Unit Eight, Dorsey was getting hungry. He looked at his watch.

" 'Bout time for the lunch truck to come around," he said.

"Hungry?"

"Sorta."

"I could do with—" Luck started but was cut off by the radio.

"Unit Ten, Unit Twelve," it said.

"Twelve."

"Ten. Movement in the ditch, north side the road, to your east. Heading toward it. Request you move in, too."

"Twelve. Comin' your way."

Luck started the humvee up and let it idle. The radio was silent for a while.

"Unit Ten, Base."

"Base, Ten."

"Ten. Got a gentleman name—what was it, sir?—name Rabun Perry here. Got him his rifle and goin' after big game. You send somebody after him?"

"Base. We'll have a deputy come get him. Make him comfortable while you wait."

"Roger, Base. Where's the lunch wagon?"

"Just loadin' up, Ten. Be there soon."

"Ten out."

"Base out."

Dorsey chuckled. "How many's that make we've caught now, Sarge? Three?"

"Think so. Understand they picked up a couple over on the other road, so this would make three."

"Crazy fuckers."

"Shit," Luck said. "I'd be up there, if I could, and none of these peckerwoods would stop me, either. I'd go at night, and you wouldn't have a hope in hell of catching me."

"Yeah, Sarge. They're not that crazy around here, to go up there in the dark."

Within half an hour a county cruiser went through the roadblocks to pick up the erstwhile hunter held at Unit Ten. It was followed momentarily by a humvee with a cardboard sign on the side that said "Joe's Eats." It stopped at each roadblock to deliver trays carrying hot meals.

"Not bad, Sarge," said Laney. It was the first time he had opened his mouth since determining why people called the sergeant Howlin' Jack.

"Not real bad, not real good. Army food. Leastwise the cap'n sees we get it hot. Not all them officers worry that much about their troops, 'specially when we just sittin' here doin' nothin'."

Laney considered that. Jackson commanded a great deal of respect within the LRRP unit. He never said much and seemed to have an even temper. But the private—who was new to the unit—gathered that Jackson had led some patrols or something in the Gulf War that had gotten to be famous. Jackson never mentioned the war.

"Let's stretch our legs, Laney," the massive sergeant said after the quarter-hourly check.

"I thought we ain't supposed to leave the vehicle."

"They say that to cover they asses. You sit in this thing for twelve hours, they gonna hafta get you out with a forklift," he said. "Come on. We watch out for each other." Laney noticed the way Jackson put that. He was expecting Laney to look after him, too. It made the private feel good.

Each took his M16. "Keep your eyes movin'," Jackson said. "Don't look for anythin' in particular. Just watch for movement, somethin' that don't look right."

They walked a little way up the road, then back to the humvee and a little way in the other direction. Jackson turned frequently to check their backs. Laney could tell Jackson was fully alert and serious, and it scared him a little.

"I need to pee, Sarge," he said.

"Watcha want me to do, hold it for you?"

"No, I mean, is it okay I go over to the ditch there?"

"Sure. I'll watch. I mean, I'll keep a lookout."

"Thanks," said Laney, walking off the road to to the ditch. He put his rifle on the ground and began to urinate toward one of the NO HUNTING signs.

At Unit Eight, a similar urge came over Dorsey. "I need to go," he told Luck. "Gimme your tray, and I'll put it on the back."

"Thanks," Luck said, handing him the lunch tray. "Careful. Don't go too far."

Dorsey climbed out of the truck, rifle in one hand and trays in the other. He put the empty trays on the roof at the back of the humvee, then sauntered down the road, walking along the yellow line and swinging his head from side to side.

He found a large bush growing outside the fence on the north side of the road and headed toward it.

Twenty yards from Unit Six, Jackson saw a bush twitch briefly behind the fence on the south side of the road. He felt his hackles lift a little. Shifting the rifle into both hands, he turned slowly, scanning the fence line for the source of the movement. He saw nothing.

"Laney!" he whispered urgently. "Laney!"

The private, shaking himself dry, looked over his shoulder.

"We got company. Get your weapon and get back to the vehicle. Now!"

The private ducked down and grabbed his rifle, his eyes wide, darting here and there.

"Go!" Jackson whispered. "I'll cover you."

The sergeant was fairly sure the threat came from the south side of the road. He moved in behind and to one side of Laney, who was sprinting for the humvee. The private leaped into the passenger side, and Jackson began his own run.

Dorsey, his bladder empty, felt better. He came back to the road and started walking again. It smelled like rain; it would be good to get a little exercise if they got stuck in the humvee until eight P.M.

He kept walking. The tiger scared the hell out of him, but he felt safe. Luck, of course, would jump at a chance to see the damn thing. The trees on the mountainsides were so beautiful, and Dorsey was so deep in his own thoughts, that he didn't realize he had walked around the corner and well out of sight of Unit Eight.

Jackson reached the driver's side of the humvee and got in with his back to Laney. "Turn around and guard your side. Put it on full auto," he whispered. "Be sure you ain't got your feet or your weapon or anything else stickin' out the door, nothin' that somebody could sneak up the side and grab without you seein' 'em."

"Jesus, Sarge, what is it?"

"Somethin' out there," Jackson said. "I didn't see nothin', I didn't hear nothin', but somethin's out there, and I don't think it's no bunny rabbit. Now shut up and watch." Laney was panting, but the sergeant didn't seem at all short of breath.

Dorsey didn't realize how far he had walked until he heard a short honk of the humvee's horn. "Oh, shit," he said, turned around, and began to trot back. Luck was going to be pissed.

As he rounded the corner, he heard the radio.

"Base, Unit Eight."

"Base, Unit Eight."

"Answer it, Sarge. I'm coming," he panted.

"Base, Unit Eight. Can you hear me, Eight?"

Dorsey threw himself into the passenger's seat and grabbed

the microphone. He was about to reply to base when he realized Luck wasn't there.

"Eight, Base," he said, craning his head around to look for
the sergeant.

"Whatsa matter, Eight? Cat got your tongue?"

"Ah, no, Base. Sorry for being slow answering you."

"You boys got somethin' goin', keep it off-duty, you know?"

Wiseass. "Eight out," he said, and hung up the mike.

Rifle ready, he got out of the humvee and walked around
the back. He stopped and peered around the corner at the
driver's side. Luck's *Guns & Ammo* magazine was fluttering
on the pavement. He stepped around and walked to the door.
Nothing. He turned and scanned the road. There was something in the south side ditch about twenty feet away.

Fearfully, Dorsey walked to the edge of the ditch. Luck's
M16 lay there. It was covered with blood. He yelled, brought
up his weapon, and emptied it wildly into the trees.

Less than a mile away, Graham heard Dorsey's cry and the
stream of gunfire. He stepped behind a tree until there was
no more shooting, then pulled out his cellular phone and
called the sheriff's office. A woman answered.

"Is Sheriff Brickhouse there?"

"He's with someone right now, sir," the woman said.

"Um, this is Colonel Graham. I believe I have an emergency. Could you—"

He heard a couple of clicks.

"Brickhouse. What's wrong, Jim?"

"I believe the tiger has visited the roadblocks on the north
highway," he said. "I was tracking it in this direction, and I
just heard a scream, followed by automatic gunfire. Those

odd-looking vehicles are rushing up and down now. I'm worried about going further lest they shoot me by mistake," he said.

"Can you see the highway?"

"Yes."

"Wait until you see a county car—blue and white, you know—and then head for it. I'll be there."

Winshiser had kept his troops out of the ditch around Luck's rifle, but search parties had gone over the fence west of it to begin scouring the woods. Brickhouse had stopped along the way, waited until Graham reached the road, and drove on to the scene.

"Over here," Winshiser said, motioning them to Unit Eight.

"We had to take the private, Dorsey's his name, back to camp. We may have to take him to the hospital. He was berserk when we got here, and now he seems to be going into shock.

"Anyway, he told me he left Sergeant Luck sitting in the driver's seat here and went off to relieve himself. Strictly against orders, but hell, I knew they'd do it. I just hoped they'd do it together. He said he walked west, not paying any attention, and walked around the corner.

"Said he heard the horn, one short honk, and started running back here. Luck was gone. Now, step over here."

They followed him to the ditch. "That's Luck's weapon. Colonel Graham, the field is yours. I've got men in the woods, but they stayed out of this particular area. Couldn't any of them track an elephant in a vegetable garden anyway."

Graham, ignoring the rifle, began casting along the fence. "Tiger crawled under the fence here," he said, pointing to a spot well east of the rifle. "Came on its belly down the ditch," he said, walking along, "and then up the bank here, right in front of this vehicle."

He looked around the door of the humvee, picked some hairs off a fold in the sheet metal, and then picked up the magazine. "One would assume the sergeant was engrossed in his reading," he said, "The tiger simply came around the tire here, reared up, and seized him, probably by the neck. I expect the horn was honked in the struggle.

"Having extracted the sergeant, the tiger dragged him into the ditch. He may still have been alive at that point and trying to use his weapon, or he may have been holding it in a death grip. Whatever the case, the tiger shook him here, quite hard enough to break his neck and shake loose the rifle, and then got another grip, probably on the small of his back. Hence all this blood.

"He continued straight to the fence, cleared it in one bound, and went into the forest. Your sergeant is dead, colonel. I'm sorry."

"Thank you, Colonel Graham," Winshiser said bleakly, going back to his radioman.

Graham turned to Brickhouse.

"His men are very likely trampling over the spoor and are very unlikely to find the body unless they are lucky enough— or perhaps unlucky enough—to surprise the tiger while it eats. But I cannot ask him to call them back. He certainly feels helpless enough without being asked to stop searching for his own man."

"Do you think you can find the body if they don't?"

"I expect so, but it will have to wait until tomorrow. I don't intend to go out there with all those itchy trigger fingers. It's getting late now. He'll have to bring them in before dark. It's been a long day, Sheriff. May I ask for a ride home?"

———

Brickhouse spoke briefly to Winshiser, then walked with Graham to his car. They drove in silence for several miles.

"I checked the ewe I left out last night," Graham said. "The tiger killed and ate it but obviously found it insufficient. I was tracking it when I heard the commotion from the road."

"One of the things I wanted to tell you," Brickhouse said, "was we got some word on where the tiger must have come from."

He gave Graham the FBI's account almost exactly the way Weinman had given it to him.

"An empty lot? This carnival had no valid address? How did it do business?"

"Far as I know, it only made four dates: the one in South Carolina, one in Alabama, and two others later. People who made the deals with the carny say they didn't have to put up any money ahead of time, nothing—just a verbal agreement with payment at the end of the show. All the business was done by phone."

"And the telephone number?"

"A public phone booth."

"I see," said Graham. He smiled and was silent for a while.

"Let me tell you a story, Sheriff, an old hunter's yarn," he began.

"Sure," Brickhouse said.

"It was a very long time ago—once upon a time, if you like—and there was a man-eating tiger operating in the vicinity of a village called Kot Kindri, perhaps fifty miles from my home. The government asked my father and me to try to kill it.

"When we reached the scene, the tiger had just taken what was believed to have been its 273rd victim. The villagers had left the kill overnight so we could see it. There was not enough of it left—it was an old woman—for us to sit over, but there were plenty of footprints.

"They were unusual. The left front paw of the tiger appeared to be scarred. There was a diagonal indentation across the pad, something that might have happened in a fight. My father always thought of him as Slashfoot after that.

"At any rate, he had a beat of about six hundred square miles, and it was hard going. He took three more people. But there was a small boy who told my father that he did not fear the tiger, because the tiger was his friend. He said it talked to him and taught him how it was to be a tiger.

"At any rate, I was downriver at Pathangiri when the tiger took a woman near Kor Kindri. Father sat up over the remains and killed the tiger—after it had made a very excellent attempt to kill him.

"The people rejoiced, setting bonfires and dancing and carrying on in general. When I arrived the next day, Father told me he hadn't killed the man-eater. The tiger he killed had no scar on any of its feet. We warned the people of this and went home, fully expecting to be called back within a few weeks. But for as long as I lived in India, no one was ever again killed by a tiger in the vicinity of Kot Kindri."

"Now, do you remember that day we found the tiger's pugmarks by a stream?"

"Of course."

"He left the prints of all four feet there for us. And the left forepaw has a diagonal scar across it. It looks exactly like the one left by the Kot Kindri man-eater."

Brickhouse felt the hair on his forearms tingle. "What do you make of it?"

"Nothing," Graham said. "There is nothing to be made of it. I have seen a number of things in the forests of India for which I could find no explanation; my father even more. And the appearance of that pugmark may not be the strangest thing I've seen in your forest, Sheriff."

"What do you mean?"

"Oh, I'm just rambling now. It may be nothing." They were silent until Brickhouse pulled up at the shack. "I shall begin looking for the remains of the sergeant first thing in the morning," Graham said. "Would you care to meet me here around midday? Perhaps I will have found something by then."

As dusk approached, Roy decided to see if he could find his friend. He started up the path, and, sure enough, about a quarter of a mile up the mountain, the tiger was sitting, just as though it was waiting for him. Somehow, though, it looked different.

Roy sat down and stared into the tiger's eyes and wondered what was different. Then he noticed the white fur around the tiger's mouth was all reddish. He thought of the women who came into Dugan's now and then with bright red lips. That seemed to be the main difference, although there was a kind of frazzled air about his friend, as though he'd been having a real hard time. Roy was sorry about that, especially since his own day had been such a good one.

Roy watched and listened intently, but he still couldn't hear his friend's message. In a bit, the tiger's great tongue came out, licked its lips all around, and it stood up, stretched luxuriously, and walked away.

He went home, helped Rose wash the cut-up vegetables for their dinner. After eating, he took off his new boots, placed them side by side by his bed, and laid his new socks out over his chair. His new jacket he hung in a closet curtained off from his room. He dropped into bed and fell asleep.

As Brickhouse drove back to town, he called the dispatcher and asked him to put out the word for the press corps to meet at the school. When he arrived, most were there.

He didn't wait on the rest before laying out the events on the highway.

"If the tiger ate a sheep," the *Washington Post* asked, "why did it have to kill someone right away?"

"Well now," Brickhouse said, "I haven't read the bylaws of the brotherhood of tigers. But I imagine one of our local sheep doesn't make much of a meal for one. If you would do a little research, you'd find that they will commonly eat the better part of a full-grown cow in one sitting."

"And the body of Sergeant Luck has not been recovered?" a network reporter asked.

"Not when I left the scene. The colonel said he would call if they found it, and he hasn't called."

"God help us," the *Miami Herald* whispered to the *New York Post*. "I can see your headline now."

"I know," the *Daily News* said. "Guard Runs Out of Luck."

October 23

It took Graham more than two hours to pick up the blood spoor on Sunday morning. Once found, however, it was easily followed. The tiger had taken its kill directly up Copperhead Mountain almost to the summit, then quartered down and around the mountain. Fully a mile and a half from the highway, the man-eater stopped in a ravine to consume Sergeant Luck.

There was almost nothing left. A few splintered bones. One empty boot, another with a foot in it. A belt buckle, scraps of camouflage clothing, and half a wallet. It had, apparently, swallowed the soldier's ID tag. Graham touched none of it but covered everything with dead grass and sticks. Then he resumed following the tiger.

The tracks went a little further around the mountain, then angled downhill to reach the faint path coming up from the shack where the boy lived.

It had stopped on the path, sat, and waited. Graham walked down the path and was eerily unsurprised to find that the boy had come up the trail, seen the tiger, and sat down facing it. They had been about seventy-five feet apart. Graham estimated they had faced each other for at least a quarter of an hour before breaking off the encounter. The tiger had continued around the mountain.

Graham retraced his tracks to the kill, made certain it was undisturbed, and returned to his shack. As he expected, Brickhouse was waiting for him.

"Are you up to a little walk today, Sheriff?"

"Do me good," Brickhouse said. "First, Mary sent you another care package. Nothing in it that won't keep."

"Nonetheless, seems like time for tea. You might not be feeling like it later. Let's see what your lovely memsahib sent us."

"I assume from that you found the soldier."

"Very little of him, I fear," Graham said. "Perhaps not even enough to make an identification."

Graham brought out tea and the two men sat silently on

the fender of Brickhouse's blue-and-white eating blueberry muffins.

Graham went through the ritual of examining his cartridges and reloading them, and they started up the mountain. He showed Brickhouse the sheep kill, and the tree where he had been waiting.

"How the hell did you get up there?"

"Why, I climbed, Sheriff. How else?"

"Damned if I could climb that tree."

"Oh, I've been climbing trees since I could walk."

They marched on, Graham beginning to puff a little.

"How can it take a man, like it did that soldier, with no sound?" the sheriff asked.

"It's not unusual. If the tiger gets in the first bite just the way it wants to, it not only punctures just about everything in the throat and neck, often breaking the neck, but it is also suffocating. A small gasp or sigh is all that would be heard."

They continued on, leaving Turkey Mountain and starting along Copperhead. They were about a quarter of a mile from Luck's remains when Graham suddenly stopped and held up his hand for silence, then raised the rifle slowly to his shoulder, muzzle to the ground and turned to face up the mountain.

Brickhouse let his hand creep to the thumb-break strap holding down his Glock and worked it loose. He rested his hand on the butt.

He watched Graham's eyes scanning the woods. The Englishman's voice came to him as if borne on the breeze blowing up the mountain.

"Tiger's watching us."

Brickhouse felt the hackles rise on the back of his neck. He slid his left foot out to broaden his stance. He could see nothing unusual, hear nothing but the faint sound of water running somewhere.

"Where?" he whispered.

"Upwind."

Wind's blowing up the mountain. Up the mountain is upwind. But how the hell does he know it's watching us if he can't see it?

"D'you see that ledge up the path there about twenty feet up?" Graham whispered, turning slightly and very slowly to face it.

"Yeah."

"Probably waiting for us there."

Brickhouse could hear the blood pounding in his ears. He couldn't think of anything to say.

"Take your sidearm out, very slowly."

Brickhouse did.

"One in the chamber?"

"No."

"Oh, bad luck," said Graham.

Brickhouse's eyes widened. Weinman had often scolded him for carrying a weapon without a chambered round.

"Don't do it now," Graham whispered quickly. "Too much noise. Get your left hand on the slide, ready to chamber. D'you shoot well?"

"At targets."

"It'll be a nice big target if it comes, but it will arrive very quickly. Be ready to take a step away from me if it charges. We don't want to get tangled. Understood?"

"Yeah."

"Now, we are going to start walking sideways, very slowly, up the path. Concentrate on that ledge. Let me take the first two steps before you take one. Ready?"

"All right."

Graham slid his right foot out, shifted his weight to it, and brought his left foot under him. He repeated the movement. Brickhouse followed suit. The breeze up the mountain was cool, but sweat fell in his right eye, stinging it. He had to close the eye and could barely keep from bringing a hand up to rub it. He clenched his teeth and followed Graham.

They were directly opposite the ledge, a slightly over-hanging rock, when Brickhouse heard a low, chilling growl, and a pebble rolled to the edge of the overhang and fell to the ground.

"Chamber a round," Graham snapped. "Be ready," and he ran up the path, darting to his left and disappearing behind the ledge. Brickhouse, startled, snapped the slide back, let it fall, and brought the lightweight Glock up into a two-handed stance, knees bent, moving the muzzle back and forth the width of the ledge.

Nothing happened. He heard a small thump to his left and looked to see Graham dropping down to the path. "What?" Brickhouse whispered, returning his attention to the ledge.

"Gone," Graham said in a normal voice. "Put your sidearm away. What sort of weapon is that, anyway?"

"It's a 9-millimeter automatic. Pretty standard in law en-forcement here now."

"How many rounds does it hold?"

"Seventeen in the magazine."

"My word," said Graham.

Brickhouse sat down on a fallen log, waiting for his pulse to return to normal.

"Jim, couldn't you see the tiger?"

"No," Graham said. "Could you?"

"Of course not. But if you couldn't see it, how did you know it was there?"

"I simply know those things. I have all my life; otherwise I would have died rather young. Father had the same knack. I have never tried to understand it."

"How did you know it was upwind?"

"Tigers, I believe, have a relatively poor sense of smell, but they assume their quarry has an excellent one. They don't know human beings have almost no sense of smell. They always stalk and ambush from upwind."

They sat in silence for a while, and then Graham rose. "Feel like going back and looking at the record?"

"Sure," said Brickhouse, although his legs ached from tension.

They had followed their back trail for no more than ten minutes when Graham pointed at the path. "See there."

Brickhouse recognized his own footprint—pointed out by Graham earlier. Overlaid on it was the tiger's pugmark.

"This is where it left our track and ran ahead to set up the ambush. It was probably going to see if it had forgotten any small tidbits of its kill when it saw us. It assumed—rightly—that we were headed for the same spot."

"Jesus," said Brickhouse. "That is truly scary."

"Indeed," said Graham, matter-of-factly. "Well, let's get on."

They reached the remains to find the tiger had been there a little before them but had only nosed about the few grisly objects. "Is it still around?" Brickhouse asked nervously.

"No, no," Graham said. "It's left us in peace."

As if in confirmation, the tiger called, twice, near the summit. "It's hunting again," Brickhouse said.

"Not necessarily," Graham said. "A tiger calls often just for the pleasure of it, just to tell the forest it is there, it is king.

They don't call only when they're hunting, and they don't always call when they're hunting—as you've just seen."

"Why didn't it attack us back at the ledge?"

"Because it had lost the element of surprise. Tigers generally will attack only in self-defense or when they feel they have every advantage."

"Cowards, then."

Graham seemed to stiffen, and turned until he was staring straight at Brickhouse.

"Never believe that, Sheriff. Never believe the tiger is a coward or is evil or is any of the things so much of mankind ascribes to him.

"The tiger is a big-hearted gentleman, the most courageous beast I know. Unless threatened or deranged, I have never known a tiger to kill beyond its needs. He has no easy life. For every careful stalk that succeeds, ten others will fail, and that is why he demands every advantage he can get.

"I shall never forget the first tiger I ever saw. I was eight years old, and I nearly stepped on him, walking in the jungle. I thought my heart would stop. I thought I was dead. But he merely got up, looked at me with disgust for ruining his nap, and walked away.

"No, Sheriff, nature created nothing finer than the tiger. Tell me, if you were this tiger, what has he done that you would not do? If you had somehow gained your freedom from a prison cell scarcely big enough to swap ends in and found yourself in a low-lying country but could see the mountains you loved in the distance, would you not try to reach them?

"If, as you tell me is now suspected, you were lying in a ditch, starving, and another creature stumbled over you, would you assume that creature was not an enemy? You have escaped from prison. Every creature is your enemy. Would you not take steps to silence that enemy? This is life or death, Sheriff, every minute of every day.

"Smelling that blood, starving, would you not accept the chance to eat?

"When that hunter your government sent here approached your hiding place, would you walk out and say, 'Here I am, slay me?' "

"You sound as though you feel sorry for this tiger," Brickhouse said.

"Answer my question, please, Sheriff."

Brickhouse was silent for a moment and then looked at Graham. "I don't suppose I would have acted any differently than this animal, Jim."

"Thank you, Sheriff. And I will tell you that yes, I feel very sorry for this tiger. I must kill it, and I will, but I do not relish it."

They were silent for a while and turned their attention to the remains of Sergeant Luck, who was beginning to sour.

"I believe everything here will go easily into this bag I brought, Sheriff," said Graham, picking up the small bones.

Brickhouse lifted the occupied shoe and dropped it into the green plastic garbage bag. "They may be able to identify him from that, if they made footprints at birth. A lot of hospitals do that."

As they moved away from the scene, Graham caught a glimpse of the boy's house through the trees and stopped. "Look here, Sheriff," he said, pointing at the tarpaper structure. "Do you know who lives there?"

"No idea," said Brickhouse. "Why?"

"Just curious," he said. "Tiger seems to spend a good bit of time in this neighborhood."

"They'd better be warned."

"They have been," Graham said.

Roy spent Sunday helping Rose with the washing. She had an old hand-cranked washing machine that she kept in the kitchen and rolled out on the front stoop to use on fair days.

Roy heated water on the stove to fill the machine, and Rose added detergent and put in the clothes, mashing them down to make them sink. Then Roy churned them around with an old broom handle until Rose felt they'd had enough. They let the water out a plug at the bottom, refilled it with cold water for a rinse, and churned the clothes some more.

Rose fed each item into the hand-operated wringer perched on top of the old green machine, and Roy cranked them through. It was kind of fun, seeing those jeans and things mashed so flat and the water squeezed out of them, but he had to be careful not to catch his ma's fingers. It took the better part of the afternoon to do a couple of loads of laundry, even though he was just tall enough to help Rose hang them on the line out back.

October 24

Monday dawned gloomy and threatening. Roy promised Rose he'd meet her at Dugan's with the umbrella if it rained in the afternoon. When she was gone, he went back to his room and looked at his new shoes. He didn't much like the idea of getting them dirty. If it rained, they'd get covered with mud. It wasn't that cold, anyway.

He put on his new jacket, even if he didn't really need it, and went up the path, the path he'd started thinking of as the tiger path. He used to think of it as the 'coon path, but the 'coons didn't seem to do much but hide in their hollow tree any more.

He was almost skipping. The forest had an expectant feeling, like it was waiting for something, maybe the rain. He hoped it wouldn't get colder when it rained. Nothing worse than cold rain. Snow was a lot better. He wondered what his friend would think of snow. He had the idea India was pretty hot. Did it ever snow in India? A jay was scolding something off to his right.

When he came to the spot where he usually met the tiger, he looked up and gasped. Where the tiger usually sat was a man. He was sitting there in the middle of the path, just like the tiger. Roy stopped and almost stumbled.

The man had gray hair and a mustache and seemed awfully old. He was smiling, a kind of quiet smile like he was very comfortable and the world was just like it ought to be. He was watching Roy intently, but he didn't say anything.

Roy couldn't think of anything to say. Of course he could have said hello, but the time for that was gone, somehow. The man must have been waiting for him. He didn't seem startled to see him. In fact, he looked like Roy was exactly what he had expected to see.

Roy couldn't tell what color the man's eyes were. He'd never thought about the color of anybody's eyes before, but somehow those eyes reminded him of the tiger's big yellow ones. The man had a little bit of a squint like he'd stared into hard sunlight all his life, but Roy knew his eyes weren't yellow.

Off to his right a woodpecker went to work on a tree.

It seemed to Roy as though they had sat and looked at each other for a long time when the man spoke.

"What is your name?"

He said it in a very kind, friendly sort of way, but the thing that made Roy shiver a little was that the man didn't seem to raise his voice. He was clear up there as far as Roy could throw a good-size rock, and it sounded as though he was sitting beside him right here. His voice also had a sort of strange accent to it.

"Roy Satterly."

The man was quiet for a little, as though he was thinking about that name.

"My name is Jim."

Again, Roy didn't know what to say. Seemed like he ought to say something, but he couldn't think of a thing.

The man looked at him for a little while longer and then stood up. He didn't flounder on the ground and push himself up with his hands. He just sort of unfolded. He was a tall man, Roy saw, and strong-looking despite the years he carried.

He also carried a gun.

The man tucked the gun under his left arm and walked down the trail toward Roy. Roy stood up, too. The man walked right up to him. He didn't crouch down to get their heads on an even plane. He just held out his hand and said, "I'm most happy to meet you, Roy."

Roy put his hand in the man's, and the man closed up his hand firmly and shook it. "Glad to meet you, sir," he squeaked. It embarrassed him.

"No, no, Roy. Not sir. Your manners are excellent, but we shall be friends, and you must call me Jim."

"Yes, sir."

The man looked at him, smiling.

"Uh . . . Jim. Sorry."

"Shall we walk a bit?"

Roy nodded and waited for the man to lead the way. He felt sort of like he was dreaming.

The man started up the path, making room for Roy at his left side. He shifted the gun to his right side. They walked without saying anything until they came to the fallen log by the 'coon tree. The man sat on the log and looked at Roy. He always seemed to have that small smile. Roy sat next to him.

"You know these mountains well, Roy." He wasn't asking a question, but Roy answered anyway.

"Yes."

"And you know all the creatures that live here."

"Most of them. Some of the really wild ones, like the wild pigs, I don't know so well. Only seen a live pig a few times."

"You've seen that boar's head on Turkey Mountain, though."

"Yeah."

"What do you suppose killed him?"

"Snakebite, maybe? Maybe he got sick."

"No."

They were silent for a while. There was no sign of the mother 'coon and her babies.

"Is the tiger your friend, Roy?"

Roy's face went numb. Panic swept over him, and for a second the forest heaved and swayed. His fingernails bit into the flaky bark of the log, and he clenched his teeth. He closed his eyes and tried to take deep breaths without the man knowing it. But he had to answer. He was a gentleman.

"Yes."

Jim was silent for a while. Roy managed to get his balance again. He realized his head had drooped until his chin was almost on his chest. He lifted his chin up, looked at the 'coon tree and then sideways up at Jim. Jim was looking down at him, still smiling.

"Why do you think he's your friend?"

"He comes to see me," Roy said. "I think he wants to tell me something."

Again they fell silent, and the silence was shattered by the tiger's moaning roar, far away.

"He calls," Jim said after a bit. "Is he calling you?"

Roy hadn't even thought about that. He considered it, and then said, "No."

"He doesn't belong here, Roy. You know that."

"Yes."

"Do you see how different the forest is now?"

"What d'you mean?"

"You have other friends in the forest."

"Yes."

"A great many of them, I imagine."

"I guess so."

"How long since you've seen them, Roy?"

He hadn't really thought about that, either.

"A long time, I guess."

"I believe some of your friends lived in that tree there, did they not?"

"Yeah."

"Curious animals. I've never seen their like. What do you call them?"

" 'Coons. Raccoons."

"They're gone."

"They are?"

"So are the deer."

Roy was silent.

"What's he living on, Roy?"

"What—I don't understand."

"The tiger is a big animal, Roy. You know how big he is. He doesn't eat grass or nuts or beetles."

"No."

"What do you suppose he's eating?"

"Sheep?" Roy suggested, suddenly remembering Bobby Willet's story.

"That's quite true. He's had a few sheep."

They were silent for a time. The woodpecker hammered again. Roy was tense. He knew what was coming.

"I expect someone has already told you the tiger is killing people."

"Yes."

"Do you believe that?"

"No. I don't think he'd do that. He hasn't tried to kill me."

"He killed a man right after he killed my sheep."

"How do you know?"

"I put what was left of the man in a bag yesterday. Not far from here."

"What do you mean, what was left of him?"

"Roy, the tiger ate him."

The boy's face paled. Jim put a hand on his shoulder. It wasn't heavy, pressing down, it was just there, kind of warm.

"That is what he must do to stay alive here, Roy. There is really nothing else for him to do."

"I still don't believe you." Roy said.

"Ah," was all the man said to that. There was another silence.

"The tiger came to see you day before yesterday, didn't he?"

"Yes," said Roy, startled again. "How did you know?"

"Oh, I think you could guess the answer to that, Roy. Now tell me, did he look different to you that evening?"

Roy thought back, remembering the tiger sitting there on the path.

"I guess he did."

"Was the fur around his mouth red?"

"Yeah."

"That was blood, Roy. The blood of a soldier, a man named Luck."

"Did the tiger kill that hog on Turkey Mountain?" Roy asked after a bit.

"I believe so."

"Maybe he killed another one day before yesterday."

"The wild pigs left with the deer and the raccoons and the rabbits, Roy."

They were silent again for a while. Roy looked at Jim. The man was still smiling at him, his hand still on his shoulder.

"You don't live around here, do you?" Roy asked.

"No," said Jim.

Roy looked at the gun, propped against the log.

"You came here to kill him."

"Yes," said Jim. "I'm sorry for that, Roy. But there is no other way."

"Where did you come from?"

"From the same place as the tiger."

"It's about to rain," Jim said. "I must be going." He stood and stretched.

"Okay," said Roy. "I better go see about my ma. She works over to Dugan's."

"I see," Jim said. He held out his hand, and Roy took it. "Perhaps we can talk again tomorrow. You might show me around your forest."

"All right," Roy said.

Jim tucked the gun under his right arm, turned, and walked up the path. Roy watched him out of sight, but the man never looked back.

The rain began before Roy got home and was falling steadily when he was ready to leave for Dugan's. He looked at his shoes. They didn't seem as important as they did this morning, but he still didn't want to get them all muddy.

He stuffed a sock in each shoe, and then found a plastic bag in the kitchen. He put the shoes in the bag, wrapped it around itself and tucked them under his arm. He picked up the umbrella and left for Dugan's.

All the way there he thought about the man, Jim, and the things he had said. He liked the man, he decided. He liked him a lot. But he couldn't believe the tiger was hurting people, eating them. He was a good animal. Roy was certain of that. But he was also pretty certain that Jim was a good man. Probably a gentleman. He couldn't make sense of it.

At Dugan's he went straight back to the washroom, washed his feet off, dried them with paper towels, and put on his shoes and socks. Annie noticed what he'd done and grinned at him. Rose was happy to see him, but she didn't notice he'd arrived in the rain with clean shoes.

Just before closing time the man who'd given Rose the money for his shoes and coat came in. He smiled at Roy, picked out a lot of groceries and even more beer, and gave Annie a card to pay for them. Roy swallowed and walked up to the man. The man looked down at him and smiled again.

"Thank you very much, sir," Roy said. Rose beamed at him.

"Mighty good-lookin' boots you got there, son," the man said. "Look brand new."

He leaned down to write on the paper Annie gave him, then looked out the door. The rain had stopped.

"Kinda muddy out there. You and your ma ready to leave, I'd be proud to give you a ride home."

Roy helped the man carry his groceries to the truck. The man opened a back door for Rose and helped her in, flustering her. He nodded Roy toward the front passenger seat. "You ride shotgun this time," he said.

Roy got into the front seat, looked back, and smiled at Rose. She smiled back at him, sort of confused.

When they got to the tarpaper house, the man looked at Roy.

"Take care of your ma, now. Help her out of the car."

He did, taking her hand like the man had.

"Thank you," she said, more or less to both of them.

"Thank you, sir," Roy said.

"My pleasure," he said, backing the car around and heading back toward the highway.

Rolls swung out onto the highway, his mind on the boy. Nice kid. Bright. Bad situation, but he'd seen worse. A whole hell of a lot worse.

He turned up the dirt track to the cabin and had to concentrate on driving; the road was a little slick. The rain hadn't come back but the sky was heavy, clouds obscuring the top of Raven Bald.

When he pulled up to the cabin, Oppenheimer popped out of the front door and hurried down the steps. "Get your contracts signed, Bernie?" Rolls asked.

"Oh yes, yes. But I just reached the Buchholz family, and they've agreed to sign, too. I'm going to take the car and go meet them."

"They don't know a hell of a lot, now, Bernie."

"Yes, yes, you said that. But they don't want a hell of a lot of money, either. I gather they're well off."

"Well, help me get this stuff upstairs and it's all yours. You're gonna miss the party, though."

"Oh, this shouldn't take that long. The big ones we need to sew up are the sheriff and this hunter he won't even identify. When do you want to move on them?"

"Bernie, I can't talk to somebody I don't know his name or where he is. The sheriff, now, from what I hear, he'll be tough. A real straight arrow. I'll try to feel him out this weekend."

The groceries and beer in the kitchen, Rolls handed Oppenheimer the keys to the Pathfinder. "Road down to the highway's a little slick, Bernie. Take it easy. You won't get stuck on it, but if you run it into the ditch we'll have to get a crane to pull it out."

"Patrick, Patrick. I always take it easy."

"You take it any way you can get it, Counselor," Rolls said, rubbing Oppenheimer's bald head. "Get some more ice on your way back."

Rolls filled the refrigerator with beer, stuffed the hamburger in where he could find room, and went back to his bedroom to shower and change clothes.

When the guests arrived Monday evening, a log fire was crackling in the huge stone fireplace, and the charcoal was glowing in the grill on the deck that ran across the front of the cabin. Bentley, the woman from St. Paul, and the *Washington Post* arrived in one car. the *New York Times*, *The Inquirer*, and the *Miami Herald* came in another.

Oppenheimer had not returned. The rain had slackened and finally stopped, but clouds had advanced well down the mountain. Darkness was coming early.

Rolls pulled the hamburger out of the refrigerator and tossed it to the *Washington Post*. "You're the only one knows how to do this right. Go to it." The *Post* fancied himself a first-rate chef.

"Yeah," said Bentley, popping a beer. "Get 'em on and get 'em done before that sonofabitch gets a whiff of 'em, wherever he is. For all we know he may like his meat well done."

"That hadn't occurred to me," said the *Post*, startled. Bentley offered to stand guard over him.

The woman from the *Pioneer Press* was awed by her present company, but she had nonetheless vowed she would not be relegated to cooking. However, when she saw the august *Post* leave the kitchen with a stack of hamburger patties, followed by Bentley, she took over the preparation of the condiments, then joined the rest of the party in front of the fireplace in the main room.

On the deck, the *Post* was flipping patties and applying a barbecue sauce while Bentley looked out over the valley. "You didn't get a beer," she observed. "Want one?"

"Yes," the *Post* said, glancing nervously at the gathering darkness. "Thank you very much." Bentley went back into the kitchen and brought the *Post* a beer. Rolls, always simplifying, had bought only one kind.

The cloud had enveloped the roof of the cabin, and its clammy fingers were reaching the deck. "Do you suppose the tiger really could smell this?" the *Post* asked.

"From what I've been reading, there's a difference of opinion over how well a tiger can smell," Bentley said. "And I expect this fog will damp down smells like it does sound. So I suppose it'd depend on how close he is. Very close, it'd be damn hard to miss. Those burgers smell super."

"Perhaps we ought to finish in the kitchen," said the *Post*, nearly dropping a patty when he tried to turn it.

"Hell, no," said Bentley, on her second beer. "Wouldn't taste as good. Sumbitch comes around here, I'll scratch his eyeballs out."

Rolls stepped out and looked at the cloud, which had dropped below the level of the deck, limiting vision to five feet or so.

"Goddamn, looks like a Lon Chaney movie out here," he said. "How we comin'?"

"If you would be so good as to fetch a platter," said the *Post*, "the first run will be ready."

Rolls stepped back to the door and bellowed through the screen. "Hey, Ross, bring a platter out here. Meat's ready." There was an answering shout from the living room.

"Hell, I don't know. Just look around the kitchen. Any old plate'll do."

The *Times* stepped onto the porch with a dinner plate, and the *Post* loaded it with patties.

"Can I make you one?" Bentley asked the *Post*.

"Thank you," he said. "That would be very kind. But don't be too long."

"Nervous?" she asked.

"Frankly, yes."

"Okay."

"Gimme some room," she said in the kitchen. "Gotta feed the cook. He's a little worried we might have another guest."

"We will," said Rolls.

There was a sudden silence.

"Bernie's not here yet," he explained with a cackle.

"Who the fuck's Bernie?" asked the *Inquirer*. "Oh, you mean Bernie from the *Chronicle*."

"No, I mean Bernie Oppenheimer, the mouthpiece. We're a team."

Bentley got the burger built and took it back to the deck, where the *Post* was beginning to look a little wild-eyed. The fog was creeping in under the roof that covered most of the deck.

"Ah," he said with relief.

"Here y'are, darlin'," Bentley drawled, batting her eyelashes in broad burlesque. "Brought you another beer, too."

"Thank you very kindly, Kathy," said the *Post*. "Where's your burger?"

"I'll have one from the last batch," she said.

"You're a cop reporter, aren't you?" he asked. "How'd you draw this one?"

"Somebody at DNR called our outdoor guy," Bentley said, leaning back against the wall, watching the tendrils of fog weave onto the deck. "He thought it was a crock of shit and mentioned it to me. I called up here, and from the reaction I got I knew damn well it was true. They had to let me have the story. Couple hundred miles outside my beat, but shit, we're dealin' with cops, aren't we?"

Light from the window beside Bentley glinted off the fog. The hamburgers sizzled as the *Post* pressed them to the grill. Muffled conversation seeped out from the living room.

"That must be Rolls's lawyer comin' now," Bentley said. Looking over the porch, she could see yellow headlights in the distance. "Got him some foglights. That's good. You 'bout done?"

"Almost," said the *Post*.

"Headlights disappeared," she commented. "Ah, there they are again. Musta gone behind something." She stared out into the fog and then slowly straightened up.

"Wait a minute," said Bentley, her eyes narrowing. "We had to come way uphill to get here. Those damn lights are up high, not down low. What the hell is this?"

The *Post* looked over his shoulder. It took him a while to pick up the lights. They blinked a couple of times. "Strange," he said.

Bentley took a couple of steps toward the edge of the deck. "I don't think those are headlights," she said.

"What are they, then?" asked the *Post*, his voice breaking.

"Just a minute," she said and walked closer. She stopped in midstride and backed up. "Holy sweet Jesus H. Christ," she whispered. "Put that shit down real careful and start for the door. Don't run. Walk slow and smooth."

"Wha-what is it?" The spatula clanked against the grill.

"Eyes," said Bentley, backing sideways toward the door. "Those aren't headlights, they're eyes."

"Oh, God," whimpered the *Post*.

"It'll be okay," Bentley whispered. "You close to the door?"

"Halfway."

"I'm about there," she said, entering the patch of light thrown through the door's panes. "I'll get it open."

The eyes bobbed lower. "Oh, shit," Bentley whispered. They raised back up.

Her hands, held behind her, felt the door. She groped for the knob, found it, turned. It wouldn't budge. Harder. No go.

"Fuckin' door's locked," she muttered.

"Oh, God," gasped the *Post*. "We're dead."

"Hell we are," said Bentley. She hammered on the door with the heel of her shoe. The eyes narrowed. The sound of laughter drifted in from the living room. The eyes, which had been somewhat to her left, disappeared. She kicked the door as hard as she could, backward, three times. She felt the *Post* draw next to her, on her left.

"What is it?" someone yelled from the living room. She kicked the door again, three times, four. She stopped when the eyes reappeared. They seemed the same distance away, but now they were right in front of her.

She heard someone in the kitchen. A puff of breeze hit the fog, and it swirled to reveal the tiger's head, upside down just beyond the eaves.

It was on the roof.

The door opened, flooding the porch with light.

"Sorry," said Rolls. "Musta locked it by mistake."

"Shut up," whispered Bentley. "Get outta the way." To the *Post*: "You ready?"

The *Post* managed a tiny whimper of assent.

Bentley stepped forward, pulling the screen open. The tiger growled like thunder in the fog. She flung herself backward into the kitchen and collapsed on her back. The *Post* whirled around the open screen and fell over Bentley, who was shriek-ing "Shut the door! Shut the door!"

Rolls, who had been watching their maneuvers with a quiz-zical grin, heard the tiger this time. Everybody did. "Jesus," he yelped, slamming the door shut. As he did, the headlights of the Pathfinder lit up the porch. The tiger disappeared.

Oppenheimer pulled the truck up close to the deck, doused the lights, and pulled the key out of the ignition. He heard faint yells and screams from inside the cabin. He hesitated. Now what? Damned reporters, acted like children. Probably drunk already.

When he opened the door, he heard Rolls's voice. ". . . in the car, Bernie! Tiger. . . ." Oppenheimer slammed the door shut again and was fumbling with the key, trying to get it back into the ignition, when the roof struck him on the head, knocking him unconscious.

Rolls yanked the door shut after hearing Oppenheimer close the car door. The fog was so thick they could see nothing, and the truck was below the level of the deck. "Douse the lights," Rolls snapped.

"Damn thing was on the roof over the deck," Bentley said. "Looking at us upside down. Goddamn head looked like a washtub. What the hell are we gonna do if it decides to come in here?"

Nobody had an answer.

In the Pathfinder, Oppenheimer returned to consciousness with a start. He was lying across the emergency brake handle. It felt as though it had worked its way between his ribs. He raised himself off it on an elbow and looked around. The roof of the truck was caved in about a foot. The windshield and the front windows were fogged to opacity from his breathing. He raised up as straight as he could and looked out the back. The windows were clear, but the fog was too dense to see anything.

Sighing, he rubbed the top of his head. There was no blood, and it didn't hurt much. Still a little dazed, he pulled out his handkerchief and swiped at the windshield.

The tiger was lying on the hood, its face three inches from the glass.

Oppenheimer screamed. The tiger roared, spraying the windshield with hot breath and saliva. Oh God, what can I do? Start the car. Start the car, that's it. He reached for the ignition. No key. He began fumbling in his jacket pockets, and the tiger roared again and flipped into a crouch. Oppenheimer remembered he'd been trying to start the car when the roof hit him. Keys on the floor. He ducked down and groped for them. There they are. Thank God.

He straightened up and stabbed at the ignition, missing. The tiger roared and drew back a huge paw. Something flickered in the fog behind it; Oppenheimer saw. It was the tiger's tail, whipping from side to side.

He got the key in the ignition, turned it, and the engine started. The tiger lunged forward, bringing its paw down on the windshield like a hammer. The glass crumpled and sagged, and the paw thrust into the truck, slashing past his face. Oppenheimer stomped on the accelerator and yanked the gear lever into reverse. The truck lurched back fifteen feet, and he felt the front end bob up and heard the tiger snarl as it fell off. He hit the brakes and switched on the headlights, but he could see nothing but fog through the rip in the crumpled glass.

He began honking the horn, then stopped after a few seconds. There was silence. Oppenheimer realized his nose hurt. He reached up to touch it and came back with blood on his hand. He remembered those ungodly huge claws flashing past like a set of knives. One of them had sliced open his nose. He held his handkerchief to it and shuddered.

In the cabin, they heard the tiger's roars, the engine starting, and the crunchy shattering of the glass.

"Oh. Jesus, it's got him," moaned the *Pioneer Press*.

Then the Pathfinder's horn beeped through the fog. "He's okay," Rolls said. "He got rid of the damn thing somehow."

No one felt like going out to investigate, however, and the people in the cabin eventually went to sleep, sprawled wherever there was room. In the Pathfinder, Oppenheimer had no intention of opening the door; the crushed windshield was bad enough. He lay awake most of the night, dozing off just before dawn. The bleeding had stopped.

October 25

Tuesday morning when the sun had burned the clouds off the mountains Roy found Graham sitting on the log where they had talked yesterday.

"Good morning, Roy."

"Morning, uh . . . Jim."

"I brought some breakfast. Not very fresh, but they're homemade," Graham said, pulling a small package from his jacket pocket and unwrapping two blueberry muffins. He handed one to Roy when the boy sat down next to him.

"Thank you," he said, biting into it eagerly.

They finished eating in silence.

"Did the tiger come to your window last night?"

"No."

"I thought not. I understand he was busy on that mountain on the other side of your house—what it's name?"

"Raven Bald."

"Ah. And do ravens live there?"

"Yes, at the top."

"It's been a very long time since I've seen a raven. Can we go there?"

"Sure," said Roy, picking crumbs off his T-shirt and popping them in his mouth. He noticed Graham was carrying his gun.

They walked back down Copperhead Mountain and came out of the woods near Roy's house. The road was soft from yesterday's rain and they stopped to discuss the stories it had to tell.

Roy, to Graham's delight, could identify every print on the road.

"Now, this fox," Graham said. "Tell me about him."

"What do you mean?"

"Was he out for a stroll or was he in a hurry? How old is he? How big is he?"

"I don't know any of that."

"Well, let's look closely, Roy. Here he comes up out of the ditch and onto the road. His prints seem pretty evenly placed, not too deep, but see here, they're sort of frayed looking, splayed out. From all that you could guess that he came up on the road at a walk. He's about medium size and getting rather up in years.

"Now here in the middle of the road he stops—see how the prints get a little blurred—and steps a bit to one side with his front feet. What do you think he was doing?"

Roy looked at the prints with a faraway gaze. Graham could tell the boy was picturing a fox and its movements, trying to see why a fox might make prints like that.

"Well . . . maybe he stopped to look behind him?"

"That's what I would guess, Roy. Perhaps he heard something. Now look at his tracks. D'you see how his stride is longer now than it was when he stepped onto the road? Whatever he heard or saw, he decided to get out of the open quickly. I'd say he left the road at a trot."

They started up Raven Bald.

"How did you learn to read tracks so well, Roy?"

"I just learned, I guess," the boy said.

"No one taught you?"

"Oh, no."

"You don't go to school, do you?"

Trouble, Roy thought. Better be honest.

"No."

"Don't you want to?"

"I don't know. I guess I will when it's time."

They walked for a while in silence.

"How did you learn to read tracks?" Roy asked.

"Oh, my father taught me most of it, and the rest I learned from experience, like you."

"How did your father learn?"

"He told me his teacher was an old poacher."

"What's a poacher?"

"A man who hunts illegally."

"What did he hunt?"

"There was a great deal to hunt in the forests where I grew up, in northern India, in a district called Kumaon. The main quarry for a poacher would be kakar and chital, which are small deer, and sambar, somewhat like your elk although not quite that big. Then there were serow, a kind of forest buffalo, but they were uncommon. There was wild pig, of course, very similar to what you have here. Our major predators were the tiger and the leopard. We also had a bear, the Himalayan bear, rather larger and a good deal fiercer than your black bears."

"What's a predator?"

"A predator is an animal that kills other animals for food."

Roy thought for a while.

"I don't think there are any of those around here." he said, "except maybe wildcats and foxes and small things like that. Nothing big."

"Not any more, Roy. There used to be what people called cougars or panthers, like leopards, but they've all been killed. I spent much of my life trying to keep that from happening to the tiger."

"You said that kind of funny," Roy said. "Like your life was over."

Graham chuckled. "I'd rather thought it was," he said.

They reached the crest of Raven Bald in silence and sat on a smooth boulder.

"If you spent all that time trying to keep people from killing tigers, why did you come here?" Roy finally asked.

"Because this tiger is killing human beings, Roy, and it is doing that because it cannot kill anything else."

"Why can't he kill deer?"

"This tiger is a poor hunter. It was lucky to kill that pig. It never had a chance to learn to hunt properly, or perhaps it forgot. Deer are too quick for it, and there aren't enough of them anyway. They simply leave the area."

"Why hasn't he killed me?"

Graham did not answer immediately. Roy noticed that the man was looking at him intently. He saw that Graham's eyes were blue, not yellow, but they still reminded him somehow of the tiger's eyes.

"Roy," he finally said, "I have seen some very strange things in the forest, things that no man could explain, but this tiger's behavior toward you is the strangest of all. I have been trying to find an answer to your question for several days. I do not have one."

Roy didn't reply. As they sat there, a hoarse, croaking cry sounded above them. They looked up to see two enormous, coal-black birds cruising effortlessly overhead.

"Ah," said Graham. "The ravens of Raven Bald. Beautiful."

"They sure can fly, can't they?" said Roy.

"Oh yes, they are great acrobats, to be sure."

They watched the birds in silence.

Eventually, Graham looked at Roy and said, "Where do you think the tiger is now, Roy?"

"I don't know. Where?"

"No, no. Think about it. Just think and see if you can tell where he might be."

Roy considered for a while.

"I don't think he's very far away."

"You're right," said Graham. "He's watching us."

"Where is he?"

"Somewhere in front of us."

"You don't see him?"

"No. I wouldn't expect to. He may not be a fine hunter, but he's certainly not incompetent."

"How do you know he's in front of us?"

"The wind is at our backs. He would approach only from downwind."

"Maybe he'll come out."

"Not while I'm here."

"Do you think he wants to kill you?"

"Not while you're here."

"Why not?"

"I'm not sure, but I'm certain there's no danger. In fact, he's been with us for some time. Followed us most of the way here."

"Will you kill him now?"

"No. I will not fire at him in your presence without your permission," Graham said in a strange voice, as though he was reading instructions.

Roy did not question that. Graham also noted that the boy had asked only how he knew the tiger was in front of them—not how he knew the tiger was present in any case.

"Perhaps we'd best go back now," Jim said, rising. He put the rifle under his arm, the way he always carried it. Roy stood up, and they began walking back the way they came.

Pat Rolls's guests didn't venture out of the cabin until the fog was gone Tuesday morning; Rolls had gone out earlier to get Oppenheimer, whom he found sleeping fitfully in the Path-finder. The blood sprinkled here and there unnerved him until he saw the lawyer's nose.

"Jesus, Bernie, he clipped you on the nose."

"Yes, yes. Thank God I saw it coming and reared back or he would have ripped my face off."

"Doesn't look very bad. You don't have much meat on that beak. You hurtin' anywhere else?"

"Not really. Head's a little sore, that's all."

"Come on in the cabin. You got your phone?"

"My God, I forgot all about it. I could've called for help last night."

"Wouldn't have mattered. Tiger was long gone before anyone could have gotten here—at least, I think he was. With that fog you'd never know."

The reporters left, arguing loudly over who had been in the greatest danger. Rolls called for another car, and when it came he took Oppenheimer to the hospital emergency room.

Much fuss was made over an ambulatory tiger victim. His nose was cleaned, thoroughly disinfected, and sewn up. It took four stitches.

"Not enough blood supply there on the bridge of the nose to spread the infection very fast," said the doctor. "Gonna have a bit of a scar, though, I'm afraid."

"Good, good," said Oppenheimer. "In LA, I can eat lunch on this scar for a year at least. I know some lawyers with very unsavory clients, but by God I'll be the only one in the courthouse who survived a man-eating tiger's attack."

Back in the new car—a Cherokee this time—Rolls said, "You know, Counselor, you're gonna have to sign yourself to a contract. You're part of the story now."

Rolls pulled into the sheriff's department parking lot. "Let's see if Brickhouse is here," he said.

Brickhouse was. He rose to greet Rolls and Oppenheimer.

"Mr. Rolls, it's a pleasure to meet you. I guess anybody who ever read a newspaper has heard of you."

SHIKAR *293*

"Thank you, sir. This is Bernie Oppenheimer, an attorney. We both work for Nova Corporation, which makes television docudramas. Did you see the one on Koresh and his Rancho Apocalypse at Waco?"

"No sir, I don't watch a lot of television, but I did know one was made. How do you do, Mr. Oppenheimer? You pick up that cut last night?" Brickhouse had already heard about the tiger's attempt to crash Rolls's party.

"Yes, yes, that I did."

"I suppose the tiger is why you folks are here."

"You bet," Rolls said. "I expect we'll start shooting within a couple of weeks after he's dead. Can't see any reason not to make the whole picture right here."

"Well, that'd be real fine," Brickhouse said. "Harte County economy needs all the film crews it can get."

"Sheriff, you're way too smart to creep up on, so I'll lay it on the line for you. We'd like to sign you to an exclusive contract to tell us your story after this is over. Doesn't stop you from carrying out any of your duties, including keeping the press informed. We just want your entire account, beginning to end, everything you know, saw, and felt about this."

Brickhouse grinned.

"Half a mil, Sheriff," Oppenheimer said quietly.

"Mr. Rolls," Brickhouse said, "you're way too smart to really think I'm going to do that. I'm a public servant. Public servants don't sign exclusive contracts. If anybody's got a right to my story, as you put it, it would be our little weekly newspaper here. You understand that?"

"Of course I do, Sheriff. I didn't expect anything different from you, but you know I had to try."

"Sure," Brickhouse said. "Now, when this is all over, if it

ever is, come on around and we'll talk. I'll compromise myself to the extent of letting you buy me dinner if you promise Arnold Schwarzenegger plays me in your movie."

A little way down the mountain, at a bare spot in the trail, Graham pointed silently at the ground. The tiger's pugmarks overlaid their footprints.

They were almost in sight of the road, at a spot where a fallen log offered a good seat, when Graham called a break. They sat quietly for a while.

"Was the woods where you grew up a lot like this?" Roy asked.

"Oh, it didn't look so very different," Graham said, "but it was a more remote place. Hotter in the summer, I would imagine. On a clear day, you could always see the snow on the Himalayas."

"What are those?"

"The Himalayas? Oh, they are mountains, huge mountains. They made my hills, and yours, look like ant heaps. Their peaks are covered with snow all year 'round."

"Do tigers like that?"

"Not at all. Tigers don't live in the Himalayas. The only cat that lives there, I believe, is the snow leopard. Very few people have ever seen one."

After a little silence, Graham resumed, his voice dreamlike and faraway.

"The biggest difference between your forest and mine, I believe, is sound. There were many more animals, and many more noisy ones, in mine. If I was looking for tiger or leopard, I always had plenty of help from other creatures in the forest."

Roy had his knees drawn up, his head resting on them. "What do you mean?" he asked.

"Well, the tiger and the leopard are solitary animals. Male or female, they live alone except during mating season. But most of the creatures in my forest are social animals and they live in large communities.

"For instance, the langur monkeys. They live in big troops in the treetops. While most of the group is feeding, guards are posted to keep a lookout. When they see danger—a tiger or especially a leopard—they make a loud call. They keep on calling as long as they can see the danger, and they usually follow it for a while to make sure it's not trying to sneak around them. If they decide they are being hunted, they make a somewhat different call, and the whole troop runs away through the trees.

"Our deer—kakar, chital, and sambar—are the same. They live in herds, or large family groups, and they post sentries. The sentries stamp their feet and make their danger calls: Some have funny barks, others a kind of sneeze.

"So, you see, in a forest fairly teeming with these animals, a person with good hearing can often follow the progress of a tiger or a leopard as it moves around. Birds are a help, too, just as they are here."

"Are there elephants in your forest?"

"No, the elephants and the rhinoceroses live further south, where it's warmer all the time. There are very, very few of them left now, I believe."

"Don't you live in your forest anymore?"

"No."

"Why not?"

"It's very complicated, Roy. It has to do with politics, and with people of different colors. Do you understand any of that?"

"I've heard of politics, but I'm not sure what they are," Roy said. "I seen some dark-colored people in Hartesville."

"Well, let's just say that a time came when I no longer felt welcome, and I thought it best to leave. I rather wish now that I had not; I believe I might have been too hasty. But it can't be helped."

"Why did you spend so much time trying to keep people from shooting tigers?" Roy asked.

"Because I love tigers. Because I think they are nature's noblest creation. Because no kind of creature should be wiped out, like your panthers were. But also, I have come to think, because man needs something to fear besides himself. We must always have creatures that dare us to put away our guns and walk out into the dark. Can you understand that?"

"I don't know. I've never been afraid of an animal."

"I see," said Graham, very quietly, looking intently at Roy again. "I see."

Graham walked back to his shack through the meadows at the foot of Copperhead Mountain. It had already been a fairly long day; he had much to consider, and he didn't relish the idea of trekking over the mountain while being followed by a man-eater no longer inhibited by Roy's presence.

As he approached the cabin, he suddenly realized he was walking on the tiger's pugmarks. It had gone ahead of him.

Bringing up the rifle, thumb on the safety, he continued slowly, watching every possible piece of cover. His forest sense was broadcasting no warning, however, and despite his caution he didn't think the man-eater was waiting for him.

The tiger's prints led directly to his door and then away into the forest.

———

There was still a little light left when Roy finished the vegetables Rose cooked, so he went out back to sit up against a log and think about things. He had just gotten comfortable when he saw the tiger watching him from the edge of the forest. It was looking at him the same way Jim did sometimes, like it was trying to see something inside him.

After a while he tried to turn his mind to the things Jim had said that day, about the way he could tell what an animal was doing and what it was like just from its tracks, but he couldn't think about anything but the animal that was watching him. It was lying down, just barely visible.

As Roy watched the tiger the sun sank below Raven Bald, but it wasn't cold, and he began to get drowsy. It was getting so dark he couldn't be sure he was seeing the tiger anymore. At some point, Roy fell asleep. He was never sure, despite later examination, just when that happened. He didn't know if the tiger licking his cheek with a tongue like sandpaper was real or a dream. It seemed awfully real. The tiger's breath was enough to wake anybody up. But he was never really sure.

What came next, he knew, was a dream. He was trotting through the forest, full of an incredible feeling of power, of strength. A really big fallen tree was in his way, but he didn't go around or scramble over it. He leaped over it in one flowing motion. At that point he realized he was running on four feet, not two, and when he looked down in surprise he saw that he was a tiger.

Being a tiger was splendid. He could run like the wind and jump over almost anything. And he was so big: When he stopped and reared up against a tree, he saw he was at least three times as tall as a boy.

Gradually he became aware of a problem. His belly bothered him. After he thought about it a minute, sitting there and looking around at the forest, he realized what it was. He was hungry. He'd been hungry before, plenty of times, but only from missing a meal or two. The way he felt now, he hadn't eaten in days.

As he was sitting there, wondering what to do, he saw a movement down the side of the mountain. Without thinking, he flattened himself out, hugging the ground behind a dead bush. The brush down there moved again, and now Roy could see it was a deer, a big buck. Automatically he began to creep, oozing along the ground, angling from one patch of cover to another, sniffing the wind, always keeping the wind blowing from the deer to him.

After a long time, it seemed, he got to within forty feet of the buck. The deer was nervous, foraging along on the ground for a few seconds, then raising its head, shifting its ears, trying the wind for scent. He knew he couldn't get any closer unnoticed.

His hindquarters gathered under him and he sort of coiled himself up, summoning all his power. Behind him, his tail twitched spasmodically. He hadn't thought about having a tail. He gathered himself, waiting for the buck to lower its head once more. When it did, he leaped toward it.

It took him two bounds to reach the spot but the buck wasn't there anymore. It was crashing down the mountainside, and Roy knew he wasn't fast enough to chase it. His stomach hurt so bad it made him cry.

That was when he woke up. Darkness had fallen, and that disoriented him for a few minutes, for in his dream it had been a bright morning. When he got his bearings, he went inside. Rose was already asleep. Roy, still a little dazed, undressed and went to bed. He remembered no more dreams that night, but when he awoke before dawn he was tired.

October 26

On Wednesday morning it was Graham who found Roy waiting for him on the fallen tree by the tiger path. It was clear that something was troubling the boy.

After some desultory conversation and a long silence, Roy asked, "Can tigers cry?"

"Why, I don't really know. I've never seen one that looked as though it was crying. I've seen tigers that looked content, perhaps even happy; tigers that were raging mad, annoyed, or disgusted. But I can't recall ever seeing one that appeared to be sad or weeping. Why do you ask?"

After some hesitation, Roy told him about the tiger's visit.

"Shall we go and see how much was a dream and how much was real?" Graham asked.

"All right," Roy said. To Graham, he seemed strangely reluctant.

They went down to the log behind Roy's house, and Graham studied the ground.

"He came to you, Roy. He sat right in front of you for a little while, close enough to touch you. Then he went back into the forest over there."

They walked back up the path to the fallen tree and sat down again.

"What about the rest of it, the dream?" Roy asked.

"The tiger gave it to you," Graham said.

"How?" Roy asked. "Why?"

"Various experiences have convinced me that in certain circumstances dreams can be induced. I have no idea how. As to why the tiger gave you the dream, I don't know that, either."

Roy was quiet for a while. He couldn't shake off the dream.

"It must be really nice to be a tiger," he said finally.

"Why do you think so?"

"In that dream, I felt so strong. So fast. I felt like . . . I don't know, like . . . like I was in charge of the whole forest."

"Ah," said Graham.

After another silence, Graham pointed out a tiny bird, with a black head, pale blue wings, and white body, flitting from tree to tree. "What do you call that bird?" he asked. "I've never seen one quite like it."

"That's a chickadee."

"*Feee-bee-eee,*" the bird piped.

"*Fee-beee-ee,*" Graham replied. Roy was astonished. Graham sounded exactly like the chickadee.

Slowly, the Englishman reached into his right-hand coat pocket and withdrew a handful of seeds.

"*Feee-bee,*" he chirped again. "*Feee-bee-ee.*" He held the seeds in his open hand, resting on his knee. He was completely relaxed.

The chickadee hopped from tree to tree, watching Graham closely. When it called, he called back. To Roy, he seemed made of stone. He didn't even seem to be breathing. Roy tried to be just as still.

After a while, the chickadee flew tentatively to the end of the fallen tree, six feet from Graham. Roy couldn't see it without moving, and he didn't dare move. The bird came hopping slowly down the log. Roy didn't see it again until it flew up briefly and settled on Graham's thumb.

The chickadee ate the seeds one by one, grabbing each and then looking at Graham as it swallowed. Graham was smiling at it. The little bird ate a dozen or more seeds before flying back into the forest.

Slowly, Graham turned from stone back to flesh. Roy was still holding his breath.

"Being a man is not so bad either," Graham said, handing the seeds to the boy.

When it was time to go home, Roy asked, "What do you think I should I do if the tiger comes to talk to me again?"

"Listen to him. You're the first human being I've known who's been taken into a tiger's confidence."

"It's kind of scary."

"Ah. Are you afraid of him now?"

"No, I know he won't hurt me. It's just that . . . well, at first, it seemed natural. Now, I . . . I guess I know it's not natural."

"Oh, I wouldn't say it's not natural, Roy. If it's happening, it's natural. But it is most unusual, and if I didn't know you so well, and if I hadn't seen all the tracks, I might think you were dreaming all of it."

"Why did he pick me?"

"Because he knew that you, of all the people here, and maybe of all the people in the world, would be his friend."

The tiger came to Roy's window that night. They watched each other until Roy fell asleep and was a tiger again.

He felt the vast strength, the power and supreme confidence, and the terrible gnawing in his belly. He had to find something to eat.

He walked quietly up a game path, its overhanging brush so low he had to almost crawl to get past it without making noise. He had no idea where his prey was in this forest. In his mind there were dim pictures of greener forest, not so dense, with an odd kind of deer and a really big deer, and lots of them, whole herds of them.

A fitful breeze was blowing down the mountain when he caught the smell of prey. He froze, and a minute later he heard it coming toward him. It was making a lot of noise, snuffling and grunting and digging sounds.

Silently, Roy the tiger melted off the trail and blended into the brush and trees. He moved down the hill until he came to a good ambush spot, downwind from the trail, a place where he could lie unseen yet reach the path in a short bound.

Presently the prey came into view. It was a big wild boar, taking notice of nothing. It was moving slowly, stopping to root along the path for food, grunting and grumbling to itself. Its big tushes had clumps of soft earth clinging to them, and the top of its snout was caked with dirt.

Roy waited. He had never felt so thoroughly alive; he thought he could hear his blood singing in his veins. He never knew hunting could be like this. He concentrated on a spot just past him. When the boar reached that spot, he would launch his charge. He did not want to concentrate on the boar itself until the final instant; it might feel his presence.

Finally the big reddish-black hog entered his peripheral vision, and Roy gathered himself, a depressed coil awaiting release. When its head moved over the spot he had marked, Roy drove backward with his hind legs and roared.

The roar froze the hog for an instant, and an instant was

all Roy needed. He landed on the boar's back, and his teeth sank into its neck, slicing through the heavy muscles. The boar screamed once as it fell, and thrashed wildly. Roy felt bone crunching beneath his teeth and the boar quivered, then relaxed. The smell of its urine and feces pierced Roy's nose.

His stomach screamed and saliva flowed from his mouth, mixing with the blood on the boar's neck. He adjusted his grip and dragged the three-hundred-pound boar off the trail and twenty yards into the forest, where he found a rock outcropping facing the valley. After dragging his kill under the rock, Roy lay down and began eating.

His powerful jaws could slice through the boar's tough hide easily. He took huge bites off the haunch, ripping them free with a jerk of his head. The bloody meat was warm and had a tang to it he liked.

October 27

Roy woke up later than usual on Thursday; the sunlight was slanting into his window. The first thing he did was look at his hands to see whether he was Roy or a tiger.

He felt more confident, more capable than he ever had. He felt as if he could do anything he wanted. He felt, in fact, just like a tiger, except that he wasn't hungry.

He dressed and went outside. Rose was probably still asleep, but he didn't check. He headed straight up Raven Bald, walking briskly but quietly, alert to possibilities.

Nobody had ever asked Roy Satterly what he wanted to be when he grew up. Roy, like his mother, lived one day at a time, and the idea that tomorrow, or the day after, he might do something entirely different never occurred to him.

What else was there to do? His world encompassed the mountains and the forest, his home, Dugan's, and, rather outside it, the Willets' place. It never occurred to him, for instance, that he might go into Hartesville by himself. He wasn't even sure how to get there. In the summer just past, when the days were long, he had hiked north and looked from the top of a mountain upon the village of Norma's Creek, but he had felt no impulse to investigate it.

Today, he felt perhaps there was something else for him to do. It seemed clear to him that was what the tiger was teaching him—to be a tiger. To rule the forest. To be—what was it Jim had called them?—yes, to be a predator.

Without thinking about it, Roy had lengthened his stride into an effortless lope. He was going uphill, but he felt as though he could run this way forever, jumping over small obstacles, dodging others. But he found it hard to hear while he ran, so he dropped his pace back to a walk. He was listening, looking, even smelling.

He crossed the rocks at the top of the mountain, not waiting for a glimpse of the ravens, and continued down the western side. He wasn't tired at all.

As he approached the intersection with another, smaller game trail, he paused. Something was coming, from his right. It wasn't large, and he wasn't sure if he was hearing something or just feeling it. He dropped off the trail and crouched behind a log.

Now he was sure he could hear something, a little scraping among the leaves, and soon a woodchuck came bustling along. Roy waited, gathering his legs under him, and when the 'chuck was just past the log, Roy yelled and leaped forward, seizing the animal by the neck and midsection. Elation and power surged through him.

After breakfast, Graham put a rope around the neck of another sheep and led it up Copperhead Mountain, almost to the top.

The hunter found a decent clearing in a rocky area, tied the sheep to a tree, and climbed a hickory thirty yards away, making himself comfortable in a crotch about fifteen feet high.

After he had checked the cartridges in his rifle, Graham's mind wandered to the subject of Roy and the question of the tiger's behavior toward him. It was entirely beyond his experience, but that was not particularly astonishing. There had been a number of events in Graham's life beyond common experience.

The relationship of Roy and the tiger, however, was an ongoing matter, and Graham knew, without understanding it, that the matter was far more important than a merely inexplicable event. It seemed ominous.

The sheep, which had been grazing placidly around its tree, made a sudden move, and Graham was instantly alert. The sheep turned to face the west and backed to the length of its rope. It stood there silently, watching or listening to something.

Graham caught a glimpse of movement to his left, the direction the sheep was watching, and scanned the area closely. Again, something moved, and there was the sound of a large animal moving carelessly through the forest. Graham relaxed; no tiger would approach its prey with such nonchalance.

In a moment a black bear ambled out of the forest into the clearing and stopped in evident surprise at the sight of the sheep, which was eyeing it nervously. After considering the situation carefully the bear—which was scarcely bigger than the sheep—went shuffling on its way across the mountain. The sheep turned to keep it in view until it disappeared.

The *Harte County Herald* was published on Thursday, and, in a front-page editorial, its editor carefully examined the efforts made to rid his readers of the tiger preying upon them. It had been, he pointed out, almost three weeks since the tiger had been identified. He recalled that entire wars had been decided in less time.

The editor questioned the wisdom of handing the hunt over to one man, a shadowy foreigner who would not even reveal his identity or his tactics to the press. All human residents of the Turkey, Copperhead, and Raven Bald areas had fled to safety long ago, he said—he didn't know about the Satterlys, and he disregarded Rolls and Oppenheimer. Once inept weekend soldiers and misguided hunters stopped going up there to feed the animal, what would happen? Might it stalk the very streets of Hartesville?

The editor concluded the time for half-measures was over. Sheriff Brickhouse and Governor Munson, he said, had done their best, but their best clearly wasn't good enough. He called upon Congress to declare an emergency and send in regular troops, preferably the Rangers from Camp Merrill near Dahlonega.

Accompanying the editorial was a starkly drawn cartoon of a man, a woman, and a child clutching each other behind a barricaded door while in the darkness outside, above the dim mountaintops, a pair of enormous feline eyes blazed.

Weinman looked at the paper on Brickhouse's desk and said, "Joe's on the warpath."

"Can't blame him," Brickhouse said. "Maybe the Rangers are the answer."

"Maybe. Nothing else's worked. So far that poison I put out has killed a few possums and raccoons, one bear, God knows how many birds, and three dogs, two of which had owners who were not happy. No indication the tiger ever even sniffed at any of it. Nobody's even gotten a shot at the damned thing. Hasn't even been much of a fight so far."

"Any more ideas?" Brickhouse asked.

"Not one. Graham want any help?"

"Said he always hunts alone. Figures if there's other guns around, he's more likely to get shot by accident than killed by a tiger."

"Well, I doubt he's got much longer."

The woodchuck squealed and struggled in Roy's grasp. He started to tighten his grip on its neck, and the remembrance of fresh meat and warm blood tickled his mouth.

He flipped the animal over without losing it and looked at its face. Its eyes blazed, and its little teeth were bared.

For a second Roy seemed to step away from himself and realize that he was about to deliberately kill an animal. He had never done that. Why was he doing it now?

Because it's what tigers do.

When they're hungry.

Jim said tigers never killed more than they needed. I'm not hungry. He could still recall in a hazy way the dream-taste of the boar, but now the thought of trying to bite through all that fur made him feel a little sick.

Gently he turned the frantic woodchuck right side up, set it on the path, and let it go. It ran into the woods as fast as its short legs would carry it.

Roy got up, brushed the leaves and bits of dirt off himself, and continued down the mountain.

After the bear left, Graham's sheep grazed a little longer and then lay down in a patch of sunlight and went to sleep. Graham watched a pair of young cottontails play in the clearing, chasing each other with acrobatic leaps and turns and generally celebrating life. They weren't interested in squandering it, however, and when a hawk began to circle high overhead, they retired into the trees.

Roy was striding downhill, going nowhere in particular. He was trying to sort out his thoughts, but they all seemed jumbled up and kind of slippery, like strawberry jelly. They oozed away completely when he noticed, well off through the trees, the cabin built into the side of the mountain. He had seen it a couple of times before. It looked real nice, but nobody ever seemed to live there.

This time, however, he noticed a fancy truck parked outside, and without thinking about it swerved off the path and started through the woods toward the cabin. Also without thinking about it, he was staying close to the trees, generally keeping at least one between him and the cabin.

Near the tree line there was a big azalea thicket, and he moved into it, rather surprised at himself. He'd never crawled into the undergrowth before. Once in it, he sat down and studied the cabin.

He realized he could hear the murmur of men's voices, at least two of them, coming from the cabin, and an occasional clink that sounded like eating noises, forks or spoons on a plate. He sat there quietly, watching. There was a lot of thicket between him and the house, but the leaves were mostly gone and he could see the cabin fairly well.

He had no idea how much time had passed before he heard some louder clanks, maybe dishes going into a sink, and pretty soon two men came out on the porch. They stood there a few minutes, then walked forward and sat down on the steps. Roy saw that one of them was the man who'd paid for his new shoes and jacket, both of them in his closet today. The other was a smaller man, bald. He was smoking a cigarette. Roy could smell it even from the thicket.

He was pretty sure they couldn't see him unless they looked close, and they weren't paying any particular attention to anything, just sitting there and talking. Slowly he backed out of the thicket, staying low, and trotted up the side of the mountain to the place where the cabin was built into the earth. It was steep, but he had no trouble hopping from the rocky mountainside onto the roof.

Carefully he slipped along the side of the roof until he reached the separate roof that covered the porch. He dropped lightly onto it and crept forward until he was almost above the two men. He could see them, and hear their conversation.

He listened for a while, but they weren't talking about anything he understood. The bald man flicked his cigarette off the porch, and anger, an unusual feeling, welled through the boy. His bare feet worked for purchase on the coarse shingles and his legs tensed. He coiled himself to spring.

Then he remembered he was only a boy, no match for either of the grown men below. He needed claws, fangs. He thought of the long knife Jim carried. When he saw the old man in his mind something washed over him, and he wondered what he was doing, hiding on a roof and spying on these gentlemen.

He faded back, scrambled onto the main roof and ran along its spine to the mountainside. He circled well around the cabin to the path and headed back up Raven Bald toward home.

As sunset neared, Graham climbed down from his tree, untied the sheep, and returned to his shack. There was too little moon to shoot by, and if he left the sheep and the tiger found it and decided to kill it, it would almost certainly eat the carcass out and leave nothing to tempt it back the following day.

The tiger came to Roy's window again that night. They watched each other until Roy fell asleep and was a tiger again.

He stalked through the forest, but he saw nothing, heard nothing, smelled nothing. He seemed to be the only creature left. He felt very lonely, and his belly hurt so badly that occasionally he uttered a low moan.

He came to the edge of the forest to a cabin he had seen once before. It was falling down, parts of it. An old man lived there, he remembered. He laid down behind a bush to watch. After a while, the door opened. It wasn't the old man who came out, it was Jim. Roy felt his body tense, pressing lower to the ground.

Jim was holding a cup on a little plate. He stood just outside the door, looking around, up at the mountains. He was a very kind-looking man.

He walked toward Roy, and Roy felt his hindquarters digging into the ground again. Jim sat down on a stump, his back to Roy, and began sipping from the cup. Steam was rising from it.

Roy's hindquarters didn't relax. The pain in his belly was burning through his spine. His tail began to twitch, and he gathered himself. He knew he could be on Jim's back in a single leap. He heard himself roar as he sprang out of the trees.

He awoke sweating and sobbing. Had the tiger killed Jim? The thought terrified him. He threw back the covers and dressed. It was dark, and the moon was barely up. He got one of his pencils and his tablet and wrote a note for Rose: "Gone out erly. see you this afternune."

Then he left, at a run, for the old man's shack. He decided to go the long way around, because in the dark it would be easy to get turned around trying to cross Copperhead, and it would also be easy to stumble and hurt himself. He had to get to the cabin as quickly as he could.

Graham was awakened by an insistent knocking at his door. He grabbed the rifle beside his bed before he was fully aware, then set it down again.

"Who is it?" he called, rising.

"It's Roy," he heard a small voice gasp.

Graham threw the door open. The boy looked at him, then rushed to grab him around the waist, pressing the side of his face into Graham's lean stomach. Dawn was near.

"What is it, Roy? What's happened?" Roy didn't answer; he could only sob.

Graham took him inside, sat him in a chair, and began

making tea. There were two of Mrs. Brickhouse's muffins left, getting old but still edible. He put both of them in front of the boy.

"Now, tell me what's happened."

Roy told him about the dream. "I was afraid he'd killed you or was about to."

"Well, as you can see, he hasn't," Graham said kindly. "It was very good of you to come and warn me."

"Why is he giving me these dreams?" Roy asked. He was afraid to mention what had come over him yesterday on Raven Bald.

"Perhaps he is explaining himself, Roy," Graham said. "Perhaps he wants you to understand him, to know why he is doing the things he is."

Roy took one of the muffins and began eating it. It was kind of stale, but it was still pretty good, and it stilled the hunger in his belly. It's not that easy for the tiger, he thought.

"Why do you think the tiger wants to kill you?" he asked.

"Oh, I don't imagine he wants to kill me specifically," Graham said. "But you and I are about the only meal-sized things still walking around in his territory, and you're his friend. No, I have never known a tiger that carried a grudge." Nor have I known a man-eater who made friends with a small boy, he thought.

Roy finished one of the muffins and slumped at the table in exhaustion. He tried some of Graham's tea, but to him it tasted mainly like hot water. Finally Graham helped him over to his sagging bed and made him comfortable there.

The boy seemed to sleep soundly. Graham had planned on tying out his sheep again, but decided it would be best not to leave Roy alone.

October 28

Weinman was right. Shortly after he walked into the office on Friday, Brickhouse got a call from Congressman Haley Alford. Alford, the last Democratic congressman in rural Georgia, lived in Gainesville, but his district included Harte County.

"Grady, I suppose you saw Joe Wells's editorial yesterday," Alford said.

"Yeah, it was a little hard to miss."

"I got about ten copies of it faxed to my office up here by ten different people. I can't help but think he's right, but I wanted to talk to you first. How do you feel about it?"

"About bringing in the Rangers?"

"Yep."

"Hell, Haley, how can I argue? Nothing else has worked."

"What about this hunter you got?"

"I'll tell you straight, Haley. The British foreign office offered him, free of charge. He's an old man, supposed to have had a hell of a reputation killing man-eaters in India. I think he's mighty impressive; really seems to know what he's doing. He's been in the mountains nine days now, but he warned us right at the beginning that it was going to take time, and more people would likely die. 'Course, he wasn't counting on folks just going out and offering themselves. I think sooner or later he'll kill the tiger. But whether it's sooner than the Rangers would, I don't know. One thing, if the Rangers come in, he's gone."

"What's his name?"

"The man's name is Jim Graham, but don't let it out. Colonel Jim Graham. He's absolutely adamant about staying out of the media until this is over."

"All right. Come Monday I'm going to have to propose a resolution before Congress to declare an emergency and ask the president to send in regular troops. We just can't let this go on. I hope they'll have your cooperation."

"Of course they will, Congressman. I hate like hell to admit I'm whipped, but I can't stand here and argue for more time. We've had enough time, and we haven't gotten it done."

"Grady, I'll do my best to see that none of this makes you look bad."

"You takin' up magic now, Haley?"

Graham went outside, leaving the door open, and sat on the small front stoop to clean his rifle and sip tea. The sun had just passed overhead when a sheriff's department car came lurching up the rutted lane. It was Brickhouse.

Graham got up and walked to the car. "Good morning, Sheriff. What brings you to my humble abode?"

"What else? Tiger tried to grab somebody at a little country store. Thought I'd carry you over there and see what you could make of it. Didn't expect to find you so easy."

"A complication has arisen," Graham said. "Do you know a family named Satterly that lives in the cut between Copperhead and Raven Bald?"

"No, name doesn't ring a bell."

"Well, it's all quite strange, and I won't go into it now. Suffice it for now to say that the Satterly boy and I have become friends. He had a nightmare this morning and thought the tiger had killed me or was about to. He ran all the way here. He's sleeping now. I don't want to leave him alone. Can he go with us?"

Brickhouse looked hard at Graham. What was he doing with somebody's kid in this shack instead of hunting the tiger?

"Okay. Go get him."

Graham came out the door with a sleepy, rough-looking boy who turned pale when he saw the sheriff's car. Graham locked his door, saw the boy's distress, and put an arm around his shoulder.

"What is it, Roy? What's the matter?"

"N-nothing," the boy said.

Walking him to the car, Graham said, "Roy, I'd like you to meet Sheriff Grady Brickhouse, who is a very nice man. He says the tiger has apparently attacked someone at a country store, and he wants us to go and see what we can find."

Roy turned even whiter, and his knees sagged for a minute.

"What store?" the boy asked.

"Dugan's," Brickhouse said. "Not too far from where you live, I guess."

"My ma's working there today," he whispered.

"From what I understand it was a customer, not anybody in the store," Brickhouse said. "Hop in, both of you, and let's go see."

The drive to Dugan's took thirty minutes. Another sheriff's car was parked in front of the store, and an old Dodge at one of the two gas pumps, but there was no sign of activity. The three entered the store, and Roy saw his mother cleaning the ice cream case. He went over and hugged her. She hugged him back but showed no surprise at seeing him.

Deputy Grimes was talking to Annie.

"Annie," said Brickhouse. "What happened?" He didn't introduce Graham, who had left his rifle in the car.

"Well, about eleven o'clock this young fellow, don't know his name but he's been in before, he drives up and fills that old Chevy out there with gas and then comes in," said Annie, pale and fidgeting. "Pays for the gas and then asks where the restrooms are. I told him there's just the one, 'round back, and give him the key. Rose just been back there, while he was gassing his car.

"Well, he walks out, and I saw him go past the side windows there, and then li'l Scooter Watson 'n' his wife comes in, and I got to talkin' to them. Next thing I know there's this scream an' a godawful noise like a rockslide or somethin', and all this bangin' around in the back.

"Fred was in the back room there sortin' stock, and he runs out the back door. Me 'n' the Watsons run out the front and head 'round the side. Well, Fred gets out the back door and damn near runs into this thing, this tiger, draggin' this fella by the shoulder toward the field. Tiger drops the fella and acts like he's gonna take Fred instead.

"Me 'n' the Watsons get around the corner, and there's Fred backed up against the woodpile, and the tiger all squatted down like he's gonna jump him. We yelled and screamed, and the tiger just makes this huge jump right past Fred and out into that field fulla high grass and that's it."

"Where's Fred?" Brickhouse asked.

"Went in the ambulance with the other fella," she said.

"Wasn't hurt, but Jimmy says looked like shock was comin' on and thought they oughtta take a look at him."

"How bad's the other guy, the customer?" Brickhouse asked his deputy.

"Had his shoulder tore up pretty bad but looked like he oughtta be okay."

"Let's take a look," Brickhouse said, turning to Graham.

Brickhouse and Graham walked out the door. Annie turned to Roy. "Never thought that damn thing would come down here in the open," she said. "God, we coulda all been killed. Tell you what, Roy, me 'n' Rose are gonna clean out all the coolers and put stuff in the freezers in back and get everythin' straightened out, and then I'm gonna close this place 'til they kill that thing. I don't care how long it takes. But don't you worry. We'll see you and your mama got enough to go on with. You make her understand that now, you hear? You make sure she don't come wanderin' back here until I come and tell her so. I 'spect she'll be okay today but keep her in the house after this, understand?"

Roy nodded.

"Now, Mr. Roy," she said with a wan smile. "What you doin' ridin' around with the high sheriff?"

Roy shrugged and grinned back, edging for the door.

"Who's that handsome old fellow out there with the sheriff?" Annie asked. "I ain't seen clothes like that since I was a little girl."

Roy shrugged again and slipped out the door. He went to the corner of the building and looked at Brickhouse and Graham studying the ground. He waited, afraid to join them unless invited. Graham looked up and motioned him forward.

The restroom was part of an addition to the store built on a concrete pad. The pad extended out to make a walkway from the front of the store, and while it had not been swept in days, there wasn't enough dirt on it to hold tracks. The bathroom stood open, showing a toilet and sink. The water in the toilet was clean.

Three feet from the door lay a stick with a key attached.

Graham motioned Brickhouse and Roy to stay on the pad and began casting around on the ground beyond the concrete. For half an hour he studied the ground, which was mown grass for about thirty feet, then gave way to waist-high brownish yellow grass that ran back a hundred yards to the forest at the foot of Copperhead Mountain. Several large trees stood in the rear yard of the store.

Graham called them over to a pile of large wooden packing cases, slowly rotting in the yard near the corner of the building. Behind them the grass was mashed down and hairs were visible on it.

"He'd been lying here for some time, perhaps before dawn. I expect he's had an eye on this store for a while—there must be a fair amount of activity here. He came here from the long grass and waited for something to happen.

"He apparently ignored your mother when she came back, Roy. Perhaps he couldn't hear her. But he could certainly have heard the customer walking on the concrete. At some point he moved around here, where he could see over this box. You see these divots here; they were left by his hind paws when he sprang over the box." Graham rose and walked back toward the bathroom.

Near the edge of the concrete, he pointed to small rips in the dirt and grass. "His first leap took him almost directly behind the customer when the man came out of the lavatory. Here he landed, rose up, and seized the man."

"I don't see any blood," said Brickhouse.

"No blood would flow until the tiger changed its grip. Somehow he failed to grab the man by the neck and kill him right way.

"The man struggled. You can see these shoe marks against the wall, the gouges here on the ground after they got off the concrete."

A few feet away, on the grass, there was plenty of blood.

"I expect the tiger had actually dropped the man and was about to kill him when the other man—Fred, was it?—comes out the back door. The tiger turns to deal with this new threat and, as the lady said, is about to spring when the others come up behind it and begin yelling. Confused, certainly frightened by the multiple threats, the tiger flees."

The man-eater's path through the dry, tall grass of the field was apparent to Brickhouse as well as Roy. "As far as I can see, he took the same path back to the mountain as he did coming here," Graham said.

"Now we shall have to part company. I'll get my rifle from your car, Sheriff, and follow the tiger. I expect Roy will stay here with his mother."

Roy nodded.

Graham got his rifle, checked the cartridges, patted his pocket to make sure the four reloads were there, and waded into the grass.

He thought it unlikely the tiger had stopped before reaching the forest, but he moved slowly, rifle at the ready. It was a perfect place for an ambush, but the tiger would have decided by now that it was not being pursued.

Once inside the tree line, the man-eater had slowed. He

appeared to be heading straight up the mountain. Graham moved cautiously, constantly checking wind direction. There was a possibility of finding the tiger resting and making an end to the shikar.

But after about half an hour, the trail faded and disappeared in a rocky area. Graham scoured the ground around the outcroppings for an hour before he finally found the tiger's pugmark on a tiny patch of dirt kept soggy by an underground spring.

Casting back over the outcrops, he found the small depression underneath an overhang where the tiger had rested. The grass was still slightly matted, there were a few hairs, but the ground wasn't warm. The man-eater had been gone for some time.

Dejected, Graham sat on a rock by the depression. He was growing more and more certain, without knowing exactly why, that there would be no conclusion until Roy was ready for the man-eater to die.

When he looked at Roy he saw himself as a child, only magnified and in some way more ideal: Roy was even more a part of the forest than he had been at the same age. He felt he was engaged with the tiger in some bizarre tug-of-war over Roy; killing the tiger before the boy was convinced it had to die would mean certain loss of that war. What that loss meant, he could not guess.

Sighing, Graham rose and began following the tiger. It was heading downhill now, still moving at a good clip. Suddenly Graham realized he was following Roy's tiger path, and as he began to ponder that, he heard a woman scream.

"Noooo!" a voice cried. It was Roy. Graham began running.

———

When Graham stepped off into the high grass behind Dugan's, Roy and Brickhouse went back into the store.

"Paul," Brickhouse said to his deputy, "call a tow truck out here to get the car. I'm going on over to the hospital." Both men left the store, and Brickhouse drove away.

Roy stayed with Rose until Brickhouse was gone, then told her he was going on home and left.

He took his time walking along the dirt road, trying to figure out what he ought to do. He was finding it increasingly difficult to believe the tiger wasn't a man-eater, but he couldn't fit that in with the way the animal treated him. It treated him, he thought, about like Jim did. Both the tiger and Jim were his friends, but he knew he couldn't keep them both.

He thought about how he felt when he dreamed the tiger's dream, about the gnawing hunger, the emptiness of the forest. He couldn't help feeling sorry for it. Jim was right—it didn't belong here. There was nothing here for it but trouble. He also thought about the things the tiger seemed to be teaching him. That scared him.

At home, he made a peanut butter sandwich and then flopped down on his bed and began reading his small stack of *Geographics* with tigers in them. Most of the stories talked about how the tiger was endangered, about how if tigers weren't given enough space and left alone they would die out. Roy wondered if his friend thought he was the last tiger on earth.

When it was about time for Rose to get home Roy got up and went outside. He stood by the door for a few minutes, restless, and decided to meet his mother and help her bring home whatever she was carrying from Dugan's.

As he reached the road, Roy saw movement ahead and thought he was late or his mother was early, but when the figure crested the last rise he saw it was not Rose, but the tiger. It was walking steadily up the road toward him.

Roy stopped, stunned. The tiger had never appeared in the open like this before, and it acted as though it intended to come right up to him. It was walking steadily, one foot falling in the print left by the last. Its head was held low, and the loose skin at its belly swayed from side to side as it walked. There was a trace of pink around its muzzle. Roy remembered what Jim had told him about that.

The tiger was about a hundred yards away when Roy saw Rose walk up the hill behind it. She had a sack in each arm. For a few seconds Roy thought she might not see the tiger, but then she stopped abruptly, staring. "Roy!" she yelled. Both sacks fell to the ground and she began running, screaming as she came.

The tiger whipped around, confused, but when it saw Rose it crouched, growling in one long, low drumroll.

"No!" Roy screamed. "No, ma, no! He won't hurt me! Stop! Noooo!"

He began running, too, hopelessly. Rose was wild-eyed, like she had been that time when she jumped on that bastard's back and bit a chunk out of his neck.

The tiger waited, its tail lashing, growling its warning. Roy never knew if the tiger thought Rose was attacking him or Roy.

When Rose was within a few feet of the tiger she launched herself at him, screaming again. The tiger rose on his hind legs and wrapped his front legs around her in a terrible embrace. His head dropped to her shoulder and she fell backward, her scream silenced as if by a switch.

Roy began howling incoherently as he ran. The tiger, standing over Rose, looked back at him. Roy, nearly blinded by
tears, stopped and groped on the road for a stone.

"I hate you, you bastard," he screamed and threw the rock.
It hit the tiger on the shoulder. With a snarl, the man-eater
leaped off the road and trotted into the forest at the foot of
Raven Bald. Roy fell to his knees beside Rose and saw the side
of her neck and part of her shoulder were bitten through. He
was kneeling in her blood.

"Ma!" he cried. "Ma!" He tried to pull the gaping wound
together and couldn't. He collapsed on her body, sobbing,
until he felt Jim's hand on his shoulder.

Graham held Roy until the crying subsided. The sun was beginning to slide behind Raven Bald.

"He killed my mother, the tiger killed her," Roy said weakly.
"Kill him now. Please."

"I shall, Roy. First we must see to your mother."

Graham lifted Rose's body and carried it to the house. Roy
picked up his rifle and followed him. In the kitchen, Graham
cleaned the wound and then carried her back to her bedroom
and put her on the bed.

"May I cover her now, Roy?"

"All right."

Graham pulled the worn sheet over Rose's ashen face.

They went back to the kitchen. Graham would have wel-
comed tea, but there was none. Roy said he wasn't hungry,
but Graham feared he might be sliding into shock and insisted
the boy help him prepare something to eat. They made peanut
butter sandwiches, a novelty for Graham. Roy ate only half of
his.

"Do you have other relatives?" Graham asked.

"Ma never said anything about relatives."

"You will be fine, Roy. I will make certain of that before I go home."

"Can I go with you?"

"I wish you could. I would like nothing better. But it isn't possible, and you belong here near the forest. I cannot offer you a forest. Now, I should think you are rather tired. Certainly I am. Shall we retire?"

"Retire?"

"Go to bed."

"Oh," Roy said listlessly. "Okay."

Roy went to his room. Graham lit an oil lamp and found a blanket in a curtained closet in Rose's room. He took it to the kitchen and spread it on the floor.

Roy lay on his bed, thinking of his mother and their lives together and weeping quietly. He was exhausted, but sleep wouldn't come. He rolled over toward his window and saw the tiger watching him.

It was looking at him with its usual impassive air, but when Roy yelled "Go away!" and leaped out of the bed, the man-eater seemed to go berserk. It snarled and lunged at him, and the glass in the window shattered. It was trying to get into his room.

Graham, awakened by Roy's yell, thought the boy had a nightmare and ran to his room without his rifle. When he saw the tiger's head and one foreleg inside the room, he snatched Roy up and backed out, slamming the door shut. "In the kitchen," he told Roy, and ran to get the rifle.

Graham dropped to one knee, bracing the rifle against the kitchen door five feet from Roy's room. Safety off, he waited for the tiger to break through the flimsy door.

Nothing happened. There was no sound from the other side

of the door. After a few minutes, Graham decided the tiger must have withdrawn from the window rather than come into the room. He wondered if it was trying to get into the house or if it had merely reacted to Roy's terror.

Motioning to the boy to join him, he slipped down the short hall to Rose's room. Her old dresser would cover much of the window. Setting his rifle against the wall, he said, "Help me shove this against the window."

It was dark, the dresser was heavy, and the board floor was rough. They had it almost in place when a roar erupted from the darkness outside. The glass shattered just as they gave a final heave and jammed the dresser against the window. Given the narrow window, Graham didn't think the tiger would be able to move the dresser. He hurried back down the dark hall to the kitchen.

The kitchen door was fairly stout. The window over the porcelain sink was too small for the tiger to enter. Graham resumed his position by the kitchen door, where he could cover anything in the hall.

If Rose's body had not been in the back bedroom, he would have allowed the tiger to come through the window. The oil lamp would give enough light to kill it easily as it entered the hall. If it would enter the hall. He had been fairly confident of killing it when it burst through the door to Roy's room, but it refused to do that.

"I think he's gone crazy," Roy said.

"Why?"

"It's just a feeling, but I think it's right. He wants to kill both of us. He wants to kill everything."

"What's it doing now?"

"I don't know, exactly. Trying to figure out how to get at us."

A mighty roar made plates rattle on the table. Graham looked over his left shoulder to see the man-eater's head at the kitchen window. He whipped around for a shot but the tiger disappeared. Something struck the door like a sledge-hammer. It jumped but held.

The man-eater began pacing around the house, roaring as he moved. Roy, terrified, began to cry. "We're all right, Roy," Graham assured him. "There's no way he can reach us without giving me a shot."

"What if you miss?"

Graham smiled. "That would be bad luck, wouldn't it? But I don't think I will, at these distances."

The tiger fell silent. Roy listened to his heart pound. As the tension drained, he became drowsy and finally dozed off. He was awakened by another shattering roar, one which seemed to echo in the little house.

"Where is he?" the boy gasped.

"In your room," Graham said. "He's come all the way in."

There were more roars, crashes, and ripping sounds.

"What's he doing?"

"Tearing up your bed, I think," Graham replied. Something hit the bedroom door, but it didn't open.

The light in the kitchen dimmed and then failed entirely, plunging the kitchen and hall into darkness. "Is there more oil?" Graham whispered.

"Yeah," said Roy. "In the pantry. I'll find it."

"Quick as you can."

Graham's night vision was beginning to develop when there was a roar from the bedroom and the door ripped off its hinges, striking the wall on the other side of the narrow hall. Expecting the tiger to be in the hall when the door fell, the hunter fired the right barrel of the .470. It was deafening inside the little house. The tiger answered with a roar from the bedroom.

It had knocked down the door without coming into the hall. Holding the rifle to his shoulder with his trigger hand, Graham groped in his pocket for another cartridge.

He dared not load it, however, until he had light. It would take too long in the dark. The tiger seemed to know, somehow, every move he was likely to make.

"Find the oil yet?" he whispered.

Roy, ears ringing from the heavy rifle's report, didn't hear him. He was rummaging blindly in the open pantry for a can of lamp oil.

There was utter silence from the bedroom. Graham thought the tiger might have gone back outside.

"Here it is!" Roy whispered.

"Can you see well enough to fill the lamp?"

"Yeah," Roy said. "I'll do it."

"Matches on the table."

In a few minutes Roy struck a match, and then light welled up in the room again.

"Good man," said Graham. He felt Roy settle down beside him.

"Are you scared?" the boy asked in a small voice.

"No, now that there is light to shoot by again. I wasn't too comfortable when the lamp went out."

"Do you think you hit him?"

"No. There's the bullet hole in the wall at the end of the hall."

"I see it."

"How about you, Roy? Are you scared?"

"Yeah, kinda."

"Good. When you are nine years old and a tiger is trying to get hold of you, it's time to be scared."

"I guess."

"Only about an hour until dawn now. Then perhaps we can turn the tables on this tiger."

A roar rattled the kitchen window, and there was a mighty thump at the kitchen door. It bulged inward for an instant. The tiger hit the door again and a third time. Graham realized the tiger was striking it, drawing back, lunging again, in a rhythmic pattern; every four seconds. At the third strike, Graham trained his rifle on the door, counted off four seconds and fired.

A hole appeared where the door had been bulging but this time there was no blow from outside. The tiger roared. Graham saw a flicker of movement left of the door and realized the tiger was at the window. It dropped back out of sight before he could turn the rifle on it.

"Amazing beast," he grumbled, reloading his right barrel.

October 29

Brickhouse arose and dressed before dawn Saturday. He had a feeling of impending disaster. He had fretted about Graham and the kid since leaving Dugan's. Why was the boy sleeping at Graham's?

And then Graham had not checked in last night, for the first time since he had gone into the field. Brickhouse had been up late, notifying the young wife of a local carpenter's helper that her husband would survive the tiger's attack, taking her to the hospital to be with him.

The sun was just beginning to bounce its light off the mountaintops when Brickhouse headed his blue-and-white out of Hartesville toward the Whitfield place. It was fully light when he got there and found what he had feared—nothing. Graham was not there. A can of gun solvent was still sitting on the stoop.

Maybe that boy knew something. Graham got back in the car and drove out onto 121, past the Willet farm and onto the dirt road that led to Dugan's store on the other side of Copperhead Mountain. He drove slowly, not sure where the house was. When he spotted an old tarpaper house just off the right side of the road, he slowed and stopped. There was no mailbox, but someone appeared to be living there. There was no driveway, either. He edged the car to the side of the road, turned off the ignition, and got out.

Quiet out here, he thought. The door of the house, he noticed, had a hole in it and looked as though someone had been trying to break it down.

Brickhouse had passed the front fender of the Crown Vic and was walking in front of the hood toward the house when the door opened. Graham, his rifle at the ready, emerged, followed by the boy.

"What is it, Jim?" Brickhouse asked, walking toward them. "You look like hell."

"Very glad to see you, Sheriff," said Graham. "We had a visitor last night. Quite a bit of excitement." He nodded at the door, and Brickhouse saw the deep, fresh furrows running down it and the spot in the middle where the boards had begun to buckle. The hole, he saw, was left by a bullet, fired from inside.

"When did it leave?" Brickhouse asked.

"I believe you scared it off," Graham said, running his hand through his thinning hair.

Brickhouse saw the boy stagger and begin to sag.

"You hurt, son?"

Roy shook his head, no.

"He's exhausted," Graham said. "Can he get in the back of your car?"

Brickhouse gestured toward the house and started to suggest the boy could sleep in his bed, but Graham shook his head sharply.

"Sure," Brickhouse said, opening a door.

Roy got in and fell asleep almost instantly. Brickhouse noted stains on the boy's T-shirt that looked as though they might be blood.

Brickhouse and Graham walked back to the house and sat on the stoop.

The widow Hadley, the only refugee from Norma's Creek unable to get out under her own power, had spent a difficult week at the home of her son, Orrin. When Vera Hadley had problems, she made sure those around her shared them. Her biggest current problem was a lack of clothing. She had been carried out of her house in a nightgown, without so much as a robe or a pair of slippers.

She wanted her blue nightgown and her flannel pajamas since it was getting colder, and she wanted her quilted robe. She wanted her warm slippers, and when she thought about it she wanted her personal toiletries, too, and the bathtub seat she had ordered through the mail.

To make matters worse, she was having trouble remembering why she couldn't go back to her house in Norma's Creek, where all the neighbors made sure she was cared for.

"There ain't nothin' to do but go out there and get that crap for her," Orrin told his wife Sandra Saturday morning.

"God's sake, Orrin, don't be crazy," Sandra told him. "I'll go buy her some stuff at Wal-Mart. You ain't goin' out there with that tiger around. Ain't nobody at all out there."

"First place, we can't afford to buy her new stuff. Second, she won't have it and you know it. She wants her stuff, and there ain't nothing for it but to go get it. And I figure if they ain't nobody out there, there ain't no reason for the tiger to hang around. I'll take the shotgun just in case."

Orrin was just as stubborn as his mother and Sandra knew there was no way to talk him out of going. "All right, Orrin, but you ain't goin' alone. You go, I go."

"Ain't no use in you goin' too, honey," he said.

"You go, I go with you."

"Oh, come on, now—"

"Let's go."

"I believe you said you didn't know anything about this boy and his mother?" Graham asked.

"That's right."

"His mother worked at Dugan's. Perhaps you saw her there yesterday. She was damaged mentally in some way. As far as I can tell she was as good a mother to the boy as she knew how to be. She never sent him to school. I would assume very few people even knew they existed. She taught him to read and to write, and she was very determined, apparently, that he become 'a gentleman.' Roy is always very concerned about what a gentleman should do in a given situation.

"As a result, his manners are remarkable for a boy who is in many ways feral. He slept in a bed at night, but he lived in the forest and the mountains. He is more at home in them than I was in my own mountains at that age, but he is very gentle. He has no desire to hunt or kill anything, as far as I know.

"Somehow, this tiger has actually befriended Roy. It came to his window at night. They eventually began meeting up the mountain from the house. It never offered to harm the child. Roy was certain the tiger was his friend and refused to believe the animal was a man-eater. He is so receptive, so much a part of the natural world, that the tiger gave him dreams.

"Roy knows what it means to be a tiger, Grady. To be a tiger in a strange land."

"Jim, for God's sake—"

"Make of it what you will. Ask him some time. He'll tell you. But let me finish.

"I felt until Roy understood the situation and was ready for the tiger to die, I could not or would not have the opportunity to kill it."

"Why not?"

"Because there is something very important about Roy. I have no real idea what it is, but killing his friend would have done irreparable damage to him. In any case, I don't believe any lives were lost because of this.

"So what's changed?"

"Come," said Graham, rising.

"Tiger do this?" Brickhouse asked, looking at the door.

"Yes. He was about to break it down. I fired blindly to try to discourage him."

Inside the house, Graham took Brickhouse into the little hallway.

"This is Roy's room. The tiger came to visit him last night. Roy screamed when he saw him. The tiger went berserk and came in through the window. I got the boy out and slammed the door before it was all the way in." Roy's little room looked as though it had contained a tornado. Even the *Geographic*s were shredded.

"Why'd he scream, if they were friends?"

Without speaking, Graham took four steps down the hall to Rose's room. He walked to the bed and lifted the sheet.

"His mother."

"Oh, Jesus," Brickhouse groaned.

"She was coming home from Dugan's. She saw the tiger walking up to Roy and obviously thought it was about to attack him, although I'm not sure she knew exactly what it was. She came running at the tiger, screaming. I heard her, but I was too far away to do any good. I believe the tiger thought she was attacking Roy. At any rate, it killed her, in front of the boy. That was the turning point."

"That would do it," said Brickhouse.

It was after nine A.M. when Orrin Hadley pulled his battered S-10 pickup into his mother's driveway in Norma's Creek.

"Damn front door's open," he said. "You reckon they left it that way?"

"Prob'ly," Sandra replied. "This is spooky. Let's just back outta here and go back to Wal-Mart."

Down in front of Sally Ann and Roscoe's, under the big tree, there was a quilt on the ground with leaves on it and more quilts on sagging ropes. Lawn chairs were tumbled around. The QUILT SALE sign had blown over.

"Nope. I'll run in, get the stuff. You just wait here and keep an eye out."

"Like hell. You run in, I run in, too. Let's go."

Orrin took one last look around, opened the door, stepped out, and reached back in for the camo-painted Mossberg 500 on the window rack. As Sandra stepped cautiously out, he racked a round of double-ought buckshot into the chamber.

"Okay," Orrin said. "Let's go. I'll go first. You watch our back. Grab hold of my belt."

They started along the ragged concrete walkway to the porch, Orrin with his shotgun at port arms and Sandra glancing nervously over her shoulder. Norma's Creek was silent except for the chatter of birds in the trees behind the houses. Orrin was beginning to doubt his judgment. He couldn't decide if it was best to creep along slow and watchful or run like hell for the house.

Once on the porch, though, Orrin had no urge to run through that half-open doorway. The sunlight was so bright he couldn't see more than a couple of feet into the darkened house. Carefully, he pushed the heavy wooden door all the way open with the barrel of the shotgun. It creaked a little.

"Jesus," breathed Sandra behind him.

The door opened directly into the left side of the living room. Orrin peered in, but his eyes were adjusted to the sunlight and he couldn't see much. He wished he had some sunglasses. The room seemed empty; he could detect no movement. After a minute he stepped through the doorway and into the shadows, Sandra still clutching his belt.

They stood near the door, their backs to the wall, until their eyes dilated enough to see. There was nothing out of the ordinary except for a small pile of feces on the threadbare old rug.

"Damn 'coons 'n' things comin' in here," Orrin snorted. "What a mess we're gonna have."

"Worry about that later," Sandra breathed. "Let's get the stuff and get outta here."

They sidled along the wall to the hall doorway, three long steps through the short hall, and into the widow's bedroom.

"Smells funny," Sandra said.

"Animals," Orrin replied.

He stood guard by the bedroom door while Sandra scurried about the little room, stuffing his mother's nightclothes into an empty pillowcase. "That's it," she said. "Rest of it's in the bathroom."

Orrin stood just outside the little bathroom while Sandra dropped some small containers into the bag. He could see one corner of the kitchen. The trash can had been overturned and its contents scattered across the floor. "I can't get this seat thing out of the bathtub," Sandra said. "I think it's rusted."

"Leave it. Let's go."

Sandra grabbed his belt and they slipped back into the living room. Orrin stopped at the door, which was still open. "Smells worse now than when we came in," he said. "You think we ought to shut the door? If we do, we're gonna trap whatever may be in here, and they'll tear the place up for sure. If we don't, God knows what else may come in."

Sandra merely grunted.

"Hell with it," Orrin said, stepping into the sunlight. "Close it behind you."

He waited on the porch, peering around for any threat. "Come on, honey, close it, and let's get out of here."

There was no response, and Orrin realized he no longer felt Sandra's hand at his belt. Half turning, he looked back. Sandra wasn't there. The pillowcase full of clothes and toiletries was on the floor a couple of feet inside the door.

Panic welled up from the pit of his stomach. "Sandra!" he yelled at the open door. "Sandra!"

She didn't answer.

"Where are you? You all right?"

Silence. Orrin was having trouble getting his breath, and his gut told him that Sandra wasn't all right. He was afraid to go into the house to find her. He was afraid not to. The shotgun in his hands seemed like a bad joke.

He looked at the floor inside the door. There was no blood that he could see. From the porch, the living room looked exactly as it did when they had come through from the hall.

Bringing the shotgun to his shoulder, Orrin forced one foot over the sill and into the living room. It took a moment or two for the other to follow. In the dim room, back to the wall, he waited and listened. A scraping, rustling sound was coming from the hall.

Orrin began sidling as silently as he could down the pale

green wall to the hall door. It took only four small steps. From the edge of the doorway, he could see nothing until something white caught his eye on the floor. Looking down, Orrin saw his wife looking up at him.

Her eyes were open wide, and her mouth gaped in apparent astonishment. There was blood dripping from her mouth and a growing pool of it on the bare wood floor.

"Oh, Sandra," Orrin whimpered. As if in response, she slowly slid behind the doorway. There was a low, muttering growl.

Orrin Hadley knew his wife was dead. His stomach told him that if he took a step into the hall he would die, too. He wanted to run, but he forced himself to back slowly away from the hall and out the door. Then he ran.

Brickhouse pulled his radio mike through the window of his patrol car to avoid waking Roy and called for an ambulance to get Rose's corpse. When it was gone, Brickhouse turned to Graham. "Now what?"

"Can you take Roy home with you?" Graham asked.

"Yeah. What're you gonna do?"

"Follow the tiger. His behavior last night was highly abnormal. I believe he is far more dangerous now than he was a day ago."

"You're in no shape to—" Brickhouse began and was cut off by the radio.

"Unit Ten." There was an unusual urgency in Ellen's voice.

"Ten."

"Call me."

The sheriff grabbed his cell phone and punched the speed-dial number for his office.

"Grady," Ellen gasped. "I got Monroe on the other line.

He's out near Norma's Creek. Some guy flagged him down on 153, said he and his wife went out there to get something or other from one of them empty houses, and the tiger got his wife. Monroe says he'd like backup before he goes in there."

"Goes in where?"

"In the house where the tiger got her."

"Tell him to get the hell out of there and meet me on the highway about half a mile north of there, with the subject who flagged him down. Send a couple more units, but tell them not to go up to the houses."

Brickhouse clicked off the phone and looked at Graham. The man's face was seamed and looked older than ever, but his eyes were clear.

"You up to this?" Brickhouse asked.

"Certainly."

When they reached the highway Brickhouse turned on his blue lights but kept the siren silent.

"What is this place—Norma's Creek?" Graham asked, hanging on to the overhead strap.

"Little collection of houses along a little two-lane county road, runs by a creek of that name. Mostly older folks live there. Keep pretty much to themselves. They all cleared out when the tiger broke up their quilt sale last week."

Graham leaned back and closed his eyes. He didn't open them until Brickhouse pulled up beside Tolbert's cruiser on the county road outside Norma's Creek. They listened to Orrin Hadley's semicoherent account, and Brickhouse turned to Graham.

"What do you suggest, Jim?"

"Let's go take a look," Graham replied.

Brickhouse pulled into Vera Hadley's driveway. Through

the open door they could see the bulging pillowcase.

Brickhouse opened his door, but Graham put a hand on his arm. "Stay here, Sheriff. Please."

"It's my duty—"

"—not to get killed," Graham finished for him. "Or to shoot your elders by accident. I know what I am doing, Grady, and in this instance you do not. If there was a madman with a gun out there, and you asked me to stay in the car, I would do so. Besides, we cannot leave Roy alone here."

Brickhouse had forgotten the boy, still asleep in the backseat.

"All right, Jim. I'll stay here for now. But if you're out of touch too long, I'll have to call in help and start looking."

"Give me an hour."

"Okay."

Graham opened the door, swung his feet out, and stood. Slowly, he looked around. Brickhouse could see a front door standing open across the highway. Graham opened the breech of his rifle, removed the cartridges and examined them. He replaced one, then returned them one by one to the breech and snapped it shut.

He closed the car door, walked up the porch steps, and stood for a while at the door, listening. Then he began walking slowly toward the rear of the Hadley house. He had the rifle at his shoulder when he turned the corner and disappeared.

Brickhouse rolled down his window a little so he could hear better and waited. Time crawled. When half an hour had passed, there was movement in the backseat.

"Where are we?" the boy asked, groggy. "Where's Jim?"

Brickhouse turned and looked back at Roy. The boy was filthy. The stains on his T-shirt, Brickhouse thought, must be his mother's blood.

"We're at a place called Norma's Creek, long way south of your house. Tiger's been here. Colonel Graham's looking for him."

Roy grabbed for a door handle. There was none.

"He said for both of us to stay here," Brickhouse said.

Roy relaxed against the back of the seat.

"What's a kernel?" he asked, after a while.

Ten minutes before the hour was up, Graham appeared, walking slowly down the center stripe of the highway, watching the houses. Brickhouse grunted and picked up his radio microphone.

"Ten. Who's in the Norma's Creek area?"

"Twelve," replied Weinman. "North of it, with sixteen."

"Eighteen. Little ways south." It was Grimes.

"All three units, block off the highway. Nothing comes in."

"Ten-four," they replied in near unison.

Graham came to the car, and before he opened the door, Brickhouse saw him engage the safety on his rifle. He'd never seen Graham carry the weapon with the safety off.

As the hunter slid into the passenger seat Brickhouse saw he was sweating lightly.

"The tiger has been around every house, possibly inside some of those with the doors open. But I cannot be sure, and quite frankly I haven't the courage to go through those open doors."

He looked at Roy in the backseat.

"How are you, my boy?"

"I'm fine. I want to help."

"Any thoughts on where the tiger may be now?"

"Can I get out?"

Brickhouse and Graham both got out of the car, and Graham opened the back door. Roy slid out and looked around slowly.

"I don't think he's very far. Somewhere on the other side of the creek there."

As if to answer, the tiger called briefly.

"You're right, Roy. He's just inside the tree line."

"What next?" Brickhouse asked.

"First, let's get that woman's body out of this house while we know the tiger isn't in there."

"Roy, too?"

"Are you all right with that, Roy?" Graham asked.

"Yeah. After what he did to Ma, I think so."

They found Sandra Hadley's remains in a corner of the hall. Most of one leg had been eaten, leaving the femur, tibia, and fibula exposed. Using a towel, Brickhouse tied the bones to her remaining leg. He and Roy carried her out, with Graham standing guard. They laid her by the road, a sheet from Vera's bed covering her.

"What now? Shall I call for EMS to come get her?"

"Not yet," Graham said. "We know the tiger is nearby. There is no use tracking it through this village; everything is in the tiger's favor here. However, perhaps I can convince it to come to me. Fall is the mating season for tigers. We can hope that the instinct is not dormant in this one."

"What do you mean?

"I am going to try to call the tiger to me."

"Jesus," Brickhouse whispered.

"The major problem is that while this place offers almost constant cover for the tiger, there is no ideal place to wait for it. I've seen no place that offers a good 360-degree view from a safe position.

"That porch over there," he said, pointing to a house on

the north side of the road, "is about four feet off the ground, and the tiger must cross the highway to reach it. I believe that gives me the best chance. I will start here, move down the highway a bit, and then cross the road to the house and wait on the porch. It's more convincing if the tigress—me—moves around a bit, rather agitated, you know. You and Roy must take the car out of sight and wait for me. Don't argue, Grady."

Graham stepped a few yards from the car, took several deep breaths, tucked the rifle under his arm, and cupped his hands around his mouth. He threw back his head, and from his cupped hands came a guttural, coughing call that seemed to engulf them.

"*Aaauuoongggh! Oongghh!*"

Brickhouse's scalp crawled and Roy's eyes bugged. From beyond the creek came an answer.

"*Aauunngh! Auuggh!*"

"He's coming," Graham said. "Go now."

The sheriff and the boy jumped into the car and Brickhouse backed it out of the driveway and drove it east until a low hill hid it from the village a quarter of a mile away. They got out in order to hear better and waited. They could hear the exchange of calls clearly.

Graham walked a hundred yards down the road, calling periodically. The tiger answered every call, but it was moving cautiously. He turned north off the road and went up into the tree line behind the house where he intended to wait. He called there several times, then moved silently back down to the house.

There he climbed the six concrete steps to the small porch and called once more. Then he turned a rickety straight-back chair toward the wall and sat down in it backward so he could use the back for a rest. He had a clear view of the highway for about seventy-five yards in each direction. The tiger was calling to his left, moving closer.

The house where Graham had chosen to wait for the tiger was the Murdocks'. The walk leading from the highway was neatly lined with large, white-painted rocks. The debris of the quilt sale was across the road and four doors west. The house next door to the west, Graham had noted as he approached, had a miniature scrap-iron yard behind it, full of the hulks of a dozen vehicles and smaller farm implements. To the east was the widow Hadley's house.

A scrawny hedge almost four feet high separated the houses on both sides. On the Hadleys' porch, a squirrel peered curiously through the open door, its tail jerking nervously.

Graham was still, his breathing not apparent from ten paces.

To the north, Brickhouse and the boy waited silently, on either side of the blue-and-white's hood, listening to the tiger. They knew that Graham must be in place by now, waiting.

Far ahead, just below the rise that hid them from Norma's Creek, Roy glimpsed a brief flicker of movement, red and black in the high, dead grass on the north side of the highway. The tiger had crossed outside Jim's view and must now be working its way back toward the village. Its calling had ceased.

Roy looked at Brickhouse. The sheriff hadn't noticed anything.

For the first time, Roy tried to summon what the tiger had given him, and it came in a rush. He could smell Brickhouse as clearly as he could see him, even through the stench of the automobile. The soft southerly breeze tickled his sensitive skin. Power surged through him.

Silently, smoothly, he backed out of Brickhouse's peripheral sight, dropped behind the car and melted into the forest. Once out of sight, he broke into a loping run, angling back toward Norma's Creek and higher into the trees.

On the Murdocks' porch, Graham realized his plan had failed. Long absence from the field had led him to a miscalculation; he had taken up his position too soon. He should have called the tiger closer.

Now, in the absence of further invitations, the tiger was not rushing to the spot where Graham had last called. Its wariness had in all probability overcome its newfound lust, and it had either abandoned the area or was stalking the site of the calls it had heard. If the latter, then the hunter was the hunted, and the new hunter held all the cards.

Slowly, Graham moved his left hand down to his belt and unsnapped the leather keeper that held the knife Brickhouse had given him in its scabbard. Then he returned his hand to the forestock of the rifle. He had no plans to leave the porch until he had the tiger located. If he did, he would be entirely at its mercy. On the porch, his back was covered.

"Awful quiet down there," Brickhouse said, shifting his perch on the hood of the blue-and-white. "You got any idea where the tiger might be now?"

There was no answer. He looked back and didn't see the boy.

"Roy?"

Nothing.

He moved swiftly around the front of the car. There was no sign of the boy. He wasn't in the car.

"Oh, shit," the sheriff said aloud. He didn't dare yell for

the boy, and anyway he knew it wouldn't do any good. If he'd been paying attention he'd have known the kid would run first chance he got. He'd wanted to be with Graham from the beginning of all this.

Going back to Norma's Creek might get somebody killed. On the other hand, not going back might get somebody killed, too. He tried to add it up and couldn't. Finally he decided doing something was better than doing nothing. He began walking down the middle of the road toward Norma's Creek.

Roy slowed his pace as the houses came into view through the trees. He'd seen no further sign of the tiger and hoped he had outpaced it. He watched the houses until he saw the one with the junk in the backyard. Jim was going to wait on the porch of the house next to it.

He stopped in a thicket at the edge of the tree line. The breeze was still blowing from the south, from the houses to him. He was panting lightly from his run. He tested the air. Nothing but faint human odors, cooking smells, oil and grease, and rotting metal. He couldn't smell Jim, and he knew the hunter's smell from any other. The house must be blocking it, he thought.

Or he's not there anymore.

If he's not there anymore, there's nothing I can do. I can only wait. Watch.

He became part of the thicket.

Graham also waited and watched. He was increasingly certain that the tiger had crossed the road beyond his sight and was somewhere behind him.

The tiger could creep up to the porch unseen from behind the house. To remain unseen, however, it would have to jump nearly straight up rather than take an easy running jump that would put it in Graham's lap in a second. After the near-vertical jump, it would have to gather itself for another short spring to reach his chair by the door. He should have time for one quick shot before the man-eater reached him.

He heard the clatter of startled mourning doves somewhere to the east and knew the tiger was near.

Roy saw the pair of doves rise from between the houses two doors east of the Murdock place. A few seconds later the tiger flowed around the corner like something moving in a dream, its head and tail low.

It trotted past the two houses, turned between the Murdock house and the one next to it, and dropped into a slow, belly-dragging crawl.

It had seen Jim on the porch and was making its final stalk.

Roy had found only two real friends in all his life, and now one was about to kill the other. One had taught him about being a tiger, the other about being a man. Anguish swept over him.

The man-eater crept along the east wall of the house to the side of the porch, then swung its hindquarters out until it was facing the concrete porch where Jim was sitting. It went into a crouch, its hindquarters twitching as its back paws worked for purchase to make the leap.

Roy tasted a salty tear, and it brought back the tang of warm blood and the sudden image of Rose lying in the dirt.

He burst out of the thicket, gathered his breath, and yelled at the tiger as it leaped for the porch. But it didn't come out a yell. It was an angry growl, and it startled Roy almost as much as it did the tiger.

———

Graham heard the growl before he saw the tiger and whipped the rifle to his left as the beast rose above the porch.

His right jacket sleeve caught on the back of the chair and the rifle didn't come around far enough, and he knew he was lost.

But the tiger ignored him. It skidded a few feet on the concrete porch and leaped off, running in front of Graham as he jumped to his feet and kicked the chair away.

The porch hid most of it, but Graham fired. The tiger roared and plunged end over end, crashing through a hedge that separated the houses. Graham fired his second barrel as the tiger hit the ground, but even as he pulled the trigger it whipped back to its feet and disappeared into the junk heap behind the neighboring house.

Graham was motionless for a second. He could not understand why he was not lying dead under the man-eater. Instinctively he broke open his rifle, withdrew the spent cartridges and inserted two fresh ones, and as he did he realized what had happened.

The growl that he had heard came from behind the house, not from the springing man-eater, and it had surprised the tiger, unnerving it and ruining its jump. He could not think what might have uttered that growl, but it was the only reason he was unharmed.

He snapped the breech shut and walked down the steps.

Roy was racing out of the tree line toward the back of the Murdock house when the deep bark of Graham's rifle echoed among the empty houses. He dived to the ground, crouching behind a moss-covered concrete birdbath just as the second report came. Through the patchy hedge he saw the tiger, its tail held high, streak into the yard full of decaying vehicles and disappear behind a rusted Allis-Chalmers tractor.

Jim was alive, possibly unhurt.

Carefully, using every piece of cover, Roy worked his way back to the tree line and then moved past the yard of rotting vehicles. There was no sign of the tiger, but Roy was certain it was in there somewhere. It was good cover, a man-made thicket. He moved behind the next house, where a tiny decaying barn stood next to the tree line. Boards nailed to the back wall served as a ladder to the little hayloft, seven feet off the ground. Roy climbed up and crouched beside an uncovered trap door in the shadows behind the open loft door with a clear view of the Murdock house and Bo Fugard's junkyard.

The breeze was still coming from the south. The odor of oil and rust and moldy seat covers was stronger now, and mixed with it were the piercing smells of cordite and tiger.

Graham was disgusted. His first shot had clipped a few hairs from the tiger's back, smashed into one of the painted rocks beside the walk, and sent fragments of lead and stone back into the man-eater. His second shot had been a complete miss.

Too many years away from the forest. Too great a difference between a paper target and a tiger. Given a reprieve from the tiger's fangs, he had wasted it.

The blood trail that started on the far side of the hedge showed the man-eater was only lightly wounded, but the pain would aggravate its evident rage. Now there was nothing to do but hunt a wounded man-eater in a strange field of discarded machinery.

He tested the wind: light, from the south. He could follow the blood trail downwind, but somewhere among the tractors and trucks and harrows and plows the tiger would be waiting for him. There would be only a small chance of getting a shot before it was on him.

Another possibility would be to work through the yard from the rear, stalking upwind. But the cover was so complete, and the chance of silent movement so small, that he would almost certainly reveal himself to the tiger long before he saw the animal.

There was little hope of survival in either method.

He looked for some kind of height advantage, something that overlooked the entire yard. The only suitable thing he could see was the little barn behind the next house over. Its loft wouldn't put him as high as he wanted to be, but it would have to do.

When Brickhouse heard the two shots he froze, waiting, but there were no more. He could hear crows arguing far away; otherwise there was only silence.

He reached down and unsnapped the keeper of his holster and, as he did, remembered the riot gun in the trunk of his cruiser. Too late now, stupid. He pulled out the Glock, chambered a round, and began walking briskly down the road. He was not yet in sight of the houses.

He wanted to run, to run as hard as he could, but he knew it would be foolish. He was too old, too fat for that, and he might need a steady hand.

Graham edged around the back of Fugard's yard, watching every gaping door, every truck bed. His forest sense was screaming. The tiger was watching him, waiting for its chance. He would not surprise it.

Right foot out, left foot joining it. Right foot sliding out, left foot joining it. A fall would likely be fatal, just the kind of edge the tiger was waiting for. He doubted it was hurt badly enough to charge while he was facing it.

Graham's right foot hit something hard and heavy. He pushed it with the side of his boot and it slid a bit. He brought his left foot under him and worked at the obstruction with his right foot until it was out of the way. He resumed his crabwise path to the barn.

When he was almost in front of it, he noticed a battered bucket half full of lugnuts a couple of yards from an old pickup truck. Just the thing he needed; from the loft he could hurl the nuts like stones and possibly flush the tiger out of its cover.

He edged to the bucket, squatted with his finger on the trigger, and reached with his left hand for the bucket. As he gripped its bail he noticed something shiny on the ground.

Blood.

The tiger was behind him.

In the loft, Roy watched Jim moving sideways toward the barn. There was nothing he could do but wait.

He shifted a little, and his right hand hit something small and hard.

It was a pocket knife. Not a very big one. Two blades, and in the dim light he could read the brand. Barlow, it said. He had never had a pocket knife. It was a little rusty, but he was able to open the bigger blade.

A claw, a fang.

Roy looked up and saw a trace of movement at the bottom of the loft's back window. Something was in the barn below him. He froze and listened. Barely audible, he heard breathing and a low, guttural grumble through the open hole in the loft floor. Jim, he saw, was almost to the barn. He had stopped, looking at something in the corner of Fugard's yard, near a doorless pickup truck that sat flat on the ground without wheels.

Graham knew the tiger was in the barn. It was the only possibility, unless it had fled the village.

From memory, because he knew any movement would trigger the tiger's charge, he estimated he was ten feet from the barn door. The tiger could cover that distance long before Graham could turn from his awkward squatting position and fire.

He could see only one faint hope, and he took it. He flung himself backward. A tremendous roar, amplified by the little barn, shattered the air as Graham landed on his back. He fell harder than he expected, knocking the wind from his body, but he slammed the butt of the heavy rifle on the ground and fired the right barrel directly upward, hoping to place a bullet in the tiger as it came down upon him.

Roy glanced through the trap door. There was a patch of light on the barn's dirt floor from the doors, but it was empty. The tiger was in the shadows. He looked back out on Fugard's yard and saw Jim edging toward the pickup.

His back to the barn, Jim squatted and reached out for an old bucket. Roy saw movement in the corner of his eye and looked through the trap door again. The tiger was directly below him, its head and shoulders out of the barn, crouched for its leap.

Roy dropped head-first through the trap door, snarling as he fell on the springing tiger.

He landed on its back, a foot or more behind the shoulders,

and with his left hand grabbed skin and coarse hair. With his right, he plunged the pocket knife into the tiger's side with all his strength. There was a roar that seemed to shake the world, the smell of hot breath and rotten meat, and a terrific blow that sent him spinning into unconsciousness.

Graham, dazed, rolled onto his stomach and saw a figure sail out of the barn and drop to the ground a few feet from him. It was Roy. Rifle to his shoulder, one barrel ready, Graham stumbled to the boy, waiting for the tiger to emerge.

Nothing else came from the barn. The tiger, Graham assumed, must have gone out the back of it. Rifle still ready, he knelt beside Roy. The boy's eyelids were fluttering. His forehead was scraped and oozing blood, but Graham could find no claw or tooth marks. His left hand was clenched around a tuft of hair.

Roy opened his eyes and Graham drew back instinctively. There was nothing of humanity in them, only the feral eyes of the big cats. But as they focused on his face they became Roy's eyes again, brown and ordinary.

Roy spoke first.

"You okay?"

"I'm fine, Roy. Are you hurt badly?"

The boy sat up. "I'm okay. My head hurts a little. Where's the tiger?"

"Out the back of the barn. What happened in there?"

"I was in the upstairs part. Saw the tiger come in, saw you coming. You turned your back, he started after you. I jumped on him. Stabbed him."

"Stabbed him!" Graham said. "What with?"

"Pocket knife. Found it in the barn."

"And was it you that made that growl when the tiger was joining me on the porch?"

"Yes."

"Where did you learn to make a noise like that, Roy?"

"Tiger taught me, I guess."

Graham pulled a snow-white handkerchief from his jacket pocket, pulled Roy close to him and dabbed at his forehead. "You are quite amazing," the old man said.

At the sound of the third shot, Brickhouse could no longer contain himself. Just in sight of the houses, he began running down the highway.

Graham and the boy walked to the barn, and in the dirt floor Graham saw how the tiger had reared like a wild horse with Roy on his back, probably dashing the boy's head against the low ceiling and then throwing him off. The trail led out the back door.

"Stay directly behind me, Roy," Graham said, checking the barrels of his rifle for dirt and then reloading. "Keep your eyes open. Check our backs particularly."

"Okay."

The tiger had turned west out of the barn and started twisting and jerking as it ran. Graham was certain it was snapping at the knife embedded in its side, and a few yards further on he saw the knife lying in the grass.

"That's yours, Roy."

"Yeah, I'd like to keep it if I can."

As the boy picked up the knife, wiped the blade on his jeans, and closed it, Graham saw its removal had resulted in a more distinct blood trail. The tiger had headed back toward the houses, running hard.

"Come," Graham said. "We've got to end this."

Rifle at the ready, Roy following closely, Graham walked

quickly along the trail. It led between the houses three doors down from Fugard's, between the general store and the last house to the east, and in front of the store it turned back to the west.

Graham stopped, trying to see the blood trail as far ahead as he could.

"It will be waiting for us now," he said. "Between the houses, anywhere. We'll go to the ditch by the road, as far as we can from the houses. Watch our backs. It will let us pass before it comes. Are you ready?"

"Yes." Roy had his knife out again, the blade open. His knuckles were white where he held it.

Graham started forward, rifle at his shoulder. His legs were growing weak, he realized with dismay. Too long away. Too old. Still afoot only by the grace of a small boy.

Brickhouse came to the Murdock house, his chest heaving, his legs quaking, and saw the porch was empty. "Jim!" he croaked, as loud as he could. "Roy!"

The tiger burst through the open door of the widow Hadley's house with a roar that Brickhouse felt through his feet.

It came from the porch in great leaps, its head low, grunting in rage, hurdling Sandra Hadley's body. Brickhouse, his knees rubbery, raised the Glock in a two-handed stance and began firing. Events seemed to unfold slowly, and he remembered Graham's remark about how quickly a charging tiger became a large target.

He was squeezing off shots just as he had been taught, and he could see some of them had struck home. There was blood on the tiger's chest. But its charge wasn't slowed, and as it reached the ditch Brickhouse knew he was about to die. He knew it as a matter of pure fact, not in any kind of emotional surge. He didn't break and run, not because it would obviously do no good but because he had thought about the moment of death ever since he put on the badge, and every time he told himself: Never run. Never beg.

The tiger launched itself across the ditch. It was in the air, four feet from him, blotting out most of the world, when Brickhouse heard something strike its body with a thud and a simultaneous explosion from his right. The tiger jerked to his left, and its body, stretched in the last long elegant leap, contracted. It fell with its head a few inches from Brickhouse's feet and its hindquarters in the ditch. The man-eater twitched and snarled weakly and its eyes glazed over.

Brickhouse, dazed, looked up and saw Graham and Roy in the ditch, three houses away. Graham was lowering his rifle.

"How do you like tiger hunting, Sheriff?" the old man asked.

Roy came running, scrambling frantically up to the road. He fell to his knees beside the tiger, and only then was Brickhouse able to unlock his elbows and lower the Glock. His legs wouldn't work, and he was afraid if he tried to move he might fall on the boy and take them both into the ditch. He had clamped himself into place, determined not to cringe away from the charge, and now he was having trouble dealing with the continuation of life.

The boy, he saw, was crying. Not sobbing, just tears running down his cheeks, one by one. He was scratching the dead tiger behind one ear.

Graham was struggling up the side of the ditch, moving with more difficulty than Brickhouse had seen since he met the man. Brickhouse's knees began to give way and he sat down abruptly. He realized he was still gasping for breath.

Graham reached the road and glanced at him, smiling that warm little smile he had, then put his rifle down and knelt beside Roy. One arm went around the boy.

"I know, Roy," he said. "I know." He ran a hand down the tiger's flank. "He was doing what he had to do, the only thing he knew to do. That's what we did, too, Roy. What we had to do.

"Do you understand that, Roy?" he asked softly. "That this is the only way it could end?"

Brickhouse saw the boy raise his tear-streaked face to look at Graham.

"Yes," Roy said in a voice so small and full of agony that Brickhouse barely heard it. Then the boy sagged against Graham's chest, and the old man held him, rocking gently. When he looked up at Brickhouse, there was a glint of moisture on his leathery cheeks.

The sheriff and Graham stared at each other silently, exhausted.

Brickhouse drove Graham and Roy, once again asleep in the backseat, to his house. Upon hearing the tiger was dead, Mary immediately began fussing over the boy, and within minutes he was soaking in the first real bathtub he'd ever used.

Graham and Brickhouse remained in the den. Brickhouse thought Graham had aged years almost overnight. His skin had that appearance of transparency the sheriff had sometimes noticed in the very old, and much of the light seemed to be fading from his eyes.

"The state and the county both offered a pretty good-sized reward for this tiger," Brickhouse said. "We'll arrange for you to pick it up tomorrow."

"I have never in my life accepted a reward for killing an

animal," Graham said. "I won't start now. If you can see that it goes to Roy, it would make me very happy."

Mary returned to the den and sat on the edge of a chair. "Who is this child? What's happened to him?"

Graham told her what he knew of Roy's background and how the boy had joined him in the hunt at Norma's Creek. Mary was pale when he finished. "I'd better see how he's doing," she said and disappeared into the hall.

"You want the tiger's skin?" Brickhouse asked Graham when she was gone.

"No," the Englishman replied. "I've had all the tiger skins I ever want. They're poor representations of the creatures they covered."

"In that case, I imagine Cal Heflin is going to want to do something with it. He's our county commission chairman, big, fat blowhard with all kinds of idiotic ideas for promoting the county. He'll probably want the whole carcass mounted and put in city hall and charge people a quarter to see it."

"Stranger things have been done, Grady," Graham said as Mary peered around the hall doorway.

"He's asleep in the guest room," she said. "Out like a light the minute he hit the bed." She vanished into the kitchen, and the men could hear her voice, talking on the telephone.

"What will become of Roy now?" Graham asked.

"Depends on how soon we can find his kin," the sheriff replied.

"He told me he had only his mother."

"Well, in that case we'd have to hand him over to DFACS."

"Deefax? What's that?"

"Department of Family and Children's Services. They'll put him in a foster home and try to adopt him out."

"No, Grady," Mary said, coming into the den. "No. I just talked to Annie Dugan. She told me about Roy and his mother. You can't do that to him, not after all he's been through."

"Mary, it's the way things have to be—"

"Not this time."

Brickhouse was taken aback by his wife's opposition. "Well, what do you suggest?"

"We'll keep him for the time being. He seems like a wonderful boy, despite all the problems he's had. If that doesn't work out, the Dugans want him. But he's not going into that bureaucratic hellhole. You know what some of those foster homes are like."

"They're not all bad, Mary, you know that."

"I know, but we're not going to gamble with this child. He's too precious."

"I'm glad you've noticed that, Mary," said Graham, who had listened to the exchange with a broadening grin. "I'm very grateful. Roy has had a hard life in many respects, but he's known nothing but love and he mustn't be shut up in some orphanage. He is the most amazing human being I have ever met."

"He sure does seem like a fine kid," Brickhouse said. "But we really don't know him, and we don't know for sure he doesn't have any relatives. The boy's old enough to have a say in it, too. I agree with Mary—he can stay with us while we get acquainted, and then we'll make up our minds."

"Thank you," Graham said.

"We've got to go tell the press that it's over," Brickhouse said. "Are you ready?"

"I would rather not," Graham said, "but I know how difficult that would make things for you." He thought for a moment and then said, "I'll do this: Take me wherever you meet these people, and I'll talk with them for fifteen minutes. Then I'll leave the building while you talk with them, and one of your deputies will take me to the airport. I believe there is a nightly flight back to London."

"I guess I know better than to argue with you now, Jim, but I sure wish you'd stay. There are a great many people in this county who would like to express their gratitude personally."

"I cannot," Graham said, with that little smile. It seemed now to have something of pain it.

"Well, then, all I can say is I'm a richer man for having met you."

Mary hugged the tall Englishman, weeping. Brickhouse called for a deputy in an unmarked car. Weinman decided to drive it himself, and when he arrived, Graham, shaven and showered, was ready.

Roy came into the room. He was shirtless, holding up a baggy pair of jeans Mary had borrowed from neighbors.

Graham put down his bag and his gun case and sat on the sofa. Roy walked over to him, tears in his eyes.

"Why do you have to go?" the boy asked.

"I am no longer young, Roy, as you may have noticed. This adventure has tired me more than I would have imagined. And I do not belong here, no more than the tiger did. I have it in mind to go back where I do belong, while I still can. Back to those hills in India that I told you about.

"I thought I had gotten over them, but my time here has brought their memory back stronger than ever. Perhaps I can even watch some tigers in the forest there, one last time."

"Thank you for everything," Roy said. Roy was silent for a moment, looking steadily at Graham. "I love you, Jim," he said.

"Ah, Roy," Graham said, drawing the boy close to him, hugging him.

"And I love you, Roy," Graham said rather formally, the words awkward to him. He released the boy and picked up the gun case. "This is yours now," he said, placing it in Roy's hands. It was so heavy the boy nearly dropped it.

"You might never use it. That will be up to you. It is a very old gun, almost as old as I am. It was my father's. Our adventure was not its first, by any means. It is a valuable gun in and of itself, but its history makes it more so.

"Should you decide to take up hunting yourself, you will find that better guns can be had. But when you decide what you will do with your life, this gun will help you accomplish it. The firm that made it not long ago offered me half a million pounds for it."

"But if you're going to India, you'll need it," Roy said. He thought it would be ungentlemanly to ask half a million pounds of what.

"No, Roy. This was my last shikar."

Brickhouse and Graham, followed by Weinman in the unmarked car, went to the school auditorium and told the press the emergency was over. Then they waited half an hour for reporters who had wandered off in search of Sunday features to get the word. Graham stayed out of sight in the wings of the little hall.

When it appeared to Brickhouse that virtually all the reporters and cameramen were on hand, their microphones in place, and their lights raising the temperature of the auditorium by ten degrees or so, he walked back onto the stage and, without a word, signaled to his right. Two deputies wheeled in the tiger's carcass, its tail hanging off a four-by-eight-foot sheet of plywood on a goods trolley.

The Atlanta stations and CNN immediately went live. Matter-of-factly, relishing the drama, Brickhouse read a preliminary report from a local veterinarian mixed with his own data. The sheriff had gotten off eleven 9-mm rounds, five of which had struck the tiger, probably doing no significant damage. A single .470 slug had, in all likelihood, shattered its brain, although a postmortem would be performed to be certain. There was a single three-inch stab wound in its right side near the loins, and fragments of lead and rock embedded in the skin on the left side of its jaw, neck, and left leg.

The sheriff outlined the events of Friday and Saturday, and told the reporters about Roy Satterly, although he did not relay Graham's observations on Roy's relationship with the tiger. If Graham wanted to get into that, it was up to him.

"The man who killed this tiger is Colonel Jim Graham," Brickhouse said. "The British government very generously told us about him, and said he was willing to offer his services. Today was his tenth day of hunting, and I can tell you he is the most uncanny woodsman and the most fearless man I have ever seen or heard of.

"Now, Colonel Graham has reluctantly agreed to keep my promise and talk to you, very briefly. Please remember, he has had little or no sleep for three days and has been under immense strain for a good deal of that time. Mind your manners." He nodded to the wings and Graham walked out.

The uproar startled Brickhouse. Most of the reporters, notebooks under their arms, were applauding. Many were yelling questions while they applauded. The sheriff stood aside, and Graham stepped behind the podium, smiling his kindly little smile until the crowd subsided enough to pick out individual questions.

"How long ago did you kill your last tiger?" a reporter yelled.

"A very long time ago," Graham replied. "I can't remember just when, but certainly more than thirty years ago."

"How old are you, Colonel?"

"I am seventy-three," he said. "And it's Jim, just Jim, please."

"Were you scared?" yelled a tall, handsome man with an elaborate coif.

"Certainly," said Graham. "I was often terrified. I am no hero, you know, and you mustn't make me out to be one. I have certain talents in terms of junglecraft and a considerable knowledge of tigers, and I tried to apply all that here. That's all I did. The hero here is one of your own people, Roy Satterly.

"Roy Satterly is the most remarkable individual I have ever met. This boy saved me from the tiger twice today.

"He did so the last time by flinging himself upon the beast and stabbing it with a pocket knife. A three-inch pocket knife. That, ladies and gentlemen, is the bravest thing I have ever heard of. And it was done by a nine-year-old boy who not twenty-four hours earlier had seen his mother killed by the tiger."

"Where is he now?"

"He is resting and grieving, and he will not be bothered until Sheriff Brickhouse decides it is all right."

"You have the reputation of a staunch conservationist," yelled the *Times* of London, apparently the only one in the crowd who had ever heard of Graham. "How do you feel about killing this tiger?"

"I am certainly not proud of it," Graham replied. "However, it had to be done. Please understand that this tiger was doing only what it had to do to remain alive. Do not make it out to be some malefic demon. It was not evil; it was merely an animal."

The sheriff stepped in, raised his hand, and said, "That's enough for the colonel, folks. He's exhausted, and he needs to rest. Now if you'll be patient a minute, I'll be right back."

He walked off the stage with Graham, and in the wings he embraced the old man.

"Thank you, Jim. Thank you for all of us."

"Ah, Grady, it is I who thank you for the chance to meet Roy. You'll watch over him, won't you?"

"Don't worry, Jim."

"I know you think this is foolishness, Grady, but I feel bound to tell you that in some respects Roy seems to have been . . . well, let's say, affected by the tiger. But I'm certain there is no harm in him."

Brickhouse smiled. "I see you're still apologizing for the animal, Jim."

"Oh, certainly. Incidentally, do you remember that little story I told you about the last tiger my father killed?"

"The story about the tiger with the cut on its foot, and how this one has the same kind of cut? Yeah. Hell of a tale."

"The animal we killed this morning had a perfectly formed

left forepaw," Graham said, smiling his small smile. "There was no scar."

With that, the old hunter turned and walked to the car where Weinman waited.